D1712831

Desire between Women in Caribbean Literature

NEW CARIBBEAN STUDIES

Edited by Kofi Campbell and Shalini Puri

New Caribbean Studies is a unique series of monographs and essay collections focused on the still burgeoning field of Caribbean Studies, a field that is contributing to Caribbean self-understanding, global understanding of the region, and the reinvention of various disciplines and their methodologies well beyond the Caribbean. The series especially solicits humanities-informed and interdisciplinary scholarship that addresses any of the region's language traditions.

Kofi Campbell is an associate professor of English at Wilfrid Laurier University and coordinator of the English program at its Brantford Campus. He is the author of *Literature and Culture in the Black Atlantic: From Pre- to Postcolonial.*

Shalini Puri is an associate professor of English at the University of Pittsburgh. Her book *The Caribbean Postcolonial: Social Equality, Post-nationalism, and Cultural Hybridity* was the winner of the 2005 Gordon and Sybil Lewis award for the best book on the Caribbean.

Published by Palgrave Macmillan:

Humor in the Caribbean Literary Canon
By Sam Vásquez

Rhys Matters: New Critical Perspectives
Edited by Mary Wilson and Kerry L. Johnson

Between Empires
By Koichi Hagimoto

Desire between Women in Caribbean Literature
By Keja L. Valens

Desire between Women in Caribbean Literature

Keja L. Valens

palgrave
macmillan

DESIRE BETWEEN WOMEN IN CARIBBEAN LITERATURE
Copyright © Keja L. Valens, 2013.

All rights reserved.

An earlier version of Chapter 6 appeared as "The Love of Neighbors: Rosario Ferré's *Eccentric Neighborhoods/Vecindarios excéntricos*" in *Contemporary Women's Writing,* volume 6 (November 2012). Reprinted by permission of the publisher.

First published in 2013 by
PALGRAVE MACMILLAN®
in the United States—a division of St. Martin's Press LLC,
175 Fifth Avenue, New York, NY 10010.

Where this book is distributed in the UK, Europe and the rest of the World, this is by Palgrave Macmillan, a division of Macmillan Publishers Limited, registered in England, company number 785998, of Houndmills, Basingstoke, Hampshire RG21 6XS.

Palgrave Macmillan is the global academic imprint of the above companies and has companies and representatives throughout the world.

Palgrave® and Macmillan® are registered trademarks in the United States, the United Kingdom, Europe and other countries.

ISBN: 978–1–137–34007–8

Library of Congress Cataloging-in-Publication Data is available from the Library of Congress.

A catalogue record of the book is available from the British Library.

Design by Integra Software Services

First edition: December 2013

10 9 8 7 6 5 4 3 2 1

Contents

Acknowledgments

This project began in frustration and confusion at the scarcity of material on its topic, but was from the start fostered by professors who encouraged me to follow the gaps and lacunae that I found. My doctoral committee, Barbara Johnson, Brad Epps, and Robert Kiely, not only challenged and supported my intellectual and academic undertaking, but also provided precious guidance in navigating commitments to teaching, service, and sanity in the halls of academia. That is true mentoring. I humbly hope that this work carries on some of Barbara Johnson's teaching. I am grateful to Heather Love's reading of the early versions of this book, and to her example as an endlessly curious, committed scholar. I also owe special gratitude to Bruno Bosteels and Doris Sommer for introducing me to *Amistad funesta/Lucía Jerez*. And to Humberto Huergo, thank you for inspiring me so many years ago.

More colleagues than I can name here have vetted the many versions of this book, pushed me to make bolder claims, and support them, and graciously coached me through confusion and aggravation. Special thanks to the Centro de estudios Martíanos in Havana, the Eastern Caribbean Islands Cultures Conferences, the Caribbean Studies Association, the International Caribbean Cultures and Literatures Conference, and the American Comparative Literature Association. Some know how much they have helped me because it has been direct and intense—Melissa Feuerstein, Emily Taylor, and Brian Martin. Others may not realize that an article, a book, or a brief exchange was sustaining, even inspiring over the years—Lawrence La Fountain-Stokes, Antonia MacDonald-Smythe, Natasha Tinsley, Emily Allen Williams, Elsa Luciano Feal, and Edgardo Pérez-Montijo. Thank you to the anonymous reviewers of *Contemporary Women's Writing* and to Alison Donnell, whose readings of Chapter 6 were transformative, and to the anonymous reviewers of the manuscript who pushed me to confront the aspects of this book that most troubled me in its completion. Articles on related topics were published in *Frontiers*, *Caribbean Currents*, and the *Journal of Postcolonial and*

Commonwealth Literature; the anonymous readers for those journals led me to hone the arguments of this book. An early version of Chapter 2 was published in the *11th Annual Eastern Caribbean Islands Conference Proceedings*; thank you to Nick Faraclas, The University of the Netherlands Antilles, and the Fundashon pa Planifikashon di Idioma for making that possible. Finally, thank you to Shalini Puri, Kofi Campbell, Brigitte Shull, and Naomi Tarlow for believing in the potential of this project, and for seeing it through to completion.

This book received material support from the David Rockefeller Center for Latin American Studies and the Humanities Center at Harvard, and the Graduate Research Council, English Department, and the offices of the Dean and Provost at Salem State University. Colleagues at Salem State have read and listened to most of this book. Thank you especially to Betsy Hart and the Reading and Writing Initiative, Nancy Schultz, J. D. Scrimgeour, Jan Lindholm, and Jude Nixon.

For the ever-evolving love of families given and chosen, thank you to the entire Valens and Langfelder and Alcaraz and Rudolf clans, but especially to Tom and Amy Valens, Jesse Valens, Win and Red Valens, Rose and Alex Langfelder, Blanca Alcaraz, Rosie Alcaraz, and Manuel Ortega, and to John McMahon, Melissa Feuerstein, Ben Dunlap, and Renée and Dave Scott. To my son, Lucca, for the wisdom of childhood, for the unconditional and the ineffable, for lessons in reading over and over and over, I love you a million times infinity.

To Matthias Rudolf, thank you for renewal and commitment, and for such thoughtful and gracious readings of every part of this book.

Introduction: The Epistemology of the Mangrove

[The Caribs] are those who have intercourse with the women of 'Matinino,' which is the first island met on the way from Spain to the Indies, in which there is not a man. These women engage in no feminine occupation, but use bows and arrows of cane, like those already mentioned, and they arm and protect themselves with plates of copper, of which they have much.

Columbus, "First Letter" (*Four Voyages*)

[In Carriacou] Aunt Anni lived among the other women who saw their men off on the sailing vessels, then tended the goats and ground-nuts, planted grain and poured rum upon the earth to strengthen the corns' growing, built their women's houses and the rainwater catchments, harvested the limes, wove their lives and the lives of their children together. Women who survived the absence of their sea-faring men easily, because they came to love each other, past the men's returning.

Madivine. Friendling. Zami. How Carriacou women love each other is legend in Grenada, and so is their strength and their beauty.

Audre Lorde, *Zami: A New Spelling of My Name*

Columbus's concern about what the Caribs did, and did not, do with the women on "the first island met on the way from Spain to the Indies, in which there is not a man," inaugurates over five hundred years of attempting to understand the possibility of relations between women in the Caribbean through European conceptions of desire and sexuality. Columbus may well have encountered configurations of gender, sexuality, and family completely foreign to him, perhaps even ones where women were economically, militarily, and erotically independent of or interdependent with men without being paired in single, permanent, exclusive male–female coupled units.[1] However, like most narratives of "discovery," Columbus's (third-hand) story of the "women of 'Matinino'" tells us more about his image of "savage" women than about precolonial Caribbean society.[2] Columbus's "first" accounts of the Caribbean inevitably misrecognize it and yet impose themselves as authoritative and interpretative frames for understanding and acting in that space. The imposition of European notions of desire, sexuality, and family arrangements that we find in Columbus extend to present-day assumptions, and ignorance, about desire between women in Caribbean literature.

The striking resemblance to Columbus's Matinino of Audre Lorde's Carriacou, an island of "women who survived the absence of their sea-faring men easily, because they came to love each other, past the men's returning," suggests neither that Columbus was right nor that the ancestral home Lorde identifies in her "autobiomythography" derives from Columbus's letters; rather, it conveys the power of the possibility of desire between women, even if it is imaginary, both for those trying to reclaim and for those trying to claim the Caribbean. Accounts such as Columbus's and Lorde's are neither simply false or merely fictional, nor are they meaningful only within the bounds of their own assumptions; they reveal the inscription of the ungraspability of desire between women (its incessant possibility, its excessiveness, its nonreducibility to representation, its materiality, its malleability) as part of a generative and textual dynamic in the Caribbean and in Caribbean literature. This may be obvious, but it has also, until recently, gone largely unremarked, as if the operative and tacit assumption of critics has been, precisely, either that one need not account for desire between women because it is always already subject to some kind of misrecognition or else that one can account for desire between women as a known unknown, for which we therefore do not need any language beyond that of otherness.[3]

The twenty-first century has seen a rapid increase of scholarship in a variety of fields, that attends to desire between women in the Caribbean, from the theoretical interventions of M. Jacqui Alexander to works in sociology and cultural studies by Mimi Sheller, Faith Smith, and Rosamond King, and in cultural and literary studies by Thomas Glave, Lawrence La Fountain-Stokes, Omise'eke Natasha Tinsley, Alison Donnell, and others.[4] Smith's edited collection exemplifies a new framing of *Sex and the Citizen* in the Caribbean as necessarily inclusive of desire between women as it tries to fill in the "Caribbean discourses of sexuality [that] constitute a still understudied topic" (1). Yet, as Donnell writes in her essay in Smith's collection, "even though in theoretical terms there are strong persuasions towards reading in-betweenness as fashionable and difference as strengthening, creolized sexualities have no currency as yet"; this work is only just beginning (172).

Accounting for the possibility of desire between women in the Caribbean offers opportunities to rethink not only what women want and do with one another but also how the conceptual frameworks through which we understand desire, sexuality, eroticism, intimacy, and family (to name just a few) can be radically different across space and time. Structures of desire and sexuality render the desires and acts in which people engage visible, hidden, known, unknown, important, unimportant, normal, or exceptional. Binary divisions and absolutes that categorize, rank, and sequence sexualities have been deployed by explorers, colonizers, plantation owners, revolutionaries, and any number of regimes to control and dominate Caribbean subjects. But multiple, unranked possibilities for relations between women proliferate in the literatures of the Caribbean; they are fertile and erotic, loving and desirous, foundational and migratory. If we can see how these relations both develop out of and resist, precede and exceed, entangle with and filter out not only colonial imposition but also *mestizaje*, *créolité*, marooning, and the like, we can see Caribbean creative structures.

Desire between women is all over the place in Caribbean literature—everywhere and in no single location. More surprising and less remarked upon than the emergence of contemporary Caribbean characters and authors who self-identify as lesbian or gay or the persistence of homophobia in Caribbean letters is the prevalence of women who desire, love, and pleasure one another. Following Donnell's observation that "in a region that is hallmarked by cultural and ethnic heterogeneity and the undoing of binary conceptions of identity, the understanding of sexuality as heteronormative or homo(deviant) stands out as a conceptual anomaly" ("New Meetings," 214), *Desire between Women in Caribbean Literature* sets out to elucidate the integral place of desire between women in a structure of desire and sexuality that is neither binary nor heteronormative.

Taking up what might be called canonical Caribbean literature from the turn of the twentieth century to the turn of the twenty-first and from the Anglophone, Francophone, and Hispanophone Caribbean, *Desire between Women in Caribbean Literature* poses a series of questions that move the discussion of desire and sexuality between women beyond the homo/hetero binary and the identity politics that have shaped the fields of Caribbean and gender and sexuality studies: how does desire between women operate not only in opposition or resistance but also alongside, intersecting with, and integral to other desires? What models of desire, sexuality, erotics, community, family, and gender relations operate in the Caribbean? What can we see about the structures of desire and sexuality in the Caribbean and beyond if we start with desire between women as a structural element, even as the structural framework?

The diversity and fluidity of both literature and desire and sexuality in the Caribbean assure the difficulty of describing Caribbean structures of desire and sexuality through a reading of their literary figuration. Perhaps the best model for Caribbean structures of desire and sexuality can be found at the place that is the edge of both water and land. Where ocean, sea, and island meet along the Caribbean shores, the mangle thrives: stands of mangrove trees filter salt water, transport oxygen, and gather sand and silt. In the entwined roots and branches of the mangroves, up, down, and sideways become indistinguishable, and countless species form, thrive, and crush each other. "Mangle" is a synonym for "mangrove" and also a term for what is otherwise variously referred to as "mangrove thicket," "mangrove swamp," or "mangrove forest." Mangles grow so intricately entangled that they appear confused, mixed up, bent out of shape, distorted, mangled, but the mangle is a delicately balanced ecosystem based on the simplest of principles: surviving in complex and variable circumstances. In the mangle, what regulates relation and growth is opportunity, availability, success of the moment. In this mangled manner, sexuality and desire in the Caribbean are relational and transverse, endlessly in motion and infinitely adaptable, responsive to multiple orders and conditions.[5] A theoretical model that draws from Édouard Glissant, Gilles Deleuze and Félix Guattari, Patrick Chamoiseau and the *créolistes*, Maryse Condé, M. Jacqui Alexander, and María Lugones, the mangle offers not just a Caribbean rhizome but also a move from the abstractions of multiple intersecting plateaus to the particulars of stories and lives related in specific geographic and historical conditions.

My approach draws on the perspectives of both queer and Caribbean studies. The intersections of these fields have begun to be articulated, elegantly and incisively, by La Fountain-Stokes, Tinsley, Donnell, and Denise deCaires Narain. Tinsley's *Thiefing Sugar* is the first book devoted to "eroticism between women in Caribbean literature," formulating it not only as an occasional occurrence but as a broad phenomenon stretching across the islands and the centuries. Tinsley's book is followed by a special issue of *Contemporary Women's Writing* on "Caribbean Queer" framed by Emily Taylor as "Reading Desire between Women in Caribbean Literature." The growing interest in this area allows the present volume to not only point out absences but join a conversation that explores the variations of desire between women and their *imbrication* with other desires and sexualities throughout Caribbean literature.

As Tinsley's title suggests, *Thiefing Sugar* finds in the writings of women from across the Caribbean and across the twentieth century eroticism between women as a resistant or recuperative anticolonial and decolonizing practice. Examining the language of eroticism between women, *Thiefing Sugar* opens onto rereadings of the metaphorics of women's bodies and desires. Tinsley brings to light authors and texts that have been ignored or marginalized, from poor Surinamese washerwomen at the beginning of the twentieth century through the emerging Jamaican and Haitian postcolonial elite in the 1920s and 1930s, the nascent Martinican middle class mid-century, to Jamaican and Trinidadian immigrant women in the late twentieth century. Extensive as it is in its temporal and geographic range and in its critical insights, *Thiefing Sugar* invites, indeed launches, more readings into the complex cross-currents that it navigates. *Desire between Women in Caribbean Literature* complements Tinsley's work by focusing on canonical Caribbean authors and texts and exploring configurations of desire between women that open onto new readings of structures of desire and sexuality, family, and nation. The distinct texts and contexts that Tinsley and I each examine evidence the wide range of literary figurations of desire between women, so much of which remains to be reviewed not only through the lenses that Tinsley and I offer but through other lenses that will bring to light still other texts and kinds of texts.[6]

Some consideration of my choice to refer to "desire between women" indicates the still awkward and fertile ground where Caribbean and queer studies overlap. The phrase "desire between women" alludes to Eve Kosofsky Sedgwick's formulation of the homosocial–homosexual continuum in her study of Victorian representations of male homosexuality, *Between Men*. "Desire between *women*" designates the gendered specificity of my investigation. I prefer it to "queer" because, as convinced as I am of the salience of queer in Caribbean studies, I remain wary of obscuring that, as Tinsley writes, "queer is only one construction of nonheteronormative sexuality among many" (6).[7] By emphasizing "*desire* between women," I foreground imagination or longing, and bestow upon affect as much importance as action. The formulation also leaves undefined how exactly desire between women might be expressed. The variations "eroticism between women" and "sexuality between women" highlight the bodily and the physical, with "eroticism" leaving purposefully open the range of senses and sensations in question and "sexuality" emphasizing the connection to sex acts. All three formulations are somewhat vague and wordy, and all three are conjoined by "between." What exactly passes between women for desire, eroticism, and sexuality defies simple definition or singular nomenclature and involves not only women but all that passes between them.[8]

Between women, desire and sexuality is something to have, to do, or to experience rather than something to be. Following José Esteban Muñóz's observation that especially where intersectionality is most salient, where one must negotiate multiple belongings, it might be best to speak of processes of (dis)identification rather than the more fixed, even if strategically so, idea of identity, I argue that in the Caribbean, desire between women does not mark off a special class of individuals and furthermore knowledge about any one woman's desire for any other woman does not carry any special truth about her: in other words, desire between women in the Caribbean may not be best understood through identity politics.[9] This does not mean that to identify or to be identified as a woman-loving-woman in the Caribbean do not happen or do not matter—they do and there are numerous local terms throughout the Caribbean to mark such identifications. A feature of many of those terms is their emphasis on doing woman-loving rather than on being woman-loving. Tinsley explains that the Papiamento *mati* appears "more frequently in verbal construction than in nominal one . . . verbalizing sexuality not as identity but as praxis" (7). We can also think of the Guadeloupean and Haitian Creole *fèzanmi* and *madivinez* or the Cuban, Dominican, and Puerto Rican *tortillera* that put woman-loving into action.[10] I refer to desire between women rather than these terms, however, precisely because of their local specificity and also because even as they emphasize doing over being, they often refer to a smaller group of women than the one that I identify as participating in desire between women.[11]

Few of the authors considered in *Desire between Women in Caribbean Literature* have biographies that include significant, if any, erotic relations with other women, and indeed one of the authors in this study is a man. These authors include desire between women in their stories not as a way to express their own feelings for women but as a part of their imaginative narrativization of the Caribbean (not dissimilar to Columbus, although from other perspectives). As these Caribbean fictions make a place for desire between women—even if that place is on the outskirts of town or on the way to the grave—they demonstrate the necessity of accounting for its possibility, indeed the impossibility of thinking about any kind of desire and sexuality in the Caribbean without also thinking through desire between women not along a hetero–homo divide but in the mangle, where desire between women operates as a structural framework.

In 1885, in Hispanophone Cuba, women desiring one another wreak havoc with the nascent nation in José Martí's *Amistad funesta* (*Fatal Friendship*, later re-titled *Lucía Jerez*), which contends with the disastrous fate of a national narrative whose structure cannot work from, include, or account for desire between women, as I examine in Chapter 1. In Francophone Martinique in 1948, Mayotte Capécia's *Je suis martiniquaise* (*I Am a Martinican Woman*), the subject of Chapter 2, mourns a lost idyll where black girls find what they want with themselves, one another, and the island itself and contends with the adaptations of Caribbean structures of desire to the impositions of late French colonialism. Chapter 3 examines how Guadeloupean Maryse Condé in *Moi, Tituba sorcière . . . Noire de Salem*

(*I, Tituba, Black Witch of Salem*, 1986) reaches back to the childhood of the "New World" as she re-views desire between women in the history of slavery and cross-cultural contact across the Caribbean and the Americas. Jamaica Kincaid's *At the Bottom of the River* (1983) figures desire between women as an integral part of an Anglophone Antiguan ordinary, as studied in Chapter 4. Patricia Powell represents a newer generation of Caribbean authors who self-identify as lesbian, but in *Me Dying Trial* (1993), the subject of Chapter 5, Powell returns to the Jamaica of her childhood to find not lesbian foremothers but instead a wide variety of relational models. While Powell is part of a growing number of Caribbean writers who explore relations between women in increasingly direct and celebratory ways, relations between women are not necessarily becoming increasingly open and accepted, and I am not writing a narrative of progress that suggests they are or they should. *Desire between Women in Caribbean Literature* ends with Puerto Rican Rosario Ferré's *Eccentric Neighborhoods/Vecindarios excéntricos* (1998), where relations between women form the outside that defines the center but where their potential move into explicit foundational spaces is nearly as threatening as it was for Martí, even if their continued presence is equally ripe.

The Epistemology of the Closet, Epistemologies of the Caribbean

"The epistemology of the mangle" proposes that many of the major flows of desire and sexuality as well as formations of family and nation in the Caribbean are structured by multiple, nonexclusive intersections, intertwinings, and deviations.[12] The epistemology of the mangle takes a rhizomatic structure as axiomatic; it also takes as axiomatic a proliferation of discourses where secrecy is not the terrain, and the key, to identity but rather where identification occurs through multiple vectors of communication; finally, rather than an ideal of transparency, contained in the dream of coming out embedded in the closet, an ideal of what Glissant calls opacity predominates in the epistemology of the mangle. Harboring not only multiple structures of desirous and sexual connection, but all that passes between women—other people (husbands, children, friends, bosses), other priorities (careers, social positions, political aspirations)—the mangled structure of Caribbean desire and sexuality exists not separate and aside from so many other structures, but rather encompasses, is traversed by, and traverses, for example, structures of race and class, family, (re)production, and the state.

The interpolation of the *Epistemology of the Closet* is deliberate. Inaugurating a shift from lesbian and gay to queer studies and developing a sustained structural analysis from a queer vantage point, Eve Sedgwick demonstrated the reach of queer analysis: how far as well as how short it can go. Sedgwick's argument that from an analysis of same-sex desire and sexuality we can understand the structures of desire and sexuality more generally, because all desire functions in relation to same-sex desire, is axiomatic to *Desire between Women in Caribbean Literature.* I also follow Sedgwick in employing a predominant spatial image to serve as a metaphor through which to represent and analyze how desire and sexuality, knowledge and meaning, identification and belonging interact. Sedgwick could not be more explicit about the geopolitical and temporal specificity of her work: "twentieth-century Western culture . . . dating from the end of the nineteenth century" (i). However, the power of Sedgwick's model for understanding identity, sexuality, and gender in the West, and the tendency of—even queer, intellectually engaged—Euro-Americans to, at best, universalize from their position have obscured the study of other metaphors and other epistemologies even as literary and cultural production supply myriad sites for that study.

Tinsley summarizes the critiques of the *Epistemology of the Closet* and its legacy for the study of same-sex desire in a global context:

> Inspired by Eve Kosofsky Sedgwick's landmark study *The Epistemology of the Closet*, too many northern studies of same-sex sexuality stay out of springs or swamps and close to bedrooms. Their cartographies often rely on standard metaphors of interior and exterior space, of the closet and of "coming out." This division reflects an Enlightenment-inspired bifurcation between the invisible and the visible, between private and public expressions of desire in which invisibility and privacy are linked to oppression, while access to visibility and publicity is aligned with empowerment. (25)

In Sedgwick's analysis, Tinsley argues, "Europe and North America occupy center stage, generating the 'rule' to which all other geographies can only provide proof of exception" (26). In the *Epistemology of the Closet*, Caribbean structures of desire are simultaneously ignored and rendered Other.

Rereading Sedgwick in the light of critiques like Tinsley's, Siobhan Somerville reminds that Sedgwick raises the questions of intersections of race, ethnicity and global position, and sexuality even if the elaboration of the *Epistemology of the Closet* "ultimately attempt[s] to separate sexuality from other categories of analysis" (198). And so I look back to Sedgwick less to identify her limitations than to, as Somerville suggests, keep looking for other answers to the questions that she raised. I also look to the work in queer studies since the 1980s that grapples with queer intersectionality. Judith Butler and Judith Halberstam paved the way for thinking through how queer does and does not apply to a complex array of genders, and how it extends in space and time. In the 1990s and early 2000s, Muñoz, Gloria Anzaldúa, Roderick Ferguson, David Eng, and Will Roscoe opened discussions of queer's intersections with race and ethnicity in the United States and Europe. And in the late 2000s, John Hawley, Gayatri Gopinath, Helen Hok-sze Leung, and Sara Salih offered ways of thinking about queer in the context of postcolonialism and vice versa.

As much as queer theory is only beginning to attend to race and class and the legacies of colonialism and slavery, Caribbean studies continue in large part to ignore, if not actively deny, that desire between women intersects with other concerns. Despite their attention to the many different cuts and pastes that constitute the collage of the Caribbean, to opacity and repetition with difference, Caribbean theorists and critics too often assume that desire and sexuality in Caribbean cultures and literatures are limited to heterosexuality.[13] In her 1990 essay "Order, Disorder, Freedom and the West Indian Writer," Condé explains that according to the "order" of the Caribbean novel:

> 1. The framework should be the native land.
> 2. The hero should be male, of peasant origin.
> 3. The brave and hardworking woman should be the auxiliary in his struggle for his community.
> 4. Although they produce children, no reference should be made to sex. If any, it will be to male sexuality . . .
> 5. Of course, heterosexuality is the absolute rule. (156)

Although Condé is neither the only nor the first Caribbean author to write about female protagonists, women's desire, and nonheterosexuality, she is one of the first to call for the recognition of a hetero-patriarchal norm that marginalizes readings of desire between women in Caribbean texts. Her primary targets are Glissant, Raphaël Confiant, and Chamoiseau, but she could, and may, easily be making larger gestures to the likes of C. L. R. James and Roberto Fernández Retamar, who represent what might be called the Caribbean literary-critical establishment that devalues writing by and about women, women's sexuality, and desire between women. Although they often remark on the persistence of homophobia, the wide-reaching critical analyses of heteronormativity and of desire between women in the Caribbean begun by Alexander, La Fountain-Stokes, Smith, Evelyn O'Callaghan, Donnell, and Tinsley in many ways fill in the lacunae Condé identified. And Condé, Kincaid, Powell, and Ferré, whose work I study in the following chapters, belong to two generations of writers who break with the literary "order" and write explicitly about desires that are neither neatly nor exclusively heterosexual.[14] But they are preceded by generations of Caribbean authors—not only Martí and Capécia (who are the subjects of the first and second chapters of this book) and the anonymous Surinamese poets, Eliot Bliss, and

Ida Faubert (all of whom Tinsley writes about) but also Gertrudis Gómez de Avellaneda, Jean Rhys, Michèle Lacrosil, and many others who write in various ways about desire between women. The work of these authors does not prove Condé wrong, however, for the "absolute rule" of heterosexuality does not preclude the presence of other desires and other sexualities. Indeed, even the Caribbean cultural and literary theorists who promote the rule of heterosexuality demonstrate a surprising tendency to refer to homosexuality, even if it is to dismiss or to downplay it. Frantz Fanon's footnote denying knowledge of homosexuality in Martinique has become infamous.[15] Glissant is only slightly less dismissive when he notes "the sparsity of traditional 'deviance' in Martinican sexual practices" (1989: 515). Doris Sommer's compelling analysis of the "national romances" that undergird Latin America's "foundational fictions" assumes the heterosexual romance plots as the only and all-encompassing narrative motor, but also acknowledges that this plot rests on the denial of others.[16] Heterosexual romance plots and the rule of heterosexuality are only partial versions of the story, and are themselves traversed by other plots, other desires.

The Mangrove

While the national romance lends itself to a heteronormative reading and to a hetero–homo divide, other Caribbean theories offer metaphorics and models that are ripe for queer turns. Less grand than the ocean or the archipelago, less dramatic than the plantation or the maroon that have been the focus of most models for theorizing the Caribbean, the mangrove is an oft-mentioned but underdeveloped metaphoric model for the Caribbean. It is precisely its background quality, its status as the messy region to avoid on the way to picturesque beaches, the intermediary that absorbs things on their way to and from the island, that makes the mangrove so appropriate for understanding how desire between women in the Caribbean can twist alongside, within, and around other desires in such a way as to compromise the dominance of heterosexuality as a model, if not as a practice.

In their 1989 tract *Éloge de la créolité*, the *créolistes* declare "Creoleness is our primitive soup and our mangrove swamp of virtualities" (90) and refer to "the deep mangrove swamp of Creoleness" (111), offering the mangrove as a metaphor for Creoleness, albeit without developing it further. Tinsley argues that the *créolistes* use the mangrove as a metaphor for their poetic complexity but "often do not recognize how their very neocolonial rootedness in binary gender and sexual identities undercuts the complexity that they express as fundamental to their project" (25) and end up effecting "the heterosexualization of the mangrove" as if that were natural (26). To the degree that, as

Condé, Tinsley, and others argue, *créolité* is hetero-patriarchal, so is its rendering of the mangrove.[17] However, the very absence of an elaboration of the mangrove as a model for theorizing the Caribbean grants it the potential for resisting and undoing from within the hetero-patriarchy of not only *créolité* but also *antillanité*, calibanism, marooning, and other models of the Caribbean.

When Chamoiseau in his reading of Condé's novel *Traversée de la mangrove* waxes lyrically that "the mangrove is . . . in our nature, a cradle, a source of life, of birth and rebirth," he blatantly ignores Condé's description of it as a site of death, pain, and suffocation (390). But the mangrove represents neither simply a feminine chaos to be manipulated and rendered fertile by male writers, nor simply the fetid, brackish dark side of feminine chaos that sucks men down. The mangrove is a mobile space of uneven recombinations where writers of all genders and sexualities revalue what was rendered minor or undesirable by both colonial and anticolonial discourses, orders, and categorizations, perhaps best captured in the self-reflexive irony of Condé's title and the paradoxical vision of the dying soldier in Antonio Benítez-Rojo's short story "A View from the Mangrove," looking out on the mangrove swamp where "below, the water is still black, but in the fat, oily bubbles rising from the turbid depths there are all the colors of the rainbow" (172).

The mangrove is native to the Caribbean but it does not hold some secret to precolonial purity; rather, it represents the multiple adaptations and incorporations of all that arrives by sea and ocean, that constitute Caribbean specificity.[18] Mangroves have survived in the Caribbean since the Paleocene epoch, evolving not only through diversification from a common ancestor but through what biologists call convergence—a series of independent evolutions in separate families that produce common features.[19] Mangrove forests remain places of differentiated combination, described by Peter Hogarth as "frequently consisting of virtually monospecific patches or bands" (1). Their most common habitat, intertidal muddy shores, might be the constitutive mixing of elements of the Caribbean: the massive shoreline of an archipelago where land and ocean meet; the alternate wet and dry of the intertidal zone; the muddy soil where oxygen hardly circulates and water can barely flow; the occasional hurricane smashing of wind and water against mud, sand, trees.

In spite of Chamoiseau's claim that "*Tracée de la mangrove*" ("Tracking the mangrove"), the title he would have given to Condé's novel, would "evoke both the path of the runaway slave and the Creole act of crossing," while the mangrove is a site of a certain degree of coming together, of mixing, it is not one of crossing. As *Traversée de la mangrove*'s protagonist comments, "You don't cross a mangrove. You'd spike yourself on the roots of the mangrove trees. You'd be sucked down and suffocated by the brackish mud"

(1995: 158). The mangrove's dense growth over and into thick muckiness borders on impenetrability and infertility and yet that very density not only marks the unique adaptation of the mangrove but also harbors so many other plants, insects, birds, and animals that it suggests instead a relational and reproductive model that might be based not on penetration and fertility but rather on intertwining, adaption, and adoption.

Gender, Sexuality, and Knowledge in the Mangrove

A central hypothesis of *Epistemology of the Closet* holds that beginning in the nineteenth century in Europe and America "every given person . . . was now considered necessarily assignable . . . to a homo- or a hetero-sexuality, a binarized identity that was full of implications, however confusing, for even the ostensibly least sexual aspects of personal existence" (2), in conjunction with which "modern Western culture has placed what it calls sexuality in a more and more distinctively privileged relation to our most prized constructs of individual identity, truth, and knowledge" (3). In the Caribbean, however, the sphere of knowledge privileged for identification is not so, or rather is much more, black and white. Intersected by the legacies of colonialism and slavery, sexuality in the Caribbean does not fit under the categorical domination of a hetero–homo binary. If there is a binary in slavery and post-slavery societies, it is as much a racial as a gender or sexual binary, and if there is one thing that says everything about you, it is race, as the history of counting "drops" of "black blood" attests.

Historically, the *Epistemology of the Closet* begins with the emergence of "the gender of object choice" as "*the* dimension noted by the now ubiquitous category of 'sexual orientation'" (8, emphasis in original). In colonial and postcolonial, slavery and post-slavery societies, both gender and choice operate differently than in the nineteenth-century Europe to which Sedgwick's statement refers.[20]

Gender, as María Lugones powerfully argues, is a colonial construct, part of the colonial organization of relations of production and property, power and knowledge (186). It is not a category that operates separately from race, class, or nationality, to name just a few. For those in "unmarked" groups, in other words whites of a certain class, gender might appear one-dimensional, but for those in marked groups, such as colonial subjects or slaves, it does not. Under slavery, Saidiya Hartman argues, slave status and race trump or erase gender differentiation, and homogeneity is strictly policed in racial terms even, or perhaps especially, as miscegenation becomes ubiquitous. Thus relations between enslaved blacks fall into a single group regardless of the gender of object choice, while the race of object choice might be noted as "sexual orientation." If queer sexuality in the Caribbean refers to strange reconfigurations of the orders of race and class as much as gender, we might even identify as queer texts such as Cirilo Villaverde's *Cecilia Valdés*, with its exploration of miscegenation and incest.[21]

Queer theory's struggles with the concept of choice have played out in a shift from speaking of "sexual preference" to speaking of "sexual orientation," but these relate to differing views of the question of the "natural" quality of same-sex desire rather than to questions of forced sexuality. Under slavery, choice, in matters of sexuality as in so much else, was denied to slaves, and to a lesser degree to all blacks. Sexuality between slaves was prohibited unless it was imposed by the master for the reproduction of the labor force. Interracial sexuality was necessarily rape (if it involved a black man), service (if it involved a slave woman or child), or seduction for the purpose of material gain (if it involved a slave woman with a man other than her master, or a free black or mulatta woman).[22] Slave sexuality, like the slaves themselves, was treated as a tool. Even white abolitionists who saw slaves as humans with individual identities retained an instrumental rather than essential understanding of black sexuality, as Joseph Philips, in an 1831 letter responding to queries relating to Mary Prince's sexual history, makes clear:

> I have heard she had at a former period (previous to her marriage) a connexion with a white person, a Capt.—, which I have no doubt was broken off when she became seriously impressed with religion. But, at any rate, such connexions are so common, I might almost say universal, in our slave colonies, that except by the missionaries and a few serious persons, they are considered, if faults at all, so very venial as scarcely to deserve the name of immorality. (32)

What blacks under slavery are reported to do or not do sexually cannot reflect individual desire or identity because slaves are not granted individual desire or identity; even the desire to rape, of which slave men are so often accused, is coded as an animal instinct. Of course, these colonial and slave-owning views were not always shared by the colonized and the slaves, and the testimony of slaves and of witnesses to slavery as well as slave narratives show glimpses of other perspectives, but as Fanon and W. E. B. Du Bois so powerfully argue, one of the achievements of colonialism and slavery is to require blacks to think through the colonial, slave-owning, and racist perspectives.[23] And even when limited choice is garnered, as slaves create subjectivity in spite of inhuman treatment, even when the colonized or the slaves revolt and claim freedom and independence, the legacies of colonialism and slavery render choice less salient in the Caribbean than other considerations such as opportunity, necessity, negotiation, or entanglement.

The masters' control of black sexuality during slavery undergirds Glissant's theory of Caribbean jouissance—that notoriously ambiguous term for orgasm and the excess, limit, or transgression of sexual pleasure—as "that which is literally taken away from the master's power" (1989: 505).[24] As a result, in Glissant's analysis, jouissance in the Caribbean is indelibly linked to theft and "the theft of the master's power is joined to the, latent but permanent, rape of women" (506). A persistent Caribbean machismo results, in reaction to which "it is not surprising that women . . . have benefited more from modern overtures and attitude changes. They have taken better advantage of certain occupations and developed positions of responsibility that allow them what we still call deviances or singularities (homosexuality, single womanhood, communal attitudes)" (512). Glissant's failure to consider "premodern" desire between women and his strange warning about how "it is to the degree to which this liberation becomes tied to intense psychic conflicts that the Martinican woman's sexual indifference is today replaced with more spectacularly intense forms of sexual pathology" (512) reveal his own blind spots in regards to women and same-sex desire. Nonetheless, his analysis underlines how the particularities of Caribbean history, and more specifically of Caribbean sexual history, lead to a sexual landscape where both object choice and choice *tout court* remain more linked to the master–slave relationship than to the expression or revelation of any identitary truth.

Caribbean women's sexual "choices," in the manner of the mangrove, reveal not who they are but how they are able to survive "unpromising" conditions with creative adaptations.[25] Indeed, Glissant's determination of a general sexual indifference on the part of Caribbean women might reflect effective techniques of dissociation required by the history of forced sexuality that are not sexual pathology, as Glissant judges, but rather sexual mobility, an unlinking of desire and sexuality and identity with the possibility of recombination. As the speaker in Kincaid's prose-poem "Girl" instructs, a lady in the Caribbean knows how to conform to expectations in ways that grant room for maneuver:

> this is how you smile to someone you don't like too much; this is how you smile to someone you don't like at all; this is how you smile to someone you like completely; this is how you set a table for tea; this is how you set a table for dinner; this is how you set a table for dinner with an important guest; this is how you set a table for lunch; this is how you set a table for breakfast; this is how you behave in the presence of men you don't know very well, and this way they won't recognize immediately the slut I have warned you against becoming; . . . this is how to make good medicine for a cold; this is how to make good medicine to throw away a child before it even becomes a child; this is how to catch a fish; this is how to throw back a fish you don't like, and that

> way something bad won't fall on you; this is how to bully a man; this is how a man bullies you; this is how to love a man; and if this doesn't work there are other ways, and if they don't work don't feel too bad about giving up.
> (*At the Bottom of the River*: 5)

The speaker offers a lesson in how to pass as a lady, where passing involves not only the ability to perform an "other" identity but also the dissolution of the self-"same" real and originary identity. The addressee in Kincaid's story is not a slut who can become, or fail to become, a lady but rather is a girl becoming simultaneously a slut and a lady. The tragedy, and the failed identification, will be if she ends up only being, or only being recognized as, one or the other.

The ability and requirement to hold multiple belongings, to belong to multiple and temporary and overlapping groupings, as well as to inhabit strange and small zones of adjacent isolation make it so that specification and identification do not follow absolute dividing lines in the Caribbean. Where in nineteenth-century Europe the homosexual, as Foucault demonstrates, becomes "a species," and as Sedgwick adds "so, as a result, is the heterosexual, and between *these* species the human species has come more and more to be divided" (9, emphasis in original), in the Caribbean those divisions are, like the roots and branches of the mangrove, porous and permeable at the same time as they form a dense filtration system. In nineteenth-century Europe, were an individual to "come out" as homosexual, he or she could be classified and known, and then either jailed or liberated. But since in the Caribbean any particular desire or sexual act does not mark a singularity of identity, it is not clear what the characters in the novels I analyze here would be "coming out" as. They desire and may enjoy sexuality with other women as part of a richly complex set of sexual desires and encounters that are experienced by them and viewed by others in many different ways; they enjoy many different kinds of intimacy with women that are and are not "sexual," whatever that may be.

If this description is reminiscent of Adrienne Rich's lesbian continuum, it should be. Rich offers a uniquely complex account of gender and sexuality in the United States. The image of a continuum, however, suggests a single line onto which many different desires and practices can be plotted, that has poles of most lesbian and least lesbian, something akin to a Kinsey scale. But any lesbian continuum in the Caribbean operates in conjunction with other continuums, not as parallel lines but as ones that like the mangrove overlap, intersect, overshadow, and nourish and that require, in Carlos Decena's words, "more relational accounts of the social construction of identity" (355).[26] Rich carefully contextualizes her lesbian continuum. It operates in relation to compulsory heterosexuality that has effected "the denial of reality and visibility to women's passion for women, women's choice of women as allies, life companions, and community, the forcing of such relationships into dissimulation and their disintegration under intense pressure" (1607). Heterosexuality is part of a certain normative discourse in the Caribbean, but it is not compulsory in the same way. Heterosexuality's history in the Caribbean as the domain of the colonizers and the slaveholders, simultaneously, and irregularly, denied to and forced upon slaves and other dominated peoples, ties resistance to it not only to feminism and to lesbian existence but also to antislavery and decolonization.[27] That some postcolonial regimes in the Caribbean have continued, and reinvigorated, colonial heteronormativity reminds us that while "the colonial" cannot be conflated with "the Caribbean," neither can they be separated: the Caribbean as we know it comes precisely out of the, awkward and unequal, combination of colonial, native, African, and Asian influences. The very multiplicity of these influences, and the resistance to colonial domination that the history of it bred, has fostered a multiplicity of orders that weakens the normative force of any one. However, as much as Caribbean societies have radically shifted their worlds through revolts, revolutions, and battles of independence, as Kevin Meehan writes: "one of the great paradoxes of decolonization . . . is the enduring, seductive force of colonial culture in the period following political independence" (292).[28]

The mixing of different cultures and traditions in the Caribbean leads to many paradoxes. As much as some traditions impose heterosexuality in the Caribbean, others specifically integrate a variety of sexual and relational arrangements. Fishing and trading economies required men to spend months on end at sea, making room for the self-sufficient all-female societies that gave Columbus such reason to pause and Lorde such reason to celebrate. This tradition is replayed with variations when slavery, migrant work, or immigration also remove men from any regular presence in most households, as Edith Clarke documented in her study of Jamaican families, *My Mother Who Fathered Me*. Religious traditions such as *voudou*, *quimbois*, and *santería* include a wide variety of erotic and sexual arrangements played out by divine figures and between humans and gods. Traditions in which spirits "ride" humans offer many opportunities for gender and sexual plurality.[29] Mami Wata worship exemplifies religious traditions in which female as well as male devotees enter into spousal or lover relationships with divine figures.

The presence of non-Christian and syncretic religions in the Caribbean also complicates the conflation of knowledge and sex that is axiomatic to the *Epistemology of the Closet*. Sedgwick locates the Biblical Genesis where "what we now know as sexuality is fruit—apparently the only fruit—to be plucked from the tree of knowledge" as the grounds on which " 'knowledge' and 'sex' become conceptually inseparable from one another—so that knowledge means in the first place sexual knowledge; ignorance, sexual ignorance; and epistemological pressure of any sort seems a force increasingly saturated with sexual impulsion" (73). *Quimbois*, obeah, voodoo, and other Caribbean religious traditions, however, privilege ancestral and magical knowledge at least as much as sexual knowledge. The girl in Kincaid's story certainly finds an epistemology saturated with the "sexual impulsion" of ensuring that "men who don't know you very well" do not "recognize immediately the slut I have warned you against becoming," but she also finds an epistemology saturated with magical impulsion. The instruction "don't throw stones at blackbirds, because it might not be a blackbird at all" conveys that moving from the age of innocence to the age of knowledge entails learning about the spiritual beings and forces that, as much as any sex, motivate the world around us, produce and reproduce the relations that we experience, tempt and satisfy our longings.

Secular knowledge also bears importance in the Caribbean. Colonialism, the slave trade, and slavery actively denied and withheld certain kinds of knowledge—of lineage, language, and tradition, of reading and writing—not just rendering this knowledge the marker not only of power but of humanity, but also making the possession and manipulation of it a secret, perhaps even the secret.[30] Slaves, maroons, and rebels sought out this knowledge in secret or developed alternative methods to establish community and to communicate their woes and their plans. The successes of this retrieval and reinvention of secular knowledge are the stuff of legend, memorialized in, among others, the stories of Ti-Jean, Alejo Carpentier's *El reino de este mundo*, and slave narratives. Thus while Sedgwick's claim that "by the end of the nineteenth century knowledge meant sexual knowledge and secrets sexual secrets, [and] there had in fact developed one particular sexuality that was distinctively constituted *as* secrecy" (73, emphasis in original) applies in the West, in the Caribbean, where gender and sexuality are not singular (or binary) and do not singularly define identity, knowledge and sex are not singularly reducible to one another, nor are knowledge and secrecy singularly sexual.

At the same time, sexuality was and is not singularly secret in the Caribbean. Indeed, in colonial construction, blacks, mulattoes, and Creoles become essentially sexual with their sexuality completely knowable and un-secret. And while some respond to this by veiling sexuality, as does Mary Prince, many others, like Aimé Césaire's Caliban in *A Tempest* or Maryse Condé's Célanire in *Célanire cou-coupé*, do so by revaluing and reclaiming open sexuality. The presence or absence of sexual secrecy must also be seen in terms of the construction of secrecy and publicity in the Caribbean.

Chamoiseau's observation that "in our countries the 'we' takes precedence over the 'I'" is now a commonplace (392).[31] His more subtle analysis that "each character . . . lives in a personal sphere with its own problems and pains, its own subjectivity and values, and presents his or her testimony against that of others, thus creating a strange, culturally open, wayward, and unpredictable collective being" indicates the interplay of individual and community in which desire between women can be both regular and abnormal, an exception and a rule, common knowledge and "tacit subject," to use Decena's ingenious formulation (392). Like the grammatical tacit subject, knowledge about same-sex desire in the Caribbean does not need to be spoken in order to be recognized.[32] Like Glissant's notion of "recognized opacity" ("*opacité reconnue*"), the tacit subject offers a way of understanding the known and the unknown, the said and the unsaid outside of the public-shared/private-secret divide that marks Western epistemology and Sedgwick's analysis. The tacit subject of sexual desires and practices is community knowledge; the truth that knowledge carries is not of the individual but of the social body. The shared codes of social relations in which communal knowledge circulates and identifications take place implicate everyone, and single out no one, in the "tacit subject" of desire between women.[33] While the closet holds the open secret and mediates "the relations of the known and the unknown," the mangrove holds the tacit subject and fosters sharing, combining, and adapting as the primary operations of knowledge.[34]

Marlon Ross takes issue not only with the aptness of the closet but with the project of epistemology, writing:

> the penchant for "epistemology" itself derives from a universalizing project . . . Primitives, savages, the poor, and those uneducated in the long history of epistemology are not normally represented as epistemological subjects, partly because they do not have the luxury of composing the kind of voluminous texts that bear the weight of such deeply buried—and thus closed/closeted up—intellectual dilemmas begging for painstakingly close readings. (171)

Euro-American epistemology has certainly been problematically universalizing and universalized, but the claim that there is no "other" epistemology resembles V. S. Naipaul's claim that there is no Caribbean history or literature.[35] In spite of the lack of certain "luxuries," Caribbeans have composed "voluminous texts that bear the weight of . . . intellectual dilemmas," but they have not been granted by Western readers the "painstakingly close readings" that would establish them as such. It is tempting, and not inaccurate, to say that part of the issue is that the Caribbean epistemologies are often elaborated in anonymously or collectively authored oral, mythological, musical, and literary texts such as Anansi stories, or calypsos. But works that "bear the weight of" Euro-American intellectual standards have also been produced by highly educated, middle-class Caribbean individuals like Naipaul, C. L. R. James, Fanon, Glissant, Martí, and Benítez-Rojo, to name just a few. The problem of epistemology in the Caribbean, in other words, is not one of production but of reading.[36]

Desire between Women in Caribbean Literature posits that works of Caribbean literature elaborate an epistemology through which we can understand Caribbean subjects, desires, and sexualities. It undertakes the close readings that examine the intellectual dilemmas that Caribbean writers imaginatively expound as they develop complex artistic representations of gender, sexuality, and knowledge in the Caribbean. Each chapter of this book is devoted to one author and book and read in the context of the particular island in question—Cuba, Martinique, Guadeloupe, Antigua, Jamaica, and Puerto Rico—with attention to the specificities of the different colonial legacies and linguistic and literary traditions in the Caribbean. The first three chapters look at novels written or set during a first wave of colonial domination, the period up to the middle of the twentieth century when most of the Caribbean islands were under direct and explicit colonial rule. In the novels of this period, colonial heteronormativity comes directly from the colonial power, although there is already a question, especially where revolt and revolution are underway, of the degree to which new national paradigms will incorporate that ideology.

Intimacy destroys, warns the original title of José Martí's only novel, *Amistad funesta* (*Fatal Friendship*, 1885), later re-titled *Lucía Jerez*. Martí dedicated his life to the foundation of a free Cuba, yet while romances knit nations in other nineteenth-century Caribbean novels, in *Amistad funesta/Lucía Jerez* menaced and menacing love ravages public and private projects. I argue in Chapter One that the foundational failure in *Amistad funesta/Lucía Jerez* stems from irreparable fissures in the heterosexual model that grounds marriage, the national romance, and perhaps even the genre of the novel. Sommer's model for foundational fictions where "a variety of novel national ideals are all ostensibly grounded in 'natural' heterosexual love and in the marriages that provided a figure for apparently nonviolent consolidation during the internecine conflicts at midcentury" (6) gestures to the fissures, but finds national romances that overcome or overlook them. I contend that *Amistad funesta/Lucía Jerez* begs a change in emphasis, directing our attention to how "ostensible" is the grounding in heterosexual love, how "in quotation marks" is the naturalness of heterosexuality, and how only apparent is the nonviolence of any national consolidation in and through the traditional heterosexual romance. The novel's disastrous end results from the persistent power of a more mobile, multiple, eroding, and re-rooting mangled love in the lives of both of its protagonists.

One way to resist the tragedy of new or old imposition of colonial heteronormativity is to hold onto, or to create, an ideal of other organizations of desire and sexuality. Chapter Two, "Lost Idyll," returns to Mayotte Capécia's *Je suis martiniquaise* (*I Am a Martinican Woman*, 1948), which was scathingly dismissed, upon its publication, by Fanon as evidence of black women's desire for "lactification" (whitening). The story does end with the protagonist bearing a child fathered by a white man, but far from being the ideal lover Mayotte comes to search for based on her childhood experiences, André is an unhappy compromise for Mayotte. I argue that *Je suis martiniquaise* depicts a character who gives up her girl loves, but it is a tragic tale whose lesson is not that the French officer provides Mayotte with the access to power and independence that she so ardently desires but rather that she might have been better satisfied if she had held tighter to her girlhood loves for the self-sufficient Loulouze, a series of daring black boys, and the moon.

Chapter Three, "Replaced Origins," analyzes how, in her playfully historical novel *Moi, Tituba sorcière . . . Noire de Salem* (Guadeloupe, 1986), Maryse Condé toys with the question of whether desire between women is a native export or a colonial import. *Moi, Tituba sorcière . . .* stages an encounter between Tituba, a slave from Barbados accused of witchcraft in Salem, Massachusetts, and Hester Prynne from Nathaniel Hawthorne's *The Scarlet Letter*, which leads to something of a love affair. Even as it (re)writes Caribbean (hi)stories of desire between women, *Moi, Tituba sorcière . . .* suggests that, like the Caribbean itself, desire between women in Caribbean literatures is born out of the simultaneously destructive and creative interactions between Africa, the Caribbean, Europe, and the United States. One of the major differences, and one of the sticking points in the relationship, between Hester and Tituba is Hester's adherence to a hetero–homo model—she wants Tituba to join a lesbian separatist fantasy world with her—which misses not only Tituba's more mangled model for sexuality, but also the accompanying series of nonbinary relations. Just as Tituba's erotic and emotional desire for Hester mixes and matches with her erotic and emotional desire for John Indian, so does her gendered connection to Hester mix and match with her racial connection to John.

If the first three chapters focus on the places and placements of desire between women in early colonial domination and emergent nations, the last three chapters of this book look at stories written and set during a second wave of colonial domination, where some degree of independence has been achieved, stories that take on questions of how to articulate the normal of and from a Caribbean-centric position.

The fourth chapter, "Plotting Desire between Girls," redefines the ordinary as including desire between women and re-views coming of age as a mangle of twists and turns that destroys any narrative of developmental progression from childishness to maturity. The Antiguan girl narrators in Jamaica Kincaid's 1983 collection of short stories, *At the Bottom of the River*, announce their love for other girls and their plans to marry women when they are grown up in simple, straightforward terms seamlessly incorporated into their narrations. The simplicity of the declarations of desire between girls, often expressed in the easily recognizable formulas "I love you/her" or "I am in love with you/her," align with the *apparent* simplicity of style throughout Kincaid's work. Kincaid's simplicity, however, is a foil: she uses the ordinary, the normal, the familiar, the commonplace only to subvert them through their own performance. Where marrying a woman is an ordinary stage in a normal girl's passage from child to adult, we are in the mangle.

In the fifth chapter, "Sexual Alternatives," I argue that while a discourse of heteronormativity and homophobia circulates as the dominant discourse in the Jamaica of Patricia Powell's *Me Dying Trial* (1993), the actual relationships in the story do not predominantly follow a heteronormative script. When Gwennie, the protagonist of *Me Dying Trial*, finds out that her oldest son, Rudi, is gay, she denounces his "sin and nastiness" and asks him to change or move out of her house (182). Gwennie represents probably the most stereotypical set of Jamaican opinions about homosexuality, those same opinions expressed in Buju Banton's infamous song "Boom Bye Bye." But in *Me Dying Trial*, Gwennie's is neither the most common nor the most supported opinion about homosexuality. The most positive characters in the story, Peppy and Cora, view homosexual relationships as part of a landscape of sexual and relational alternatives where gender or sexual activity are not the determining factors in what qualifies a relationship as sinful or praiseworthy, natural or unnatural, nasty or nice. Peppy and Cora offer not only other opinions about Rudi's homosexuality, but also information and opinions about a whole series of same-sex relationships between women as well as between men. Indeed, as she thinks about how to understand her brother's homosexuality, Peppy realizes that she grew up in a mangle of relational and sexual alternatives. What *Me Dying Trial* reveals then is not that Banton is unrepresentative of Jamaican popular opinion or that homophobia is not prevalent in Jamaica, but rather that blanket professions of Jamaican homophobia obscure much more complex reactions to individual deviations from a heteronorm that is far from normal. *Me Dying Trial* is not anti-homophobic against Jamaican heterosexual tradition, but instead anti-homophobic with Jamaican traditions that can better be described by the metaphor of the mangle.

Weaving personal relationships with public projects, Rosario Ferré's *Eccentric Neighborhoods/Vecindarios excéntricos* offers a variation on the national romance and on a story that Ferré has told many times: Puerto Rico's traditional plantation elite face the economic and social shifts of the twentieth century, and the women in a family struggle with the new and old opportunities and limitations reserved just for them. In Chapter Six, "The Love of Neighbors," I argue that *Eccentric Neighborhoods/Vecindarios excéntricos* repeats this basic story with several significant twists. Most remarked upon is that while Ferré has, since 1989, translated her own works in English, she wrote *Eccentric Neighborhoods/Vecindarios excéntricos* first in English and then translated it into Spanish. A logical ancillary to this is that *Eccentric Neighborhoods/Vecindarios excéntricos* carries a pro-statehood message, marking the shift in Ferré's political views. Not at all remarked upon is a third change: while many if not all of Ferré's works are haunted by indirect references to erotic possibilities between women, *Eccentric Neighborhoods/Vecindarios excéntricos* is her first work to directly describe women sexually involved with one another. The shift in the referents for the first term in the national romance—the nation might no longer rest on the opposition between an independent Puerto Rico and a colonizing power (be it Spain or the US) adds to the already shifty ground of the second—romance might not rest on the opposition between male and female—destabilizes the rigid opposition between hetero and homo that undergirds traditional understandings of both the nation and the romance. It is not that in *Eccentric Neighborhoods/Vecindarios excéntricos* Puerto Rican specificity is relinquished in favor of American sameness nor that opposite-sex relations are jettisoned in favor of love between women—in fact both of those possibilities loom as just as undesirable and unsustainable as the dream of Puerto Rican independence or the rule of the patriarchal, heteronormative family. Rather, the destabilization of the binary gives rise to mutually inclusive, unranked possibilities where Puerto Rico could give new meaning to the term nation-state and where women could have relationships with one another that supplement, supplant, and are completely independent of the relationships they may or may not have with men. The mangle in which these possibilities thrive is a terrifying, muddy, dangerous mess. And yet the persistence of the conditions that lead to it, and the return of the topic in this way at this moment, suggests the power, if not the appeal, of the mangle for Ferré.

Desire between Women in Caribbean Literature finds desires between women so integrated with other desires that it does not fit to understand them in a homo–hetero structure; they offer instead a proliferation of terms, of branches and roots, that in its very resistance of centralization remains to a certain degree peripheral and chaotic. But in the mangle, nothing has a major function; in each particular combination of oxygen gathering, salt filtering, each piece is both expendable and necessary. The apparently minor or unimportant is integral to Caribbean literature. Relations between women twist around, across, and within other relations, desires, loves; they do not overturn or exit other arrangements, but they pervade Caribbean letters in a way that exposes the insufficiency of heterosexual *and* homosexual paradigms. *Desire between Women in Caribbean Literature*'s elucidation of the place of desire between women in Caribbean letters asks readers to rethink how we read the structures as well as the practices of desire and sexuality in the Caribbean and beyond.

CHAPTER 1

José Martí's Foundational Failure

According to José Martí, *Amistad funesta* (*Fatal Friendship,* 1885), later re-titled *Lucía Jerez,* was to have been "the Hispanoamerican novel that was desired" (109), a story where "higher ventures" lifted mere lovers' tales to "better ends" (110). Yet, faced with the problem of containing desire between women, the romance in *Amistad funesta/Lucía Jerez* fails.[1] The unrealized hope for Martí's only novel anticipates Doris Sommer's conception of national romances where "books fueled a desire for domestic happiness that runs over into dreams of national prosperity; and nation-building projects invested private passions with public purpose" (7). Sommer's work defines one of the major trends in Latin American literature and Martí is one of the most venerated authors in Latin America and the Caribbean, but Martí's preface to *Amistad funesta/Lucía Jerez* is staged as an apology, an admission of defeat. Either this novel or the novel erodes the foundation faster than it can be shored up.

Amistad funesta/Lucía Jerez opens as the story of Lucía and Juan Jerez, cousins engaged to be married. Lucía's female cousins, the sublimely moribund Ana and the pretty, if petty, Adela, share her life of needlepoint, balls, and waiting for Juan. Juan embodies Martí's ideal man, a "genuine poet" dedicated above all else to social good and purity (119). Lucía's strong, independent character would seem to make her a perfect candidate for the role of revolutionary love-companion to Juan.[2] However, rather than complementing one another, Juan's idealism and Lucía's ardor are irreconcilable in the marriage plot. Juan is ill equipped for Lucía's powerful passions, which are excited at every turn, not least by the beautiful but poor Sol del Valle. Lucía's desires rage increasingly out of control, and then explode.

Most analyses of *Amistad funesta/Lucía Jerez,* when they do not tend to questions of poetics and genre, focus on the character of Lucía as emblematic of Martí's views of women or the character of Juan as emblematic of Martí's views of the ideal man, and see the disaster at its end as related to these, or as the reflection of a moment of personal and political despair in the author's life.[3] However, I argue that the foundational failure in *Amistad funesta/Lucía Jerez* stems less from the individual qualities of its characters or author than from irreparable fissures in the heterosexual model that grounds marriage, the national romance, and perhaps even the genre of the novel. When the terms homosexual and heterosexual were just entering into Caribbean discourse (through, in part, Martí's own chronicles on such other writers as Wilde and Whitman), the binary that adherence to that model would encode into the foundational narrative of the postcolonial nation was already showing its inability to adequately account for desire and sexuality in the Caribbean.

In *Foundational Fictions*, Sommer analyzes Latin American literary nation-making where "a variety of novel national ideals are all ostensibly grounded in 'natural' heterosexual love and in the marriages that provided a figure for apparently nonviolent consolidation during the internecine conflicts at mid-century" (6). Among these books, Sommer includes the Argentinean José Mármol's *Amalia* (1844), and Columbian Jorge Isaac's *María* (1867), both mentioned in *Amistad funesta/Lucía Jerez*, and drawing on his articles praising these and other similar novels, Sommer refers to Martí as a "notable propagandist for nation-building novels" (10). However, *Amistad funesta/Lucía Jerez* directs our attention to the fissures in the model that Sommer signals but that the national romances that she analyzes overcome or overlook: the only "ostensible" grounding in heterosexual love, the quotation marks that must surround any claim to the naturalness of heterosexuality, and the violence that underlies any national consolidation in and through the traditional heterosexual romance.

"The Hispanoamerican novel that was desired": Prefacing *Amistad funesta/Lucía Jerez*

Born in 1853, Martí lived in Cuba until the age of 18, when he was deported for his pro-independence writings.[4] Martí eventually settled in New York, where he supported himself writing chronicles for newspapers and journals throughout Latin America and the United States, composed poetry, and developed the arguments for, including the organization of, a Cuban revolution.[5] Martí's work has been widely read in the Spanish-speaking world since its publication, but only small portions of it—and not *Amistad funesta/Lucía Jerez*—have been translated into English.[6] The reasons for this are many and include the Anglophone world's disinterest in non-European literary production and political writing, the decrease of translations *into* English, and the reaction in the United States to all things Cuban. But it is strangely fitting that the man whose most famous essay (which has been translated into English) is entitled "Nuestra América" (1891) be read and studied predominantly in Latin America (OC 6:15–23). "Nuestra América" folds together Latin America and the Caribbean in its urgent call for a united front of "natural" Americans to launch armed rebellion against colonial rule, resist US expansionism, and found republics where all classes and races unite and defend local and regional righteousness. Martí was an avid reader of European and American writing, often translating it into Spanish for publication in Latin American newspapers and magazines, but he was a vocal critic of the United States as well as of European colonialism.

Martí's chronicles and essays served as the political and intellectual foundation not only of many Caribbean and Latin American independence movements but also of *modernismo*. Rejecting the rationalism of European Enlightenment, realism, and naturalism in favor of irrational and imaginative literary production, *modernismo* reflects and produces late-nineteenth-century Latin American and Caribbean experience. *Modernismo* celebrated the development in Latin America and the Caribbean of "modern" forms of government (independent democracies), social organization (more egalitarian, or with an elitism based on something other than ancestry), and literary and artistic expression (affective, symbolic, and metaphoric).[7] Martí's poetry, emblematic of *modernismo* as much as that of Rubén Darío, is collected in the volumes *Ismaelillo* (1882) and *Versos Sencillos* (1891). Martí also wrote plays, edited a children's magazine, and published a great number of translations. Martí returned to Cuba in 1895 to take up arms against Spain. He was killed a few weeks later. (Cuba's war of independence ended in 1898 when the United States took control of Cuba.)

Although he was widely respected for his intellectual and artistic achievements and was part of a vibrant Cuban exile community in New York, Martí suffered from over two decades of failed attempts at Cuban independence as well as from more personal difficulties. Deeply in love with his island, in the first decade of his exile, Martí tried twice to return to Cuba but both times was accused of conspiring against the colonial regime and forced to leave. Martí's second return to Cuba, in 1878, was made with his wife, the Cuban-born Carmen Zayas-Bazán, whom he met while both were in exile in Guatemala. In 1878, in Havana, José Francisco Martí y Zayas-Bazán was born. When Martí left Cuba shortly thereafter, Zayas-Bazán and José Francisco remained on the island. Zayas-Bazán and José Francisco came to New York several times to be with Martí and also met him in Venezuela while he was living there for a time, but financial difficulty as well as their differing opinions about Martí's primary loyalty to the Cuban cause plagued the marriage, and Zayas-Bazán and José Francisco rarely stayed long in New York. Zayas-Bazán returned to Cuba for a last time in 1891 and the couple did not see each other again. Many of the poems collected in *Ismaelillo* as well as the children's magazine that he edited, *La Edad de Oro*, attest to the tremendous pain Martí felt at being separated from his family. Martí left many of his personal affects to Carmita Miyares, who had been his companion in New York.

Amistad funesta originally appeared between May 15 and September 15, 1885, in nine serial installments in *El Latino Americano,* a New York Spanish-language newspaper. *El Latino Americano* was distributed throughout Latin America and also in Europe and engaged a reading public acutely involved with Latin American and Caribbean independence movements.[8] The newspaper, however, addressed itself primarily to women readers and purveyed messages of moral conformity and conservatism.[9] Martí signed *Amistad funesta* with the pseudonym Adelaida Ral.[10] A dedicatory poem to Martí's friend and compatriot Adelaida Baralt, not included in the original publication, gives an oblique explanation of his unusual use of female pseudonym: Baralt had apparently been commissioned by the magazine to write the story and, knowing that Martí was in need of money, passed the assignment along to him.[11] But as much as it acknowledges the circumstances of the commission, the use of the pseudonym distances Martí from the genre and content of the novel, literally preventing readers from knowing that he wrote it. Martí might best be read, through Sylvia Molloy, as posing as Adelaida Ral, presenting himself (and his story) as something that he equally affirms he (and it) is not—"feminine," performative, full of artifice and feigning, nothing serious.[12]

When, years after the original publication, Martí planned to reissue *Amistad funesta* with a new title, under his real name, and with the addition of a prologue, he indicated that the novel was a work to be read over differently.[13] In the planned prologue, Martí claims, speaking of himself in the third person, that "the genre of the novel does not please him, however, because there is much to pretend in it, and the pleasures of artistic creation do not compensate for the pain of traveling in a prolonged fiction; with dialogues that have never been heard, between people who have never lived" (109). This is not just a critique of fiction, but of the artificial and superficial associated with the "feminization of the novel" that Michael Danahy observes at the end of the nineteenth century. The serious novel Martí would have liked to write would be not only manly but by, for, and about only men, a book that would "raise readers' spirits with feats of knights and heroes" (110). Editorial requirements that the novel have "much love, some death, many girls, no sinful passion; and nothing that would not be most pleasing to fathers and priests" make it not only feminine but heterosexual (110). Women and heterosexuality are, by convention, associated with artifice and artificial market or religious impositions. The hero who flowed naturally from Martí's pen had a "better destiny," ready for "higher enterprises, great feats" (110). But put into a novel, guided by editors, "his career was cut short by certain prudent observations," and Juan became a "mere ladies' man" (110). The opposition Martí establishes between men and women and between heroes and husbands, rather than generic conventions, precludes Juan's, or any man's, being a ladies' man without being *merely* that.

Sommer crystallizes common knowledge when she observes that heterosexual romance works so well to consolidate nations in other stories because it offers a story of opposites attracting, of different sides of a family or a conflict, of different temperaments and concerns, a coming together in harmonious union that will spawn a new race of integrated citizens. It can be less successful, however, in accounting for the attraction of similarity, the favor of insular self-sufficiency, or the mangled interweaving and cordoning of species and genera, genders and genres that occurs along the Caribbean shores.

In *Amistad funesta*/*Lucía Jerez* and throughout Martí's work, correspondences occur not between men and women but between men and between women. It is the friendship of men, not the love of women, that can impel the poet-warrior and to which Martí would like to exhort his readers. In an 1875 article, Martí lamented:

> our intelligent youth go around as if avoiding that which unites them, and cautious of one another: they are like isolated plants, those who daily praise the serendipities of friendship. They do not seek each other out, they do not like each other, they do not love each other: they do not want to know how many sweet things are enclosed in this community of those born to move, to look to the sky, to sing and to dream. Friendship is as beautiful as love: it is love itself, devoid of the enchanting fickleness of woman.
>
> (OC 6:307)

In Emerson, Wilde, and Whitman, Martí finds fellow poets, rhetoricians, and nation-builders who base their poetics and their politics in an ideal of male friendship (OC 13:15–30; OC 15:362–367). But reading Whitman, Martí confronts the erotic desire that holds together this world of men. In his 1887 article, "El poeta Walt Whitman," Martí notes that

> Since [Whitman's] books and lectures earn him barely enough to buy bread, "loving friends" care for him in a little house nestled away in a pleasant country corner from which he rides out in an old-fashioned carriage drawn by the

> horses, he loves, to see the "athletic young men" at their virile pastimes, to the *camerados* [*sic*] who are not afraid to rub elbows with this iconoclast who wants to establish "the institution of the dear love of comrades."
>
> (*The America of José Martí*: 242, emphasis in original)[14]

The proliferation of quotation marks around every reference to friendship and to masculine attractiveness is striking, especially in comparison to their omission in Martí's citations of Whitman elsewhere in the same article.[15] Martí signals a problem of interpretation surrounding male friendship, or an attempt to contain, set off, and distance certain aspects of it. A few pages later, Martí asserts:

> fools, with the affected modesty of prurient schoolboys, have thought to see a return to those vile desires of Virgil for Cebetes and of Horace for Gyges and Lyciscus in those most ardent images of the human language with which Whitman celebrates the love between friends in "Calamus."
>
> (*The America of José Martí*: 250, translation modified)

"El poeta Walt Whitman" makes clear that Martí's ideal of friendships between men was not an ideal of homosexuality, but it also reveals Martí's concern about the ways that it was equally not an ideal of heterosexuality. As Sylvia Molloy observes, "what calls attention . . . is not that the issue of homosexuality is avoided but, precisely, that it is brought up" ("Too Wilde": 195–196).[16] Furthermore, Martí's attention to male friendship and desire in the works of both Whitman and Wilde as well as in Greece and the Latin American youth of his day suggests that Martí was well aware that desire between men is not only the terrain of "fools, with the affected modesty of prurient schoolboys" but rather circulates, in various forms, throughout American populism (Whitman), British elitism (Wilde), and Cuban anticolonialism (OC 13:137).

Martí avoids desire between men in *Amistad funesta*/*Lucía Jerez* by containing Juan Jerez's male friendships to the "high feats" of politics and religion, but he cannot insert Juan into the role of hero in a national romance. The problem with the novel and with this novel becomes the problem of containing women and their desires. Embodied in a way that Martí's male friendships never are and unchecked by a strong heterosexual romance, Lucía's correspondences with women develop into full-fledged love affairs. Attached to a homogeneity that cannot accommodate women, let alone the mangled mixings of men and women, Indians and criollos, that the new Cuban nation will have to hold, *Amistad funesta*/*Lucía Jerez* remains caught in a hetero–homo divide that it also cannot sustain.

Feeble and Faulty Heterosexuality

In the opening scene of *Amistad funesta/Lucía Jerez*, Ana and Adela sit with Lucía chatting and embroidering. Juan arrives at Lucía's house late because he was caught up in an impassioned conversation about "public nightmares" with Don Miguel (114).[17] Juan loves social causes directly and actively, and women indirectly and passively: "He loved who loved him" (115). He is not equipped to tame Lucía, "who like any subjugating nature needed to be subjugated" (119). But it is not just Lucía's feralness that is the problem. No real woman, by virtue of being real, will be a good match for Juan, for "he, in woman, saw more the symbol of ideal beauties than a real being" (118).

If Juan and Lucía could function as a foundational couple, they might together develop a new model for a romance, which would also be a new model for the nation, one that integrates the multiple branches of desire that bind the cousins to one another but also to other interests. Eventually confessing to Lucía how the imperfections of men leave him melancholy, Juan describes how her love could sustain the poet-warrior in his quest to carry the "Excelsior": "the two of us together will carry the flag. I'll take you with me for the whole journey . . . In woman, Lucía, since she is the greatest beauty known, we poets think we find like a natural perfume all of the excellencies of spirit" (168). Lucía responds with her own confession, about how she struggles with jealousy. While Juan's secret is that what he loves in Lucía is her perfection and her qualities of spirit, her secret is an imperfection grounded in her corporeality. The only shared understanding they may gain is that the heterosexual romance at the center of the foundational fiction is based on a fictional woman, a woman who is the idealized fiction of men who don't want women as real people.

Of course, as a novel *Amistad funesta/Lucía Jerez* is a fiction, and in it Martí can and does create unreal, pure, and perfect women: Ana and Sol. Even within the boundaries of the story, however, Ana's perfection rests solidly in her impending death and her consequent removal from any potential romance. Sol is more complicated: indeed, she is *the* plot complication in the story, the character who might be perfect enough to replace or to complete Lucía. But Sol attracts Lucía's desire to have her as much as to be her, and Juan's goodness rests on his distance from romantic intrigue. If Sol takes a place in the foundational couple, it is Juan's.

In the margins of this story no heterosexual couples contrast with the disaster at its center: nothing to suggest that the failure of that romance is exceptional.[18] Indeed, in the midst of describing the ball that gathers together all of the eligible young men and women, all of the potential couples in the city, the narrator uses his omniscience to comment: "For most men beauty is not a holy creation and a cup of spirituality; but rather a tasty apple. If there were a lens that allowed women to see men's thoughts as they pass through their heads, and what lies in their hearts, they would like them much less" (161). And yet the hyperbolic praise of women as seen through the eyes of men and of the perfect union where women "almost see ourselves in [the eyes of a man who loves us], as if we were in them" also establishes heterosexuality as the ideal that none of the real relationships can attain (181).

The few men who appear to rise above "most" to occupy a higher class of sensibility in the novel are Juan Jerez and the Hungarian pianist Keleffy. But it is precisely these two men who, when they enter into relationships with real women, find their cups empty, or else filled with venom. Keleffy enters the story through his travels, and he "traveled because he had married a woman whom he thought he loved, and found her after like a mute goblet, in which his soul's harmonies found no echo" (157). Perhaps the problem is that the few "select" men form a class apart to which women can never accede, or that only women such as Ana can reach, through impending death. Or perhaps the problem is that when an ideal man meets a pure woman, what follows cannot be so mundane as a love affair or a marriage; such a perfect union can only play out as it does when Keleffy and Sol meet, in the most beautiful piece of music anyone has ever heard (162). If there exists on the one hand a potential consummation of idealism and purity in artistic creation that subsumes the heterosexual marriage by reaching above and beyond it, there is also another much more incarnate and much more threatening alternative to the national romance that leads it inexorably off course.

Amistad funesta/Lucía Jerez offers two contrasts to the lustful thoughts that Sol's beauty inspires in most of the men at the ball. Keleffy's musical achievement is one; Lucía's gaze is the other. The narrator insists: "But it was not a man, no, who with the greatest insistence and a certain rancor already mixed with love, looked at Sol del Valle" (161). No man's gaze is described to counter or to replace Lucía's. Rather, Lucía's gaze replaces those of all the men in the room. Lucía "knew her in that moment, and already she loved her and she hated her" (161). Between the first sentence and the second, the order of Lucía's feelings for Sol shifts, from rancor mixed with love, to loving and hating. The ambivalence of the two emotions, as well as their uncertain order, is never resolved, but rather marks a great disturbance that the relationship reveals in the binary ordering of things (words, social norms).

Powerful Desire between Women

The encounter between Lucía and Sol builds from the very beginning of the story. In the first scene in which Juan and Lucía are together, Lucía has been waiting impatiently for Juan. He explains his tardiness: "I went to beg that [the landlords] not harass Señora del Valle for the rent this month" (114). While Juan seems concerned with the del Valle mother, Lucía thinks immediately of the daughter, and walks away from Juan: "—the mother of Sol? Of Sol del Valle?" (114). While the narrator and the other characters use Sol's given name, Leonor, until the third chapter, Lucía has already monikered her Sol, the center of her universe, the focus of her heliotropic existence. Focused on the other girl, "Lucía entered, without turning back nor lowering her head, into the interior rooms," where Juan can only follow her "with his eyes sadly" (114–115). It is as the novel does enter this standard cliché of a feminine space that desire between women takes over. Less surprising than the disaster that eventually results from the inability to contain or to cordon off desire between women is the persistent suggestion that it cannot be avoided, that it is in some senses no less natural and no less American than patriarchal heteronormativity.

In the last paragraph of the first chapter of *Amistad funesta/Lucía Jerez*, the cousins discuss the "ideal head" that a local magazine has published. Lucía waxes, "a head that looks like it belongs to one of Rafael's virgins, but with American eyes, with a figure that looks like a lily's cup" (136). Just as Juan's devotion to his work with men in the courts and the countryside is the mark of an American hero, so the attraction between women also links to their American qualities. When Pedro reveals, "it is not an ideal head, but that of a girl who will graduate from high school next week, and they say she is incredibly beautiful: it is the head of Leonor del Valle," the narrative structure of Sol's first mention is repeated: "Lucía rose to her feet with a movement that was more like a jump; and Juan gathered from the floor, to return it to her, the handkerchief, torn" (136). The rip in the tissue constitutes a rupture in the text. The comma between handkerchief and torn is in Spanish grammatically unnecessary, and serves only to emphasize the importance of the last word of the chapter, "torn" (the original reads: "*Se puso en pie Lucía con un movimiento que pareció un salto; y Juan alzó del suelo, para devolvérselo, el pañuelo, roto*").

The entire second chapter is a flashback that recounts the history of Leonor's family, from her humble but hardworking and fiercely revolutionary father's emigration from Spain through his death and the family's fall into misfortune and Leonor's attendance of an exclusive school. Although flashback is a standard feature of narrative, this one is extremely lengthy (17 pages out of a 95-page book, or almost 20 percent of the novel), and gives an enormous amount of detail of relatively limited importance to what had appeared to be the primary romantic plot. It takes the attention away from Juan and Lucía as a couple to refocus on Leonor as a character, and then introduces her physical body into the space occupied by Lucía and Juan. The flashback rejoins the primary narrative as Sol makes her debut at the ball, where she and Lucía take their place as a couple.

Opening the third chapter, the narrator asks, "what is the whole city talking of if not Sol del Valle?" and continues "it was like the morning that follows the day on which a powerful orator has been revealed. It was like the dawning of a new drama. It was that inevitable commotion that, in spite of its innate vulgarity, men feel when some supreme quality suddenly appears before them" (155).[19] But while the men are thrown into turmoil by this rising star, Sol finds her great light reflected and a gaze that she can return in Lucía. It soon becomes commonplace to find the two together, and it comes as no surprise to find that when the narrator asks, "who is it who is sitting, and looking at her with long gazes, that enter the soul like beautiful queens looking for their home in it; and letting her play with her head, whose brown hair she unbraids and twists, and then pulls up with much care, so that you can see her noble neck?," the answer is "at Lucía's feet is Sol del Valle" (163).[20] The attraction of similarity, but also the solipsism of mirroring, inflames Lucía and Sol's relationship.

Their encounter at the ball leaves the two women dumbstruck: "And Sol's face lit up, without knowing what to say, and all the color drained from Lucía, searching in vain for the strength to move her hand and to open her lips in a smile" (164). Someone interjects at that moment: "But this must not be so, no" (164). The voice belongs to either Lucía, Sol, the director of Sol's boarding school, who made the introduction, or the narrator; it is impossible to determine whom. The speaker provides no clear reason for the interdiction, offering more of an interjection than a well-reasoned thought. The sentence begins with the conjunction "but," implying an exception, objection, limitation, or contrast to some previous statement. However, no clear grammatical antecedent exists to the conjunction, so that the sentence seems to express a partially formed idea, or the second half of a thought whose first part is not stated. Where we might expect to find a justification for the thought, in the sentence's second clause, we find instead the repetition of a single word, "no." Rather than developing into a fully reasoned concern, the sentence devolves into an almost stuttering monosyllabic objection, "no." It is not even clear exactly *what* must not be; it is only the imprecise "this" that must not be "so." But the antecedents lie in the mutual attraction of Lucía and Sol. Whoever the speaker is, it recognizes that in some way, for some reason, to some people, it ought not to be. Inasmuch as the interjection is an expression of Martí's own dismay at the turn of events, it might mark a recognition of his own incapacity to escape a binary imagination of sexuality. Indeed, it is the novel's failure to either subsume all desires under the heterosexual romance or to reimagine the romance as encompassing multiple desires that leads to its being overrun by rampant desire between women.

The interdiction of love between women does not stop it from developing but haunts it at every moment. Indeed, leading Lucía toward Sol for their introduction, the director reminds Lucía of her future position as a wife, calling her "she who will be Juan Jerez's wife . . ." (164). Although the statement fixes Lucía within the heterosexual order, it also recognizes that she has not yet fulfilled that role; she *will be* a wife. The sentence ends in an ellipsis. The idea of Lucía becoming Juan's wife, always tenuous, is increasingly incomplete.

The narrator reiterates that there is a code by which Sol ought to fall for a young man, commenting that "she required a master," but recognizes in the same sentence, "and Lucía was her mistress" (176). The strictly gendered nature of the requirement set up by the narrator points to a key problem in the narrative. Sol is described as needing a distinctly male master ("*un dueño*") whose place is taken by a markedly female mistress ("*su dueña*"). While this novel articulates the need for a balance or attenuation of femininity by male control, it repeatedly produces instead a proliferation and extenuation of women and their power.

Jealousy is the primary emotion that Sol inspires in Lucía, contend most critics, and the murder at the end of the novel is the result of Lucía's jealous rage.[21] In this analysis, it would be ironic that one of the few positive things about Lucía's character is her presumed lack of jealousy. The director of Sol's school explains as she entrusts Sol to Lucía's care, "Lucía, I am bringing you a friend, so you can hold her in your heart and care for her like a member of your own household. I can leave her in your hands: you are not jealous" (164). The director might simply be wrong, as suggested by Aníbal González and Gladys Zaldívar's arguments that Lucía is essentially and overwhelmingly a jealous person, or Sol's possible relationship with Juan may override Lucía's natural disinclination to jealousy, as in Morales's analysis.[22] I submit, however, that jealousy is not the only or even the primary emotion that besieges Lucía. Furthermore, of whom Lucía might be jealous, and who she is afraid to lose to whom are unclear.

As Sedgwick so effectively demonstrates in *Between Men*, jealousy is based on the inclusion not only of fascination with, but also of desire for the rival.[23] Fitting with Sedgwick's analysis, Lucía tells Juan, "I am dying of a great jealousy for all that you might love and that might love you" (170). The dual direction of her jealousy (toward anyone Juan loves, and toward anyone who loves Juan) makes it unclear whether Lucía wants to *have* Juan or to *be* him. The jealousy that she expresses toward Sol reflects her bifurcated wish to be in Sol's position as the object of Juan's desire and to be in Juan's position as the subject desiring Sol (and the object of Sol's desire).[24]

As the relationship develops, Lucía herself struggles against it, sporadically refusing to see Sol or treating her with anger: "Lucía kissed Sol with such frigidity, that the girl stopped for a moment, looking at her with pained eyes, that did not alight on her friend's brow. And suddenly, for many days, Lucía stopped seeing her" (177). As much as the passage shows a distancing between the two women, it underlines the otherwise physically passionate nature of their relationship. After some time, Lucía does return to visit Sol, and as she takes leave of her for the evening, "she took her hands, and she kissed them; and as she conversed with Sol, she gently rubbed her hand across her cheek; and when she said good bye, she gazed at her as if she knew she ran some risk, and she ought to warn her of it, and as she went toward the coach, her tears were flowing" (177–178). The focus on Sol's hands recalls the place of hands as a metaphor for Juan's other women love interests (118). The sustained nature of Lucía's interaction with the hands furthers the metaphor and also suggests the repetitive and nongenital sexuality often associated with two women together.[25] But the tender kisses of reconciliation are accompanied by the sense of "some danger." Lucía realizes that there is some, indefinable, un-nameable, danger that surrounds their relationship, and yet she is unable to break it off.

Sol is so taken with Lucía that she will not be daunted in her pursuit, and may even be piqued by the chase; Lucía "exercised, as much as she did not wish to, a powerful influence on Sol's spirit" (176). At every opportunity Sol "went looking for Lucía, who now always found some way to be occupied with lengthy chores in her room, into which Sol entered almost by force one day, and saw Lucía in such a state that she wasn't sure if it was her" (199). Sol's ability to penetrate Lucía's room marks a stark contrast with Juan's distance and exclusion from the novel's interior spaces.

Even as she pushes Sol away, Lucía expresses a desire to give herself and her possessions entirely over to the other woman: "And Sol looked at Lucía in such a beautiful way, that no sooner had Ana fallen almost asleep, than Lucía approached Sol, took her lovingly by the waist, and once in her room, began to empty with almost feverish gestures her boxes and drawers. —All, all, all is for you" (183–184). The motion represents Lucía's desire to reach into the deepest parts of herself—perhaps the chests and drawers even represent female genitalia—and to give what she finds to Sol. With Sol and Lucía waiting for Ana to fall asleep before they run off together, the relationship acquires a clandestine character. There is something intensely personal that only belongs to Sol and Lucía, which they cannot announce to others but must steal off to share. An element of illness also marks the two women's connection, through Lucía's "almost feverish" actions. Although illness and especially feverishness are common literary indications of falling in love, here the association of sickness with love, as well as the forced entry, carries connotations of the impropriety and unnaturalness of desire between women. As the desire deepens, it becomes more problematic, sicker.

Ana also acquires an increasingly important role because of her understanding of Lucía and that of her relationship with Sol. Ana's illness as well as her artistry separate her from the others. Possessing "those rights of a married woman that the proximity of death gives to the young," Ana escapes the sex and gender norms and rules that her women cousins must follow. From her unique vantage point, Ana observes and depicts Lucía with striking acuity. Though she is often too tired to put brush to canvas, Ana describes her tableaux:

> On a hill, I will paint a monster, sitting. I'll put the moon at its zenith, so that it shines fully on the monster's hill, and allows me to simulate with lines of light in the salient parts, the most famous buildings of Paris. And while the moon caresses the hill, and while you can see by the contrast of the luminous profile all the blackness of its body, the monster, with a woman's head, will be devouring roses. There in a corner will be thin, disheveled young girls who flee, with their shirts ripped, raising their arms to the heavens. (132)

Lucía's virility, passion, and corporeality over-determine the association between her and the monster, while the almost excessive symbolism of the painting begs a reading of perverse female sexuality.[26] Paris has just been named in the text as the place where "all is sin" (131).[27] The moon with its classic feminine symbolism (a moon that could easily represent Ana herself, the woman artist whose pale light illuminates the scene) not only presides over the scene but caresses the hill on which the monster sits, suggesting an erotic encounter. Earlier in the text, Lucía nibbled a camellia (114); now, as the monster-woman "devouring roses," her action is at once erotic and cannibalistic—the monstrosity of someone who eats their own kind.[28] Judith Ginsberg argues that the fleeing young girls appear to be in the wake of a rape, adding, "however, there are no male symbols in the painting, only a female monster, and there is a clear suggestion that women themselves are responsible for the havoc wrought by sexuality" (134).[29] Not only are women responsible in a general sense for the havoc wrought by sexuality, but one particular woman, the monster-woman, Lucía, is responsible for wreaking sexual havoc among the other girls in the novel.

Ana is not simply a detached observer here. She explains, "—Of beasts, I know two categories, Ana said once: one dresses in skins, devours animals, and walks on claws; the other wears elegant dresses, eats animals and souls, and walks with a parasol or a cane. We are nothing more than reformed beasts" (133). The narrator draws attention to the strangeness of this knowledge, asking "Where had the poor girl, who had barely left the circle of her fortunate house, suffered so much that she had learned to know and to forgive?" (133). Ana's self-implicating first person plural "*We* are no more than reformed beasts" suggests that she not only knows but may have shared in a beastliness that, in response to the narrator's question, she could have learned from her, still unreformed, cousin Lucía in her own home.

As with Sol, Lucía's feelings for Ana include jealousy. When Juan and Ana engage in a long discussion about Ana's paintings,

> Lucía followed with perturbed eyes Juan's face, profoundly interested in what, in one of those moments of self-explanation that those who carry something inside themselves and feel themselves dying like to have, Ana was saying. Who did Juan think he was, with her at his side, and thinking of something else! Ana, yes, Ana was very good, but, what right did Juan have to forget Lucía so much, and while he was at her side, pay so much attention to Ana's rarities? (134)

Lucía does not, however, express any real fear that Juan and Ana might strike up a relationship; even in her most distraught moments, Lucía thinks, "Ana would have liked Juan, if she did not know that he already liked me; because Ana is good!" (195). If Lucía is jealous, it is for the spotlight. We can even wonder if Lucía is troubled by jealousy or, rather, fear of discovery, for what Lucía does not want Juan to pay so much attention to is not just Ana in general, but most specifically Ana's "rarities" ("*rarezas*"), a word that evokes "*los raros*" with which Rubén Darío would designated, a few years later, a group of writers including Martí and such gender- and sexual nonconformists as Rachilde and Wilde.

While Juan, in his fascination with Ana's artwork, may appear to forget about Lucía, Ana does not. All the while she and Juan talk, Ana describes paintings whose central figures evoke Lucía. In addition to the planned painting of a flower-eating monster, Ana mentions a painting she has already completed, symbolizing "a person who I know" who can be none other than Lucía, "that haughty red rose, with black shadows, that rises above the rest on its leafless stem" (135). The apparent audience for both women, Juan may in fact only be the vehicle through which they communicate with one another. Ana's fixation with Lucía is such that we can wonder whether the "something" that she carries inside and wishes Juan (and Lucía) would understand before she dies is her art, or her love for Lucía. Or perhaps it is less definable, "something" that cannot resolve into either an affair with Juan or an affair with

Lucía, that troubles both a heterosexual and a homosexual model, that would thrive in the mangrove, if it could ever get there.

When Lucía, in a passionate fit, locks herself in her room, Sol might gain entrance but Ana, possessed of some special knowledge, is the one to go in:

> —It's just that I know why Lucía is sad. Let me go. Under no circumstances should you [Sol] go. It's to everyone's benefit.
>
> She went, she knocked, she entered.
>
> —Ana!
>
> Ana, almost livid and holding out her arms so as not to fall to the ground, was standing, in the doorway of the dark room, dressed in white.
>
> —Shut the door, shut the door.
>
> There was much talking, moans were heard, as from a breast being emptied, there was much crying.
>
> There in the dawn, the door opened. Lucía wanted to go with Ana.
>
> —No, no, I want to take you, how can you go alone if you cannot even stand up? Sol will still be awake. I want to see Sol this very moment.
>
> —Crazy! Even when you are good, crazy! Juan, yes, when you see him tomorrow, which will be in my presence, kiss Juan's hand. As for Sol, may she never know what has gone through your mind. Let us go: accompany me to the middle of the corridor. (200–201)

The intimate silences between Lucía and Ana suggest, according to Yolanda Martínez-San Miguel, "a very profound understanding between the two friends, which the narration leaves beyond representation" (36).[30] Behind closed doors that even the omniscient narrator does not pass, Ana spends all night, drawing on her particular understanding of Lucía to affect some change whose exact nature is never revealed. The most obvious analysis of the little that can be heard from outside the room is that Lucía unburdens her troubles to Ana, sobbing loudly in the process. However, the qualification, "as," of the description of the sounds suggests that there may be a difference between what was heard and what actually happened. Rumor, hearsay, and other clandestine (mis)interpretations are invoked with the passive construction of the verb "to hear." The long night together in the bedroom, the moans and sobs lend a sexual undertone to whatever that secret communication may have been. Ana's knowledge of the details of Lucía's troubles, and their continued love despite, or perhaps even because of, whatever else may be going on set the scene for their final encounter.

The Final Destruction of the Heterosexual Couple

In the novel's final scenes, everyone gathers at a country estate to raise Ana's spirits with a party. As the guests convene, Lucía, dressed all in black, comes out of her room. When she does, "she saw, coming toward her arm in arm, alone, in full silver light, in the middle of the little forest of flowers in the entrance to the room, Juan and Sol, the most beautiful couple" (206). "Juan and Sol" and "the most beautiful couple" are synonymous, shifting the emphasis from the specificity of the individual characters, Juan and Sol, to their representation of the perfect heterosexual couple.[31] At this vision, Lucía

> with a terrible jerk unleashed her mane of hair onto her back: "Be quiet, be quiet!" She said to the Indian [carrying a case full of arms], while pretending to look inside, she put her tremendous hand into the case; and when Sol disengaged herself from Juan's arm and came toward her with open arms . . .
>
> Fire! And, with a shot in the center of her chest, Sol wavered, groping the air with her hands, like a fluttering dove, and, at the feet of the horrified Juan, dropped dead. (206)

The pastoral location, both of the country house and of the entry hall scene, adds an element of the natural to the episode. The country offers the healthy air that might alleviate Ana's suffering, and it is home to the Indians whose connection to the land and knowledge of how to work is what the narrator identifies as most needed in "our lands" (117). But the "local Spanish bosses," not the Indians, own the land and force the Indians to work in plantations producing not the fruits of the land that will sustain them but rather the alcohol that they do not even taste (189). Juan tries his best to return the land to the Indians, but the success of his efforts is not guaranteed: "the Indians ran the risk that the temporary land grant that, while awaiting the definitive, Juan had obtained for them from the judge would be taken away, for, the day before the judge had received from the local Spanish boss a beautiful horse" (189). Perhaps, however, the Indians, fed up with arguing their cases in corrupt courts, join together with the young women who have tired of living always in the shadow of their impending marriage and subjugation to the men who play those legal games, and take matters into their own hands.

The perfect romantic heterosexuality of Sol and Juan as a couple allies them with oppressive sociopolitical structures, while Martínez-San Miguel and Masiello assert that the Indian's provision of the gun case aligns him with Lucía against the patriarchal colonial order.[32] Although the Indian's active participation in the murder is questionable at best (he seems to be carrying the case of arms for another purpose, and to be used as an unwitting pawn in Lucía's act), he stands at Lucía's side as she commits the act. In the natural countryside setting, the unfettered woman and the Indian may be able to take the master's tools and turn them against him.

If the focus of *Amistad funesta/Lucía Jerez* is the triangulated desire between Lucía, Juan, and Sol, it would be fitting to end with an image of the resolution (even if it is in the form of destruction) of the triangulation, and if a goal of the novel is to establish a national romance, it would be fitting to end with the restitution of a solid heterosexual order. Rachel Blau de Plessis suggests, in *Writing beyond the Ending*, that

> one of the great moments of ideological negotiation in any work occurs in the choice of a resolution for the various services it provides. Narrative outcome is one place where transindividual assumptions and values are most clearly visible, and where the word "convention" is found resonating between its literary and its social meanings. And artistic resolution (especially of a linear form that must unroll with time) can, with greater or lesser success, attempt an ideological solution to the fundamental contradictions that animate the work. Any resolution can have traces of the conflicting materials that have been processed within it. It is where the subtexts and repressed discourses can throw up one last flare of meaning; it is here the author may side-step and displace attention from the materials that a work made available. (3)

Not only does *Amistad funesta/Lucía Jerez* continue somewhat oddly one paragraph past the final fatality, the ending is already exceeded in the prologue, the last two paragraphs of which explain:

> Juan began with a better destiny than the one he has at the end, but in the novel his career was cut short by a certain prudent observation, and he who was born in the novelist's mind ready for more and for higher undertakings (greater) feats, had to be converted into a mere ladies' man. Ana lived, Adela as well. Sol died [an unintelligible word follows].
>
> And Lucía killed her. But the author did not know Sol or Lucía well. He knew Don Manuel, and Manuelillo and Doña Andrea, as well as the director herself [several unintelligible words follow]. (110)

The remarks set the ending out of order, and also insist on the appropriateness of over-reading the novel. The end, particularly Juan's end, is not what it should have been. Not quite following Blau de Plessis's model, Martí suggests that it was not his unconscious, but rather outside forces that sent Juan off in the wrong direction. However, even Martí's own retrospective opinions are peppered with hints of his struggle with revising and expressing his thoughts, as evidenced by the scribblings in the margin of the (pre-)conclusion, which his untimely death and editorial decisions leave intact for the reader. The repeated rehearsals of Sol's murder at Lucía's hand in both the prologue as well as in the foreshadowing throughout the novel also highlight the strangeness of the last paragraphs:

> Fire! And, with a shot in the center of her chest, Sol wavered, groping the air with her hands, like a fluttering dove, and, at the feet of the horrified Juan, dropped dead.
>
> Jesus! Jesus! Jesus! And twisting around and tearing at her clothes, Lucía threw herself to the ground, and dragged herself to Sol on her knees, and tore out her hair with her burnt hands, and kissed Juan's feet; Juan, whom Pedro Real, so he would not fall, held in his arms. For Sol, for Sol, even after her death, every attention! Everyone on her! Everyone wanting to give her life! The corridor full of women crying! To her, no one came near, not to her!
>
> Jesus! Jesus! Lucía entered the door of the women's dressing room, fleeing, until she reached the hall, where Ana, half dead, crossed, holding the arms of Adela and Petrona Revolorio, and letting out a howl, Lucía fell, feeling a kiss, into Ana's arms. (206)

The characters in the last scene are the same as those in the first: Lucía, Ana, and Adela, with the addition of Petrona Revolorio. The frame for *Amistad funesta/Lucía Jerez* is neither a heterosexual family nor its homosexual replacement, but a group of women variously related. Ana has been described before as capable of understanding and pardoning (133); she now calls on this ability.[33] Up until that embrace and kiss, I would have argued that the novel presents the deadly consequences of the impossibility of either containing or repressing desire between women. Lucía's position in Ana's arms and Ana's kiss infinitely complicate any final analysis of the novel.

Uribe explains that "in nineteenth century literary convention, the novel was to represent either the defeat or the assimilation of the rebel heroine" (37). Despite Israel Ordenel Heredia Rojas's claims, in his analysis of *Amistad funesta/Lucía Jerez*, that as Lucía "destroys what she loves, she destroys herself" (14), and despite Blau de Plessis's suggestion that "the punishment of one desire is the end of all" (16), Lucía remains alive, nonconforming, and desirous to the end of the novel. She is neither killed, nor banished, nor thrown back into Juan's arms. The defeat and contrition Lucía may be imagined to suffer with Sol's murder are mitigated by a return to an all-female space, where the pardon she receives comes from the lips of a woman she loves. Blau de Plessis acknowledges the possibility of an alternate meaning of an ending in death, where "death itself becomes a symbolic protest against the production of a respectable female and the connivances of a respectable community" (16). *Amistad funesta/Lucía Jerez* presents a death orchestrated by Lucía, which functions as her protest against those elements of Sol which represent the ideal woman, and against the subsumption of those elements of Sol which do *not* represent the ideal woman into a heterosexual couple. Blau de Plessis, again, finds that "death comes for a female character when she has a jumbled, distorted, inappropriate relation to the 'social script' or plot designed to contain her legally, economically, and sexually" (15). However, the abundance of women and the proliferation of desire between women in *Amistad funesta/Lucía Jerez* means that only a series of deaths would correct the uncontained female behavior in the novel. Lucía is the most nonconforming of the women; she remains half alive, and with a woman she loves, to the end.[34]

Although Ana is "half dead" when she takes Lucía into her arms, amazingly, she remains alive. Whether Ana's death is actually close at hand is debatable. The prologue informs us of Sol's death, and of Ana's life: "Ana lived, Adela as well. Sol died" (110). Although the past tense of the verb "to live" certainly allows for Ana's subsequent death, or could refer to Ana's existence as a person with a life outside of the novel, the juxtaposition with Sol's death suggests that this information refers to the status of the characters after the novel's close. Juan ends up where he started, a background character off in a world of men. Ana, Lucía, Adela, and the Indian housekeeper Petrona Revolorio offer an all-female space where a new kind of revolution (Re-vo-lo-ri-o is significantly evocative of *re-vo-lu-ci-ón*) may be brewing against the bosses (Petrona is a feminized inversion of *patrón*, Spanish for boss).

Of course, the ending is not quite so simply positive. Even if alive, Ana is terribly ill, and Lucía is a murderess. And the national romance has failed. Its heterosexual marriage plot was flawed and impotent, and it was not able to reformulate itself to rise up with or to contain other possibilities. And with the national romance founders not only a fecund couple to embody and engender that new nation, but also the alliances that set Juan up as its hero. For not only is he no longer a part of a potential foundational family, but even his status as defender and promoter of justice is in question. The heterosexual couple and any national romance that it might represent have come from being flawed, ethereal, or impotent, to being on the side of the colonial order. And yet, what stands against them and in their place as the new foundational fiction is an out-of-control murderess.

Martí offers a negative epistemology of the mangrove, the demonstration of the destruction of lives and ideals that cling to, or even reach for, a national romance that is exclusively heterosexual or homosexual. For Martí, the embodied woman, the narrated novel, is too traversed by material needs, too mixed up and entangled by complex desires to be ideal. And yet the ideal's inability to account for these things is its demise. It is a bleak end. And yet, as he composes a foundational failure, Martí reveals the profound recognition that to radically reimagine the nation outside of a colonial status might require to radically reimagine the relational and generic forms on which it can rest.

CHAPTER 2

Lost Idyll: Mayotte Capécia's *Je suis martiniquaise*

In its first four years in print, Mayotte Capécia's *Je suis martiniquaise* (1948) won praise for its poignant descriptions of the life of a young Martinican woman discovering her island and negotiating the erotic and economic mire of early-twentieth-century colonialism.[1] *Je suis martiniquaise* was the first book published in France by a woman of color. It won the *Grand prix littéraire des Antilles* in 1949. Capécia published a second novel, *La Négresse blanche*, in 1950. Then, in 1952, Frantz Fanon scathingly dismissed *Je suis martiniquaise* as evidence of black women's desire for "lactification." According to Fanon, Capécia's novel epitomizes postcolonial subjects who, adopting the mind-set of the colonizer, strive to become whiter.[2] Fanon excoriated Capécia, whom he regularly called by her first name, because he saw her choice of the "other" for a partner as an attempt to be more "other" herself: "Mayotte loves a white man to whom she submits in everything. He is her lord. She asks nothing, demands nothing, except a bit of whiteness in her life" (42). Women, in Fanon's reading, can literally take the body of the white man into their own to lighten not only themselves but "the race": "We have been forewarned, Mayotte is striving for lactification. In a word, the race must be whitened" (29).[3] And women writers who describe this process incorporate colonial ideology, reproducing it in their texts.

Over the last several decades, scholars have returned to Capécia's work, recognizing the many different ways of reading it. Clarisse Zimra and Beatrice Stith Clark were among the first to point out that while the story ends with the protagonist, Mayotte, bearing a child fathered by a white man, far from being the ideal mate she ends up seeking, André is an unhappy compromise for Mayotte. Rather than a model to follow or even an example of what colonized black women want, they read *Je suis martiniquaise* as a tragic tale with lessons about the dangers, perhaps even the impossibility, for colonized black women to find any kind of happiness, success, let alone self-realization, through relationships with white men.

Yet, *Je suis martiniquaise* remains under Fanon's shadow. Most recent criticism focuses on reading or responding to his critique of the novel,[4] and while *Peau noire, masques blancs* is widely available in its second edition, *Je suis martiniquaise* never saw a second edition and remains out of print and difficult to obtain. Stith Clark's 1996 English translation is also out of print, although it is still widely available.[5] Part of the legacy of reading Capécia through Fanon is an almost exclusive focus on the second half of the novel. Translating *Je suis martiniquaise* as *I Am a Martinican Woman*, Stith Clark makes a titular focus on Mayotte's adulthood, which she only enters in the second half of the novel. *Martiniquaise* conveys the national identification, Martinican, and is gendered feminine, but does not contain the age specification of "woman."[6] The idyllic first half of *Je suis martiniquaise* where black girls find what they want with themselves, one another, and the island itself remains virtually unexamined. The few French critics who do mention it dismiss the first half of *Je suis martiniquaise* as both overly romantic and "devoid of literary substance." And Mercer Cook's 1949 praise of the "poignant beauty" of the first part's "intimate" descriptions of childhood in Martinique fell from grace along with other pre-Fanonian commendations of the novel and the declamation of "*doudou*" or "sugar and vanilla literature."[7] It is my contention that the first half of *Je suis martiniquaise* offers an opportunity to reconsider the first half of Fanon's claim: that black women want white men. Before she depicts Mayotte fully acceding to the mind-set of the colonizer, Capécia paints her an idyllic childhood where black girls find what they want with themselves, one another, and the island.

Perhaps as much as a black woman's desire for white men, these other desires too, in Fanon's judgment and in the colonial regime with which he is for a moment aligned, are a problem. She needs not to choose "the same" versus "the other" but rather to choose a certain same and a certain other. The conundrum Mayotte is caught in then is the one Cheryl Duffus and others describe, doubled: she is trapped in the colonial status that she embodies but also in the compulsory heterosexuality that undergirds and is promoted by both colonial and postcolonial projects. The insistence on heterosexuality as *the* norm that can and must not be violated—and its concomitant regulation of the boundaries of gender and family roles—belongs to a moral and political structure whose imposition forms an explicit part of French colonialism.[8]

José Martí, as discussed in the previous chapter, demonstrates the foundational failure of a new national romance incapable of escaping the heterosexual structure (similarly part of Spanish colonialism). Ironically, when he refers to "the result of the absence of the Oedipus complex in the Antilles," Fanon is among the early writers to address the ways in which Caribbean family structure differs from European family structure and to consider how, as a result, European models of individual and national desires that derive from the nuclear family model may not fit well in the Caribbean (180). Indeed, drawing from Carib and African traditions as well as from those traditions forged out of necessity during slavery, Caribbean domestic life, outside the elite European-dominated strata on which Martí's story focuses, organizes not around the heterosexual couple, but around extended families.[9] Furthermore, the great incidence of nonnuclear child-rearing households in the Caribbean renders uncompelling an oedipal model that divides mothers, fathers, sons, and daughters into so many components of a heterosexual family romance.

But Fanon, instead of seeing the absence of the oedipal model in the Caribbean as begging a thorough reconsideration of the configuration of family, gender, and sexuality, links it to his assertion of the absence of homosexuality in the Caribbean, offering it not as a general observation but only as the guarantor of the absence of homosexuality: "Let me observe at once that I had no opportunity to establish the overt presence of homosexuality in Martinique. This must be viewed as the result of the absence of the Oedipus Complex in the Antilles. The schema of homosexuality is well enough known" (180). And so, in spite of his insight, Fanon and the postcolonial project that remains deeply indebted to him, as Duffus writes, "relegates women to their traditional role in nationalism and community formation as maintainers of order through their reproductive capabilities" (1100). If she chooses Loulouze or a banana or a storm or the moon, Mayotte might refuse her position as a vessel for the reproduction of one or another socioeconomic system where the family, reproduction, and the state are linked through the disavowed womb. If in the second half of *Je suis martiniquaise*, and in all of Fanon's view of Mayotte, the problem is that she asserted her choice, and it was the wrong choice, about what would go into that womb, the other option that Mayotte might be considering is not using that womb at all for traditional reproduction. Mayotte's girlhood desires are neither neatly homo nor neatly hetero, just as they are neither clearly colonized nor clearly decolonized. It is, however, particularly difficult to explain her significant desires for women and natural elements as part of a trajectory of lactification due precisely to the question of what kind of reproduction, if any, might occur between them.[10] The critique that Mayotte wants to reproduce colonized subjectivity and colonized subjects not only mistakes the tone of her turn to André in the second half of *Je suis martiniquaise*, but it misses her multiple and mobile desires preserved and proliferated in the childhood idyll that can be best understood through the epistemology of the mangrove.

This chapter first considers how the historical and biographical contexts in which Capécia, and Fanon, wrote set the ground for my close reading of the first half of *Je suis martiniquaise*. At the moment when she writes, a nostalgic idealization of rural early-twentieth-century Martinique might itself express a radical attachment to specifically Martinican tradition, creolized but not departmentalized. Then I turn to an analysis of Mayotte's childhood ideal and the complex intersections of similarity and difference that structure its erotics and that allow Mayotte to pursue her desire for others—other races, other things, other genders—and for sames—same race, same gender, same place. Finally, I read the departure from that ideal in Mayotte's arrival in Fort-de-France, where even the *dream* of the independence and interdependence of Martinican girls is traded for the hetero-colonial economy.

Martinique and Mayotte Capécia, 1916–1955

Martinique as well as Mayotte were teetering, during the 1930s in which the first half of *Je suis martiniquaise* is set, on the brink of a new submission to (neo)colonial rule, and Capécia was not alone in revaluing the past and savoring the freedom that is fed by dreams of independence. After the Haitian revolution of 1791, which led to its independence in 1804, France was extremely attuned to quashing any slave uprisings or independence movements in its remaining Caribbean colonies, so Martinique looked on as most of the Spanish colonies either achieved independence or fell under US control during the later part of the nineteenth century. Nonetheless, a vibrant Martinican intellectual community developed, although not always in Martinique, in the first decades of the twentieth century. In Paris, Antilleans and Africans met and formed literary and political alliances that culminated in *négritude*. Both a political and a literary movement, *négritude* reclaimed pride in African ancestry and asserted the value of African aesthetic traditions largely through the principles of French Enlightenment. As T. Denean Sharpley-Whiting argues, although Aimé Césaire, Léopold Sedhar Senghor, and Léon-Gontran Damas are widely recognized as the fathers of *négritude*, the movement was equally born of the labors and ideas of Francophone women including the Martinican Nardal sisters and Suzanne Césaire. The important role of women in *négritude* was, however, eclipsed from the beginning by the attention given to male voices, and *négritude*'s most well-known writers focused on race and colonialism in ways that did not attend to gender and often reinforced images of women in minor maternal or spousal roles.[11]

In 1939, Aimé and Suzanne Césaire, recently married, returned to Martinique; Aimé Césaire became a teacher at the Lycée Schœlcher in Fort-de-France, where he counted Frantz Fanon among his students. That same year, Aimé Césaire published the first version of his *Cahier d'un Retour au pays natal* in a French periodical. The poem's lyric celebration of African tradition both revalues the very things that are deemed "backward" by European standards and romanticizes an African pastoral. Césaire's celebration of African nature resonates in Capécia's celebration of an organic Martinican pastoral. Césaire's return to Africa in *Cahier*, however, comes after a deeply critical look at Fort-de-France:

> the disparate stranding, the exacerbated stench of corruption, the monstrous sodomies of the host and the sacrificing priests, the impassable beakhead frames of prejudice and stupidity, the prostitutions, the lubricities, the treasons, the lies, the frauds, the concussions . . . Right here the parade of laughable and scrofulous buboes, the forced feedings of very strange microbes, the poisons without known alexins, the sanies of really ancient sores, the unforeseeable fermentations of putrescible species.
>
> At the end of daybreak, the great motionless night, the stars deader than a caved-in balafon, the teratical bub of night, sprouted from our villainies, our self-denials. (5–6)

Capécia's celebration of rural Martinique reads almost like a response to Césaire's excoriation of Fort-de-France, as if to suggest that he needn't have looked so far to find the other side of the island. But both Capécia and Césaire were in Fort-de-France in the late 1930s and early 1940s, and their literary turns to other times and places can be read against the ways that both became increasingly entangled, in the mid-1940s, in the colonial machine.

When France fell to the Nazis in 1940, although the local Martinican government voted to follow de Gaulle and the Allies, the colonial governor, along with Admiral Robert, a Vichy naval officer whose troops were stationed in Martinique, accepted the armistice. For three years Admiral Robert and his troops were blockaded on the island. The soldiers stepped into the positions of white economic and erotic power vacated by the plantation elite that, after a resurgence of the rum trade during World War I, was in rapid decline. They reimposed colonial racism unobscured even by the veneer of French universalism.[12] Nonetheless, in 1941, Susanne Césaire began to articulate her visions for a Martinican anticolonial literature in the literary review *Tropiques*, which, along with Aimé Césaire, René Ménil, and others, she founded in 1941.[13]

Admiral Robert was finally overthrown in 1943, and Martinique joined the Free French as the Vichy troops left. In 1945, Aimé Césaire was elected mayor of Fort-de-France and deputy to the French National Assembly. In a complicated combination of compromises and ultimately unsuccessful strategic alliances not unlike those that Mayotte makes in her liaisons with French men in the second half of *Je suis martiniquaise*, Césaire was instrumental in achieving not Martinique's independence but its transformation, in 1946, into a French *département d'outre-mer*.[14]

Composing her novels in the late 1940s in Paris, Capécia had a view of the compromises and lost ideals of the *négritude* movement as well as of its erasure of women's voices and concerns. Capécia was not of the class of Martinican intellectuals who attended the Lycée Schœlcher. She was not an active member of the Antillean intellectual and artistic community in Fort-de-France or Paris. Her idealization of her own childhood freedom coincides with and allows her to avoid *négritude*'s equally, if differently, idealizing support of a free Martinique in a pan-African alliance.

Fanon appears unable to distinguish between Capécia the writer and Mayotte the character.[15] The confusion is certainly enjoined by the coincidence of the author's name with the character's, with the autobiographical nature of the title, and with the claims of the marketing material that the book offers a "testimonial," but other contemporary critics understood *Je suis martiniquaise* as belonging to the long tradition of pseudo- or semi-autobiographical novels, referring for example to Capécia as a "*romancière*" (novelist), perhaps less than an "*écrivaine*" (writer) but all the more solidly located in a fictional tradition.[16]

As Christiane Makward's 1999 biography, *Mayotte Capécia ou l'aliénation selon Fanon*, details, Mayotte Capécia was the pseudonym of Lucette Céranus, who, like the character Mayotte, was born a twin in Martinique, lived for a time in Fort-de-France, became pregnant by a French sailor named André, and moved to France without him. However, while Mayotte spent her early years in the Martinican countryside first with both of her parents and then after her mother's death with her father, Céranus was never recognized by her father and moved to Fort-de-France with her mother and sister when she was an infant. Céranus worked with her mother and sister in the market until, when she was 13, her mother died. The sisters then worked in a variety of jobs in Fort-de-France. Céranus had two children by two different men before she met André; after he left her, she became engaged to another French man who she was to follow to Paris for the wedding. Before leaving for Paris, Céranus convinced her father to allow her to take his last name, Combette, which she did in 1944. When she arrived in Paris later that year, her fiancé was nowhere to be found. She worked in various domestic service jobs through

1947, when she attempted to become an editor/author of André's memoirs, of which she had a copy. The publishing house she approached, Corrêa, refused André's manuscript but suggested that Combette use it as a springboard for her own memoirs, which they would publish. Combette then worked with the publishing house to write the first half of the book and to rewrite the second, based on André's manuscript. She signed the final book with the name of its protagonist, Mayotte Capécia.[17]

Fanon's inability to distinguish between author and character attests to the success of Capécia's autobiographical invention, but it also diverts critical attention from the book's creative expression of ideas about Martinique and Martinican women.[18] Capécia's second novel, *La Négresse blanche* (*The White Negress*), published, under the same name, with the genre specification "a novel" just under the title, could not occasion the same confusion of author and character. Fanon, however, brushed aside *La Négresse blanche* in a footnote that accuses Capécia of being unable to "reckon with her own unconscious" and therefore constructing characters who "belittle the Negro" (52, n. 12). After Fanon's summary execution, Capécia fell from grace. She did not publish again and died of cancer in 1955. Her work was little read or known outside of its mention by Fanon until the 1980s.

Mayotte's Other Ideal

In the opening paragraph of *Je suis martiniquaise*, Mayotte constructs herself as a child who is motivated by sensual desire. Her first bodily craving is to ingest the abundant fruit of the land: "My mother dangled before my mouth a bunch of bananas. I tried to catch them, for I adored them. I think I learned to walk out of gluttony" (7). The infantile paradise where doting mothers prance around with bunches of fresh ripe bananas risks repeating so many other utopic romanticizations of Caribbean women and plants, but the obviously utopic quality of this and so many other images from the first half of the novel makes it difficult to find the facile repetition of a Caribbean Garden of Eden, and points toward a more self-conscious idealization.[19] Furthermore, the self-sufficiency of girl and land is an ideal whose erasure is assured in its very imagery, for bananas represent not only a native plant of Martinique and a staple of Martinican cuisine but also one of Martinique's major exports to Europe, and thus the island's status as a "banana republic."[20] The tenuousness of the ideal, its construction through its impending loss, is made obvious only a few paragraphs later as Mayotte realizes that she will soon become an "abandoned child," literally abandoned by her mother's early death but also forced to give up freedom and accept discipline. In one sense, this is a necessary part of any growing up; any story that follows a character beyond childhood will tell of her struggle with or submission to some kind of discipline, some loss of freedom, and where the context is colonial that discipline will be colonial. And most Bildungsromane depict the preadolescent moment as some kind of ideal. But the details of Mayotte's ideal and its loss are revealing: Capécia does not just lament the limitations that adulthood and colonialism impose on black girls, but she mourns a particular set of lost possibilities that are characterized by the ways that they precede and exceed binary divisions such as heteronormativity versus homosexuality (or what in this oppositional structure might be homo-radicality). Mayotte's childhood desires are divided and entangled in a mangrove-like structure where she reaches in many different directions, wanting and enjoying not a series of transitional objects that build up to heterosexual adulthood but a disparate group of things whose very transverse qualities are constitutive of their appeal.

In her ideal childhood, Mayotte enjoys the freedom to indulge her "passion for games, sports, rough-housing" (8). It is a freedom from the control of bodily impulses and from binary gender roles. It is the freedom to play in a group of children that is not divided by gender or color: "about twenty kids of both sexes and all nuances" (10). The gender blending of the group extends also to the individuals in it, who are each boys or girls and "of both sexes." Mayotte refers to herself in the feminine, with the designation "girl," and with the expectation that she will become a woman at the same time as she speaks of herself as a *garçon manqué*, a tomboy, but more literally someone who has just missed being a boy, in other words between genders (8).

The gender ambiguity of Mayotte and her friends grants a certain queerness to their interactions. However, as important as any romantic play in which they may engage with one another is the passion that they, and especially Mayotte, experience with the land and the elements. For what Mayotte loves to do with her group of friends is to get caught in a storm: "Storms of my country, how I loved your violence and the great waves of your rains and that water from the heights, all full of your lightning!" (10–11). The apostrophe—the French *orages* (storms) embeds the "o" of apostrophe in the first word of the address—extends into a personification of Martinican storms that allows a love interest and a corporeal connection to emerge. The sentence builds to an exclamation whose last word, *foudres*, designates not only a weather event, lightning, but also half of a set phrase, *coup de foudre*, love at first sight or lovestruck.

It is a commonplace of writing about the Caribbean to conflate the women with the island or its various parts, but here Mayotte seems to see herself not as *being* the island or the storm, but as *having*, or at least wanting to have, them.[21] In order to take the island as her lover, Mayotte simultaneously aligns herself with and distinguishes herself from a female embodied land. Her group of friends are called the Weeds, *les Mauvaises Herbes*. The noun phrase *Mauvaises Herbes* is feminine in French, but weeds are hardly the traditional woman-nature image; in contrast to the open ports or fertile flowers that form the stereotype of the island-woman, weeds belong to the realm of the mangrove: disorganized, impenetrable, and ineradicable thickets of ambiguously gendered growth. The particulars of what this weedy Mayotte loves in the storm—violence, lightning—make it hard, even as it is personified to become a lover, to assign the storm any particular race or gender. This confusion between animate and inanimate, human and elemental objects of love and desire marks the first half of *Je suis martiniquaise* and makes it difficult to qualify Mayotte's sexuality. What is certain is that what she most savors as a child is unbounded sensation, social and physical disorder, and contradiction—things that she finds naturally abundant on and in the island itself.

During this time she also has "like the other girls, an admirer, a little black boy named Paul" (11), but his designation as "an admirer" ("*un amoureux*") leaves out any comment on *her* feelings for *him*, and her contextualization of the relationship with Paul suggests that she accepts him because that is what is done, regardless of her personal feelings for the boy.[22] It is in comparison not only to her impassioned address to the storm but also to the gaze she directs at an older girl, Loulouze, that Mayotte's relationship with Paul seems so unremarkable. Mayotte's idyll certainly includes relationships between boys and girls, but these already position a passive girl in a socially structured dynamic and contrast with the richness of feeling that she has with the storm and with Loulouze.

The Cambeille river where Mayotte and her friends play is also where the *blanchisseuses* ("washerwomen," literally "white-washers") wash their clothes and where "after their work, the youngest bathed freely in the river" (12). One person in particular stands out among these women:

> Loulouze was the most beautiful and most gay and, despite the difference in our ages, we were friends. Still a child, despite her seventeen years, she loved to laugh; after she had spread her washing on the rocks, she often came to join us while it dried. When we had strung a rope above the rapid water, she hung by her arms and crossed delicately, as we also did, but it was different. Loulouze's movements caused me a certain emotion. Sometimes also, she bathed with us. She had a golden skin with tones of orange and banana, long black hair that rolled into braids and that were only kinky at the base, a rather flat nose and thick lips, but a face of a shape that showed she must have rather close white ancestors. I looked at her chest with envy, I who was completely flat. When she was serious, her big black eyes, that became brown when one saw them up

> close, made her look rather melancholy, but she was rarely serious and, at every chance, she showed teeth that shone like the sun. (12–13)

Working and playing in the river, Loulouze merges with and emerges from this force of nature. As in the storm, Mayotte admires and desires in Loulouze a blend of innocence and risk, and of similarity—here of age and gender—and difference—of occupation, education.

The physical description of Loulouze seems to offer a special appreciation of those things that allude to her white ancestry: her "gold" skin, mostly straight hair, and most tellingly "a face whose shape reveals rather close white ancestry." Perhaps even where it is directed toward a sameness of geography or gender, Mayotte's prepubescent ideal is already guided by a desire to have and to be as white as possible. But Loulouze's whiteness combines with her other qualities to connect her not so much to a French colonial ideal as to Maman Dlô, the river woman whose power of seduction is as irresistible as it is dangerous.

Appearing also as Manman d'leau, Mami Wata, and River Muma, Maman Dlô is a mythico-religious character prevalent throughout the Caribbean and West Africa. She beckons with her beautiful face and voice and the promise of material as well as sensual gain. Maman Dlô's beauty as well as her connection with money and mechanical progress stem in part from her mixed race: like Loulouze she has long smooth hair, light skin, and Aryan features. Often identified with East Indians or Europeans, her origins have been traced to the first encounters of Africans and Indo-Europeans in the fifteenth century, when she became a syncretic artifact, recoding various European and East Indian icons—mirrors, hairbrushes, coins—into Afro-Caribbean mythology and religion.[23] It is not that by their association with Maman Dlô, Loulouze's traits are less white, but that whiteness itself becomes less exclusively the territory of the colonizer. Loulouze's connection with Maman Dlô positions those elements of her character that would seem to fall outside of a Caribbean tradition (her light skin, her later financial success and rejection of marriage, the sexual attraction she engenders in Mayotte) all the more firmly within it, while simultaneously acknowledging that even the "within" of Afro-Caribbean mythology is always already created out of some sort of syncretism.[24]

While Maman Dlô at times grants things like material wealth and sexual pleasure, men who do not do her bidding or who mistakenly follow her beneath the surface are killed; women who follow Maman Dlô often become Maman Dlôs, temporarily or permanently, themselves.[25] But Maman Dlô attracts devotees as well as partners and victims. Unlike her victims, who think they can possess her, Maman Dlô's devotees balance their desire to have her with their desire to be her.[26] They exchange devotion and service, often sexual, for the chance to be touched, in whatever way she deems fit, by Maman Dlô. Inasmuch as Loulouze can be read as a Maman Dlô figure, Mayotte can be read as her devotee.

The play of self and other, same and different, in Maman Dlô, in Mayotte and Loulouze's relationship, and in *Je suis martiniquaise*, is complicated. Although Fanon tries to separate out into easily distinguishable categories—"*la femme de couleur*," "*l'homme de couleur*," "*la Blanche*," and "*le Blanc*"—the categories are neither as coherent nor as fully distinct as he seems to imagine, and the alignment of others and sames even among those four is not clear. As Capécia's descriptions of boys and girls show, Martinique is far from homogeneous in terms of race, culture, or collaboration.[27] For Mayotte to love "*le Martinicain*" is not necessarily to love "the same"[28] and for her to love whiteness is not necessarily to love "the other."[29]

The innocence of the riverside encounters between Mayotte and Loulouze almost belies an interpretation of Loulouze as Maman Dlô: they mostly chat and look and move alongside one another, and while the emotion that Loulouze inspires in Mayotte is intense—the "certain emotion" she feels when she sees Loulouze move, and the beating of her heart "as it had never beat before" when she sees her despondent—their physical contact by the riverside appears restricted to "an arm around the neck" (19). But Mayotte also reassures Loulouze, "Ah know how tuh keep secrets. Ah already have uh collection uh dem, dis will make one more, dat's all" (18). Mayotte is indeed a faithful devotee; the secrets are never divulged.

The girlhood innocence, and intensity, of Mayotte and Loulouze's relationship, and even the secret it may contain, set it in the realm of *macocotte* relationships that Antonia MacDonald-Smythe analyzes in the work of Oonya Kempadoo and Jamaica Kincaid. A term designating "the intense frienships shared by young adolescent girls," according to MacDonald-Smythe, *macocotte* includes "expressions of pleasurable intimacy, the sensuality of frequent bodily contact, the tenderness of devotedness, and the 'rightness' and the joy that one girl feels in the company of another" (224). MacDonald-Smythe's further observations that "in the Caribbean the quality and context of female friendships are as yet undertheorized criteria for tracking the development of libidinal subjectivity" suggest that her assertion that *macocotte* relationships "operate within a heterosexual paradigm" and "create structures for socialization that reinforce the [heterosexual] status quo" might only be a part of the story (226). MacDonald-Smythe is certainly right that *macocotte* relationships ought to be interpreted "as manifestations of sexual awakening rather than solely as indicators of homosexual desire" (229) and that "in Caribbean society these same-sex female friendships among adolescent girls become a site for the erotic, a site that needs to be established as different from the ones occupied by homosexual desire" (230). But it is my argument that a Caribbean structure of desire and sexuality is not limited to the binary choice of heterosexual or homosexual. As my readings of both the relationship between Mayotte and Loulouze here and those between the girl narrator(s) and various other girls and women in Kincaid's *At the Bottom of the River* and Patricia Powell's *Me Dying Trial* in later chapters demonstrate, the adolescent female friendship model is neither fully contained in adolescence nor neatly streamlined into adult homosexuality *or* heterosexuality. Indeed, among MacDonald-Smythe's own profound insights is that the Caribbean

> spectrum of passionate friendships . . . like a rainbow, has variations, latitude, and seeming boundarylessness and, because of its complexities, allow[ing] females to locate themselves in ways that are appropriate to their life experiences. Implicit to this is the notion that female sexuality is fluid, capable of changing over time, and that this plasticity is both situational and social. (227)

Macocotte relationships transform with changes in age, location, family configuration, and much more, but not into only or always either heterosexual or homosexual adulthood; those limited and limiting options in *Je suis martiniquaise* are the tragic result of the acceptance of binary colonial structures.

The location of Mayotte and Loulouze's meetings at the river's edge and deep in the island's woods links their connection to Mayotte's relationship with the elements and situates their interactions in a kind of Martinican sylvan pastoral that will remain opposed to the urban romance with the French officer in Part Two.[30] But that is the point: the awakening of Mayotte's desires occurs in a childhood idyll. It is interrupted not by any waning of Mayotte's desire for Loulouze, or even of what might be Loulouze's desire for Mayotte, but rather by Loulouze's entry into the "traffic in women." Loulouze is given a "gold" bracelet by a young man in return for which she gives him something that she deems Mayotte too young to hear. As a result, Loulouze's father, with the approval of the women of the village, sends Loulouze away to Fort-de-France. Loulouze has entered into the exchange of material goods for women's bodies. She may be able to maintain some control of the proceeds of that exchange, but her body and her "desires" have become something that can be purchased. If there are gains, they are often not what they seem. The bracelet turns out not to be real gold, and the first new knowledge Loulouze shares with Mayotte is that "Life's hard fuh a woman, you gonna see Mayotte, 'specially fuh a culluhd woman" (20). If the girlhood relationship is, in MacDonald-Smythe's words, "a learning space for heterosexual identity development," what is learned is as much the undesirability of heteronormative adulthood as how to survive it. And it might even be that one of the survival mechanisms that it prepares is an interweaving of girlhood relationships into adult experience. Undeniably, colonial binarism often not only limits this possibility but affects the postcolonial national construction of official sexuality, but what interests me here is that plasticity persists in practices and stories, even ones like *Lucía Jerez* and *Je suis martiniquaise* that ultimately cannot resist colonial heteronormativity.

In this story of multiple and intersecting desires, it is not surprising that even Mayotte's progression from her idyllic childhood to the hard realization of colonial heteronormativity is not neatly linear. Indeed, at the same time as Mayotte desires nature she desires a black boy, at the same time as she desires Loulouze she has her first love for a white man (her parish priest), and after she loses the first black boys, Loulouze, and the white man, she falls in love with the moon.

> I walked, all alone along the edge of the sea which lengthily reflected the moon. I was in love with the moon, I filled my heart with her light which seemed to me at once purer and more troubling than that of the sun, I felt myself shiver at her contact, I spoke to her, I offered her my virgin heart and said to her: "talk back tuh me, tell me that yuh love me . . ." (87)[31]

Even more so than the storm, the moon is personified: given the power of bodily touch, spoken to and asked to speak back. This is for Mayotte as full-blown a love affair as the one she has with Horace, to whom she will soon give her virginity. Mayotte's love of the moon is also presented as one of her first independent and adult relationships. Just prior to this passage, she notes that her father now "spoke to me as if I was a little woman" and she is able to go out for these nighttime encounters because her father's own nighttime antics leave her "more free" (87). The maturing Mayotte still loves the Caribbean elements, but now she does so without the company of her friends, walking alone along the shore of the Caribbean sea to declare her love to the moon.

The moon's traditional feminine symbolism is highlighted by its feminine gendering in French grammar. The reflection of the moon in the sea, *la mer*, also gendered feminine in French and homophonous with *mère*, mother, establishes a space of feminine connection. Mayotte loves the moon through its distorted reflection, looking at it not in the sky but drawn out, "lengthily," by and in the sea. Moon, sea, and girl are connected not so much because they are like one another but because they like each other. As in her riverside encounters with Loulouze and the washerwomen, for Mayotte desire between things feminine is desire for feminine difference.

Mayotte repeats the symbolic contrast between a feminine moon and a masculine sun as she calls the moon's light "at once purer and more troubling than that of the sun." The purity, as well as the trouble, of the moonlight might derive from its singularly feminine associations not only as it shines down from the moon but also as it meets the ocean and Mayotte, in contrast to what would be a heterogeneous encounter of male sunlight and female bodies. However, I have just argued for the heterogeneity inherent in the meeting of moon and girl through oceanic reflection. Perhaps what is troubling and troubled is the homo–hetero divide. The purer, and more troubling, qualities of the moonlight might also be understood in racial terms. Set off by the dark of night, the moon and its light appear a "purer" and whiter color than the sun and perhaps the contrast of pure white moonlight and dark night, or perhaps the "pure" light-ness itself is what Mayotte finds "disturbing." Either way, Mayotte's love affair with the moon presents a similar conundrum as that with Loulouze. Where Mayotte may desire a same in terms, for example, of national origin or gender, she equally seems to desire an other in terms here of race in a broad sense—human versus nonhuman—and in a narrow sense—black versus white.

Mayotte in her early loves begs a series of complex questions: Does loving darkness have to entail complete rejection of all whiteness? Is any love of whiteness a love of colonizer? Is any love of colonizer necessarily part of a desire for "lactification"? How does a love of same gender, of same geographical origin, complicate other divisions of hetero and homo? How can we talk about desire between women as it intertwines with other desires?

Je suis martiniquaise does not answer these questions, but it does show them to be constitutive not only of the colonial progress in the city but also of the, consequently, idealized pastoral past: even in the idyll of the child on the moonlit shore, the values and the influence of the colonizer have arrived, and they cannot even remain an outside force threatening to destroy the idyll because the idyll in its necessary retrospectivity necessarily responds to and perhaps incorporates their values. Any precolonial ideal is predicated on its impending and always already accomplished loss.

What interrupts Mayotte's affair with the moon is not any failure of prosopopoeia or any deficiency in the embodiment of the moon, but rather new events on other fronts. Mayotte is denied the opportunity to explore what she and the moon might share by the "terrible shock" of learning about her father's affair with a girl her own age and then by a boat with a couple singing a well-known Créole song about his departure for France, which leads her back to her friends and to Horace, who will fall in love with her. It is a perverse world out there, full of men preying on women, and colonialism preying on both, the text seems to say, and Martinican girls can do nothing about it. You can only avoid it for so long, then it will sweep you up.

Indeed, at the end of Part One, Mayotte moves to Fort-de-France and gets swept into the urban economy and a carnival that unmixes her up and readies her for the affair with the French officer that is already under way at the beginning of Part Two.

Unmixing It Up at Carnival

Despite her enchantment with the sands and forests of the Martinican countryside, Mayotte is tempted by the stories of urban "progress" told by her father and sister: "I, too, wanted to see that city about which Francette had told me so much, those elegant people, those stores, those beautiful women in bathing suits on the beach" (112). The colonial city's class structure and economic power entail a gender order where French men make money and decisions and French women spend profits and time in an early version of tourism.

Fort-de-France is the center of colonial power in Martinique. In her first description of it, Mayotte compares Fort-de-France not to any place she has lived previously, but to Paris. And the first street she walks in Fort-de-France is la Liberté, at the end of which, "on the big white house where the Government of Martinique had set up, flew the tricolored flag" (113). The rural Martinique of Mayotte's childhood is no less a product of colonialism, but it is the kind of colonialism that has trickled down country roads and mixed in many culverts with the other native and imported traditions of the island. In Fort-de-France, Mayotte faces the source of colonial power in Martinique. Its promise of liberty is there for Mayotte to seize, but that liberty comes at the price of an insidious "colonization of the mind," which freezes the mangled structure of desire and sexuality as one more folk artifact and accepts hetero-patriarchy with all of its gender and sexual binaries as the desired future.

In Fort-de-France's main square stands a statue of the woman Mayotte will, in many ways, come to emulate in Part Two of *Je suis martiniquaise*:

> The Empress Joséphine. My heart began to race. My father had often spoken of the wife of the great Napoleon, she was the pride of our island. That a Martinican could have become Empress of France, of the entire French Empire, that she could have become the wife of the greatest sovereign in the world, filled us all with pride. We worshiped her and I, like all the girls from home, I had often dreamed of her unparalleled destiny. (113–114)

Mayotte's recent arrival in Fort-de-France, the fact that she garnered her information about Joséphine from her father, and her use of the "we" of "Martinican girls" in place of the insistent "*je*" ("I") of the title and the speaker's designation of herself to this point figure her dream of Joséphine as less the expression of a personal desire than that of a cultural myth, indeed the kind that disciplines the polymorphous desires of Martinican girls into a hetero-colonial model. Mayotte seems here to align herself neatly with Empress Joséphine as a Martinican, as if that identification were not traversed by a color line, as if Joséphine, *née* Marie Joseph Rose Tascher de la Pagerie, came from a family that was, like Mayotte's or like that of her childhood friends, mixed either by lineage or by association. Like many women Mayotte knows, marriage seems to have served Marie Joseph Rose to escape difficult economic circumstances and to reshape her identity, and her marriages first to the French aristocrat Alexandre, Vicomte de Beauharnais, and then, after his beheading and with two children by him, to Napoleon Bonaparte, led her to the exceedingly high position of Empress Joséphine. But Joséphine was from a prestigious French colonial family, and that distinction separates her from the likes of Mayotte in ways that neither the Tascher de la Pagerie family's economic difficulties nor questions about Joséphine's possible creolization, by virtue of being born in Martinique or through the affair of some relative, can affect.[32] And if Joséphine represents the possibility that a Martinican girl might attain equality with the French through marriage, her instrumental role in the restoration of slavery on the island between 1814 and 1830 should serve as a reminder of what French power represents in the Caribbean.[33] Aimé Césaire had, in 1939, described the statue as "Empress Josephine of the French dreaming high, high above negridom," but Mayotte in Fort-de-France sees through the eyes not of the anticolonial poet or even the independence-loving girl she was just days before but of the colonized woman. More striking, however, than Mayotte's acceptance of the dream—she has previously accepted the dream of Catechism—is the absence of any expression of a desire to have the marble woman. The statue openly displays Joséphine's bosom, and while it may not be of the Loulouzian amplitude that so attracts Mayotte, it receives not even passing mention; the statue's fair smooth skin, and curly coiffure also go unremarked where earlier such attributes are consistently described with erotic intensity. Mayotte's arrival in Fort-de-France announces the novel's shift. But before Empress Joséphine's model passes from being a dream Mayotte shares with other Martinican girls to one she actually tries to act out, a few more things must occur.

Her first night in Fort-de-France, Mayotte reconnects with Loulouze: "I slept that night in her bed. She had a voluminous chest to which I took great pleasure comparing my little breasts" (118). The absence of the oedipal model even in Fort-de-France is here evident as are its possibilities. Loulouze has two children, but when Mayotte asks if she's married: "Fuh nothin' in the wuhld would Ah marry, Loulouze declared. Why would Ah marry now that Ah ha' kids?" (118). Loulouze has born children as light if not lighter than herself, but by purposefully remaining out of wedlock she leaves open the question of whom and what she's born them for, and she reserves room for erotic developments with Mayotte or other non-white non-men. Mayotte and Loulouze's reconnection, with a much more explicit suggestion of sexuality than what they shared by the riverside, reminds that the entry into the traffic in women, and into the hetero-colonial economy, may change the expression of desire between women of Mayotte's childhood idyll but in its imposition of gender, racial, and colonial hierarchies may offer more opportunity for, indeed may even require or at least rest on, women supporting one another economically, emotionally, and erotically. But whatever is required to support the colonial economy becomes just that in Fort-de-France and in Mayotte's adulthood, secondary to and subsumed under the colonial rule.

I have repeated that the colonial order is a binary structure that works, actively and passively, to take over the mangled structure of desire and sexuality in the Caribbean, but at the same time the colonial order and the mangle are inextricable from one another. The colonial order works as much by pushing aside and by subsuming as by eradicating the mangled structure. The mangle survives by both withstanding and incorporating influences, from within and without, above and below, by adapting to change without changing completely. In *Je suis martiniquaise*, the mangled structure of desire and sexuality, which includes desire between girls and between women, survives by becoming a part of an idealized past.

It is, perhaps less ironically than one might think, in the place that seems to allow for all manner of sexual transgression that Mayotte finally trades her passions for Loulouze, the storms, and the moon for social mobility through André. Maryse Condé finds in *Je suis martiniquaise* a depiction of "the impossibility for [a West Indian girl in those days] to build up an aesthetics which would enable her to come to terms with the color of her skin" (131). The Carnival chapter at the end of Part One might offer an even more biting indictment than Condé: it is not that Mayotte is unable to build up that aesthetics, but that the beauty of raw nature, *métissage*, and femininity that she found in the people, the land, and the elements of her youth is coopted and abandoned. For after her re-encounter with Loulouze, Mayotte could be in one of her strongest positions in the novel. She begins to achieve financial independence. Although she has left the natural elements of rural Martinique that so move her, she finds in the city at least some of what she loved in the country: Loulouze and all that she represents.

In the chapter following her night with Loulouze, Mayotte attends the long-awaited Carnival. This could be a place for the authentic expression of Martinican aesthetics: a "native" festival that not only celebrates local notions of the beauty of blackness, *métissage*, drums, and playful performativity but resists European valorizations of whiteness, purity, and restraint as it offers an opportunity to turn everything upside down.[34] Mayotte describes her first impression of Carnival: "Loulouze had told me so much about Carnival, but I had never imagined something so beautiful. Plunged, from one day to the next, into a world that was all farce and adventure, I was extraordinarily excited" (125). However, since Mayotte has never before witnessed Carnival, its native status comes into some question, and, as Mikhail Bakhtin has shown, the reversals of Carnival may succeed not in controverting the status quo but in reinforcing it. Indeed, the Carnival Mayotte attends effects not a resurgence of Martinican tradition but the imposition of colonial order in Martinique, and yet it is somehow accepted by Mayotte and all those around her as Martinican—perhaps in the same way that the "Government of Martinique" flies a French flag with no seeming irony.

Even as Mayotte expresses excitement about the "farce and adventure" of Carnival, she seems to anticipate something much more conventional than the wild mixing of elements that she so loved in the storms of her childhood. Carnival will not offer farce for the sake of play or adventure for the sake of surprise, but rather farce and adventure for the sake of finding the order that undergirds them, the same colonial order that supports the dream of Joséphine. Mayotte explains: "I was dreaming of the Prince Charming that I would find under a Pierrot [a stock character of French pantomime] or a clown costume" (125). In both scenarios, the young Martinican girl enters into an affair with a colonial agent—Joséphine married Napoleon, quite directly the head of the French empire, while "prince charming" is a standard formulation to designate the male hero in European fairytales. Mayotte has partaken of this dream ever since her first love for the white priest, but as long as she was in rural Martinique she had competing desires and she believed in *les guaiblesses* and *les zombis* as much as in any European mythology (15, 106). In Fort-de-France, the colonial order begins not just to penetrate but to take over Mayotte's dreams, and Carnival is the last hurdle that sends her full flung into the tragic pursuit of lactification.

It turns out, furthermore, to be common knowledge that the colonial order is not the dream of Joséphine realized, but only another mask over a much more sinister colonial reality: "I did not yet know that, more often, the opposite occurs and men who are but clowns disguise themselves, to abuse us, as Prince Charmings" (125). This function of Carnival is common knowledge to women, but Mayotte stands here still on the brink of childhood:

"I thought I was already a woman, but I still had many illusions" (125). Coming of age, Mayotte teeters between an imaginary childhood ideal and an illusory colonial dream, from which she will soon tumble into the pit of pain and disappointment that awaits her in womanhood and in the second half of the novel.

During Carnival, Mayotte gives up the play of gender traits and roles that she relished in her rural childhood for a straightforward set of reversals that rely on a stable set of binary opposites: "Many were, like me, transvestites for the night. I had, in fact, gotten myself a man's costume . . . Soon I noticed that a masked woman was following me. I looked back occasionally and found with pleasure that she was still there" (126). Mayotte's expression of surprise when she discovers her pursuant to be a man is either disingenuous or else her final moment of ingenuity: "What was my surprise to hear a man's voice from behind the velour mask" (127). She had explained her own manly costume as what girls wore, not an expression of gender bending but of gender conformity.[35] And she went to the Carnival hoping to find the "prince charming of whom I dreamed" so that her own transvestism could only have been designed to encounter another, a sort of double negative that would resolve into a standard positive (127). Mayotte is "a little disappointed" not at the gender of her partner, but at his race and class: "it was the voice of a colored man named Yvon, one of my neighbors" (127). Mayotte's acceptance of a colored man during Carnival does not mark her resistance to "the mind-set of the colonizer" but rather one penultimate step on her path into the arms of a white soldier.

Mayotte goes to sleep twice on the last page of the Part One, as if putting to final rest, though with some difficulty, her girlhood self. After the dance with Yvon, "I went home and fell asleep immediately" (128). She wakes to one last hope of a mixed-up world, full of Martinican tradition.

> Around one o'clock I was awoken by voices coming up from the street. Finding again my excitement from the night before, I ran to the window. At first, I wondered if I was still dreaming. The road was full of little black devils shouting about who is best. The day after Mardi Gras is, in fact, the day of the guiablesse here. That day, everyone wears black dresses tied at the waist with a white scarf, heads wrapped in white scarves, other scarves covering shoulders, and glasses sit on faces so uniformly floured that it is no longer possible to distinguish blacks from whites. (128)

But her participation in Carnival has set Mayotte straight, as it were. She describes the day after Carnival as something that happens "*chez nous*" (translated as "here," but literally "in our home"), forgetting her own unfamiliarity with Carnival and lumping together all Martinicans and all of Martinique as "*nous*" ("us") in the face of an other to which it seems to feel a need to explain itself.[36] And she exchanges her childhood enjoyment of "all the nuances" where color difference matters not as part of a dividing line but instead as part of the spectrum that makes up a Martinique of whose racial complexity she is much too aware to draw simple lines like white versus black, for this binary division where blacks should be distinguished from whites, and there is a concomitant panic when that might prove impossible. For the "little black devils" are not here just playful creatures of Martinican mythology, or companions of the *guaiblesses* that earlier hunted men but did not scare Mayotte and her childhood girlfriends (10–11), but they have become the stuff of Mayotte's nightmares. After just a few more lines describing the festival day, Mayotte goes to sleep for a last time in Part One, "dreaming that those little black devils whose cries had awoken me were running after me and I could not rid myself of them" (128). Mayotte's transformation is complete when she not only sees the sprites of her childhood as "little black devils" that might chase her, but also wishes more than anything to be free of them. Mayotte has accepted the binary of the Carnival and of colonialism, and now all she can do is try to be on the right (white, heterosexual) side.

The beginning of the next chapter is the beginning of Part Two. Mayotte wakes up, and we soon realize enough time has passed for her to be living with André in his house that "dominated the vast harbor of Fort de France" (129). The tragedy ensues: Mayotte becomes pregnant by André, who abandons her, exemplifying Fanon's model of "the colored woman and the white man."

And so we have returned to Fanon, whose shadow is so long because his analysis is so incisive on so many fronts, and because his example as much as his analysis shows how resistance to colonialism is so often also complicit with it. *Je suis martiniquaise* could have offered Fanon, does offer us, not only the opportunity to see how Capécia mourned Mayotte's fate but also a glimpse of her other ideals. It has become difficult to see Capécia as doing anything other than mourning Mayotte's fate. But that mourning is not only because of colonialism's insidious power, it is also because even with colonialism in place, Mayotte was able to articulate another ideal, on to which she could not hold.

CHAPTER 3

Replaced Origins: Maryse Condé's *Moi, Tituba sorcière . . . Noire de Salem*

Disturbed by the brief and dismissive mention, in historical accounts of the Salem witch craze, of Tituba as "a slave originating from the West Indies and probably practicing 'hoodoo' " (ix), Maryse Condé undertakes in *Moi, Tituba sorcière . . . Noire de Salem* to "offer [Tituba] her revenge by inventing a life such as she might perhaps have wished it to be told" (Scarboro, "Afterward": 199). Playing with the genres of autobiography, slave narrative, and historical novel, *Moi, Tituba sorcière . . .* offers the first person account of the life and death of Tituba. Like Ann Petry's 1956 *Tituba of Salem Village*, *Moi, Tituba sorcière . . .* posits that Tituba's presence in Salem was instrumental in both the "bewitched" girls' and the ministers' and judges' ability to make their case for the manifest presence of the Devil among them.[1] *Moi, Tituba sorcière . . .* rewrites not only the history and literary depictions of witch trials, but also Nathaniel Hawthorne's *The Scarlet Letter*, and it includes not only Tituba's version of the infamous events in Salem, but also her prior and subsequent life in Barbados.

Conceived out of a slave-ship rape, Tituba is born on a plantation in Barbados, where she witnesses the deaths of Abena, her mother, and Yao, her adoptive father. After fleeing the plantation, Tituba is taken in by Mama Yaya, a witch doctor who lives in the island's swamps. Mama Yaya teaches Tituba the secrets of the healing arts and communication with the spirits so that Tituba can continue her work after Mama Yaya's death. But not long after Mama Yaya passes into the spirit world, Tituba meets John Indian and, heedless of the warnings she receives from the spirits, marries him. Tituba follows John Indian into slavery in the family of Reverend Samuel Parris as the latter departs for Massachusetts. In Salem, Tituba uses her craft to help heal her sickly mistresses and falls prey to the witch hunts of the 1690s. Jailed in Ipswich for witchcraft, Tituba meets Hester, redrawn from Nathaniel Hawthorne's *The Scarlet Letter*. The two women share a cell, as well as an intimate connection that introduces Tituba to "another kind of pleasure" and draws Hester's spirit into Tituba's world of "invisibles" (122).

Tituba travels between slavery and *marronnage*,[2] between the Caribbean and North America, and between the worlds of the living and the dead. Pascale Bécel adduces that Tituba occupies an interstitial position that "metaphorically underwrites a shift from traditional notions of identity to a recognition of cultural hybridity" (613). I argue that Tituba must also be read as occupying a sexually interstitial space, metaphorically underwriting a shift from traditional Western hetero–homo notions of sexual identity to a recognition of sexual hybridity, plurality, and intersectionality.

If all of these clashes, intersections, and hybrid formations start to feel excessive and difficult to sort out, it is because they are. And as I foreground them in my analysis, I may render this chapter difficult to navigate, or frustrating in its attempt to bring together but not to untangle so many different roots and branches of the story. This is the epistemology of the mangrove at work, and this is what working in the epistemology of the mangrove is like. In a sense, I repeat throughout this chapter and this book various versions of: it is complicated. If I could neatly pull *Moi, Tituba sorcière* . . . apart and simply categorize its constituent parts, I would belie my own argument. I can, however, point out what *Moi, Tituba sorcière* . . . complicates and how it is complicated, direct attention to certain entanglements that have been largely avoided by other critics, and suggest how a reading of and from *Moi, Tituba sorcière* . . .'s depiction of desire between women reveals important paths into, if not through, the mangled structure of desire and sexuality in the Caribbean.

In *Moi, Tituba sorcière* . . ., Condé toys with the question of whether desire between women is a native export or a colonial import. Staging the encounter between Tituba and Hester as something of a love affair, even as *Moi, Tituba sorcière* . . . (re)writes Caribbean (hi)stories of desire between women, it suggests that, like the Caribbean itself, desire between women in Caribbean literatures is born out of the simultaneously destructive and creative interactions between Africa, the Caribbean, Europe, and the United States.

Moi, Tituba sorcière . . .'s investigation of desire between women in the Caribbean quite fittingly locates its origins in the strategies of domination and resistance, the modes of incorporation and transformation of selves and others, that marked the colonial period (and texts written in it, such as *Amistad funesta*/*Lucía Jerez* and *Je suis martiniquaise*). It reminds us that the question to ask of any practice or person in the Caribbean is not who does it belong to but who controls its distribution and representation. What investments hold it in place and what forces impel its change? Whose rules and whose perspectives dominate its circulation and interpretation? What other versions and visions can we find and what do they allow us to see?

Framing *Moi Tituba sorcière . . . Noire de Salem*

A series of epigraphs, an epilogue, and a historical note frame *Moi, Tituba sorcière . . . .*[3] The first epigraph, attributed to Condé, claims: "Tituba and I lived for a year on the closest of terms. During our endless conversations she told me things she had confided to nobody else." Condé establishes herself as audience and author, the translator, the medium, and the mouthpiece for Tituba's story. The violence of colonialism and racism that kept silent or erased voices like Tituba's from the historical register is as necessary for this story to exist as is the power of oral literature and history and of religious traditions in which ancestors can continue to communicate with us today. The character, the story, and the writer all emerge from these multiple frames that they self-consciously allude to and that they also exceed.

Born in 1937 in Pointe-à-Pitre, Guadeloupe, the youngest of eight children in a middle-class family, Maryse Condé (then Boucolon) was raised to revere all things French, among which she counted herself.[4] Her mother was a schoolteacher and Condé grew up with a strong model of educated women and only minimal awareness of the inequities in Guadeloupe. At the age of 16, Condé moved to France to complete her schooling, as had most of her siblings before her. While she was in Paris, a French friend introduced Condé to the writings of the *négritude* movement. Like many of her generation, Condé became enthralled with Africa. Eager to find her "roots," and armed with a teaching certificate, she married the Guinean actor Mamadou Condé in 1959 and moved with him to Guinea. However, as she explains, she was in love with an idea of Africa rather than a man; the marriage was a difficult one and the Condés separated and eventually divorced.[5] In the late 1960s and early 1970s, Maryse Condé taught in the Ivory Coast, Guinea, Ghana, and Senegal, and in 1972 she returned to France to pursue graduate studies.

In 1976, Condé obtained her doctoral degree and the same year published her first novel, *Hérémakhonon*. The novel was not well received, although Condé's doctoral dissertation, "Stéréotypes du noir dans la littérature antillaise" (Black stereotypes in Antillean literature), and her critical writings on Caribbean and Francophone African literature established her as one of the first academic experts on Caribbean literature, which she taught in France and the United States. In 1979, Condé authored the first extensive study of Francophone Caribbean women writers, *Parole des femmes*. Condé's second novel, *Une saison à Rihata* (1981), was scarcely better received than her first. However, Condé achieved popular and commercial success with her third and fourth books, the African sagas *Ségou: les murailles de terre* (1984) and *Ségou II: la terre en miettes* (1985). Her next two books, *Moi, Tituba sorcière . . .* and *La vie scélérate* (1987), confirmed her success as a novelist and were awarded the Grand Prix Littéraire de la Femme and the bronze medal of the Prix de l'Académie Française, respectively. Condé has since divided her time between Guadeloupe and the United States, as well as between teaching and writing.

Women's desire and sexuality figure prominently throughout Condé's extensive body of critical and creative work. Repudiating exoticist visions of Caribbean women who always and only offer sexual pleasure to others and contradicting depictions of them as desexualized mothers, Condé's female characters explore and enjoy their vibrant sexuality for their own benefit, or detriment. In *Hérémakhonon*, Véronica searches for her African roots in the bed of Ibrahima Sory and experiences an array of interracial and intercultural sexual relationships. Thécla and Ottavia in *La vie scélérate* share the discovery of their bodies and desires. In *Traversée de la mangrove* (1995), young women look for escape from oppressive family traditions and self-affirmation in the arms of disinterested men. In *Desirada*, Reynalda contends with the effects of rape and the prohibition of her relationship with Fiorella, while Marie-Noël faces the difficulty of finding emotional satisfaction in sexual relationships with men. Célanire's almost insatiable sexual appetite in *Célanire cou-coupé* (2003) reaches across genders and continents.[6] And in *Moi, Tituba sorcière . . .*, in the midst of the Salem witch trials, Tituba meets Hester.

The encounter between Tituba and Hester has been analyzed in terms of *Moi, Tituba*'s formal experimentation with intertextuality and anachronism and its treatment of female specificity in Puritanism and slavery, North America and the Caribbean.[7] However, the desire between Hester and Tituba that arises in and from their meeting continues to elicit almost as little reaction from critics as it does from the characters in the novel.[8] Condé herself does not, in the numerous interviews in which she discusses *Moi, Tituba sorcière . . .*, raise the element of desire between Hester and Tituba, but neither is she ever asked about it.

Literary Cannibalism

Moi, Tituba sorcière . . . belongs to a class of Caribbean works that rewrite American and European "classics," offering critiques of the colonial discourses those "classics" contain, what Condé calls "literary cannibalism" ("Unheard Voice": 62). Condé traces the practice back to Martinican intellectual Suzanne Césaire, who, in 1941, declared: "Bambous, we decree death to doudou literature. And shit to the hibiscus, the frangipani, the bougainvillea. Martinican poetry will be cannibalistic or it will not be" (cited in Sourieau: 69).[9] Rejecting exoticizing idealizations, literary cannibalism inhabits the stereotype of the wild savage as an anticolonial stance.

The cannibalistic text reverses the dynamic in which the Caribbean is the source of raw material (sugarcane, coffee, tobacco, beautiful landscape, exotic experiences) that the European colonizer works into a finished product (sugar, espresso, cigarettes, literature), to take the European text as the raw material that the Caribbean author (re)works into a (re)finished product.[10] A reconfiguration of major and minor in terms of both colonial status and literary canonicity lies at the heart of literary cannibalism. Like much cannibalistic literature, *Moi, Tituba sorcière . . .* snatches up a "marginal" character from a European or American text—in this case Arthur Miller's *The Crucible* but also the historical records of the Massachusetts Bay Colony and myriad other fictionalizations of the events—and spits her out at the center of the story. At the same time, *Moi, Tituba sorcière . . .* cannibalizes *The Scarlet Letter* in an inverse manner, taking the "main" character of this "major" literary work, and rendering her a "minor" character in Tituba's story.[11]

Combining, in *Moi, Tituba sorcière . . .*, *The Crucible* and *The Scarlet Letter*, Condé assures that the frame for her novel is not of one individual, possibly exceptional, text, but of the American literary canon in which *The Scarlet Letter* and *The Crucible* both figure prominently. Condé's re-placement of Hester in 1690s' Salem reminds one of the connection that Hawthorne himself makes between the witch trials and his novel when, in "The Custom House," he writes that an anxious personal connection to witch-hunting ancestors motivated the composition of *The Scarlet Letter* (7–8). Drawing attention to the ways in which the Salem witch trials frame *The Scarlet Letter* and then portraying as crucial Tituba's role in the Salem witch trials, Condé posits that the reworked texts were already dependent on the story now told in the reworking.[12] Condé's Tituba enables Hawthorne's novel and by extension the launching of American prose fiction.[13] At the same time, *Moi, Tituba sorcière . . .* disables *The Scarlet Letter*, for the events that transpire in Condé's Ipswich jail not only figure a Hester rather different from Hawthorne's, but lead her to a suicide that would in fact prevent her from ever setting foot in the "open air" of Hawthorne's story (77).

In a *mise en abîme* toward the end of *Moi, Tituba sorcière . . .*, Tituba predicts the "major" and "minor" waves that will wash ashore the history of Salem village and of her life:

> I felt that I would only be mentioned in passing in these Salem witchcraft trials about which so much would be written later . . . There would be no mention

> of my age or personality. I would be ignored . . . There would never, ever, be a careful, sensitive biography recreating my life and its suffering. And I was outraged by this future injustice! (110)

Tituba considers that the failure to acknowledge the importance of any one element (be it major or minor) in a system (of slavery, of witch trials) is an injustice. Literature, however, might have the power to give back what was due, to rectify and to remedy. For the injustice is not only Tituba's treatment in the trials, but also her lack of treatment in the literature about those trials, and the absence of her biography.[14] Justice becomes less the affair of legal proceedings and historical accounts than that of individual life stories and novels. Justice becomes an individual fiction, and an individual fiction renders justice. The slippage between biography and novel, between the "careful, sensitive" work of rectifying the historical register and the art of "recreating" a life is also the slippage between a community and an individual, and between history and story.

Re-placing the Black Witch of Salem

The titular focus of *Moi, Tituba sorcière . . .* is on Tituba as a witch: what it means to be a witch in different places and times and how blackness and witch-ness are conflated. I use the French title in part because its elliptical quality highlights the absence of a resolution to the questions of how being a witch and being black fit together, of what links or goes between being a witch and being black, for Tituba.[15] Depicting Tituba not simply as the black scapegoat for Puritan fears about witches but actually as a witch, *Moi Tituba sorcière . . .* stages in the story the reclaiming and rehabilitation of stereotypes that literary cannibalism also accomplishes. To the questions "Is the designation of black women as witches a colonial creation, or is witchcraft a Caribbean export?" and "Did Caribbean women really go to Salem and practice witchcraft, or did the people of Salem assume any black woman was a witch?," *Moi, Tituba sorcière . . .* answers "yes." This kind of accumulative combination of elements expected to be oppositional belongs to the epistemology of the mangrove, which entangles, and shows the entanglement of, sexuality with race, religion, and place, among other things.

In a Euro-American worldview, and especially in seventeenth-century Puritan America, witches work with the Devil for the demise of man and God. Blackness, femininity, and sexuality are marks of witchcraft, as is any spiritual or medical practice that falls out of bounds of the dominant Christian theology.[16] Even the Puritan children in *Moi, Tituba sorcière . . .*, playing Tituba's games, eating her food, and hearing her stories, quickly conclude "Tituba, it is true you know everything, you see everything, you can do everything? You're a witch then?," specifying when pressed that they know a witch to be "someone who has made a pact with the devil" (62).

But Tituba learned to be a witch in the Caribbean from a creolized African and understands witchcraft as healing art that comes from ancestral knowledge of the physical world—plants, animals, weather patterns—and of the spiritual world—the invisibles—as well as of their interactions. For her, witchcraft is powerful and dangerous, something to be revered and used carefully. And while it is something that whites in Barbados misunderstand, fear, and accuse slaves of using against them, it is not something that they manipulate.

One of the great crises of Tituba's life, and one of the major conflicts of the novel, comes from the disparity between the Caribbean and Puritan views of witches. When the girls confront her with their understanding, asking "Are you a witch, Tituba, I think you must be," she cannot respond: "This was too much. I drove all these young vipers out of my kitchen and chased them into the street" (62). Eventually the girls' accusations, presenting through a Puritan worldview the very things Tituba did but with a different understanding, land Tituba on trial for witchcraft.

But the misconception of witches and their reductive association with femininity is not an invention of colonialism or slavery. The Puritan order can *only* condemn someone like Tituba as a witch working with the Devil, but in Barbados she also faces limiting Caribbean conceptions of witches and women. As Tituba says, in the Caribbean, "the witch, if we must use this word, rights wrongs, helps, consoles, heals . . ." (96). Ina Césaire explains, however, that although the Caribbean witch is a powerful healer, she is also typically "an old toothless woman, a ghoul who lays her head on her lap to pluck her lice" (144).[17] Mama Yaya fits this model: "hunched and wrinkled," "hardly of this world," and marginalized as much as she is sought out, for "People were afraid of her, but they came from far and wide because of her powers" (8–9).

Until she meets John, Tituba operates as a stereotypical Caribbean witch. When she is out walking, "the minute they saw me, everybody jumped into the grass and knelt down, while half a dozen pairs of respectful, yet terrified eyes looked up at me" (11). But John's remark upon meeting Tituba that "You could be lovely" inspires her to "cut my mop of hair as best I could" so that everyone recognizes her as an "elegant young person" (15–16). She wants to be a witch and to be part of a community, to be loved and to have a lover. So she marries John and continues to practice her craft in Bridgetown, Salem, and back. Yet even "when [John] said the word [witch], it was marked with disapproval" (17), and when Tituba finally thinks she has found acceptance as a witch, upon her return to the Caribbean, she discovers that the folks who welcome her into their communities have their own misconceptions about witches. The sailor Deodatus and the maroon Christopher believe that as a witch Tituba is all powerful, and that she can control the weather, make them invincible, and end slavery and colonialism; when Tituba has to "explain that they were exaggerating the extent of my powers," they turn from her, with harsh words like Christopher's "You're nothing but a common Negress" (155).

The terms as well as the stakes of the misunderstanding and marginalization of witches are certainly different in the White and Black communities: demonization versus stereotyping, hanging versus exclusion. But Tituba's quest to represent the complexity of the witch must occur with her peers as well as with her masters.

Re-placing Hester

Tituba struggles with being viewed as the strange outsider in Salem, but she also positions herself as the interpreter of the strange world of the Puritans, peppering her tale with asides that ask the reader to "imagine a small community of men and women oppressed by the presence of Satan and seeking to hunt him down in all his manifestations" (65). Tituba (via Condé, or vice versa), reading Hester and her context through a Caribbean frame, restages Hawthorne's novel.

To meet Tituba in jail in Ipswich, Hester steps forward fifty years from the mid-seventeenth-century setting of *The Scarlet Letter* to 1690s' Salem. But she still appears in *Moi, Tituba sorcière*... a week before the summer morning when she sets foot in Hawthorne's story.[18] The events that transpire in Condé's Ipswich jail not only figure a Hester rather different from Hawthorne's, but also lead her to a suicide that would in fact prevent her from ever stepping out into the "open air" of Hawthorne's tale to bear the Puritan punishment for adultery, living out an increasingly productive life on the outskirts of Salem, the A blazoned on her chest and her daughter at her side, while she watches her fellow sinner suffer under the weight of his unacknowledged crime and the machinations of her unidentified husband.

Condé's Hester bears a strong physical resemblance to Hawthorne's but Tituba's description inscribes Hester and the judgment of beauty outside of a Puritan or Anglo-American system of values. Hawthorne's Hester is "tall, with a figure of perfect elegance, on a large scale. She had dark and abundant hair, so glossy that it threw off the sunshine with a gleam, and a face which, besides being beautiful from regularity of feature and richness of complexion, had the impressiveness of belonging to a marked brow and deep black eyes"

(77), while Condé's "revealed a mass of thick hair, as black as a crow's wing, itself the color of sin for some people and worthy of punishment. Likewise, her eyes were black, not gray the color of dirty water, not the green color of wickedness, but black like the benevolent shadow of night" (95). The dark beauty of Hawthorne's Hester spills out in an exotic excess of passion, more "impressive" than good and, as Tituba's comparison of Hester's hair to a crow reminds, suspect thanks to the negative connotations of anything black in *The Scarlet Letter*. Tituba's observation that the color of Hester's hair symbolizes sin *to some people*, however, indicates the existence of competing values. Tituba's qualification of the various eye colors confirms that *her* preferred frame of reference is Afro-Caribbean.

In the Caribbean frame of reference of *Moi, Tituba sorcière*..., Hester becomes not only a certain kind of beauty, but also, as Jane Moss suggests, a lesbian separatist (14). Hawthorne's adulterous Hester exceeds the (legal) limits of Puritan sexuality, but she does so in a markedly heterosexual manner, committing adultery with a man. Only in Condé's interpretation does Hester desire women. Although in their conversations Hester tries to make Tituba more like herself, the novelistic reinvention of Hester already has turned this process around. Condé makes Hester a lesbian separatist who tries to make Tituba one.

The argument that desire between women is a Euro-American phenomenon that is then imposed on other cultures circulates in public opinion and in Caribbean critiques of gay and lesbian studies. Alibar and Lembeye-Boy summarize: "homosexuality? Public opinion asserts that it is in evil come from elsewhere, imported to the Antilles like prostitution, the 'caprice of the Gods' or the Redoute catalog" (189). Reversing the dynamic, Hester's desire for women is exported *from* the Caribbean.

In *Moi, Tituba sorcière*..., the lesbian feminist separatist Hester escapes Ipswich jail only through death. She is not reworked to be reinserted into Hawthorne's text, but to be removed from it. When she learns of Hester's death, Tituba asks: "Hanged herself? Hester, Hester, why didn't you wait for me?... Hanged herself? Hester, I would have gone with you" (111). But Tituba does not follow Hester's suicidal lead. Rather, Hester's spirit follows Tituba throughout New England and back to Barbados.

Tituba and Hester's Jailhouse Encounter

In each chapter in this book, there is a section akin to this one, where I perform close readings of encounters between women that emphasize their erotic, sexual, and romantic charge. If, individually or together, these seem to belabor the point, it is in large part because the paucity of critical attention to these moments makes me suspicious that they are too easily overlooked, not recognized for their eroticism or not recognized as relevant to understanding the structures of desire and sexuality in the novels or in Caribbean literature. And while to a certain degree this paucity of critical attention can be attributed to the heteronormative assumptions of critics, I think that more often it is due to the mangled quality of desire between women in Caribbean literature. These moments are hard to notice, must be read over and overread, because they are entangled and fleeting, fluid and multivalent, traversed by so many other relationships and desires that operate along other important critical axes.

Tituba presents her relationship with Hester as one more in a string of treacherously disappointing friendships that she has with white women. When she entered Ipswich jail, Tituba recounts, "here again, despite my recent misfortunes and John Indian's recommendations, I fell into the trap of making friends [*de l'apparente amitié*]" (95). However, Elizabeth and Betsey Parris, Tituba's former "friends" whose accusations landed her in jail, were literally masters to her slavery. Overdetermined by their respective positions as slave and mistress, the "apparent" friendships Tituba shared with Elizabeth and Betsey were invested with those elements that explain their "trap." Although Tituba's friendship with Elizabeth Parris, like the relationship with Hester, begins with each woman expressing her appreciation of the other's beauty, that mutual admiration only precipitates their fuller participation in the prescribed roles of mistress and servant. Tituba sustains: "We did not belong to the same universe, Goodwife Parris, Betsey, and I, and all the affection of the world could not change that" (63). The inalterable dynamic of power in the mistress–servant relationship also explains the danger, to Tituba, of her belief that Elizabeth or Betsey would ever side with her against the Puritan authorities.

Hester, on the other hand, is, already, in *The Scarlet Letter*, an outsider in Puritan society, her Alterity literally marked on her breast. In *Moi, Tituba sorcière . . .*, Hester ministers to the welts that remain from Tituba's first days in jail, practicing the same informal nursing that she does in *The Scarlet Letter*, but also occupying in relation to Tituba the stance of helper and caretaker that Tituba held in relation to Betsey and Elizabeth. Furthermore, Hester asks Tituba to call her by her first name rather than by the title Mistress that Tituba assumes she should use. Hester renounces, in other words, the position of mastery over Tituba that she might be assumed to hold by virtue of her whiteness. When Tituba refers to Puritan New England as "your society," Hester explains that she does not feel herself to possess any of the rights or privileges of belonging to that society: "It's not my society. Aren't I an outcast like yourself? Locked between these walls?" (96). Tituba seems to accept Hester's claim when she "corrects" herself and continues, "this society," but these exchanges serve to highlight Hester's ambivalent position in relation to Puritan society (96).

The Scarlet Letter emphasizes the ways in which, after she exits jail, Hester becomes increasingly a part of, if always slightly apart from, New England society, so that by the time Hester's daughter Pearl is seven years old, "her mother, with the scarlet letter on her breast, glittering in its fantastic embroidery, had long been a familiar object to the townspeople" and "as is apt to be the case when a person stands out in any prominence before the community, and, at the same time, interferes neither with the public nor individual interests and conveniences, a species of general regard had ultimately grown up in reference to Hester Prynne" (145). *Moi, Tituba sorcière...*, however, does not reinsert Hester so easily, even as it also asserts that to be outside of the mores of Puritan New England as an adulteress or even a woman-lover is not the same as to be outside of them as a slave.

Hester possesses the white skin that makes Tituba assume she should call her "Mistress," while Tituba's black skin means that, as John Indian explains, "you are guilty and you will always be that in [the Puritans'] eyes" (92). Hester was born into freedom and committed an act that limited it, while Tituba was born into slavery, which she can only escape through flight to a maroon camp, or through death. An adulteress who passes from being one of "us" to being one of "them" always has the possibility of passing back to the other side, but a black or an Indian was, is, and always will be Other. Nonetheless, temporarily secured in the same spatial relationship to Salem's authorities, Tituba and Hester can form a bond of common resistance, even one of desire and sexuality.

The jail-cell setting for Tituba and Hester's meeting lends both parodic and serious undertones to their encounter: Patrice Proulx maintains that the prison functions as a metaphor for the various restrictions Tituba and Hester face as women; the liminal and restricted space of the prison is reminiscent of the closet and its epistemology; the prison setting of the encounter could play on the oft-repeated notion that same-sex sexual activity is common in prisons, *faute de mieux*; finally, the jailhouse scene has become a sort of pornographic convention. Calling on all of these references, the setting of Tituba and Hester's meeting reinforces, even as it parodies, the scene's erotic charge.

When Hester first invites her into the cell, Tituba observes: "the woman who had spoken was young, beautiful" (95). And Hester says of Tituba: "What a magnificent color she's got for her skin" (95). Hester not only admires Tituba's skin but continues, in a wink at Fanon's *Peau noire, masques blancs*: "and what a wonderful way she has of covering up her feelings" (95).[19] To a certain extent, Hester exoticizes Tituba when she idealizes and mystifies her color. But Hester does not exactly reiterate colonial exoticization. Rather, she offers an example of it as analyzed by a Caribbean subject (Fanon and/or Condé).[20] At the same time, Tituba's description of Hester's "luxurious hair" not only comments on Hawthorne's exoticism, but it also exoticizes Hester in its own right.

According to Rita Felski, through exoticism "the racial other is typically feminized as a dark continent to be penetrated and subjugated" by, of course, a white man (136–137). But it is Hester and Tituba themselves, not any men, who hold, even as they are held by, the exoticizing and desiring gazes. Hester enacts another typically exoticizing move when she imagines Tituba to be representative of a sort of natural purity, of "some societies [that] were an exception to this law [of patriarchal domination]" (96). Tituba, however, exposes the misunderstandings on which idealizing exoticism is based, responding: "Perhaps in Africa where we come from it was like that. But we know nothing about Africa any more and it no longer has any meaning for us" (96). Exoticization plays between the women, but it is no longer a tool used by the Euro-American to subjugate either through penetration or through idealization of an objectified Other. At the same time, the play with exoticization reminds one that the relationship is located at a point of interaction between two systems with a long and troubled history.

According to Fanon, black women become involved with white men in order to themselves become whiter, if only by bearing lighter children, as exemplified by what I argue, in Chapter 2, is his misreading of Mayotte Capécia. The interracial relationship in *Moi, Tituba sorcière . . .* could follow Fanon's model of lactification, especially if Tituba were to fall into the trap of agreeing to emulate Hester. But Tituba does not want to *be* but to *have* Hester, and it is difficult to explain the desire of the black woman for the white *woman* as part of a trajectory of lactification, for, as Tituba reminds Hester: "We couldn't make [children] alone, even so!" (101). Tituba's desire for Hester is not part of any larger desire to produce, to be, or to have whiteness.[21]

Whiteness is not part of what Tituba finds beautiful in Hester, although she does find Hester beautiful. Indeed, almost immediately after meeting, the two women seal their faith in each other based on the feelings inspired by their mutual appreciation of one another's beauty:

> She took my face between her hands. "You cannot have done evil Tituba! I am sure of that, you're too lovely! Even if they all accused you, I would defend your innocence!"
>
> I was so moved, I was bold enough to caress her face and whispered: "You too, Hester, are lovely! What are they accusing you of?" (96)

Tituba's sudden deep emotion and faith contrast with her cognizance of the treachery often hidden under the guise of friendship or a pretty face. But Tituba also has a history of acting on attraction immediately and against her better judgment, telling Mama Yaya after one brief encounter with John, "I want this man to love me" (14). Tituba comments on the power of attraction that John exerts over her, asking and answering:

> What was there about John Indian to make me sick with love for him? Not very tall, average height, five feet seven, not very big, not ugly, not handsome either! A fine set of teeth, burning eyes. I must confess it was downright hypocritical of me to ask myself such a question, since I knew all too well where his main asset lay and I dared not look below the jute cord that held up his short, tight-fitting trousers to the huge bump of his penis. (18–19)

Sexual desire might also account for the overinvested and under-explained quality of the relationship between Tituba and Hester.[22]

As soon as Tituba enters Hester's cell, Hester "endeavored to wash the welts on my face," inaugurating a series of repeated and protracted touches that are both intimate and erotic. The mobile opacity of touch replaces transparent explanation and binary opposition in Tituba and Hester's relationship. Throughout Condé's work, expressions of desire are tactile. The narrator in *La vie scélérate* explains: "Friendship between women can resemble love. It has the same possessiveness as love, the same jealousies and lack of restraint. But the complicities of friendship are more durable than those of love, for they are not based on the language of the body" (212). Tituba and Hester's relationship might combine the fleeting corporeal language of love with the more durable complicities of friendship.

Certainly, locked in a small cell, Tituba and Hester are almost forced to touch one another, repeatedly. Indeed, their jailhouse encounter mirrors some of the experience of colonialism and slavery, where contact between cultures is forced and constrained, although individuals find ways to work around and within those constraints to express and fulfill their own, unsanctioned, desires.

Drawn out over the course of their conversation, Tituba and Hester's touches are reciprocal and parallel—the original French specifies that it is with a "*va-et-vient de sa main*" ("back and forth of her hand") that Hester "attempted to wash the welts on my face" (MT: 151; IT: 95; "MT" refers to the original French text of 1986, whereas IT refers to the Philcox translation of 1992); Hester takes "my face between her hands" and in return Tituba becomes "bold enough to caress her face"—playing on the notion of desire between women as based on doubling.[23] While the mirroring aspect of Tituba and Hester's touch asserts this dynamic, the racial and cultural difference between Tituba and Hester sets them at a remove from it. In Condé's novel, and in the Caribbean, the consciousness of difference is omnipresent, particularly of racial difference and of the legacy of colonialism and slavery that divide, even as they unite, blacks and whites. The gender similarity and racial difference between Tituba and Hester troubles even as it invokes a notion of mirror images, functioning more like Homi Bhabha's notion of same but not quite, and its inverse, different but not quite.[24]

As her lengthy narration attests, Tituba is not someone for whom verbal expression is difficult. Yet Hester's touch and words leave her deeply moved: indeed, the original French specifies that Tituba is "*émue au-delà de toute expression*" ("moved beyond all expression": 153). Perhaps Tituba knows no word with which to designate feelings that are somehow foreign to her. Or perhaps Tituba's reaction to Hester intimates the extreme intensity, the ineffability, of the connection between the two women.[25] Tituba regains the ability to speak in the same sentence in which she lost it, but only after she has returned Hester's touch: "I was so moved [*émue au-delà de toute expression*], I was bold enough to caress her face and whispered: 'You too, Hester, are lovely! What are they accusing you of?' " (96).

In response to Tituba's question, Hester recounts the story of her life, in which Tituba recognizes resonances with her own. Then Tituba agrees to tell a story to Hester and her unborn child. Tituba prefaces her story by bringing her lips to Hester's womb: "Resting my head against this soft curve of flesh, this hummock of life, so that the little one inside could be near my lips, I started to tell a tale" (98). Tituba's action continues the pattern of repeated touch established in their first conversation, the eroticism of lips touching womb enhanced by adjective "soft" and the noun "flesh" emphasizing Hester's belly as the object of Tituba's interest not only because it holds a baby but because it is itself pleasurable to feel. The characterization of the belly as a "hummock" recalls John's "mound." In the original French, the word itself, "*morne*" ("hummock"), inscribes Hester's body and the pleasure Tituba finds in it within a Caribbean topography, for "*morne*" is a Creole noun used throughout the Francophone Caribbean to designate hills and hillside communities.[26]

Tituba does not admit it to Hester, but the story she tells is that of her own life, more specifically of the pain engendered by her decision to be with John Indian even at the cost of her own freedom. Hester at first protests Tituba's love of men, saying "Don't talk to me about your wretched husband! He's no better than mine. Shouldn't he be here to share your sorrow? Life is too kind to men" (100). Tituba realizes that Hester "was telling me the truth," but also understands that even as his gender grants him social powers and privileges denied to her and to Hester, his skin color renders him vulnerable to racism in a way that Hester will not experience but that she herself knows all too well. Tituba also, regardless of the similarities and differences that she finds between herself and John, loves him. And so Hester takes another tactic:

> She ended up laughing and drew me close to her.
>
> "You're too fond of love, Tituba! I'll never make a feminist out of you!"
>
> "A feminist? What's that?"
>
> She hugged me in her arms and showered me with kisses.
>
> "Be quiet! I'll explain later." (101)

Hester's pulling Tituba into her arms and showering her with kisses appears to respond to Tituba's question about the definition of feminism: feminism is desire between women, a desire between women opposed to love as conceived through heterosexuality. But the kisses also replace transparent explanation and binary opposition with the mobile opacity of touch.

The kisses serve simultaneously as a response and as a lack of response to the question of what feminism might be. They silence, counter, and supplement the sexual pleasure Tituba finds with men, perhaps even accepting Tituba's refusal to give up loving men and adapting to her more intersected and intertwined view of various kinds of desires. Hester never finishes the explanation, for Tituba leaves shortly thereafter for her trial. When she returns to jail crying "tears that only Hester would know how to dry" (110), Tituba finds that Hester has hung herself.

Hester's infanticide and suicide in *Moi, Tituba sorcière . . .* strengthens the parallels between the experiences of Puritan women and those of slave women and at the same time questions the infrequent attribution, in historical analyses, of infanticide and suicide to white women. In *The Scarlet Letter*, Hester considers suicide and infanticide but decides against them. Why does Hawthorne not imagine Hester following through with her thoughts of killing herself and her child? When Hester is possessed by "a fearful doubt . . . whether it were not better to send Pearl at once to heaven, and go herself to such futurity as Eternal Justice should provide," her enduring love for the Reverend Dimmesdale keeps her from suicide (150). When Condé has Hester kill herself and her child, then, perhaps she mocks Hawthorne's Romanticism and reminds one that however much support of equality between women and men he puts into Hester's mouth, he still creates her as a hetero-reproductive mother and a martyr to "sacred love" and the redemption of a man (235).

Condé offers Hester a way out of Hawthorne's story through what is often attributed to slaves as a final resistance to an unlivable order: suicide and infanticide. Glissant's gloss, in *Le Discours Antillais*, of the Creole proverb "eat dirt, don't make children for slavery" signals not only how common abortion by slave women was, but also how the practice has been incorporated into a traditional, even romanticized, image of Caribbean women. Glissant writes:

> earth to be sterile, earth to die. It is woman who has thus at times refused to carry in her womb the master's profits. The history of the Martinican family institution is based on this refusal. The history of an enormous primordial abortion: words stuck in throats, along with the first cry. (166)

Tituba has two pregnancies that she does not bring to term. The first pregnancy, by John, she aborts in order that the child not be born into slavery. After her return to Barbados, Tituba becomes pregnant by the maroon leader Christopher; she is still pregnant when she is hanged for her participation in a slave revolt. Although Tituba is not directly responsible for terminating this second pregnancy, it too ends because she is more committed to the struggle against slavery and the colonial plantation system than she is to procreation.

The unwanted pregnancies Hester describes to Tituba bear more resemblance to that of Abena, Tituba's mother, than to her own, for like Abena Hester "would have found it impossible to love the offspring of a man I hated," but when Hester tells Tituba that "the number of potions, concoctions, purges, and laxatives I took during my pregnancies helped me to arrive at this fortunate conclusion," Tituba whispers to herself, "I, too, killed my child," recognizing a commonality that enables their solidarity (97–98). Through suicide and infanticide, in *Moi, Tituba sorcière . . .*, Hester is able to throw off her obligations to Puritan morality and at the same time to live on not in Hawthorne's story but in Tituba's. For death in *Moi, Tituba sorcière . . .* is not an ending, but a passage into the realm of the "invisibles." When Caribbean characters die, they naturally enter this realm; in order for Hester and the American literary canon to enter it, they must be killed off and brought back through literary cannibalism, a rewriting that is revenge and rectification.

Still, Tituba mourns the loss of Hester's life, and of the lives of Hester's unborn baby and her own aborted child: "I often think of Hester's child and of my own. Those unborn children. It was for their own good we denied them the light of day and the salty taste of their skin under the sun. Children we spared, but whom, strangely enough, I pity" (113). Tituba speaks of her child by John Indian and of Hester's child by an unnamed man in one breath, almost as if they were siblings (un)born to the two women together.

The repetition of "we" unites the women not only as aborted mothers but also as co-parents. Tituba sings a song she wrote for her unborn child "for both of them," claiming Hester's child as her own, and offering Hester a place as the second mother to her child (113). The tradition of co-mothering in the Caribbean is well established as coordinated with and supportive of parenting by mothers and fathers, *macomère* designating what Antonia MacDonald-Smythe describes as the adult version of the *macocotte*, "a woman who, by virtue of the longevity and depth of her friendship, has rights and privileges relating to your child" (239, n. 4). But just as I argued in the previous chapter that *macocotte* relationships are best understood as neither necessarily or neatly homosexual *or* heterosexual, so I will do for the *macomère*. For *macomères*, the erotic plasticity of female friendship meets the eroticism of maternal relationships, not necessarily but easily rendering the relationship between *macomères* if not homosexual, certainly not heterosexual either.[27] Perhaps, just as her own mother Abena accepted Yao as her mate after he adopted Tituba, Tituba also, thus, grants Hester a place as a permanent partner.

Out of Jail, Out of Life: Replacing Desire between Women

Hester's death does not put an end to the two women's affective or erotic relationship. Indeed, the most explicit sexual encounter between Tituba and Hester occurs later. Three days before she is finally released from prison, Tituba says: "I had the feeling that the darkest hours were behind me and I would soon be able to breathe again" (122). That night:

> Hester lay down beside me, as she did sometimes. I laid my head on the quiet water lily of her cheek and held her tight. Surprisingly, a feeling of pleasure slowly flooded over me. Can you feel pleasure from hugging a body similar to your own? For me, pleasure had always been in the shape of another body whose hollows fitted my curves and whose swellings nestled in the tender flatlands of my flesh. Was Hester showing me another bodily pleasure? (122)

Although the spectral aspect of the affair could render it, as in Terry Castle's model of the *Apparitional Lesbian*, incorporeal and invisible, *Moi, Tituba sorcière . . .* establishes a distinctly Caribbean relation between the worlds of the living and of the dead, where the "invisibles" are quite palpable presences.[28] Even Hester's ability to share "bodily pleasure" across the threshold of death is not unusual, and Tituba also, after her own death, occasionally "slip[s] into someone's bed to satisfy a bit of leftover desire" (178). The death as much as, perhaps even more than, the life that *Moi, Tituba sorcière . . .* gives to Hester makes her a Caribbean creation even as it confirms the important place she occupies in the novel and in Tituba's affections.[29]

The reworking of Hester into a companion that Tituba can and does want to have, if not to be, might itself evidence a kind of internalization: *Moi, Tituba sorcière* . . . makes a white woman for Tituba to desire even as it remakes Hester into that woman. Like the mangrove, cannibalism includes internalization; it plays, and dangerously, with the forces of colonialism *and* anticolonialism. Tituba's metaphorical reference to "the quiet water lily of [Hester's] cheek" as she welcomes Hester's body next to hers, holding it tight, demonstrates how cannibalism must eat up the aesthetics of the colonizer in order to spit them back out, or, rather, how nearly impossible it is to determine what belongs to whom, both in terms of material of origin and in terms of representational value. This metaphorical cheek as water lily might evoke Stéphan Mallarmé's "Nénuphar blanc" ("White Water Lily") to eroticize Hester as an ideal beloved of French poetry, it might reference Aimé Césaire's citation of the flower as representative of a European imagery that does *not* belong in his "native land" to critique that very same eroticization, it might anticipate Condé's classification of it, in *Guadeloupe*, as a native Guadeloupean plant associated with Ti-Marie, sister of the legendary maroon Ti-Jean (23), or it might do all three and more, pointing out that desire between women in *Moi, Tituba sorcière* . . . is simultaneously native and foreign to both Hester and Tituba and for both is simultaneously about an attraction to same and to other, about a desire to inscribe into their own, same, worldview and to encounter an other.[30]

The word that Richard Philcox translates as "bodily pleasure" is in the original "jouissance." Philcox' translation picks up on the very corporeal and sexual nature of this interaction between Hester and Tituba, but it masks the allusions to the privileged site the word jouissance itself holds in French psychoanalytic, feminist, and literary theory as well as in Glissant's thinking about its place in (theorizing) the Caribbean. With her head against this water lily cheek and holding Hester's body tightly, Tituba comes up with a series of questions that culminate in the possibility of jouissance, whose very definition is posed as an open question: "Was Hester showing me *another* bodily pleasure [jouissance]?" shows that even if what Hester offers her *is* jouissance, it may be different from any jouissance that she has known previously (or, it may repeat her previous experiences of jouissance—"another" indicates both difference and repetition).

For Lacan, jouissance indicates an almost transcendent exceeding of all limits, including those of the body. Drawing on the psychoanalytic concept, in *The Pleasure of the Text* Roland Barthes locates the jouissance of a text "just where it exceeds demand, transcends prattle, and whereby it attempts to overflow" (13). Feminist psychoanalytic theorists such as Luce Irigaray and Julia Kristeva argue that desire between women not only exceeds the limits of heterosexuality but transcends "phallogocentrism," so that jouissance is a particularly apt term in desire between women. When Tituba refers to jouissance as a possibility, in a question, she intimates the uncontainable charge that the term conveys. Of course, jouissance is thus charged precisely as part of French academia and French academic lesbianism, so that its use links Tituba and Hester's relationship to a French tradition of desire between women. But Tituba has already told Hester that she is unfamiliar with Western theories, particularly feminist ones, and that she finds them ill fitted to analyze her situation even if she also recognizes a certain truth in them. It might then be Glissant's critiques of the application of psychoanalytic theory to Caribbean texts and contexts that Tituba's question about jouissance invokes.

Glissant specifically addresses the meaning and function of jouissance in the Caribbean. Glissant's assertion that for Caribbean men jouissance is always "tacitly recognized as a non-due, as a discontinuity, stolen from the master" could endow jouissance with an almost transcendental revolutionary quality as a kind of sexual *marronnage*. However, Glissant finds that instead of something Caribbean men can steal off with to form a new sexual economy, jouissance becomes "abrupt in this menaced instant" and opposed to "a flow of pleasure which would have supposed continuity, the in and of itself of duration," so that for Caribbean men "jouissance is thus only a last catching up, catching up on lack of responsibility in economic processes of production, catching up on lack of responsibility in physiological processes of reproduction" (506). Of course, Tituba and Hester experience pleasure and jouissance as women. Even if women's jouissance is, like men's, stolen from the master, the different experiences of slavery had by men and by women figure their relationship to sexuality and the master quite differently.

If my rereading of jouissance offers a particularly overloaded set of possible references with too many points of entry and nothing to follow clearly through, it is because that is precisely the way that *Moi, Tituba sorcière . . .* figures desire between women in the Caribbean and desire between women as the Caribbean paradigm. In the place of possible jouissance—when Tituba and Hester lie together—the questions that Tituba asks about jouissance, and the allusions that she calls on through the term, the physical, sexual aspects of what might occur between women, the conceptual frameworks of desire and pleasure, and the historical constructions of gender and race knot together and branch off. It is a messy, mangled place, a place of possibility and of risk. Tituba's question as to whether it is possible to feel pleasure with a body "similar to your own" and Hester's role in indicating the jouissance, as well as Tituba's description of the jouissance as something which, in the original French, "*m'envahit*" (literally, "invaded me"; Philcox gives it as "flooded over me"), intimate that the desire the women share emanates from Euro-America and arrives in the Caribbean only through conquest. Yet, Tituba indicates that her lack of sexual experience with another woman is quite personal: "*For me*, pleasure had always been in the shape of another body whose hollows fitted my curves" (122, emphasis added). Tituba's surprise or ignorance is about her own experience of pleasure with another woman. The otherness of the new and unexpected surprises and pleases Tituba not only with Hester, but also earlier with John, and later with Iphigène. Tituba's apparent naiveté as to what may occur with herself and Hester does not distinguish theirs from other sexual encounters in the novel, but instead aligns it with them, and entangles all of her desires, jouissances, and lovers.

Tituba's question—does Hester indicate to her another jouissance?—remains at the end of the paragraph. The answers it receives, if any, are oblique. The question is followed by a paragraph break, then a hard return, which is unique in the chapter and rare in the novel. The next paragraph begins "Three days later" and narrates Tituba's release from prison (122). Perhaps the response to Tituba's question is that Hester introduces her to a new form of pleasure that releases her from the prison of her love of John Indian's body. Perhaps the spatial and temporal gap between the two paragraphs denotes a space where the question is answered in silence, or where the question is contemplated but not answered. The manifestations of Tituba and Hester's connection remain unknown (Does Hester indicate a new jouissance?) while its qualities may well be unknowable (What is jouissance? What is another jouissance?).[31]

The unknown in *Moi, Tituba sorcière*... is like Decena's tacit subject of Glissant's "recognized opacity" that I discuss in the introduction, a space where (unconscious) desire between women is neither closeted nor outed. The imprecision of whether there is content to the unknown in *Moi, Tituba sorcière*... draws on the unconscious nature of desire and on the dynamic tensions in the structures of the tacit subject and, to keep with Glissant's terminology, the "*diversalité*" of Caribbean poetics. *Moi, Tituba sorcière*... emphasizes with Johnson and Sedgwick the difficulty of specifying (or even claiming) content for desire between women, and insists with Glissant on the problem of content in Caribbean identity.[32] It also proclaims, with Johnson, Sedgwick, and Glissant, the compelling polyvalence of identities whose contents are dependent on the very contingency that makes them uncertain. However, while desire between women in Sedgwick's epistemology is inexorably sucked into the black hole of the closet, desire between women in Condé's work is caught in something more like the mangrove swamp, where it can be filtered through porous roots to nourish growth, or shore up in the muddy silt.

Desire between Women, among Others

Hester's fantasy of "a model society governed and run by women [where] we would give our names to our children, we would raise them alone . . ." positions men, "those abominable brutes [who] would have to share in a fleeting moment" in order to conceive those children, separately from and inimical to women so that desire between women can only be understood in opposition to desire between men and women, with the hope that the former could replace the latter in a better world. Tituba knows from experience and hears from her ancestors that relationships between women and men are often detrimental and might be better avoided: Abena repeats to Tituba like a refrain throughout the novel, "Why can't women do without men?" (15); Mama Yaya warns Tituba when she first meets John Indian, "men do not love. They possess. They subjugate" (14).[33] Yet for Tituba questioning the desirability of men and their capacity as partners is not coextensive with rejecting desire for or relationships with men.

Tituba understands herself as erotically and politically differentiated from and linked to black men at the same time as she understands herself as erotically and politically differentiated from and linked to women. Recognizing that "the color of John Indian's skin had not caused him half the trouble mine had caused me," Tituba also realizes that if she describes seeing Satan as a black man, the Puritans will think of John Indian (101). And in response to Hester's lament that for sexual reproduction men "would have to share in a fleeting moment," Tituba teases "Not too short a moment, . . . I like to take my time" (101). Tituba revels in the pleasure and humor of mixing and matching, of polyvalence and parody. Thus Tituba flirts with Hester, exposing her preference for slow seduction, even as she makes fun of Hester's oversimplified ideal.

Moi, Tituba sorcière . . . does not resort, like *Lucía Jerez*, to triangular models for multiple desires. Like Mayotte's, Tituba's various relationships with different characters either succeed each other or bend around one another as they overlap. The end of Tituba's relationship with John is not precipitated by the relationship with Hester, although the latter begins while Tituba and John are still together. After the night where Hester possibly indicates to her the path of another jouissance, Tituba is released from jail into Benjamin's service. Tituba soon becomes the medium through which Benjamin reaches his dead wife, Abigail, calling Abigail from the land of the invisibles to speak with Benjamin and then taking Abigail's place in Benjamin's bed. Rather than replacing her relationship with Hester, Tituba's relationship with Benjamin serves as a point of contact with Hester, and vice versa: "At the decisive moment [in calling Abigail] I got scared, but then

I felt a pair of lips on my neck and I knew it was Hester come to give me courage" (125).

When, with the help of Benjamin, Tituba finally returns to Barbados, she gives up Hester's touch, since the invisibles can only cross over bodies of water in a limited capacity. Tituba then pursues relationships with Deodatus, Christopher, and Iphigène before she dies. Yet, despite the limits imposed by death and the ocean, Tituba maintains a profoundly erotic relationship with Hester. Tituba discovers a way to install Hester at her side in Barbados: "One day I discovered an orchid among the mossy roots of a fern and I named it Hester" (157). Tituba's use of herbal medicine in her craft renders consequential the orchid's rich symbolism: the word orchid derives from the Greek *orkhis*, "testicle," and indicates the flower's physical resemblance to genitalia; orchids grow symbiotically or epiphytically with ferns or trees, existing always in relationship with another plant, but one of a different family; in both Afro-Caribbean and Western symbologies, the orchid represents beauty, love, and fervor; it serves in Afro-Caribbean magic as an aphrodisiac and to stimulate fertility (Julien: 305, Ratsch: 129). When she names the orchid she discovers after Hester, Tituba finds and roots Hester's sexuality in the Caribbean, in a symbiotic and fertile relationship with her own home and her own sexuality, and as an accessible substitute for Hester's "real" genitalia which she can no longer touch. Indeed, this remembered and replaced relationship might embody "the transformative power of queer desire" that Alison Donnell identifies as lying "in its ability to exceed rather than directly challenge heteronormative social structures" when

> the frisson of an imagined consummation . . . expresses how such moments are compelling and exquisite, precisely because they exist outside hetero-familiar temporality, with its chronology of child care, domesticity, and coupledom [and] reminds us how much sexual desire is comprised of flutters, imaginings, and longings, as well as acts, practices, and identities.
>
> ("New Meetings," 228)

The lines describing Tituba's discovery and baptism of the orchid end a chapter. The next chapter begins: "A few weeks after I had returned home, dividing my time between my herbs and healing the slaves, I realized I was pregnant" (158). In the following paragraph, Tituba specifies that the pregnancy is the result of her sexual relationship with Christopher. However, Hester in her fertile incarnation as an orchid appears to engender the pregnancy much more directly than does Christopher. Condé has perhaps found a place for childbearing and child care "outside hetero-familiar temporality," and Tituba has perhaps found a way to combine Hester's dream of a reproductive matriarchy with her own enjoyment of sex with men. This child will not be born. But Tituba does finally become mother to another woman's child: Samantha, born to one of her patients, the black Creole Délices. This mothering of "a child I did not give birth to but whom I chose" is equally disconnected from heterosexual reproduction; either instead of or in addition to Hester's city of women, it is engendered by the Caribbean medical and spiritual traditions that Tituba practices. These traditions allow Tituba to pass into the spirit world where "I am never alone. There's Mama Yaya, Abena, my mother, Yao, Iphigene, and Samantha. And then there is my island," and where she finds the political community and power that may finally set her people free (177).

Finally understanding the secrets that she could not know in life, Tituba looks back over her life and finds,

> I have only one regret, for we invisibles too have our regrets so that we can better relish our share of happiness: it's having to be separated from Hester. We do communicate of course. I can smell the dried almonds on her breath. I can hear the echo of her laugh. But each of us remain on our side of the ocean. (178)

In the course of the story, Tituba suffers many privations: she loses the love of John Indian, for whom she sacrificed her freedom; she compromises her vision of the truth in order to save her life; she aborts her child; she fails in her attempt at initiating a slave revolt. Yet she derives only this one regret. And since she can still communicate with Hester, and can still satisfy her sexual desires, becoming like the legendary *dorliss* who passes through locked doors to make love to unsuspecting mortals in their sleep, what Tituba misses can only be some particular quality of the physical or sensory closeness that she and Hester shared when they were on the same continent.

So what is the definition and where is the place of desire between women in *Moi, Tituba sorcière . . .*? It certainly comes out of contact between women, but whether it emanates particularly from any one tradition or from any one cause, what political charge it carries, and how it interacts with other desires, remains unclear. Condé's work portrays complex mixes; it does not try to sort them out.[34] The lack of clarity mirrors the paradox of Caribbean identity as Condé describes it in an interview with Marie-Clotilde Jacquey and Monique Hugon: "after all, the Caribbean is a completely artificial creation of the capitalist system. The paradox is that after all that, born out of a truly artificial creation, the Caribbean people exist" (24). Desire between women may be an "artificial construct" in *Moi, Tituba sorcière . . .*, in America, or in the Caribbean, but in that capacity it is not different from any other element of culture or identity.

With an ending much less tragic than those of *Amistad funesta/Lucía Jerez* and *Je suis martiniquaise*, *Moi, Tituba sorcière*... might stand at the gateway of a new era of liberated desire between women in a new generation of liberated Caribbean women writers. But as much as Condé belongs to a generation in which changes to a hetero-patriarchal "order" of Caribbean literature resulted in and from more authors publishing more different stories of desire between women, desire between women in Caribbean literature was not and is not the terrain of an oppressed minority waiting to be liberated; it is part of a mangrove structure of desire and sexuality in the Caribbean that is often misread as and through hetero-patriarchy, that is sometimes threatened by hetero-patriarchy, but that was and remains a structure of complex interconnected desires, practices, and traditions, so many roots and branches reaching up and down for sea and sky through mud. As she re-presents desire between women in *Moi, Tituba sorcière*..., *The Scarlet Letter*, and the Salem witch trials, Condé does not suggest a liberation or a synthesis which resolves slavery, racism, and sexism through transhistorical intertextual interracial lesbian coupling. What she does is to re-place Tituba and Hester into a Caribbean space where their desire circulates: ambiguous, circular, circumstantial, and shared.

CHAPTER 4

Plotting Desire between Girls: Jamaica Kincaid's *At the Bottom of the River*

The Antiguan girl narrators in Jamaica Kincaid's 1983 collection of short stories *At the Bottom of the River* announce their love for other girls and their plans to marry women when they grow up in simple, straightforward terms, seamlessly incorporated into their narrations. The simplicity of the declarations of desire between girls, often expressed in the easily recognizable formulas "I love you/her" or "I am in love with you/her," aligns with the simplicity of style throughout Kincaid's work. Yet Kincaid's simplicity is a foil: she uses the ordinary, the normal, the familiar, the commonplace only to subvert them through their own performance.

In the context of the epistemology of the mangle, Kincaid reminds that while this structure may be so twisted and entwined that it is nearly impossible to disentangle or to cross, it is neither impenetrable nor inconceivable. In fact, the principle on which the mangrove works is the most basic and regular: a plant needs water, soil, air, and light to survive and in the intertidal zones the best way to do that is to grow roots both up and down, to take in air and water at multiple levels. The simple and the complex, the normal and the exceptional, the norm and the normal are no more opposed than the homosexual and the heterosexual, but neither are they neatly aligned. The terms themselves—normal, norm, like center and eccenter as I discuss in Chapter 6 in regards to Rosario Ferré's *Eccentric Neighborhoods/Vecindarios excéntricos*—when reconsidered, allow us to re-view the structures of desire and sexuality in the Caribbean.

Kincaid's first book, *At the Bottom of the River,* is a collection of short stories told in the first person by an unnamed narrator or series of narrators.

From the adolescent prose-poetry of the first story, "Girl," to the dreamlike sequences of the last story, "At the Bottom of the River," each tale recounts the quotidian experiences of girls and their families. Every day, in *At the Bottom of the River*, girls negotiate between conforming to and resisting colonial norms of womanhood and struggle with the ways that their own mothers participate in the imposition of those norms. Every day, girls become aware of the places, people, and spirits that comprise their world. And every day, girls form erotic attachments with one another.

Taking the "normal" lives and loves of Antiguan girls as their subjects, Kincaid's stories bring into question what Peter Brooks deems, in *Reading for the Plot*, the "unnarratable" quality of the "quiescence of the 'normal' " (103) and also the quiescence and normality of the "normal." *At the Bottom of the River* questions not only what is normal, but also how the normal is constituted in and as narrative. It does so not by opposing the normal but by pluralizing it. The claim that there are many normals seems paradoxical. A particular kind of complication (I am still repeating variations on "it's complicated"), the paradox requires that we rethink what is possible, particularly what is self-contradictory, and the possibility of apparent self-contradiction entails a rethinking of the basic premises of what we take to be obvious, such as what is normal and how the normal works.

After "regular, usual, typical, ordinary, standard," then "free from any disorder, healthy," the OED asserts that "normal" also means "heterosexual." When Kincaid figures desire between girls as normal, then, she either redefines normal or else she shows "heterosexual" not to follow necessarily and only from the other definitions of normal, but to be one among many kinds of normal. *At the Bottom of the River* works with "the normal" and its avatars to reveal their ideology, or rather to reveal them as ideology: the structuring belief that constitutes normal subjects even as it is constituted by individuals' recognition of themselves as normal subjects. Possibly then, just as Louis Althusser claims that there is no outside of ideology, there is also no outside of normal. By pluralizing the normal, Kincaid only reveals its omnipresence: showing the range of things that can be normal demonstrates the pervasiveness of the normal as much as it shows its mutability. But, just as an understanding of ideology and of ideological state apparatuses allows, for Althusser, at least a new relationship to ideology, so Kincaid's exposition of different kinds of normal, and of the ambiguities and excesses in normal's reproduction of itself, opens up "normal."

In *At the Bottom of the River*, the normal repeats with a difference in the manner of what Homi Bhabha calls mimicry, creating something that is "the same but not quite" ("the same but not white": 89). Even as they recognize and constitute themselves as normal subjects, Kincaid's characters also exploit the ambivalences of different discourses, ideologies, normals.

When Brooks studies "design and intention in narrative," he unveils a profoundly ideological, normal, and universal plot structure that moves inexorably from a beginning of (unsatisfied) desire though a middle period of searching to a reproductive end in (heterosexual) marriage, childbirth, and death. Any potential undoing of the narrative (of) progression in its detours and backtracking is always already recuperated in the final denouement that not only straightens out but also explains as necessary any kinks in the scheme.

Various "other" narratives, including feminist and queer narratives as well as non-Western narratives, offer different readings of the "end" of Brooks's model that undermine his schema. Thus Rachel Blau DuPlessis reads "beyond the ending" in many texts to find a space for women's desires that may not have a single "aim" or that may not find their ultimate satisfaction in motherhood, while Angus Gordon studies how the coming-out narrative turns the "digressions, red herrings, and the like [that] are particularly important in the treatment of same-sex desire or experience during adolescence" into an end in and of themselves (3). But the narrators of *At the Bottom of the River* neither enter nor accept standard heterosexual adulthood, nor do any of the characters "come out" as "feminists" or as "lesbians." Rather, *At the Bottom of the River* belongs to the ranks of "straight" Caribbean novels and short stories that explore erotic, domestic, and child-rearing groupings that do no fit colonial heteronormativity, including not only those in the other works studied in this book but also many others, from Simone Schwarz-Bart's *Pluie et vent sur Télumée Miracle*, to Mayra Montero's *La última noche que pasé contigo* or Merle Hodge's *Crick, Crack Monkey*. In these works, as in Kincaid's, marriage is not the singular form of consecrated relationship, romantic coupling is not the primary basis of stable households, and children are not the exclusive property of heterosexual couples. At the same time, as Antonia MacDonald-Smythe points out in *Making Homes in the West/Indies*, Kincaid's practice of retelling, both within and between her novels, draws on "the never-ending story" of "a West Indian folkloric tradition, where each performance of the folk tale is both a repetition and a metamorphosis" (2). The challenges to heteronormativity and to Western narrative convention in Kincaid's works are not unique: they are rather emblematic of Caribbean narrative structure and cultural tradition.[1]

The declarations of love and desire between girls hang in Kincaid's narratives in such a way that they shine like orchids in the tangled branches of a mangrove, at once magnified and distorted by the shifting shadows and leaves. In the midst of a panoramic description of the night in Antigua, one narrator states: "Now I am a girl, but one day I will marry a woman" (11); another describes how "today, keeping a safe distance, I followed the woman I love" (25). In their simplicity, the assertions of desire between girls in *At the Bottom of the River* seem to lack or else to hide some other deeper truth. This may well be the reason for which many critics analyze them as not "really" declarations of love for other girls or women, but as schoolyard crushes, expressions of friendship, or declarations of a "deeper" love for the mother.[2] However, I contend that the deeper truth they hold is that in a simple and straightforward manner, the narrators desire girls and women. Or, depth and surface are not opposed and the one does not hide or hold the truth of the other.

It is tempting to read Kincaid's work as autobiographical, not only because of the coincidences between her life and those of her characters, but also because of her statements in interviews to the effect that "I write about myself for the most part, and about things that have happened to me" ("Interview": 27). However, Kincaid does not label any of her works as autobiography, and she is always careful to specify something to the effect of "Everything I say is true, and everything I say is not true . . . I aim to be true to something, but it's not necessarily the facts" ("Interview": 27). Kincaid draws on her own experiences to narrate literary (re-)visions of Antiguan girlhood.[3]

Born Elaine Cynthia Potter Richardson in St John's, Antigua, in 1949, Kincaid was raised by her mother, Annie Richardson Drew, a half-Carib Dominican, and the man she knew as her father, David Drew.[4] Kincaid entered Antigua's British Colonial school system in 1952 at the age of 3 ½, stating that she was already 5 so that she would be allowed to attend. Kincaid became the older sister to three brothers and watched her father's health begin to fail. In the mid-1960s (and in her late teens), Kincaid left Antigua and went to work as an au pair in the United States.[5] During her first five years in New York and New England, Kincaid obtained her high school diploma, attended some college, and decided to become a writer. It was at this point that she changed her name to Jamaica Kincaid. She explains the name change, in numerous interviews, as stemming at once from a play with identity, and from a fear of potential criticism from family and friends.[6]

Kincaid's first published pieces, in the entertainment magazine *Ingenue*, were interviews with celebrities. These were followed throughout the early 1970s by articles in magazines such as *Ms* and the *Village Voice*. Around the same time, Kincaid's friend *New Yorker* writer George Trow recognized her work as *New Yorker* material and introduced her to the magazine's editor, William Shawn. In her 21 years with the *New Yorker*, Kincaid produced 85 anonymous "Talk of the Town" articles as well as the signed short stories that served as the basis of *At the Bottom of the River* (1978), *Annie John* (1983), *Lucy* (1990), and *The Autobiography of My Mother* (1996). *Annie John* is in many ways a rewriting of *At the Bottom of the River*. *Lucy* can be seen to pick up where *Annie John* ends, as it follows an Antiguan girl's young adulthood as an au pair in the United States. As its title suggests, *The Autobiography of My Mother* plays with the genre of autobiography, and with the identity of the self, the mother, and the daughter in a first-person account of the life of Xuela Claudette Richardson in the British colony of Dominica in the first half of the twentieth century. In the 1980s, Kincaid also published, not in the *New Yorker*, *A Small Place* (1989), a biting description of the political, social, and economic state of postcolonial Antigua, and two short stories "Annie, Gwen, Lilly, Pam, and Tulip" (1989) and "Ovando" (1989), which explore the first encounters between conquistadors and native inhabitants of the Caribbean.

Not long after the death of her mentor and editor, Mr Shawn, Kincaid stopped publishing in the *New Yorker*. Kincaid continues, however, to publish in a variety of other magazines, as well as to compose novels and to compile collections of her essays. *My Brother* (1997) employs the genre of the memoir to narrate not only the death from AIDS of Kincaid's youngest brother, Devon, but also Kincaid's life as it is—and as it could have been. *My Garden (Book):* (1999) collects essays that combine musings on gardening in Vermont with reflections on the relationships between gardening, botany, and colonialism. *Mr Potter* (2002) blends biography, memoir, autobiography, and fiction as it explores the life of a man in colonial Antigua who fathered a daughter who could be Kincaid, and *A Hike in the Himalayas* (2006) recounts her seed-seeking trek. After a ten-year hiatus from fiction, her novel *See Now Then* (2013) tells of family life in New England.

Leigh Gilmore astutely labels Kincaid's literary project as one of "serial autobiography" (104). But Kincaid toys with more than just autobiographical form. She also forays into memoir and biography, and her works fall between the genres of the short story, the prose-poem, the novel, and the essay. Kincaid also belongs with a difference, or belongs on the fringes, of various national and canonical traditions. I write of Kincaid as a Caribbean author, but Kincaid explains that when she decided to become a writer, she knew only a European, and primarily a British, literary tradition of the nineteenth century and before. She tells Moira Ferguson:

> I had never read a West Indian writer when I started to write. Never. I didn't even know there was such a thing, until I met Derek Walcott. He said "Do you know—?" I had never heard of them, so I can't remember who he said. And I said no. And he made a list of people for me to read. There was not one woman on it, by the way.
>
> ("A Lot of Memory": 169)

When Kincaid was growing up, Antigua's library as well as its school system were under the control of the colonial administration, and the colonial curriculum was composed almost exclusively of British authors.[7] Kincaid belongs to perhaps the last generation of Caribbean authors who had to proceed as if there were no Caribbean literary tradition for them to inherit.

Kincaid asserts that as a Caribbean writer faced with a British literary legacy: "What you ought to do is take back. Not just reclaim. Take—period. Take anything. Take Shakespeare. Just anything that makes sense. Just take it. That's just fine" ("A Lot of Memory": 168). Derek Walcott describes a similar relationship to literary heritage not only for the Caribbean writer schooled in the British tradition but for all writers when he notes that the originality of all great poets "emerges only when they have absorbed all the poetry they have read, entire, [so] that their first work appears to be the accumulation of other peoples' trash but that they become bonfires, that it is only academic and frightened poets who talk of Beckett's debt to Joyce" (*What the Twilight Says*: 62). However, the colonial relationship complicates the process of absorption. Kincaid, Walcott, and their peers could access not "all the poetry" in the world, but only "all the poetry" in the British canon. Furthermore, the image of picking through trash in a Caribbean context suggests not the young poet riffling through the crumpled papers of his mentor, but the starving slave searching in the debris of the master for a few bites to eat, a few swaths of cloth to stitch together. Relegated to a different class, not only a different economic class but also to a different human class, colonial subjects cannot absorb British trash in the same way that Beckett can. When they "take," they do not simply borrow; they steal, imitate, assimilate, or revolt. Kincaid's "taking" is a form of literary cannibalism, similar to Condé's rewriting, as discussed in the previous chapter. But Kincaid also reevaluates the loaded implications of the verb "to take." She starts by saying "take back," indicating that taking Shakespeare for example is not thievery because he himself took from the Caribbean the material for works such as *The Tempest.* But Kincaid continues with a series of short sentences: "Not just reclaim. Take—period. Take anything. Take Shakespeare. Just anything that makes sense. Just take it. That's fine." Stripping "take" of any implications beyond the most literal, Kincaid works to remove the value judgments attached to the verb: "take" becomes neither a "good" nor a "bad" action, but rather almost neutral. Kincaid and her Caribbean peers do not have the luxury of choosing what literary mentors they want to adopt. They take what they can get.

Throughout her work, Kincaid explores what it means to belong—to a family, a community, a culture, a place. Through characters who contemplate the lives of their parents, grandparents, and the figures of folklore, Kincaid examines how personal and mythic history impacts the understanding of self. Vivid descriptions of plants and climate suggest the role that place plays in identification. Neighbors, friends, and teachers represent the community with which Kincaid's narrators identify and from which they distinguish themselves. Rebellious adolescents question how rules and taboos are established and why and how they ought to be followed. Narratives that treat individual comings of age also suggest that development, learning, and changing may be as essential to the community, perhaps to the nation, as they are to the young girl. And young girls who desire mentoring, friendship, and love explore the many different kinds of relationships they can build with the people and the places that surround them.[8]

Way into the Middle: Reading without Plot "In the Night"

Like many of the stories in *At the Bottom of the River*, "In the Night" is divided into a number of indirectly interrelated sections, strikingly lacking in the kind of "design" that for Brooks is the organizing principle of plot. In the first section of "In the Night," the third-person narrator repeatedly employs simple declaratives such as "it is" and "there are" to describe the activities, sounds, and senses of a night in Antigua. In the second section, a first-person narrator tells of a dream she has of herself "in the night." The same narrator recounts, in the third section, what "no one has ever said to me": that a girl and her family love and appreciate her father, the night-soil man. The fourth section reverts to the third-person narrator to describe the flowers at night as well as another series of activities. In the last section, the first-person narrator returns to describe the future she sees for herself.

Brooks claims that "temporality is a problem, and an irreducible factor of any narrative statement in a way that location is not" (22). But in *At the Bottom of the River*, location is an irreducible factor of narration, while temporality is not. "In the Night" begins:

> In the night, way into the middle of the night, when the night isn't divided like a sweet drink into little sips, when there is no just before midnight, or just after midnight, when the night is round in some places, flat in some places, and in some places like a deep hole, blue at the edge, black inside, the night-soil men come. (6)

The deep hole evokes Caribbean history and also the outhouse holes that constitute Antiguan plumbing in the 1950s and that the "night-soil men" clean, while the spatiality of the night folds time into location rather than vice versa: "Round in some places, flat in some places" describes a topography, and "blue at the edge, black inside" can refer to an island at night or with a population of African descent. The night of the story is a time that is also a place, and one that does not obey rules of temporality such as succession or progression. Although various characters' nighttime preparations for "tomorrow" and the last section's projection into "one day" suggest that "In the Night" progresses from dusk to dawn, the story operates in an endless present where before and after, beginning and ending have little relevance.

According to Brooks, death is the end point in standard (heterosexual) plots, anticipated in or preceded by reproduction, which is the only way to gesture to a future.[9] In "In the Night," however, death is not terminal; instead, a woman killed by her husband appears "back from the dead, looking at the man who used to groan; he is running a fever forever," while a man stands "under the tree, wearing his nice suit and holding a glass full of rum in his hand—the same glass of rum that he had in his hand shortly before he died—and looking at the house in which he used to live" (8). If there is no ending in death, there may be no end at all, but only the continuation of a middle where desire between women is not a stop on the way to a heterosexual completion but rather one story, one branch, among many.

In Brooks's account, the middle only appears in relation to the beginning and the end as the space of the detours that confirm the (hetero)normative rule (92). The middle of "In the Night," however, exists outside of the progression that beginning and ending require. The tangential relation of the stories' sections to one another may move the story to different times and places, but refuses any developmental, resolutionary, or hetero-reproductive model.

The subjects of "In the Night's" first sentence are the night-soil men who come "way into the middle of the night" to clear the outhouses of the day's waste. These men, or the narrator watching them, are able to see the truth of things that are not as they appear:

> The night-soil men can see a bird walking in the trees. It isn't a bird. It is a woman who has removed her skin and is on her way to drink the blood of her secret enemies. It is woman who has left her skin in a corner of a house made of wood. It is a woman who is reasonable and admires honeybees in the hibiscus. It is a woman who, as a joke, brays like a donkey when he is thirsty. (6)

In the night when spirits walk freely, the night-soil men and the narrator see and see through shifting appearances. Seeing clearly means not stopping at the outlines of a form or the singularity of time but possessing the night vision that allows you to perceive surface and depth, multiple moments in the timeless present, all at once. Along with the masks that let magic creatures pass unnoticed in the daytime, the false veneer that makes heterosexuality appear a perfect model becomes transparent in the night:

> There is the sound of a man groaning in his sleep; there is the sound of a woman disgusted at the man groaning. There is the sound of the man stabbing the woman, the sound of her blood as it hits the floor, the sound of Mr Straffee, the undertaker, taking her body away. There is the sound of her spirit, back from the dead, looking at the man who used to groan; he is running a fever forever. (7)

The namelessness of the man and woman, their introduction with the indefinite article "a," and their eternal existence in the night render them representative of any, or perhaps even of every, man and woman who sleep together. The repetition of "there is" puts the events into a strangely static succession that refuses to build toward any kind of climax or even to assert causality. Although the man's violent outbreak appears senseless, the couple sleeping together is already "groaning" and "disgusted." Neither death nor reproduction culminate the relationship; the cycle of violence, retribution, and suffering will be endless (and without a beginning, it already, always, is).

A happy reproductive heterosexual family appears in the night only as part of what "no one has ever said to me":

> No one has ever said to me, "My father, a night-soil man, is very nice and very kind. When he passes a dog, he gives a pat and not a kick. He likes all the parts of a fish but especially the head. He goes to church quite regularly and is always glad when the minister calls out, 'A Mighty Fortress Is Our God', his favorite hymn. He would like to wear pink shirts and pink pants but he knows that color isn't very becoming to a man, so instead he wears navy blue and brown, colors he does not like well. He met my mother on what masquerades as a bus around here, a long time ago, and he still likes to whistle . . . I love my father the night-soil man. My mother loves my father the night-soil man. Everybody loves him and waves to him whenever they see him." (9–10)

The heterosexual model is a fiction and a fantasy, the quoted ideal that the narrator imagines might be said. The fiction rests, however, on the father's unhappy gender conformity. And the parents' meeting was part of a broader masquerade where British terminology dresses the island's transportation infrastructure, just as it does the island's familial and erotic structures. In this ideal, not only the narrator and her mother, but "everybody" loves her father, an extension that reminds that although it may sound good, it is the ideal of universalism.

In the fourth section of "In the Night," the narrator describes another family or series of families that confirm the heterosexual model as a colonial ideal perpetuating a colonial-patriarchal economy, or what María Lugones demonstrates to be the heterosexualism of the colonial organization of power:

> Someone is making a basket, someone is making a girl dress or a boy shirt, someone is making her husband a soup with cassava so that he can take it to the cane field tomorrow, someone is making his wife a beautiful mahogany chest, someone is sprinkling a colorless powder outside a closed door so that someone else's child will be stillborn, someone is praying that a bad child who is living prosperously abroad will be good and send a package filled with new clothes, someone is sleeping. (11)

The division of children into girls and boys who wear dresses and shirts, respectively, illustrates the gender binary that also organizes adults into husbands and wives. Just as Lugones argues that these are interrelated and both imposed by and created through colonialism, Kincaid shows the grouping to sustain the plantation economy where the wife serves to prepare meals for her husband to eat while he is off working in the cane fields. In the present of a (hope) chest, a European Romantic tradition lurks in the background of Kincaid's story, as does its hetero-patriarchy. The sprinkling of powder in order to cause a stillborn can be read in the light of a similar incident in *Annie John* as an action performed by the other women whose children the same man has fathered, exposing the heterosexual family to not only foster the production of bastard children but also destroy women's solidarity or else to create for women only a solidarity through assisted infanticide. When the heterosexual family groupings "in the night" do produce children, they are children who can only provide for the perpetuation of the family through their service in, as well as to, the colonial center, "abroad."

While these families might fit Denise deCaires Narain's analysis that "sexual relationships in [Kincaid's] texts are invariably (hyper) heterosexual and always doomed" (203), the girl narrator of "In the Night" does not imagine a heterosexual future for herself: "one day," she says, "I will marry a woman" (11). Although this imagination of a future might suggest an end of the endless middle and an opening onto a standard end in a future of reproductive marriage, the collapse of temporal progression asserted at the beginning of "In the Night" brings the future of "one day" into the present of "In the Night" so that it not only projects but also realizes a nonheterosexual structure where "Now I am a girl, but one day I will marry a woman—a red-skin woman with black bramblebush hair and brown eyes, who wears skirts that are so big I can easily bury my head in them. I would like to marry this woman and live with her in a mud hut near the sea" (11).[10] The verbs in this last section shift between future (I will) and future conditional (I would), so that the narrator's own desire, what she would like, is realized in her own formulations, creating a future from and in the present desire. And the future that is projected will become its own endless present, for it is imagined not as the next step in many, but as the "one day" that will become "every day" and "every night," the time markers that repeatedly begin sentences in the last part of the section.

The idea that "every night, over and over, she will tell me something that begins 'Before you were born' " (12), and the maternal imagery in the red-skin woman's embracing skirts have led many critics, like Lizabeth Paravisini-Gebert, to read the relationship as "the relationship between the girl and the mother, here represented as a couple delighting in their domesticity—the mother/daughter bond having replaced the husband/wife connection" (57).[11] Yet, it might rather be that the narrator's desire to marry a maternal figure stems no more from a desire to marry her mother than from a desire to marry a maternal woman. The futurity of the relationship is formulated around the projection of the narrator into her own womanhood, so that we find not a relationship of girl to woman, but of woman to woman. The red-skin woman is presented as a desired wife, not as a desired mother, suggesting not a return to a pre-oedipal "mother/daughter bond" but a re-vision of marriage, where the relationship of two wives stands in the place often assumed to be that of "the husband/wife connection."

If a relationship between two wives simply replaces one between husband and wife, with the switch turning on the gender of the object of desire, we might have a shift from heterosexual to homosexual. I make a point here of emphasizing the romantic, erotic, and domestic coupling of the two women because other readings downplay those elements and because those are indeed part of the ideal marriage in "In the Night." However, the relationships between men and women already show deep fissures in the hetero-colonial model not only because the men and women in them are not happy but because of the ways that they are not happy and the ways that they cope with work around their unhappiness. Furthermore, desire between women "In the Night" mirrors and differs from the relationships between men and women not so much based on different object of desire but based on a different relationship to colonial models and to heterosexual structures—they live not in a house but in a mud hut and keep not a hope chest but a John Bull mask, they form not an oedipal triangle but a mirrored couple that is at once one, two, and three. The narrator never rejects a man as a husband, but describes an ideal marriage that is as much a version of the mother–daughter relationship or of the *macocotte* relationship as it is of the father–daughter relationship, a distinctly non-oedipal and nonheterosexual model, in other words, of both childhood fantasy and adult sexuality and family formation.

The marriage in "In the Night" will be based on reciprocal mothering: "Every night I would sing this woman a song; the words I don't know yet, but the tune is in my head. This woman I would like to marry knows many things, but to me she will only tell about things that would never dream of making me cry; and every night, over and over, she will tell me something that begins, 'Before you were born' " (12). The two women will put one another to bed, one singing, the other telling stories. That these stories will begin before the narrator was born fits the timelessness of "In the Night" as much as it does a model of maternal love. If the marriage between the narrator and the red-skin woman in "In the Night" does represent "the relationship between the girl and her mother" as "a couple delighting in their domesticity," we must read the slippage from parents to siblings as going both ways. That is, it expresses not a desire to return in adulthood to a childhood connection, but a desire to find in childhood an adult connection, so that rather than desexualizing the two women's marriage, it sexualizes the mother/daughter relationship.

Evelyn O'Callaghan and MacDonald-Smythe both touch on the connection of desire between women and mother–daughter relationships in the Caribbean. MacDonald-Smythe's most recent intervention "concedes [to O'Callaghan's argument] that in the novels of many Caribbean women writers sexuality is linked to the desire for a lost maternal imaginary" but argues that

> where O'Callaghan reads the erotics of homosexuality as the reaction to that loss, I offer an alternative rendition. In assembling the social relations and cultural practices attendant to macocotte relationships, I am suggesting that in Caribbean society these same-sex female friendships among adolescent girls become the site for the erotic, a site that need to be established as different from the ones occupied by homosexual desire, and that these same-sex relationships develop naturally out of, rather than compensating for, the mother–daughter imaginary. (230)

I am suggesting one more loop in this conversation, positing these *macocotte* relationships are no more necessarily, as MacDonald-Smythe finds, "a learning space for heterosexual identity and development" than they are a homosexual compensation for its lacunae, and that while they certainly are sometimes each of these, their expression in childhood and adolescence as well as their projection into adulthood describe a mangled structure of desire and sexuality where erotic, sexual, and emotional relationships between women intertwine with those between women and men in ways that are neither heterosexual nor homosexual.

Although it is projected into a future of which some elements are conditional, the narrator of "In the Night" describes her marriage as a certainty: "one day I will marry a woman." This simple assertion joins others throughout the story to establish the marriage of two women not as some deviation from an expected path, but as the most natural and normal thing. It follows from all of the narrator's observations of life around her, a life that includes married families, couples, and children. The narrator's idea of marrying a woman only contrasts indirectly with, and never opposes, any other options, although the description of the married life of the two women suggests that it plots a narrative structure that has no more progression though perhaps more play and pleasure than the heterosexual (un)couplings in the rest of the story. Playing on the status of marriage as the apotheosis of a heteronorm, a normal marriage between women either concedes to that norm with a difference, or else pluralizes it.

Everything in the narrator's future home with her wife will be set up for a self-contained unit of two rather than the three who symbolize the reproductive heterosexual family. These two women will nurture only one another, and no one else:

> In the mud hut will be two chairs and one table, a lamp that burns kerosene, a medicine chest, a pot, one bed, two pillows, two sheets, one looking glass, two cups, two saucers, two dinner plates, two forks, two drinking-water glasses, one china pot, two fishing strings, two straw hats to ward the hot sun off our heads, two trunks for things we have very little use for, one basket, one book of plain paper, one box filled with twelve crayons of different colors, one loaf of bread wrapped in a piece of brown paper, one coal pot, one picture of two women standing on a jetty, one picture of the same two women embracing, one picture of the same two women waving goodbye, one box of matches. (11–12)

The play of ones and twos in the list of their items insists on the status of the two women as a couple: whatever can be shared, they possess in single; the things that cannot be shared they have in double, assuring that there are two, but only two, of them. The only possessions they own in triplicate are pictures of themselves: together they exceed the required one or two, providing more than the bare minimum to one another. Represented in three pictures, the two women do not blend together into one, nor are they the perfect symmetry of two. The narrator and the red-skinned woman stand together and apart, one, two, and three. The setting of the pictures is on a jetty, from where, in *Annie John*, Annie John will depart from Antigua and from her mother's ideal of a colonially conforming "young lady." It is unclear from the descriptions of the photographs in "In the Night" to whom the two women in the picture are waving goodbye, and whether they are waving goodbye to someone leaving while they stay, or to someone staying while they leave. The photographs sit, however, in the hut by the Caribbean Sea that the two women share, implying that if they ever left, they have returned. They keep in their home a reminder of leave-taking. If, via *Annie John*, we read this as a leave-taking of colonial conformity, then these two women have already completed the circle on one edge of which Annie John stands, having left behind colonial conformity without leaving, or having already left and returned to, what they do want of Antigua.

While their mud hut near the sea may evoke a mermaid's dwelling or some sort of mythical woman's space, at the same time it suggests a modest home, and the women's marriage in "In the Night" occurs in the midst of the everyday real. The mundane list of household items in the hut wraps the scene of two married women not in mythic lore but in quotidian normalcy. Their house holds no secrets, its entire contents laid out before the reader in a nearly exhaustive list. Two women married to one another do not attain riches, nor is there any mystery to they way in which they go about their lives.

The narrator and the red-skin woman do, however, weave into their daily routine a subtle resistance to colonial rule:

> Every day this red-skin woman and I will eat bread and milk for breakfast, hide in bushes and throw hardened cow dung at people we don't like, climb coconut trees, eat and drink the food and water from the coconuts we have picked, throw stones in the sea, put on John Bull masks and frighten defenseless little children on their way home from school, go fishing and catch only our favorite fishes to roast and have for dinner, steal green figs to eat for dinner with the roast fish. (11–12)

Colonial schooling marks the time of their days, but the narrator and the red-skinned woman appear to participate exclusively in truant, after-school, or holiday activities: running, playing, and eating favorite foods. The schoolgirl activities remind also that the narrator is a child imagining her adulthood, and filling it with play with another girl, solidly in the domain of the *macocottes*. In their play, the two women extend the carnival celebration during which satirical masks are common into their everyday, and use a symbol of British prosperity and joviality, John Bull, as a tool of terror and persecution.[12] Their marriage may not in itself challenge colonial authority, but it is through this marriage that the two women evade colonial educational discipline, hiding in the bushes rather than going to school, and also transgress colonial economic discipline, getting their food not by working on a plantation but by fishing and gathering for themselves from trees they may not have the right to harvest. And the two women will be the team who together attack or use a threat that is outside them, rather than turning on one another in a binding violence that spirals into endless destruction, as in *Amistad funesta*/*Lucía Jerez*, or succumbing to the greater power of colonial patriarchy, as in *Je suis martiniquaise*.

The two women in Kincaid's story will spend not only their days but also their nights together so that "I will marry a woman like this, and every night, every night, I will be completely happy" (11–12). The specification and insistence through repetition ("every night, every night") that it will be at night, after the singing and the storytelling, that the narrator will be "completely happy" draws attention to a particular happiness shared in a single bed at night, in other words, a happiness that is also implicitly sexual. At the same time, the scene evokes children's bedtime rituals. Linked as it is with the adult marital pleasures of two women, the childish demand for songs, stories, and company in bed at night reveals its sexiness. Imagining herself as a woman married to a woman, the girl narrator can play out, in their bed, the erotic desires girls have for one another as well as the erotic charge of the mother–daughter relationship. In both cases, the narrator and the red-skinned woman enact distinctly nonheterosexual erotic and kinship structures, where imaginative transformation rather than heterosexual romance and reproduction makes daughters into wives and wives into mothers.

The repetition of "every night, every night" brings the future of the marriage into the present of the story, not only in the eternity of "every night, every night" but also in the location, "in the night," of the story, where a place can be a time and where in a hut by the sea a girl will be the wife of a mother. The caressing rhythms of poetic language, "every night, every night," turn and return, drawing past and future into an eternal present and refusing singular models of progression and certain ends in heterosexual coupling.

Undermining Simplicity: "Wingless"

"Wingless" might be the daytime side of "In the Night." Like "In the Night," "Wingless" consists of a series of unclearly related sections often narrated in the first person by a young girl. The narration in the first part of "Wingless," by far the longest, moves from third to first person as it follows a schoolgirl in her lessons, her play, and her search for "a love like no other" (21). The first-person voice in this section belongs to a girl who expects to grow into "a tall, graceful, and altogether beautiful woman," but who describes her current state as "primitive and wingless" (22, 24). A brief dialogue between two unnamed characters about telling children a scary tale makes up the second section of "Wingless." In the third section, a first-person narrator, presumably the same as in the first section, follows "the woman I love" on a long walk. The narrator describes, in the fourth section, a day by the sea, followed by a dialogue with someone who has frightened her. In the fifth section, the narrator details what frightens her. The last section offers a descriptive list of

Antiguan insects and animals, followed by a first-person description of the narrator's hands.

Like that of "In the Night," the narrator of "Wingless" observes the world around her and attempts to understand her place in it, more specifically the relationships she would like to have. While the narrator of "In the Night" concerns herself with marriage, in "Wingless" the topic shifts to love as the girl narrator looks for the unquantifiable "love like no other" that she will find with a woman with a "red, red smile" (25). The story is concerned less with the marital structure that might hold a relationship than with the affective state of love. Yet the superlative and exceptional formulation, "a love like no other," becomes normalized through its refrain-like repetition, and any exceptionality of the relationships between the narrator and various women with whom she might feel this love is belied by their simple and straightforward presentation.

In a story that might appear as a kind of quest narrative for "a love like no other," the unremarkable, simple, and normal way that this love is sought, found, and described is striking. Although the story does follow a certain causal progression, with the continuation of the narrative motivated by the unsatisfied desire for "a love like no other" and the culmination of the narrative lying in the discovery of that love, the simplicity of what is sought and found and the obviousness of it both repeat a simple quest plot and refuse its basic conventions: "Wingless" has no oedipal drama, no distinctive beginning middle, and nothing that can be mapped onto a triangular structure of rising action, climax, and falling action or of unsatisfied desire, coming together in marriage or death, and reproduction. Like "In the Night," "Wingless" is told in a timeless present, with the verb "to be" used so repeatedly in the formulations "there is" and "there are" that they become a sort of refrain undermining any causality and progression that may occur in the story. The narrator only considers other girls and women as possible candidates for the "love like no other" while the confusion between lover and mother makes it difficult to determine whether the narrator is coming of age, discovering love outside of a parental relationship, or resisting that very narrative of temporal progress, clinging to love inside a parental relationship which both stops her from "progressing" to adult relationships and shows that what might look like progress is not, creating a kind of succession without progress that is also the time of "there is" and that creates not a tree-like structure on which to plot a family but rather a mangle, a thicket of intertwining roots and branches that just stays in place.

The simple and straightforward timeless present in "Wingless" is not, however, an anticolonial natural simplicity that is opposed a complicated artificial colonial progress narrative. Rather, the first section of the story reveals the place of simple, straightforward assertion in and as colonial ideology. As "Wingless" opens, children read a book whose "simple words and sentences" present deeply charged ideological lessons as self-evident and universal truth:

> The small children are reading from a book filled with simple words and sentences.
>
> "Once upon a time there was a little chimney-sweep, whose name was Tom."
>
> "He cried half his time, and laughed the other half."
>
> "You would have been giddy, perhaps, looking down: but Tom was not."
>
> "You, of course, would have been very cold sitting there on a September night, without the least bit of clothes on your wet back; but Tom was a water-baby, and therefore felt cold no more than a fish." (20)

The "simple words and sentences" are quoted from Charles Kingsley's *The Water-babies* (1863), a fairy tale that epitomizes British Victorian education and ideology.[13] Kingsley wrote *The Water-babies* while serving as professor of Modern History at Cambridge; he went on to become canon of Chester, then canon of Westminster and chaplain to Queen Victoria.[14] *The Water-babies* thematizes sin and redemption through a metaphor of filth and cleansing where the epitome of dirtiness is black skin, which can be removed to reveal redeemed whiteness.[15] Kingsley's narrator describes Tom in his unclean state—in the paragraph that begins "you would have been giddy, perhaps, looking down; but Tom was not"—as "a jolly little black ape," a phrase easily recognizable as designating the position of the black person in nineteenth-century discourses of race that fused theories of evolution with the "great chain of being" to draw a hierarchical ordering of the races with apes at the bottom, followed by blacks, and progressing up to European men and/or God at the top (33).[16] Tom's baptismal cleansing, in *The Water-babies*, leaves behind "a black thing in the water" that is taken for his body although in fact it is only "his whole husk and shell" which fairies "had washed quite off him, and the pretty little real Tom was washed out of the inside of it" (52). As children learn to read and write with the "simple words and phrases" of Kingsley's story, they also learn the racial ideology, what Toni Morrison calls "the master narrative," that undergirds his story, an operation that is far from simple and whose workings the simplicity of Kingsley's tale masks and thus renders all the more powerful.[17]

Kingsley dedicated *The Water-babies* to his youngest son, Greenville, and to "all other good little boys." These white British boys become the universal child whom the narrator addresses with the suggestion that "perhaps you would have been giddy" and the prescription that "you, of course, would have been very cold." Like Wordsworth's "Daffodils" that erect for the eponymous Lucy, in Kincaid's later novel, beauty, contemplation, and nature as a flower she has never seen, *The Water-babies* imposes British reality onto Antiguan children's experience. Antiguan children must misrecognize themselves in Kingsley's words, either agreeing to a normal where houses are built two stories high with chimneys and where a September night is cold so that they can be different from the filthy Tom, or else seeing themselves in Tom, not afraid up on the roofs of their homes nor cold in September and like him little black apes in need of fairy-born lactification.

The ideological charge of Kingsley's story permeates the British colonial curriculum in which the children in "Wingless" "have already learned to write their names in beautiful penmanship. They have already learned how many farthings make a penny, how many pennies make a shilling, how many days in April, how many stone in a ton" (20–21). Counting, these children learn, means measuring time, money, and weight according to a British norm, so that arithmetic as much as reading lessons provide education in the colonial order, rendering normal a British worldview and British colonialism. Yet just as the mother in the first story in the collection, "Girl," in imparting the lessons of how to be a lady, may show as much how to *use* as how to *do* conformity, the children in school learn how to normatize and normalize as well as how to follow the norm.

The first intervention of the first-person narrator is to comfort a classmate "after thirteen of her play chums have sat on her" (21). The narrator says: "There, Dulcie, there. I myself have been kissed by many rude boys with small, damp lips, on their way to boys' drill. I myself have humped girls under my mother's house" (21). The comforting "there, . . . there" and the repeated "I myself have" normalize whatever has happened to Dulcie, implying that Dulcie, the narrator, and any number of other children have had similar experiences. Dulcie's becomes not a tale of exceptionality but one of normalcy. It is not juxtaposed with the quotidian school lessons, but is rather contiguous with them.

The identical openings, "I myself have . . . I myself have" establish the two sentences as parallel, so that a girl humping other girls is equally frequent and (un)important as boys kissing girls on the way to class. Here we find not only the exclusive *macocotte* relationships between two intimate best girlfriends, but a large set of girls and boys who engage in sexual play with one another. The verb "to hump" indicates heterosexual intercourse but does so in the register of children's language. When the narrator talks of humping, she demonstrates not a knowledge of any precise meaning of the term but rather the expression through it of a more nebulous conception of sexual activity which uses heteronormative terminology even as it empties it of its heterosexual particularity. That is to say, "humping" here is a sexual act even, or especially, where no precise definition of a particular sexual act can be attached to it. The recourse to a child's perspective and to children's language at once simplifies and complicates the activity, and at the same time underlines that the definition of the simple is slippery, at best.

Although the narrator describes being in the passive position kissed by boys and being in the active position humping girls, she presents not a passive–active opposition between the two but rather the ability to move between passive and active positions with both boys and girls. Being kissed by boys and humping girls are activities, not expressions of love or identity. A sentence that serves as a refrain in the story follows the narrator's words to Dulcie: "But I swim in a shaft of light, upside down, and I can see myself clearly, through and through, from every angle" (21). The complex grammar and dense imagery of this sentence contrasts starkly with the simplicity of the preceding comments to Dulcie. Yet the sentence itself describes an experience of perfect transparency and clarity, and of absolute self-knowledge.[18] The unclear assertion of clarity contrasts with the clear assertion of ambiguity; it undermines the connection between clarity of form and clarity of content and at the same time suggests that ambiguity may be clearer than transparency.[19] The sentence seems to be related to the comments to Dulcie, because its first word, "but," is a conjunction, one that designates a relation of exception or dissension. Perhaps the narrator's being kissed by boys and humping girls is something she does not understand about herself although she generally sees herself clearly. Or perhaps being kissed by boys and humping girls does not make the narrator sad, like it does Dulcie, because the narrator sees herself clearly. Although the narrator asserts her ability to see herself "through and through," what she sees is not made clear to the reader, and what follows the assertion of being able to see herself clearly are a series of possibilities and questions about herself.

Many of the narrator's questions are about love, about whom she loves and who loves her and how. The first possible love object is "that woman over there, that large-bottomed woman [who] is important to me" for whom "I save up my sixpences instead of spending them for sweets." The narrator wonders, "Is this a love like no other? And what pain have I caused her? And does she love me?" (21). The answer at least to the first question appears to be "no," for the narrator continues to search, wondering next: "that woman over there. Is she cruel? Does she love me? And if not, can I make her?" (22). The large-bottomed woman and the woman who might be cruel and might "love me" fit into the highly erotic, even sexualized maternal imagery that runs throughout Kincaid's work. However, the narrator understands the age difference to be one of the impediments to her ability to make "that woman over there" love her, following the question "can I make her [love me]?" with the comment "I am not yet tall, beautiful, graceful, and able to impose my will," suggesting that what she seeks is an adult love (22). And when the mother is directly mentioned in "Wingless," she is more like the mother in "Girl," an authority figure who the narrator both resents and loves without trace of erotic tension: "Is this my mother? Is she here to embarrass me? What shall I say about her behind her back, when she isn't there, long after she has gone? In her smile lies her goodness" (23). The narrator later describes the smile of "the woman I love" and refers to "the woman I love, who is so much bigger than me," keeping in play the possibility of a mother-love, but the beloved woman is at most a partial double for the mother.[20] The adult love this narrator imagines might be maternal, even if it is not of the daughter for the mother, but there is never any question of it being the love of a boy or man.

Boys and men rarely appear in "Wingless." They are alluded to several times, but they act in the story only as the "many rude boys" who kiss and as a man who "had stood up suddenly in front of [the woman I love]," then "said things to her . . . so forcefully that drops of brown water sprang from his mouth" and then "put wind in his cheeks and blew himself up until in the bright sun he looked like a boil" (25).[21] But while this man is an impediment to the woman's walk, presenting words and images from which the woman must shield herself, he is simply a bother, for the woman "only smiled—a red, red smile—and like a fly he dropped dead" (25). In this way desire between women never has to contrast with desire between women and men. The regular pattern is to search for a love like no other with women and girls; whatever may be had with men and boys is irrelevant to this, although it certainly may coexist with it.

A beloved first appears as the answer to the narrator's questions:

> Is a girl who can sing "Gaily the troubador plucked his guitar" in a pleasing way worthy of being my best friend? There is the same girl, unwashed and glistening, setting traps for talking birds. Is she to be one of my temptations? Oh, this must be a love like no other. (22)

This girl is a colonial product, knowing the English folk song "Gaily the troubadour," although her singing it establishes a contrast between a British tradition of heterosexual love—the song tells of a troubadour returning home from war to the lady love who awaits him—and the world of the Antiguan girls of the story.[22] Taking the singing girl's dirtiness not as a sign of sin that must be washed off but as an emblem of beauty, what makes her glisten, the narrator sees in this girl a refusal of colonial ideology, if also an integration of colonial elements. If the singing girl has been taught by an Antiguan mother like the one in "Girl," she has ignored the lessons about cleanliness but remembered those about recognizing magical birds. That this girl might tempt the narrator is what leads directly to the assertion that "this must be a love like no other." The association between temptation and sexuality is Biblical, but rather than turning from what in Biblical terms would be sin, perhaps even original sin, immediately after asking "is she to be one of my temptations?," the narrator exclaims and claims to have found what she was looking for: "Oh, this must be a love like no other" (22). Other loves might conform to Biblical ideology and the conventions of British folk tradition, but this one is "like no other." It is unique, but not exceptional.

In the third and fifth sections of "Wingless," "the woman I love" appears as someone so perfectly known to the narrator that her being loved is simply an adjectival phrase repeated every time "the woman" is named. It is not clear whether "the woman I love" in these two sections is a single person and whether she is the singing girl, someone the narrator loves instead of the singing girl, or someone the narrator loves alongside the singing girl. But whether she loves one woman or many, another girl or her mother or a motherly woman, this simple assertion of the existence of women whom the narrator loves is as embedded in a Caribbean worldview as are the "simple words and sentences" of Kingsley's story embedded in a British worldview:

> the sky, which is big and blue as always, has its limits. This afternoon the wind is loud as a hurricane. There isn't enough light. There is a noise—I can't tell where it is coming from. A big box has stamped on it "Handle Carefully." I have been in a big white building with curving corridors. I have passed a dead person. There is a woman I love, who is so much bigger than me. (26–27)

Rather than imposing reactions to what "there is" onto "you," like the "book filled with simple words and sentences," these simple sentences describe the ways in which "I" experience what "there is" in a specific place and time. That the sky is always big and blue is, Kincaid asserts in *A Small Place* and in *Mr Potter*, particularly true in Antigua, and incomprehensible to people from elsewhere.[23] Hurricanes and their accompanying noises and transformations of light are common in the Caribbean but not throughout the world. Passing a dead person entails understanding dead people to inhabit the same spaces as the living. The "I" and her reality are inscribed within a Caribbean space, but they describe rather than prescribe their reality. The narrator's simple assertions of her experience do not, like simple school lessons, provide a framework through which anything is explained but rather, in their very simplicity, defy explanation. They toss simplicity into the mangle and watch it thrive, simply, in whatever way it can. A girl narrator's finding "a love like no other" with a girlfriend, and knowing beyond a doubt that "there is a woman I love" belong to this Caribbean "simplicity."

The simple in Kincaid's stories can mask complex ideological machinations and also unmask the ideological presumption of the norm to simply repeat what is "regular, usual, typical, ordinary, standard," to set an order for what is "free from any disorder." But by reducing the simple to its barest workings, the assertion of what there is, Kincaid's stories succeed not only in laying bare the assumptions on which ideological structures are built but also in allowing for other constructions. With the simplest tools, Kincaid builds mud huts for women to share that are much more appealing than any master's houses. She writes narratives that move not forward but around, that grow like mangroves, accessing maximum water and light amid muddy marshes and dense growth, thriving if they can move in several directions at once, or not at all. Desire between women in Kincaid's stories does not go anywhere and it does not do anything except to be there, regularly, normally, free from disorder (but out of Brooks's colonial heteronormative plotting order).

CHAPTER 5

Sexual Alternatives in Patricia Powell's *Me Dying Trial*

Buju Banton's infamous 1988 dancehall hit "Boom Bye Bye" conveys the prevailing view, persistent for more than a quarter century, of Jamaican public opinion about same-sex relationships: extreme intolerance. Dancers across the country still sing along to Banton's refrain: "Boom bye bye/Inna batty bwoy head/Rude bwoy no promote the nasty man/Dem haffi dead" (Boom bye bye/In a fag's head/Dancehall singers don't promote no fags/They have to die).[1] Even in the popular and academic debate sparked as Banton continues to receive international recognition, while many argue that Banton's view is offensive, few suggest that it is uncommon.[2]

Sex acts between men are criminal in Jamaica, and while intimate acts between women are not regulated, women who are known or suspected to be involved with other women are regularly detained under indecent and lewd exposure laws.[3] The legal status of homosexuality contributes to a reticence to prosecute or police crimes against homosexuals, and widespread and extreme violence against homosexuals led Human Rights Watch to declare Jamaica, in 2004, "the most homophobic place on earth."[4] Ongoing civil discrimination, including Prime Minister Golding's 2008 statement that he would not allow gays in his cabinet, ensures serious consequences for those even suspected of engaging in same-sex relationships.[5] Shortly before Portia Simpson Miller was elected Prime Minister in 2012, she said that she would not exclude anyone from her cabinet on the basis of sexual orientation and condemned discrimination against homosexuals.[6] Simpson has not, however, moved to repeal the laws, and violence against homosexuals appears to be only increasing.[7]

Jamaican homophobia is articulated as part of anticolonial nationalism so that homosexuals are associated with "the West" while, in M. Jacqui

Alexander's words, "as the [postcolonial] state moves to reconfigure the nation it simultaneously resuscitates that nation as heterosexual" (6).[8] This hetero-nationalism, as Cecil Gutzmore argues, rests on "the imperative of the purity and authenticity of a primordially homosexuality-free global African culture" (125). However, Alexander and others present compelling arguments that Jamaican "anticolonial" homophobia derives from the very same British colonial laws and traditions which it proclaims to resist.[9]

More insidious, even, than the colonial privileging of heterosexuality that results in Jamaican hetero-nationalism, is the hetero–homo opposition that undergirds the hetero-colonial imperative. Analyses of desire and sexuality in Jamaica in terms of heterosexuality or homosexuality always already accept a hetero-colonial structure, whose apotheosis might be the homophobia exemplified by the dancehall lyrics, and miss the ways that Jamaican family configurations and social structures make room for alternatives not only to heterosexuality but to the hetero–homo divide. Gutzmore argues that "Jamaican and other societies of the Caribbean combine their fierce social policing of homo/sexuality with a certain permissiveness, producing a situation to which Herbert Marcuse's expression 'repressive tolerance'—suitably reinterpreted—may well be applicable" (122).[10] Roger Lancaster's Marcusian reformulation "tolerant intolerance," developed to refer to Nicaraguan treatment of nonheterosexuals, is perhaps most apt. The intolerant requirement that same-sex desire be hidden in order to avoid being named and persecuted as homosexuality only enhances the *imbrication* of same-sex desire with other desires and arrangements that is a defining feature of the tolerant epistemology of the mangrove. Where legislation and law establish an oppositional structure between an authorized national heterosexuality and a delegitimized foreign homosexuality, nonheterosexual structures and practices appear as alternatives, others in relation to the one norm. But the proliferation of alternatives also undercuts the standing of the "norm" as what is normal, regular, or most common.

The difficult combination of intolerance and tolerance that arises as different understandings of familial and sexual norms and normals, and different frames of reference, are sorted out by a range of Jamaican characters in Powell's novels. Powell's novels examine the struggles of "battymen" and other Jamaicans labeled as sexual deviants but they also depict a Jamaican tradition that includes such a wide range of family configurations and sexual relations that the norm from which some deviate must be understood as what is promoted and legislated by the state, rather than what is regular or usual for a majority of Jamaicans.[11] Powell shows that even as virulent homophobia targets men and women identified as homosexual, a multiplicity of family structures fosters acceptance of a variety of intimate relationships.

The most prominent alternative sexual and intimate relationships in Powell's first two books, *Me Dying Trial (1993)* and *A Small Gathering of Bones* (1994), are between men. For that reason, I wondered about including an analysis of *Me Dying Trial* in this book about desire between women in Caribbean literature. A series of questions arose: If the gender binary that divides men and women is part of the same hetero-colonial system against which I examine other structures of desire and sexuality, how do I account for the differences that gender makes without reifying what María Lugones calls "heterosexualism and the colonial/modern gender system"? Do the gender differences between men and women, even (or especially) if they are socially, colonially constructed, render desire between men structurally different from desire between women? How do desire between men, desire between women, and other kinds of nonheterosexual desire, sexuality, and family intersect? These questions must run throughout any study of desire between women in Caribbean literature, and indeed I find myself addressing various aspects of them in each chapter of this book. *Me Dying Trial* brings them front and center.

In *Me Dying Trial*, the public and religious intolerance of homosexuality renders it the lightning rod that protects and also illuminates other non-heterosexual individuals and families. Indeed, the relationships between men in *Me Dying Trial* are presented through the eyes of Gwennie and Peppy, a mother and daughter trying to figure out their own places in family and sexual relationships.[12] They look at how desire between men fits into or disrupts social norms and normal social relations as they try to decide with whom to ally themselves and how to balance their own desires for various forms of social acceptance and social change.

Powell has also suggested that in these early works, the focus on relations between men provided an important degree of distance for her as a writer.[13] Powell's biography loosely coincides with that of Peppy in *Me Dying Trial*: she was born in Jamaica, raised by a female relative for most of her early years, and immigrated to the United States in her teens. Powell finished high school and college in the United States and wrote *Me Dying Trial* as her MFA thesis at Brown University. In the following years, as she has continued to write and to teach creative writing, Powell has slowly made public her own relationships with women.

As someone who openly has primary erotic and sexual relationships with women and as a relative newcomer on the literary scene—*Boston Magazine* calls her "a Generation-X vanguard for the Caribbean literary world"—Powell might not quite queer the "straight" Caribbean "canon" in the same way as the other authors in this study. And yet even as she represents a new generation of Caribbean writers who speak and write explicitly about desire between women in their novels and in their own lives, Powell also belongs to an earlier moment in the Caribbean canon exemplified perhaps best by Michelle Cliff and Dionne Brand, who self-identify as lesbian and whose poetry and novels have depicted women loving women since the late 1970s. Cliff and Brand's work has been well studied as offering a woman-loving challenge to a Caribbean heterosexual tradition, and it is one of the aims of this book to recall that the tradition that they oppose is already traversed by desire between women and also that other oppositions to it, notably ones that turn to focus on women although not primarily on women-loving-women, also are traversed by desire between women. And yet Cliff and Brand, like Powell, while they are recognized as writing about same-sex desire and sexuality in the Caribbean in ways that other canonical writers are not, like the other authors I study here and, I would argue, many more, depict not an exclusive focus on same-sex desire, not same-sex desire as distinct from and in binary opposition to heterosexuality, but desire between women intersected by and intersecting multiple other desires and sexualities. Thus, while I am purposefully not framing this study with the work of authors like Cliff or Brand, neither do I want to exclude it. And so, as *Me Dying Trial* probes the many different ways to express and to contextualize same-sex desire in the Caribbean, it serves as both model and object for my study.

Me Dying Trial follows Gwennie and her daughter Peppy as they negotiate their complicated relationship through their relationships to the rest of their family and community but especially to Gwennie's son and Peppy's half-brother, Rudi. Peppy and Rudi represent Gwennie's deviation from the traditional role of mother and wife: Peppy is such a symbol of the affair in which she was conceived that Gwennie sends her to be raised by her Aunt Cora; Rudi is Gwennie's replacement in the home that she leaves to follow her own sexual, intellectual, and professional desires. Peppy and Rudi form a natural alliance built on their shared positions both outside of the heternormative social order and inside other Jamaican normals. So Peppy has a context in which to accept Rudi when he tells her that he loves other men, and they support one another in withstanding the contradictions of a mother who ends up enforcing on her children the very norms that have so plagued her own life.

Powell's other three books also explore connections between sexuality, gender, and family configuration in the Caribbean. *A Small Gathering of Bones* depicts the sympathy, love, and support that family, friends and lovers, church, and hospital offer and refuse to a young man dying of AIDS in Kingston in the 1970s. In *The Pagoda* (1998), a Chinese-Jamaican gender-crossing character struggles to negotiate the racial, gender, and sexual mores of nineteenth-century Jamaica. Powell's most recent novel, *The Fullness of Everything* (2009), follows a Jamaican-born American who on his return home has to rethink his understanding of what it means to be a sibling, a parent, a spouse, and a child. In all of her books, Powell looks at the contradictory ideologies that operate in Jamaica. And yet rather than a society of incompatibilities, Powell's Jamaica is one of complexities. Individual characters often run headlong into specific people and positions that reject them or parts of them, but there always turn out to be other spaces where they can fit, other sides or twists or turns of the same positions that do accommodate and even support them, other ways of viewing or other positions from which to view.

Gwennie, the Bible, and Jamaican Tradition

Me Dying Trial's Gwennie exemplifies Jamaican homophobia. A schoolteacher who contends with her abusive husband and her mixed loyalties to her community, her children, and herself, Gwennie views same-sex relations as "unnatural" and incompatible with the familial, national, transnational, religious, or political groups with which she identifies (65, 182). At the same time, Gwennie finds it difficult to embody the ideals of the wife and mother that those same identifications require: she has an affair that leads to a child she has trouble raising; she relies on her husband and eldest son to perform household and child-care duties while she studies, works, and finally immigrates. The omniscient third-person narration, in a language and perspective that often overlap with Gwennie's, conveys, as Opal Palmer Adisa writes, that "Gwennie's story is not an anomaly, nor are her trials exceptional" (322). In other words, Gwennie is an everywoman and her life exemplary not because it is ideal but because it is typical. Gwennie represents the many women who stay with alcoholic and abusive husbands because they cannot figure out how to leave, who feel themselves forced into a motherhood that they do not relish, who can only find their independence in radical moves that gain them as much approbation as success, and who do not see "battymen" as fellows in oppression but as nasty sinners.

These deeply entrenched attitudes play out in Powell's representation of Gwennie's relationship with two "battymen," Percy and Rudi. Gwennie meets Percy at the teacher training college she attends during her first escape from her husband. Percy quickly becomes her best friend, sharing Gwennie's passion for knowledge and her committed leftist politics. But when Gwennie realizes that Percy is involved with another man, even her recognition that he "maybe her only true friend" and that she herself has breached certain sexual mores cannot stop her expression of distaste:

> she not passing judgment. For the Bible always say, whoever don't have sin can cast the first stone. And you can't exactly say she clean and pure. But

> it's different. The Bible say the entire city of Sodom was destroyed with fire and brimstone sake of all that funny-funny business going on. All that unnaturalness. (65)

The main source of Gwennie's disapprobation is the Christian tradition in which she was raised. Gwennie, her parents, and many of the other characters in the novel take Christianity as a central element in their lives. The novel's title, a Jamaican saying that is Gwennie's first utterance in the story, refers to Jesus's last days and calls on a Christian God to witness earthly suffering.[14] The landscape of the story, as Gwennie surveys it from a bus in the book's first paragraph, consists of "the shops sailing by, canefields with stalks bowing in the wind, the cemetery with break-down tombs, Aunt Emmy's house, the old church, the pond . . ." (1). The qualities of a gentleman are to be "kind, church-going and everything" (2). Praying to God punctuates almost every day and attending Church occupies almost every Sunday of the characters' lives.[15] And the Church condemns same-sex relationships. Gwennie's view is confirmed as that of their Church when "one Sunday in church" Peppy hears Pastor Longmore "mention how all those men who go to one another for love and affection had better change them ways, for God just going to shut the doors of heaven in them face" (96).[16]

Gwennie's use of "unnatural" with the common Patwa suffix–ness connotes an infraction not only of the Biblical order but also of a natural Jamaican order.[17] In Biblical terms, "unnatural" or "against nature" most often censures non-procreative sex acts, while the Jamaican natural order Gwennie feels to be disturbed relates primarily to masculinity.[18] Inasmuch as Percy "don't talk much about man-friends, and she don't often see him with any, except for the way him and another fellow from the meeting did just kind of take to one another from the very first," what he does with his "man-friends" is a tacit subject that Gwennie might accept as part of Jamaican tradition (65). However, "she can't just close her eyes to the way him always dress neat, or how his hair and face always tidy, how shirts always match pants, ties always large and flamboyant . . . the way him walk, sorta dainty-like" (65).[19] Percy's transgression of the codes of Jamaican masculinity are remarkable in a way that his transgression of the codes of Christian sexuality are not, partly because he seems to be less tacit about his gender presentation but also partly because there is no Jamaican tradition, at least in Powell's novel, of male effeminacy through which his gender can be both understood and ignored.

The other distinctly Patwa phrase that Gwennie uses to refer to same-sex sexuality, "funny-funny business," also relies on and reconfigures Biblical concerns. "Funny-funny business" can certainly be understood as relating to problems in sexual conduct or hospitality as seen in the story of Sodom and Gomorrah. But in Jamaica the phrase commonly indicates dishonesty or unfair dealings. In Jamaica, then, battymen threaten manliness, truth, and trust as well as the procreative function of the couple or the nation.

While Gwennie's turns to the Bible and to Christian teachings in times of all kinds of personal conflict, her tendency to reconfigure Biblical passages through paraphrasing as well as her occasional willingness to request personalized exemptions from Christian teachings display an ability to see scripture as one part of a guiding framework in which Jamaican tradition and personal experience play important roles.[20] As Gwennie tries to piece together John 8:7 ("He that is without sin among you, let him first cast a stone")[21] and Genesis 18–19 (the destruction of Sodom and Gomorrah),[22] she could begin to recognize that her homophobia derives from a document whose potential contradictions call for some creative interpretation.[23] She could begin to find that her experiences with individuals require her to reject blanket judgments. She could even begin, as Palmer Adisa finds, to realize that "women like Gwennie, who are victimized, . . . have less of a stake in adhering to cultural norms, and therefore are more open to difference" (322). But when Gwennie learns that her son Rudi also loves men, rather than taking one more step away from homophobia to accept his difference, Gwennie denounces his "sin and nastiness" and requires him to "go or change your ways" (182).

Powell has said that she wrote *Me Dying Tria*l in order to understand why someone like Gwennie makes the choices that she does.[24] Indeed, *Me Dying Trial* renders Gwennie's choices comprehensible, but it never suggests that they are right or good. If *Me Dying Trial* evokes sympathy, it is less for Gwennie than for Percy, Rudi, and Peppy. We feel sympathetic for Percy and Rudi not only because they are good men on whom Gwennie passes harsh judgment but also because Gwennie's judgment of them exposes the degree to which they are outcast even by educated and sympathetic Jamaicans, and even by Jamaicans whose experience of the "cultural norm" has been anything but positive. The few critical treatments of the novel and the many brief references to Powell's perspective concur: *Me Dying Trial* is anti-homophobic, against a Jamaican tradition for which Gwennie is the mouthpiece.[25] In their eagerness to endorse Powell's anti-homophobic intention, these critical treatments of the novel end up reducing its complex politics by overlooking the ways that few of the actual relationships in the story follow the "cultural norm" and that Gwennie may speak for a homophobic majority, but hers is not the only Jamaican opinion about same-sex relationships in the novel and she is not the only representative of Jamaican tradition. Even as it critiques Jamaican homophobia, Powell's novel asks readers to revise a simplistic reading of Jamaican tradition as essentially and thoroughly heterosexual and homophobic.

A Cultural Norm That Is Not Normal

Me Dying Trial opens with a family tree, that organizing principle of heteronormativity that maps out family and community in terms of biological parenting organized in nuclear units of one man, one woman, and the children that they bear together (Figure 5.1).

A standard family tree has the triangular shape of a spruce, but this one looks more like a mangrove, lopsided, twisted, and hard to follow. Also striking about this family tree is how little it conveys about the actual primary relationships and household configurations in the story.[26] The only family in *Me Dying Trial* that lives out the norm and exists as it is represented on the tree is that of Gwennie's parents, Clara and Fred. They marry young, have four children, and live together through their old age.[27] They hold themselves and all members of their household to strict compliance with Christian norms of family, telling even their roomer Luther "that even though him only staying for a little while, this is a house of God. Him can't be bringing in young gals from out this street in here as him please" (3). But even Clara and Fred end up raising their grandchildren Delores, Dave, and Jeff for significant periods of time as well as taking in roomers like Luther whom they expect to behave at least while they are there as part of the family. At the same time, that household is so restrictively linked to the Church that Gwennie prefers to stay with her abusive husband than to return to it: "she couldn't put up with the eight o'clock bedtime every night, the prayers, church service, night

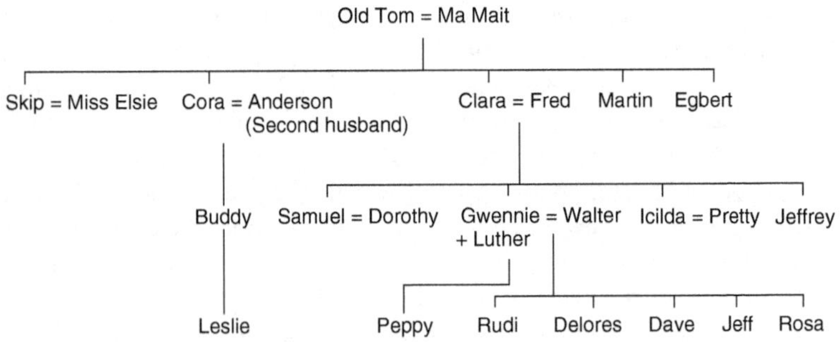

Figure 5.1 Family Tree

service, and Bible study, three and four times a week" (4). Gwennie becomes the tragic casualty of a norm that she can neither follow nor escape.[28]

But there are alternatives, right on the family tree next to Clara and Fred. Martin and Egbert never married. Cora married twice and bore a child only with the second husband. Buddy seems to have had a son, Leslie, by himself. The actual composition of Cora's household, not shown on the family tree, is even further from the triangular norm:

> Aunty Cora was about sixty, and she live in this huge house with the seven bedrooms with her grandson Leslie; one of the eleven children she raise, George; her live-in-helper, Miss Irene; and her cousin Miss Gertrude Fines, who was still on extended visit, from Ma Pen. Her Aunty Cora's been married two times, but both husbands already pass on leaving her with fifty acres of fertile land, two acres of rock-stone, one shop, one house, one church, thirty heads of cow, three bulls, two donkeys, fifteen laying hens, six roosters and one young pullet. (16)

Cora's family models the intergenerational women-headed households and the nonbiological parenting common throughout the Caribbean.[29] These extended family networks allow that "when people don't have food, or when family life mash up, instead of letting the children suffer, parents send them to Aunty Cora to hold until better days," and mobile family configurations make it easy for those children to become regular members of Aunty Cora's household when "sometimes better days don't come" (69–70). Intergenerational woman-headed households have been well examined in terms of their implications for understanding the role and place of women in the Caribbean, but the implications for structures of family and sexuality have elicited less attention.[30] It is my contention that Cora represents a Jamaican nonnuclear family structure that makes room not only for women to hold a variety of powers at home and in the community but also for a range of family and intimate relationships between women and between men. Jamaican law does not recognize the structures over which Cora presides, but it can accommodate them, and Cora is careful to "think about the will and how she have to rewrite it" and to send Gwennie a letter "asking if she could adopt Peppy and change her name" (40). The disjuncture between the norm and the normal does not necessarily entail binary opposition or incompatibility, but it does position the Jamaican state and the Jamaican "natural" that Gwennie invokes on the side of norms that are rooted in colonial legal traditions that are out of touch with if not inimical to Jamaican tradition.

Cora personifies a traditional Jamaica rooted in slave culture and the ideals of the maroons. Cora is literally from the generation of Gwennie's mother, but rather than taking her ways with her when she dies, like MaDee who can barely speak in her last years, Cora raises children through her seventies, ensuring that her knowledge of Jamaican social structures and sexual alternatives are passed down to many generations. The ties between the members of Cora's intergenerational and wide-ranging family are sealed not through blood, though Cora's belief that "blood thicker than water" is part of why she takes in Peppy, but through the shared project of living together. The strength of the nonbiological parental bond is perhaps most clearly evidenced in Cora's nursing all of the children that she raises, for even when the fact that "I don't have any more milk in me titty for such a young baby" gives her pause when Gwennie asks her to take in Peppy (17), she knows how to ensure that she nurses Peppy anyway:

> Every morning after she get up and tidy herself, and after her grand boy, Leslie and her adopted boy, George, bring in and scald the cow's milk, she pour out a mugful, cool it and then pour it little-little over her nipple so the baby can suck and lick it like the real thing. And when she suck down the entire mugful, Aunty Cora burp her and then sway and hum to her until the little baby fall asleep. (34)

The tradition of nonbiological parenting Cora embodies recalls the creative response to slavery's attempt to destroy family ties as well as the use of slave women as nursemaids.

But if Cora is like a slave woman, she is more like *the* Jamaican rebel slave, Nanny of the Maroons.[31] Nanny of the Maroons is a national Jamaican hero, and it is no wonder that maroon culture in Jamaica is often imagined to center around a strong woman figure who serves as grandmother-mother to a whole community. The parallels are far from perfect, but like Nanny, Cora is the matriarch in a large nonbiological family and the organizing figure for a strong rural social network. Like the Nanny figures in Cliff's *Abeng*, *No Telephone to Heaven*, and *Free Enterprise*, Cora draws on a model for black women's power that is sexual, strong, independent, and suggestive of a female self-sufficiency in regard to family and desire.[32]

Her constant cup of rum confirms Cora's status as the representative of Jamaican tradition.[33] Cora herself associates the white rum that she drinks with Jamaica, writing to Peppy from a visit to her brothers in the United States, "The Foreign rum really weak, she complain, and was glad that she bring plenty of the real thing from back home, for if is Foreign rum to save life and ease up bad feelings, she stone dead as a bird" (89).[34] Rum is for Cora the native remedy to all ills, what she drinks in spite and in place of the pills that the doctor prescribes for her arthritis: "Doctor Lord says she must ease up off the white rum for it will cut her off earlier than she think, but sometimes the little white rum is all that give her relief, not the several bottles of tablets and jars of medicine him give her" (67–68). Cora sells the rum she drinks, representing a Jamaican economy that is based on the trade and consumption of cane products, but also drawing the circle in to trade on a local level.

Cora's shop is the community center of the town of New Green, where everyone gathers to buy provisions, drink, and gossip. Cora's shop thrives because she understands "business not just buy and sell" but something that intertwines seamlessly with friendship (92). Through her place in the shop, Cora becomes such a central figure in New Green that even when she becomes too old and sick to run the shop, when she allows the doctor to come to see her, "him finally step outside to where almost all of New Green was waiting in the yard for the final diagnosis" (171). Cora is member and transmitter of a localized community tradition where "Everybody know everybody, and everybody know about everybody's business" (34).

Mile Gully, the large town where Clara and Fred live, has a social structure similar to that of New Green, the country village where Cora lives: "Mile Gully's people love to know and carry people's business" (5) and even "[Gwennie's husband] Walter come from the little district just right across the other side of the bridge. The people from Mile Gully know him well. It wouldn't be too hard for him to find out if people was going to be doggish and walla-walla them mouth" (9). But because of its more urban location, Mile Gully's traditional social structure has somewhat broken down. Outsiders like the roomer Luther regularly come in without the community information about them, and leave without a trace. They may be closely monitored while they are around, but they are so transient that the structure does not function fully. And because of the rise of other urban centers and the draw that they exert, people like Walter can extricate themselves from that community and no longer be privy to its information. The knowledge that Cora's practice preserves requires new generations to avail themselves of it in order to endure.

Where information is shared, be it through tacit understanding or gossip, be it in New Green or in Mile Gully, it reveals large numbers of families and relationships that do not comply with the norm of one man, one woman, and their children. If Walter had stayed to listen, he would have learned about Gwennie and Luther's liaison. Peppy knows from an early age of her best friend Vin whose father "live abroad," and among her grade school friends "plenty of them grow with them granny" (88). *Me Dying Trial* acknowledges at least two different structures of desire and sexuality, the Christian colonial and postcolonial heterosexual model for which Gwennie is the mouthpiece, and the mangled alternative that is inclusive of multiple desires and sexualities for which Cora is the representative. By referring to

Cora's model as alternative I mean to indicate a difference between the two and to convey that it is possible to choose Cora's model in place of Gwennie's model, but not to position the two in binary opposition. Indeed, although they are opposed in some ways, what becomes clear through the course of the story are the many ways Gwennie's heterosexual model and Cora's mangled model for desire and sexuality are also mutually inclusive. Furthermore, I mean to play on the definition of alternative as "Of or relating to activities that represent an unorthodox style or approach; of a kind purported to be preferable to or as acceptable as those in general use or sanctioned by the establishment," for while Gwennie's model is "sanctioned by the establishment" of the Jamaican state, Cora's turns out to be "in general use" as much if not more than the state-sanctioned model. The alternative, then, reveals the coexistence of multiple normals.

Many of the alternatives are revealed later in the story—they are the background that contextualizes the main events and characters but that does not come to the fore or become evident until well into the novel. Indeed, they are things that the children in the novel learn not by being told what is right and wrong by parents or teachers or pastors but by observing the people in their community and maturing enough to become conversant, as it were, in the tacit subjects of their community discourse. So Peppy, though she "didn't mean anything by it really," is so struck one day by things that she does not quite understand about Percy and Martel that she asks Rudi, "What's the position between Martel and Percy?" (82). Rudi's initial answer, "Them good friends, . . . Good friends like you and Jasmine. Or like you and Vin. You understand. Good friends," certainly conveys his reluctance to make a direct public statement of desire between men. Yet as much as it downplays the sexual aspect of Martel and Percy's relationship, it also points to the potential erotic component of *any* intimate friendship (82). And once Peppy recognizes the possibility of desire between men and of friends who are also lovers, it does not take her long to recognize how very normal same-sex desire is in her world. So by the time Rudi explains to Peppy first that Percy and Martel are "together" and then that he is "that way too," she has a rich context in which to understand his choices as part of a Jamaican set of alternatives, telling Rudi "I know about those things. MaCora tell me about those things all the time" (96).

Normal Alternatives, Alternative Normals

While Kincaid pluralizes the normal through imaginitave feats that playfully present as normal things that would not be so in a heteronormative structure, reconceiving the very concept of the normal, Powell pluralizes the normal by quietly revealing the commonness of a variety of sexual and relational practices. In both cases, structures that are common to the heteronorm—the family unit, the married couple, the child-rearing unit—are not rejected but are shown to be inhabited and played out in ways that are the same but not quite, where that not quite marks a structural difference that is the difference between a hetero–homo binary and the structure of the mangrove. Through these normalizing moves, desire between women even where it does not fit neatly into the heteronormative structure, even where it is conceived by that structure as inimical, turns out to be so regular that the heteronormative structure falls apart not by direct opposition but by the realization that it always contained and indeed is built on and in the mangle in a way that lets it exist, persist, but rather than as the totalizing model that it claims to be, as part of the mangle.

The information Cora shares with Peppy about same-sex relationships and families begins around "this man. Them call him batty-man" who patronizes Cora's shop, but soon extends to "men who love other men," "people," and "this woman she [Cora] used to study cooking backing and decorating with, Miss Clementine" (96), depicting not a single exception that proves the rule of the heteronorm but instead a wide range of men and women in different kinds of relationships.

Peppy is slow to group together into a special category the nonheterosexual relationships that surround her, partly because they so often occur in families that resemble quite closely the other families in the story. She begins to make the connection when Pastor Longmore refers to "all those men," but it is only when Rudi presents his love for men as a problem and an exception that she puts together the long list of nonheterosexual families that she has learned about with Cora. But once Rudi formulates the category of people who are "that way" to which he belongs, Peppy fills it in not only with information she has gleaned from Cora and the rum shop, but also "she tell him about her friend at school, Jasmine, and how Jasmine's mother was that way too" (98). Jasmine only told Peppy once "them close" that her mother lives with Miss Pearl "almost like them married," while "to other children, she refer to Miss Pearl as her mother's second cousin from the country who just spending time," for this is a tacit subject, and Rudi is right to expect that Jasmine is "afraid them laugh" or worse if she "tell children at school about she family life," but while Jasmine may not have been able to go into the details of how "them loving one another," she also did not need to lie about or to hide Miss Pearl's role in her household, for her classmates are perfectly familiar with the tradition of nonnuclear families and mangled household configurations. In some cases, cousins or acquaintances do indeed just "spend time." In Cora's house a distant cousin is also just spending time. The point is not to suggest that Cora is actually involved with the woman, but rather that two or more women living together without husbands for any number of reasons is normal, just as are all kinds of relationships that motivate or form from those women living together.

Peppy initially questioned Rudi about "the situation between Percy and Martel" because "them not family, yet everyday Martel driving up in his car, everyday him over his house, everyday . . ." (82). Equally confusing to Peppy, it seems, is that Percy and Martel do *not* use the language of family to house their relationship as that "Percy give Martel . . . Gold ring at Christmas. Bracelets at Easter. Special kinds of underclothes that fit certain ways" (82). Of course, the language of family would in a certain sense hide the relationship, for the language of family does not on the surface have words for two men together, but the vagueness that clearly exists within the term "cousin" and the open term of "just visiting" provide room for a language of family to be used for same-sex relationships. The line between using the language of family as a protective screen and using the language of family to integrate same-sex relationships into the normal is a blurry one.[35]

As the story progresses, more and more characters prove to know about and to engage in a range of family and erotic configurations. Toward the end of *Me Dying Trial*, after Gwennie has brought all of her children to join her in the United States, Gwennie's Trinidadian boyfriend Clive shares with her brother Sam and his wife Dorothy his view that "them [battymen] is an abomination before God and man" (147). In response, Dorothy reveals that "she used to dabble-dabble in it before she got married and was even still on good terms with the woman" (149). Clive tries to explain it away with "you married now and was only going through phases then" (149), but Dorothy makes clear that is not the case: "Dorothy let him know, after Samuel leave the room, that if she was ever to leave Samuel she would probably go back to Dawn" (149). She is not planning to leave Samuel because the relationship with Dawn was so good or because she is still really in love with Dawn, but if she happened to leave Samuel she might well seek out Dawn. Dorothy positions desire between women as intersecting the nuclear family, but she does not set it in opposition to or in competition with other desires.

Even Gwennie, although she ultimately tries to expel it from her own family, is aware of a wide network of Jamaican men who are involved with other men. As Clive points derisively to the young men he identifies as battymen, Gwennie half-protests, "But I don't see anything wrong with them?" (148). Formulated as a question, her response to Clive conveys her struggle to understand what might or might not be "wrong with them." And so Gwennie tries to understand what distinguishes "them." First she thinks about the gender transgression which so concerned her with Percy, noting how "some of them look a little effeminate," but here she is able to put effeminacy into a Jamaican and a Christian context that makes it acceptable to her, concluding "but that don't mean anything for I know a few ministers at church back home who used to look and even go on like these fellows" (148). And so she tries to understand other groupings of "battymen":

> her mind run on the men she knew back home who people called batty-men, but she didn't pay much attention to the name-calling, for usually they were big and respectable people in the community. She'd even hear that her very own Teacher Brown was that way, that him live in the big white house on the hill with a fellow from Vere. The older gentleman that run the festival each year, Robeson, she hear was that way too, and the young man at the post office . . . (148)

Percy and Rudi's relationships with other men are less exceptional even in her social circles "back home" than Gwennie's initial reaction to Percy suggested. Indeed, many of the rumored "battymen," from the school and government employees to the more traditional organizer of the local festival, are at the center of community and cultural life in Jamaica. The importance of their status makes Gwennie less, rather than more attentive to the information. If they are accepted and active in the community, it seems, their family and sexual arrangements matter little. Indeed, if there is a problem it may not lie in how any one character's intimate or familial configurations do or do not match the norm, or even how they do or do not conform to ideals of Jamaican masculinity, but rather in how well integrated they are into the community.

Percy and Rudi stand out because they find it difficult to integrate into the community. Percy has an active professional life as a teacher and activist, but he struggles to find a heterosexual cover for his desires for men, first saying he has a wife already, then asking Gwennie to marry him even though their relationship has "plenty friendship and lots of love" but no romance (30). Percy's own sense of needing to cover his relationships with men under a veneer of heterosexuality, rather than any questioning or exclusion because of his relationships, sets him apart. Rudi is young and almost completely confined to the house by his devotion to his younger siblings in the absence of Gwennie and Walter. And, strangely, gossip does not seem to circulate about Percy and Rudi as it does about the other men Gwennie or Peppy mention. This absence of gossip makes it more difficult for tacit knowledge to circulate, and establishes their sexuality more in the structure of the closet than in that of the mangrove.

Engaging in sexual relationships with other men or not, Percy and Rudi differ from the other men around them because both are both visibly marked by an effeminacy that is not always easily associated with the flamboyance of ministers or other Jamaican-Christian contexts. Percy's effeminacy is so striking to Gwennie that "she can't just close her eyes" to it. Similarly, when Gwennie's children step off the plane, Rudi stands out, "and it wasn't anything that Rudi said or did, it was just the way him carry himself: clothes neat and close-fitting, colours blending in so well causing both she and Dolores to look like butu compared to him" (147). This kind of effeminacy is not mentioned in relation to the other (tacitly) known "battymen." What makes Teacher Brown, and by extension the other men in Gwennie's list, "that way" is his living with another man. Clive distinguishes between "battymen" who are "effeminate" and those who are "manly like me, big shoulders and everything" (148). Although the distinction does not stop Clive from locating a primary objection to battymen in their gender nonconformity, for according to him "if you look in them [manly battymen's] face you can tell . . . it's just soft and tender like a woman's . . ." (148), his comments and the ways that Percy and Rudi stand out in the story suggest that "battymen" who are "effeminate" are marked off from Jamaican community in a way that other "battymen" are not.

Percy and Rudi are also both marked by their internationalism. Rudi tells his mother about himself after she brings him to live with her in the United States and develops his first adult relationships with men in the United States. Percy drives an Austin Cambridge, a classic British car. Before Walter stops Percy from coming to the house, he "used to bring [Rudi] different-different stamps for his collection." It is Percy who helps Gwennie to understand how to obtain a visa to the United States and who tells her about what to expect when she gets there. This internationalism might serve to locate them as homosexuals and to locate homosexuals as non-Jamaican. But while Percy spent time in the United States, he does not speak fondly of it, and throughout the story lives in Jamaica first with a wife, then with Martel, and then with another man. And Rudi comes to understand his sexuality in Jamaica; Percy and Martel are his first role models, but they quickly introduce him to a community of men in Jamaica. Rudi's description of his first "friend" establishes Rudi's love of him in relation to his Jamaicanness in terms of his physical body and his affiliations: "him tell Peppy about the boy, Terence, jet black with white-white teeth. And how Terence used to go to the Youth Camp where Walter teach" (98). If Percy and Rudi's internationalism is a factor in negative judgments against them, the story is also careful to show that this is more something that might be attributed to Percy, Martel, and Rudi by others who are unwilling or unable to accept their Jamaicanness. Indeed, the characters who most harshly judge same-sex relationships, Gwennie and Clive, appear in the story equally if not more "international" than those they judge, having both immigrated to the United States, so that the suggestion that relationships between men is un-Jamaican is matched by the suggestion that homophobia is as well. Like the accusation that they are unnatural or sinful, the suggestion that those who desire their own gender are un-Jamaican is presented and pulled apart in *Me Dying Trial*.

Just as *Me Dying Trial* shows multiple traditions and practices in Jamaica, it also locates Jamaica in a global context with multiple forces and traditions. Not only does it bear the legacy of the colonialism that in many ways formed the country, Jamaica is also intersected by the more contemporary "foreign" of the United States where many characters go to work or to visit relatives who have immigrated. However, international opinion in *Me Dying Trial* does not stand as the accepting alternative to Jamaican intolerance nor is the United States positioned as the haven in which homosexual characters come out or live out.

Although the novel ends with Gwennie and then her children having moved to the United States, the narrative rarely follows their movements or interactions in the United States. The portion of the novel that takes place in the United States is set almost exclusively inside Gwennie's home or her brother's home. The children go to school and work where they make friends that let them encounter a wide American world, but it only appears in the novel as what Gwennie does not like them bringing home.[36] Rudi finds an American boyfriend, and when Gwennie and Clive go to the mall, they do see what they perceive to be a group of "battymen," but this is hardly different from what occurs in Jamaica. And if the American context impacts Jamaican opinion about same-sex relationships, it is not clear in which direction: when Gwennie's brother Samuel, in response to Clive's homophobia, "claimed that him live in America too long and life was way too short to allow anything to bother him except water pollution and nuclear war" (149), it might just as well be life in America or a sense of mortality that is the main factor in his tolerance. Furthermore, alongside the acceptance of desire between men delivered by Samuel from the United States are Clive's rejection of Rudi and anyone else "like that," and Gwennie's final adoption of a similar position.

Clive's view of same-sex desire is presented as both international and Caribbean, but not as Jamaican. That Clive is Trinidadian and uses the same terminology, "battymen," in the same way that Gwennie does establishes Jamaica and Trinidad as sharing a Caribbean culture. However, the difference of Clive's opinion from that of Cora, Samuel, Dorothy, and to a lesser degree Gwennie in conjunction with his different national affiliation also points to the differences of views of same-sex desire across the Caribbean as well as within each Caribbean country. And it does not seem coincidental that Clive comes from one of the two Caribbean countries that have more restrictive legal sanctions on same-sex relationships than Jamaica. The men with whom Gwennie enters into relationships occupy the normative positions of their countries, as if they are the representatives of the (neo)colonial hetero-patriarchy. And while Gwennie and Walter, together and separately, suffer from that order much more than they benefit from it, after Gwennie leaves Walter and Jamaica, she enters into a relationship with Clive. Gwennie resists Clive's requests that they get married and eventually ends the relationship, and she seems to resist his condemnation of same-sex relationships after the conversation with Samuel and Dorothy: "She couldn't understand why her feelings on the subject [of battymen] was seeming to lean towards Dorothy and Samuel's argument. But maybe it was because of the hatred and contempt she hear so much in Clive's voice that cause her to adopt another view of the matter altogether" (149).

But Gwennie's early alignment with a Jamaican hetero-colonial norm in her condemnation of Percy, her time in the United States, the Baptist church that she attends there, and Clive eventually lead her to become less rather than more tolerant. When she realizes that Rudi is involved with a man, she does not listen to Samuel's advice that "you and him will have to work out some kind of compromise. You going to have to give a little, take a little . . . His plans for life may not follow the same route you have mapped out for him, but you going to have to give him room" (157). Instead, Gwennie waits, hopes that Rudi has found a girlfriend, and when she is finally confronted with his desire for other men, says, "So this is what you interested in? . . . This sin and nastiness. This is the example you setting for the younger ones? Well, it can't go on inside here. You have to go or change your ways" (182). Rudi at this point is old enough and knows enough about other opinions of desire between men, that rather than bow to Gwennie's demands, he leaves. Gwennie ends up being the victim as well as the perpetrator not only of the condemnation of same-sex desire but also of the inability to accept normal alternatives or alternative normals.

A Variety of Opinions

Cora is the true heroine of *Me Dying Trial*, not only embodying the sexual and relational alternatives that are normal in Jamaica but also expounding what I argue is a Jamaican anti-homophobia. Unlike Gwennie, Cora is able to extrapolate from her alternative position in relation to the heteronorm to accept all manner of people in all kinds of same-sex relationships.

In contrast to Gwennie's view of the Bible as conveying monolithic, absolute judgments, Cora tells Peppy: "Bible say one thing, John Brown say another. Bible big and open wide. It say plenty things, it mean plenty more things" (97). Cora refuses strict rules for knowing "what to believe" or "right from wrong," and offers instead the suggestion that such determinations be made based on pragmatics, accumulated experiences, and instinct. She explains to Peppy, "sometimes you find out right and wrong through trial and error. Other times is only by what feel good deep down inside your belly bottom. Nothing else" (97). Cora offers Peppy a criterion wherein gender or sexual activity are not the determining factors in what qualifies a relationship as sinful or praiseworthy, natural or unnatural, nasty or nice. Cora's position is perhaps radically anti-normative in that it requires a personal and individualized evaluation of each and every relationship. Yet what is more significant in the context of Jamaican homophobia is that it offers, within a Jamaican and a Christian framework, a space for varying judgments on same-sex relationships.

Cora tolerates the ideal of monogamous heterosexuality being preached in the churches and taught in the schools knowing that although it allows or even generates nominal condemnation of deviations from it, it bears little on the actual configuration of relationships and households. She knows in other words that while there is a heteronorm, there are also many alternative normals. Palmer Adisa finds that "Aunty Cora's openness to difference makes her an exception in her community" (323), but while Cora may be unusually open *about* her "openness to difference," she stands as the emblem of, rather than the exception in, a Jamaican community where tacit tolerance of difference predominates and where "everybody's business" includes not only the wide range of sexual and relational alternatives practiced in the community but also the wide range of judgments passed by that community. Peppy explains:

> Well, you know if you spend plenty time inside a shop, you hear people talk about things. And one time them was talking about this man. Them call him batty-man and was laughing about it.
>
> So that night when shop lock and me and MaCora was walking home I mention it to her. And she start to whoop, lasting about four whole minutes. Then she tell me that's what them call men who love other men. And she say nothing wrong with it, but plenty people don't like to hear about it. But as far as she concern, people can do whatever them damn well please with whichever part of them body them damn well want. For them not paying taxes for it. (96)

When people talk about the man they call battyman they laugh, but that laughter is not qualified as derisive; if it establishes a certain distance between the audience and their subject, it is not one of judge and condemned like the distance that Gwennie puts between herself and first Percy, then Rudi.

The almost friendly judgment of the laughter is established when Cora, too, laughs at the mention of the rumor. Cora goes on to explain the term battyman in a way that offers other language for referring to such men but importantly does not specify that battyman is necessarily pejorative. Finally, she seems to interpret the laughter as an expression of a prevailing attitude of tacit acceptance. The community's judgment of battymen is not polarized into celebration and condemnation but rather spread between Cora's open acceptance and "plenty people's" preference not to hear about it, a position.closer to the "tolerant intolerance" that Lancaster finds to help integrate same-sex relationships into the cultural fabric of Latin America, than to Clive's or Gwennie's condemnation.[37]

Tolerant intolerance has its limitations and, as other critics assert, Powell depicts many Jamaicans as often profoundly homophobic and Jamaica as a deeply uncomfortable place to pursue same-sex relationships. But *Me Dying Trial* also depicts Jamaicans as intimately familiar with a variety of social and sexual alternatives, as often tacitly tolerant and sometimes actively supportive of same-sex relationships. What *Me Dying Trial* reveals then is not that Banton is unrepresentative of Jamaican popular opinion or that homophobia is not prevalent in Jamaica, but rather that blanket professions of Jamaican homophobia obscure much more complex reactions to individual deviations from a heteronorm that is far from totalizing. *Me Dying Trial* shows minorities of Jamaicans who are virulently homophobic and clearly anti-homophobic, and also reveals a majority of Jamaicans who practice tolerant intolerance of the many different kinds of familial and intimate alternatives to heteronormative nationalism. *Me Dying Trial* is not anti-homophobic against Jamaican tradition, but instead anti-homophobic with Jamaican traditions. And Jamaican homophobia is neither superlative nor exceptional in the Caribbean, but instead representative of the complex intertwinings of heterosexual and homosexual alternatives that render the overall structure of desire and sexuality in the Caribbean neither heterosexual nor homosexual but at the same time inclusive of both in all of their manifestations.

CHAPTER 6

The Love of Neighbors: Rosario Ferré's *Eccentric Neighborhoods/Vecindarios excéntricos*

Daughter of the governor, one of Puerto Rico's premiere feminists, and one of its most prolific novelists, Rosario Ferré pens iconic literary critiques of Puerto Rico's "free association" with the United States and paints compelling portraits of women who resist Puerto Rican patriarchy. For many years, Ferré's novels bound the freedom of women with the independence of the island.[1] But as they struggle to disengage the binary structures of colonial patriarchy that constrain them, the women of *Eccentric Neighborhoods/Vecindarios excéntricos* (1998/1999) walk in on possibilities rarely admitted in Ferré's extensive body of work: English, statehood, and desire between women. In the convergence of linguistic, national, and erotic (re)configurations in *Eccentric Neighborhoods/Vecindarios excéntricos* appears an ideal of intersectional complementarity, a nonhierarchical order of mutually inclusive possibilities.

This chapter examines three strands of possible complementarity in Ferré's novel: the complementarity of Spanish and English, the complementarity of Puerto Rico and the United States, and the complementarity of homo- and heterosexuality. If the complementary structures intersect complementarily, my book ends with the novelistic idealization of the epistemology of the mangle, the foundational fiction of Caribbean structures of desire. But I am wary of plotting a progression from José Martí's foundational failure to Ferré's successful one for many reasons. For as I have shown throughout this study, Caribbean structures of desire proliferate in the presence of colonial heteronormativity, always already undermining it but also necessarily in its shadow. And also, I am not at all sure Ferré's novel avoids foundational failure.

Ferré's practice of rewriting her own books exemplifies what linguistic complementarity might achieve: a space where Spanish and English exist not mixed together, not first and second, but in conjunction. The titular eccentricity conveys the spatial configuration of decentralized parity and plurality. Eccentric neighborhoods, connected by their distance and difference, is a strange figure of statehood, if an apt one.[2] In *Eccentric Neighborhoods/Vecindarios excéntricos*, statehood promises productive egalitarianism where domestic partnerships mirror public enterprises that escape the decadence of a plantation elite whose dreams of independence have devolved into nostalgia for patriarchal power. Statehood as it is imagined by Ferré might organize equality in diversity, but it leaves open a door to a dark room where languages, monies, and bodies mix and match haphazardly in anarchic, orgiastic undifferentiability. The treatment of desire between women in *Eccentric Neighborhoods/Vecindarios excéntricos* reveals a fantasy of separation and a fear of disorder that might undergird complementarity, or that might be what it most radically rejects. The second half of this chapter focuses on the one scene of explicit sexuality between women in which I read a deep fear that while eccentric women in eccentric neighborhoods can escape colonial patriarchy, they risk stepping into the disorder of radical anti-heteronormativity, where the attraction of parity devolves into that of similarity and down a slippery slope to indistinguishability. Framing this chapter and this book are the questions: What kind of a danger is desire between women? What allows it to emerge? To what or whom is it dangerous? What does it threaten? What does it enable?[3]

M. Jacqui Alexander's analysis can connect desire between women to a threat to the (post)colonial Caribbean nation:

> Women's sexual agency, our sexual and erotic autonomy have always been troublesome for the state. They pose a challenge to the ideological anchor of an originary nuclear family, a source of legitimation for the state which perpetuates the fiction that the family is the cornerstone of society. Erotic autonomy signals danger to the heterosexual family and to the nation, (64)

the kind of danger that results in the state-sanctioned homophobia to which Powell responds in *Me Dying Trial.* Ferré might offer, in complementarity, a conceptual link between erotic autonomy and national identification. She might find a genealogy on which to anchor the nation that does not rest on the nuclear family but on the eccentric neighborhood.

Weaving personal relationships with public projects, *Eccentric Neighborhoods/Vecindarios excéntricos* attempts to offer a variation on the national romance and on a story that Ferré has told many times. As Doris

Sommer establishes in *Foundational Fictions*, romances provided not only an allegory for national consolidation but the very site where new Latin American and Caribbean nations were imagined into being. In the national romance, a particular kind of family is made into a particular kind of nation and vice versa.[4] Even, or perhaps especially, as it imagines politically independent nations, the national romance solidifies what María Lugones identifies as the heterosexualism of the colonial legacy.[5] When it does not, as in José Martí's *Amistad funesta/Lucía Jerez*, which I discussed at length in the first chapter, there is great risk of foundational failure. Ferré's work, and this analysis, asks what happens when we pursue other national romances.

As Elvira Vernet, the narrator of *Eccentric Neighborhoods/Vecindarios excéntricos*, traces three generations of her family tree, examining more than a century of their intimate, political, economic, and social development, she retells the history of Puerto Rico's troubled emergence from colonial domination. The story progresses toward statehood for Puerto Rico and emancipation for women, but it is wracked with the expenses at which any progress is obtained.

Establishing Puerto Rico's colonial origins, Elvira traces her maternal line, the Rivas de Santillanas, back to her Corsican great-grandfather, Bartolomeo, and her paternal line to her French great-grandfather. In 1898, Elvira's paternal grandfather, Chaguito, helps to negotiate the Spanish surrender of Puerto Rico to the United States. Technically, Puerto Rico became a possession of the United States, but for Chaguito, as he writes to his mother in Cuba, "I've become an American, a free man" (154). Elvira's maternal family, part of the island's plantation elite, is more ambivalent about Puerto Rico's attachment to the United States, but even for them it marks the advent of modernity on the island. Moving to the town of Guayamés in 1898, Elvira's maternal grandfather, Alvaro, finds that "with the arrival of the Americans on the island, the quality of life in Guayamés had improved greatly: streets were paved, there was running water, a sewage system and storm drains had been installed" (8). This establishment of 1898 as the year when Puerto Ricans become Americans and Puerto Rico becomes integrated into the US infrastructure makes the subsequent acts and amendments revising Puerto Rico's status less important in the novel than tornadoes, trade policy, and changes in the sugar industry and construction. Various characters' pro-statehood political activity occupies much of the novel, but the 1917 Jones Act establishing Puerto Rico as an "organized but unincorporated" territory of the United States and granting citizenship to Puerto Ricans is not mentioned.

Political and economic endeavors are primarily the terrain of the men in Elvira's family. Her grandfathers, Chaguito and Alvaro, and their respective sons love strong, passionate, smart women, but once marriages are settled and daughters are born, like Abuelo Chaguito they make clear their belief that women "should get married, have children, and take care of them" (190). Elvira's mother Clarissa fights to maintain a position in running the family's plantation and joins Puerto Rico's women's suffrage movement. Sexuality serves as the site for a certain resistance to patriarchal rule for Celia, whose entry into a convent is described as a strategic use of celibacy, and for Sigilinda, who becomes a nudist. But as they progress into married life, the women give themselves over to conforming to their husbands' expectations and wills. The marriage that brings together Elvira's parents in 1930 subsumes even Clarissa's identification as "Puerto Rican before anything else" under the strident Vernet devotion to statehood as the best future for Puerto Rico (224).

Eccentric Neighborhoods/*Vecindarios excéntricos* details a fictionalized political history of Puerto Rico through the 1960s, which, aside from minor name changes, makes one substantive revision to events outside the novel: in the story, by 1945, Puerto Rican parties are presenting candidates for governor to Puerto Rican voters, three years before Luís Muñoz Marín actually became the first democratically elected governor of the island. The slippage of a few years may itself be insignificant, but it allows the elision of the 1947 shift from a Puerto Rican governor appointed by the US President to one elected by Puerto Ricans. The novel comes to a close at the end of the 1960s, referring to the first plebiscite where Puerto Ricans voted on maintaining Puerto Rico's commonwealth status, but never having mentioned the 1950 Public Act 600 allowing Puerto Ricans to draft their own constitution establishing Puerto Rico as a Commonwealth of the United States (in Spanish, *Estado Libre Asociado*, "associated free state"). These minor shifts and lacunae downplay the limits that the United States has placed on Puerto Rican autonomy, facilitating the idea of a complementary partnership in statehood although perhaps also reminding of the fictional quality of that complementarity.

Ferré's personal history coincides with that of her characters. Like Elvira's father, Ferré's held the governorship of Puerto Rico from 1969 until 1972. In 1972, Ferré famously defied her father's pro-statehood stance in an open letter detailing her pro-independence position. But in 1998, the same year *Eccentric Neighborhoods* was published, she ended an op-ed piece in the *New York Times*, "Puerto Rico, U.S.A.," with the declaration that she would "support statehood in the next plebiscite."[6] Ferré's support for statehood arises in part from her belief that statehood no longer entails "losing our language and culture," ensured by her perception that "bilingualism and multiculturalism are vital aspects of American society" and by a shift in the US position on language, which would allow a Puerto Rican state to maintain Spanish as an official language.[7]

Linguistic tensions, evident in the different connotations of the terms Commonwealth and *Estado Libre Asociado*, underline the relationship between Puerto Rico and the United States and play prominently in Puerto Rican politics.[8] The defense of the Spanish language figures in the platforms of the Puerto Rican Independence Party and the Popular Democratic Party (which backs maintaining Commonwealth status), while the pro-statehood New Progressive Party embraces English.[9] The coincidence of Ferré's shift to writing in English first with her shift to supporting statehood seem to reinforce this division. Elena Machado Sáez, however, reads Ferré's use of English for and in *House on the Lagoon* (1996) alongside her political statements to argue that Ferré favors not English but bilingualism. Ferré's writing in both English and Spanish, her comments on translation, and the thematization of language in *Eccentric Neighborhoods*/*Vecindarios excéntricos* propose a bilingualism very different, however, from the Caló or Spanglish advocated by many of the Chicanos and Latinos with whom Machado Sáez sees Ferré trying to ally. Caló and Spanglish belong to the aesthetic and ethic of *mestizaje*, which, as Suzanne Bost writes, "highlights the fusion of differences . . . the mixtures, negotiations, and frictions that define American history" (188). Ferré may, as Bost argues, valorize racial *mestizaje* in Puerto Rico, but in Ferré's bilingualism, Spanish and English coexist but rarely mix or overlap; it is a complementarity that would eliminate hierarchies but maintain separations.

Ferré achieves bilingualism not by writing any single book in Spanish and English but by writing each book first in one language and then in the other, what might be called translating. Translation, however, is inherently hierarchical, for, as Lawrence Venuti writes, "assymetries, inequities, relations of domination and dependence exist in every act of translating" (4). This is not to say that monolinguism or an absence of translation does not also involve wielding power through language, but it allows discussion of the particular hierarchies of translation and of possible ways to move between languages that minimize, acknowledge, or reconfigure those hierarchies.[10] The "fundamentally ethnocentric" nature of translation derives, for Venuti, from translation's work of domestication. "Foreign" texts are translated into "domestic" cultures, a process of assimilation (11).[11]

When Ferré writes in English first, she troubles the distinction between domestic and foreign to some degree, but that is precisely what renders the choice to write in English first a political one that is connected to statehood, to making English a domestic language of Puerto Rico and rendering Puerto Rican literature domestic in the United States. But Ferré insists, in a 2000 interview with Bridget Kevane, "I don't translate my work; I write versions of it" (64).[12] She claims a right to be domestic in both Spanish and

English, and at the same time for both Spanish and English to be foreign, the untranslated other.

Ferré's versions exemplify complementarity. Versions insists on non-assimilability, on difference, on proliferation. Because they are not equivalent, the English version cannot replace or stand in for the Spanish or vice versa: both are necessary. As complements they also destabilize ranking systems based on notions of priority and primacy. The completeness that Ferré's two versions of the same story offer is not one of filling in the gaps or supplying the missing piece. Nor does it require that the only complete understanding come from reading both the Spanish and the English versions of the story because either one is insufficient or incomplete on its own. Rather, their complementarity simply insists that one is not enough; you need to know of the other although you may not necessarily need to know the other.

If Spanish and English do not stand as first and second, original and copy, domestic and foreign in Ferré's work, they escape binary hierarchies. Binary hierarchies are powerful because they organize not just one pair but an entire cultural system. If one pair in the binary hierarchy can be rearticulated into complementarity, the entire system can, perhaps must, follow. The understanding that one is not enough linguistically leads to complementary bilingualism which both allows and is allowed by eccentric statehood. And if the nation is a romance imagined in language, a newly imagined nation with a newly imagined language structure can and will have a newly imagined erotic structure. It will certainly be one with complementarity between men and women. The possibility of complementarity also between women has been less fully conceived by Ferré. Desire between women might be hardest to fit into the model of complementarity and might be the most radical version of it.

The possibility of desire between women has long haunted Ferré's work. Since "Cuando las mujeres quieren a los hombres" ("When Women Love Men") in her first collection of short stories *Papeles de Pandora* (1976; *The Youngest Doll*, 1991), Ferré has consistently included subplots revolving around women of different classes and races, whose relationships with a same man leads them into a complex set of doublings and pairings.[13] These relationships offer compelling critiques of how patriarchy and misogyny render women instrumental and indistinguishable.[14] The rich white women have been unhappy in their marriages because they were oppressed by the obligation to be morally upright. The poor dark women were oppressed by the obligation to sexual service to those underserviced husbands. When the husband/lover dies, emptying the place of the oppressor, we might find a complementarity where the rigid opposition of man/woman gives way to gender equality, allowing a union of equals. Suggestive as they are, the relationships between the wife and the "other woman" consistently figure any desire of the women to have one another through a desire for the absent man. And marking these is a stark division between rich, white, bored, sexually repressed, dissatisfied women and poor or working class, black or mulatta, sexually self-possessed, exploratory, and fulfilled women. Though they may need one another to be complete, it is clear which half each one brings to the union. Oppression gives way to repression, and the suggestion the women may have repressed desires for one another remains just that as heterosexuality and hierarchy remain intact.[15]

"El Regalo" ("The Gift"), a short story in the *Maldito Amor* (1986; *Sweet Diamond Dust*, 1996) collection, offers the one instance in Ferré's extensive body of work prior to *Eccentric Neighborhoods/Vecindarios excéntricos* where the desire between women is not mediated by husbands, dead or alive. The story might offer a rare moment, for Ferré, of hopeful imagining of a productive women's relationship across class and race and within gender. The protagonists Merceditas and Carlota could serve as the model new family where the white aristocracy is inspired by and in love with the mulatto working class to such a degree that it is ready to embrace a new order, bringing an old name and the respect and power that it carries into union with new ideas about productivity, gender relations, sexuality, race, and the family. However, the alliance between Merceditas and Carlota is metaphorized into the exchange of a mango, sublimated into a story of female solidarity, and locked within the walls of a convent school. Before the girls get to the threshold on which they stand in the final scene, the mango putrefies. They hand it to the Mother Superior, establishing the place of eroticism between girls as a corruption of excessive Catholicism and ensuring that their union will return to the repressed. And for Ferré repression holds desire between women deep in the swamps of the subconscious and the subtextual until *Eccentric Neighborhoods/Vecindarios excéntricos.*

Eccentricity for Judith Halberstam is queer. "Eccentric economic practices" and "subcultural practices, alternative methods of alliance, forms of transgender embodiment, and those forms of representation dedicated to capturing these willfully eccentric modes of being" characterize Halberstam's expansive notion of queer that extends to time and space and a "way of life" (1). Ferré's eccentricity is also spatial and similarly denotes both literal and symbolic geographies, but where for Halberstam eccentricity is outside the norm, away from the dominant center, Ferré's eccentric neighborhoods are both far and near. Bartolomeo's plantation is the center of the Rivas de Santillana clan in Puerto Rico, but it is located "on the outskirts of Guayamés" (10). In the Spanish not only Bartolomeo's plantation but each family home is described in relation to a center where it is not: the Rivas de Santillana home

Bartolomeo establishes in Emajaguas, "*a las afueras de Guayamés*" (5; "on the outskirts of Guayamés"), Guayamés itself, which is on the outskirts of La Concordia, and even La Concordia, "*una ciudad pequeña y provinciana*" (197; "a small, provincial city"), whose very "*secreta convicción de ser la 'verdadera' capital de la isla*" (222; "secret conviction that it was the island's 'true' capital") highlights how far it is from San Juan. Perhaps in the English these phrases are superfluous because to an English-reading audience all of Puerto Rico is already far from their center. Simply giving Puerto Rican place names conveys their eccentricity. However, the abundance of eccentric neighborhoods filled with Elvira's eccentric relatives, paradoxically, makes them central to the novel and to its figuration of Puerto Rico and Puerto Ricans. Eccentricity becomes not quite the norm, but certainly the paradigm for understanding the Puerto Rican in *Eccentric Neighborhoods/Vecindarios excéntricos.*[16]

The figurative eccentricities of the members of the Rivas de Santillana and Vernet families reveal the centrality of order in the national imaginary and its work to contain or disavow eccentricity (as difference from the norm). The power of "central control" looms as many eccentric women struggle with the ways that they are still judged by the center. The predictability of the outskirting location of the houses, and the eventual marriages to man or to God of almost all of the eccentric women suggest that while their eccentricity may not be plot-able in the most usual patterns, it can be contained within the traditional plot structure.[17]

The national romance does not plot desire between women, at least not yet. Desire between women parallels the other eccentricities in *Eccentric Neighborhoods/Vecindarios excéntricos*, highlighting the non-heteronormative quality of eccentricity, and also remains separate from them, eccentric even to the eccentric, both locationally and figuratively. The scene in which Clarissa encounters a room full of women erotically engaged with one another appears buried in another scene, covers barely one of the novel's 340 pages, and is never mentioned again. The gratuitousness of the scene, its lack of development or placement within the story line, begs questions about what it is doing, while the novel's interest in the eccentric lends a particular significance to the very fact that this scene appears so far from the center of the characters' lives and of the story line.

By the time we get to the scene in question, Elvira has recounted the life stories of her maternal and paternal grandparents, uncles, and aunts, and detailed her mother's childhood and early marriage. Clarissa set aside her educational and career goals in favor of marriage and motherhood, raised a family, and supported her husband Aurelio through a successful business career that took full advantage of American policies. With the children grown and Aurelio embarked on a busy pro-statehood political campaign, Clarissa is at somewhat of a loss. It is at this point that

> Mother one day accepted an invitation to a bridge party at the house of Rosa Luisa Sheridan, the wife of a distillery owner. Not everyone in La Concordia got invited to Rosa Luisa's parties, but Mother belonged to the sugarcane aristocracy of Guayamés and Rosa Luisa considered her one of her own. (255)

Rosa Luisa Sheridan's home, where the party takes place, is located in Las Bougainvilleas, the same neighborhood that all of the Vernet brothers moved into in 1948. Its eccentricity comes not so much from its geography—it is "the most elegant district in town"—as from the extravagance of its homes, "lined up next to one another on Avenida Cañafístula like four ornate chariots" (239). Rosa Luisa's home is not, however, on Avenida Cañafístula but occupies some other unspecified street, for while the Vernet homes, made of cement, are aligned with the States, Rosa Luisa's is supported by the rum distilleries "which stood on the outskirts of La Concordia" (255).

Aware that political, social, and economic change has slowly eroded the plantations, most of the "sugar barons" have either left the country or decided to "live it up as best they could with the last swigs from the bottom of the barrel" (256). But the eccentric Clarissa married into the enterprising Vernet family, eschewing the old aristocracy of plantations and their mixed or missing political affiliations for the new enterprise of industry and statehood. Clarissa's choice keeps her apart from what is figured in the novel as the decadence of her peers, although it also leaves her profoundly isolated.

The excesses of the "sugar barons" include excessive drinking, expensive architecture to accommodate the excessive drinking, and wild parties that facilitate extensive infidelities (256). The wives of these men flock to Rosa Luisa's parties. Like their husbands, these women enjoy excess. They find their sexual options, however, restricted: "Female infidelity was not permitted—shooting your wife if you caught her *in flagrante* was a sport husbands practiced successfully—and ladies were forced to socialize only with other ladies" (256). It is not clear from the passage whether ladies turn to one another to avoid the prohibition on infidelity or the possibility of discovery. If it is the former, the novel renders sex between women *not* parallel to sex between a woman and a man, incapable of constituting an infidelity, so that the women being together is something that they do in place of marital infidelity, a sort of next best thing, whereas if it is the latter, the novel suggests that the women find a way to commit marital infidelity under the cover of their husbands' inability to imagine that is what they might be doing.

Rosa Luisa's last name, Sheridan, suggests that like Clarissa she has allied herself with the United States. The game used to designate her parties is so essentially English that it can only be named in that language—the Spanish version reads "*decidió asistir a la merienda* bridge *en casa de Rosa Luisa Sheridan*" (335). And Rosa Luisa is among "La Concordia's well-to-do ladies, who did their shopping in Miami and spoke a Spanglish peppered with honeys and darlings" (247). While Clarissa's turn to statehood figures as part of a deliberate and morally upright embrace of progress and equality—political, economic, and social—that an American decentralized order might offer, Rosa Luisa's represents a space where anything goes, where nothing is eccentric any more, and where the destabilized norm unleashes mutually inclusive, unranked possibilities that are not the hallmark of equality and opportunity but rather of indistinguishable proliferation and unproductive chaos. If you gamble, even in so restrained a manner as at a bridge game, you might get taken in, and if you gamble on decentralized egalitarianism you might find that there are no controls to help pull you back once you walk through that door.

Everything has its chaotic underside. On the brink of its loss of power, the plantation patriarchy is both overregulating and devolving into decadent debauchery. Clarissa's turn to Aurelio, enterprise, and statehood, however, is less fulfilling, and less functional, than she had hoped. The old order does not even promise equality in marriage, but in spite of its best intentions the new order might be equally unable to deliver, so that even the promising alliance of statehood becomes one more way for the (neo)colonial male power to use the resources of the colony/woman and then move on. Clarissa's sister Lakhmé discovers this early on in the novel. Her first husband Tom "was the perfect American husband" (77). The Spanish version even more explicitly identifies Tom as representative of the American husband in general, specifying "*Tom era el marido perfecto, como suelen serlo a menudo los americanos*" (99). But Tom does not have the nerves necessary to survive "the severe wounds that he had suffered in combat during his stint in the Pacific," and as soon as the dowry is gone he dies (77); the perfection of an American marriage may work better as an ideal than as a reality. Clarissa rather than marrying an American marries a Puerto Rican who embraces statehood; however, Aurelio's exemplary economic, political, and lifestyle choices create a family life that may look good but is beset with inequalities and dissatisfactions.

Clarissa and Aurelio serve as the contrast to the "sugar barons'" wild excesses: "the exception to the rule [of wild parties] was our house at 1 Avenida Cañafístula where Father and Mother would have had their heads chopped off before allowing a bar. Whenever they gave a party, they stopped serving drinks at midnight" (256). And while Aurelio has ample opportunity, he remains chaste outside of his marriage bed. It would appear, then, that Elvira's parents represent a moral ideal highlighted by the horrors of the decadent society that surrounds them. However, despite Aurelio's fidelity, Clarissa is so wracked with jealousy that she becomes filled with the "bad temper" that her priest warns "can also be a path of red-hot bricks that leads to hell!" (252), and Elvira, their daughter, is so consumed by an Electra complex that she plots her mother's downfall:

> When Father's political campaign intensified and Clarissa was too tired to accompany him, he asked me to stand beside him on the platform when he spoke. I was eighteen [*sic*] and this made me feel important. Father needed me, I told myself, and my presence in this world made Mother's just a little bit less necessary. (252)

In the model pro-statehood family, gender equality does not function and solidarity between women does not exist.

Clarissa tries to move outside the family, looking for a different kind of egalitarian productive alliance with other women. She tries to count as her "good friends" the members of her "sewing club, Las Tijerillas" who "didn't have a college education and didn't belong to La Concordia's sugarcane aristocracy" (247). But Clarissa comes back to Rosa Luisa "probably because she was bored" (255), for while the other women in her sewing group can only spare one day a week from their busy schedules of housework and child care, Clarissa has servants, nurses, gardeners galore (248). Her other distractions are limited because there are so few of them (255) and additionally in the Spanish version because she is so attentive to what is "*bien visto*" for "*las damas como Clarissa*" (332).

Clarissa finds herself, like so many of Ferré's aristocratic female protagonists, deeply dissatisfied with the life of a married woman of means, which offers no intellectual stimulus, no productive or creative outlet, and no sexual satisfaction (246). But instead of the working-class black mistresses to envy and/or emulate that other Ferré protagonists find, Clarissa stumbles on Rosa Luisa and her friends:[18]

> She got there late, delayed by a dental appointment, and found the front door ajar. She stepped in, pushing it fully open with her umbrella and calling out for Rosa Luisa. Soft music wafted out from the bar. Instead of the elegant little card tables she was expecting, with ladies shuffling the deck and betting in low voices, she saw a group of women dancing and others lying on cushions strewn on the floor. They were kissing and rubbing slowly against one another, and they were so drunk they didn't even notice Clarissa standing there. She turned and ran out of the house, her face flaming. (256–257)

Clarissa and the other eccentric women in Elvira's family strike the balance, with more and less success, between repression and eccentricity. If she is not eccentric, if she cannot run off into the Río Loco at times, Clarissa will implode. But if she gets stuck in the river, if she lets the repressed return fully, Clarissa recognizes in this scene, she will become forever enmeshed in eccentric disorder. Eccentricity for Clarissa is not so much a way of escaping order as an escape valve for the sorrow that builds up from performing the repressions required by order. Clarissa's late arrival at Rosa Luisa's party and the specification that she was delayed at the dentist's, that place where deeply hidden rot is uncovered, lay the ground for the return of the repressed. In this state of disarray and openness, when she finds the door to the dark corridor slightly ajar, Clarissa follows the sound of the music. Hesitant, Clarissa tries to maintain a certain distance by pushing the door with the tip of her umbrella, but of course the repressed returns on its own in those moments when our defenses might be a little low without our even knowing it. This one is pretty deep, down a corridor through which not articulated language but only the indistinct sound of music can pass.

Because I am reading this scene closely, and because I find a difference between the English and Spanish versions of this scene, I will here refer to both versions. The difference has to do with the depth and complexity of the repression of desire between women, as if it were more complicated to access in Spanish than in English, in a separate but equal state. Specifically, where the English text reads: "She stepped in, pushing it fully open with her umbrella and calling out for Rosa Luisa. Soft music wafted out from the bar" (256), we find in the Spanish "*La empujó con la punta de la sombrilla y la puerta se abrió sola; llamó a Rosa Luisa en voz alta pero no le contestó nadie. Escuchó que estaban tocando música al fondo del pasillo y se dirigió hacia allí*" (335). While the English suggests that Clarissa by her strong and conscious action brings something to broad daylight, with wide open doors and lungs, the Spanish describes Clarissa using only the tip of her umbrella, after which the door opens on its own, emphasizing Clarissa's loss of control and suggesting the presence of subconscious forces. The Spanish adds the specification that no one answered Elvira's loud call, putting in doubt how clear anything was to anyone. The description of the origin of the music in English is specific and clear, whereas the Spanish "*al fondo del pasillo*" indicates the depth or end of a passageway, not a specific and known room, and this confusion is emphasized in Spanish by Elvira's action, heading toward there, to end up who knows where.

In both versions, the sexuality between women that Clarissa walks in on does not mirror the men's coupling with their mistresses. For the men, parties are often covers, and their party rooms are always fitted with back doors "where the gentlemen and their paramours could make a discrete exit" (256). The women, on the other hand, engage erotically at their parties, just inside "the front door ajar" (256). Leaving a party with a single paramour ensures that, even in their affairs, the men are perfectly heterosexual. The women not only are with one another, they do not pair off. Instead, Clarissa finds an orgiastic "group of women dancing and others lying on cushions strewn on the floor. They were kissing and rubbing slowly against one another, and they were so drunk that they didn't even notice Clarissa standing there" (257). The transitive quality of the verbs adds to the confusion about how many women were touching how many at any one time, while the specification of the degree of drunkenness suggests that they themselves were not attending to details of who was where when. This is the chaos of no center at all, in which social orders and bodies become disarticulated.

These women seem to have found a different way around the problems of colonial and neocolonial patriarchy than Clarissa, or any of Ferré's other women. They find room for pleasurable disorder. Not only do they enjoy the eroticism of the orgy, but they enjoy other chaotic mixings as well. Rosa Luisa and her friends seem able to enjoy a disordered hybridity that emerges from the destabilization of binaries such as English/Spanish, man/woman, and heterosexual/homosexual. This is the flip side of complementarity: all that might happen to complementarity if it did not or could not make the tenuous case for the intactness of each version, if the complements began to freely associate as so many constitutive parts that could mix and match, recombine and disarticulate at whim. Is this what Clarissa flees, her face bright red?

Clarissa's face flared up similarly once before in the novel when her priest warned her about the flames of hell awaiting if her "bad temper" went too far. Perhaps, like her anger, Clarissa understands the sexuality between women as a sin to which she is, almost overpoweringly, drawn. It remains ambiguous whether the problem then is one of sin and its attractiveness or one of the labeling of so many attractive things as sin. Clarissa never talks to Rosa Luisa again, and the narrative never mentions her or her parties again. The question of what is so terrifying about the women together remains, not only for Clarissa but also for Ferré, integral to the question of what women want and where they can get it, and to the possibilities to which a destabilization of ordering systems—political, social, economic—might give rise.

Engaging in sexuality between rich white women is not part of what the eccentric pro-statehood family does. It might be part of what the family misses about what everyone else does. Sexuality between women might satisfy or at least occupy some of the notoriously unsatisfied and underoccupied women in Elvira's family. We do not know if the women at Rosa Luisa Sheridan's parties are satisfied. We do know that the parties are regular and that invitations are highly sought after: "Not everyone in La Concordia got invited to Rosa Luisa's parties, but Mother belonged to the sugarcane aristocracy of Guayamés and Rosa Luisa considered her one of her own" (255). Here, being "one of her own" seems to refer to being upper class. But once we realize, with Clarissa, that this is not the kind of bridge party she imagined, and that no one thought it important to inform her, we understand that "one of her own" must also refer to being open to sexuality between women. It is not that entertaining sexuality between women should replace "upper class" as the referent, but that the two become synonymous. The implication is that all of the women of Rosa Luisa's class engage erotically with one another.

Perhaps Rosa Luisa's party is the center which Clarissa rejects; perhaps Rosa Luisa and her friends are the eccentric in relation to which Clarissa's life becomes quite normal; or perhaps Clarissa's world is eccentric and the party eccentric to the eccentric, which would render it insignificant if it were not for the fact that the eccentric is the paradoxical center of this novel. Desire between women is dangerous precisely because it must be maintained and disavowed, especially at the moment when other delicate balances—such as between independence and statehood—are in flux. Desire between women is necessary either to prove the rule of heterosexuality or else to keep in question what exactly the rule is, what is "in" and what is "out" of the norm, leading either to an impasse or else, as I prefer, to a realization that the categories themselves (normal–abnormal, central–eccentric, homosexual–heterosexual), and the idea of putting things into neat categories, are the ultimate targets, intentional or not, of the representation of sexuality between women in *Eccentric Neighborhoods/Vecindarios excéntricos*.

Eccentric Neighborhoods/Vecindarios excéntricos shows that sexuality between women, were it allowed, might complement sexuality between men and women, and its very rendering impossible the placement of desire between women makes the categorical imperative at the basis of any divisionary model impossible to achieve. The disruption of hierarchies of importance, even of circles or spheres that might organize the central and the eccentric, destabilizes any model that sees the homo as simply an alternative, because that model of the alternative actually reifies the norm by its dependence on it to be an alter. We end up with a chaotic collection of mutually inclusive, unranked possibilities: so dangerous precisely because it is a deeply compelling possible exit from heteronormativity. There will be—there are—extensive outside conditions that limit or enable the possible: for Clarissa, the opinion of the Catholic Church looms large, but so does a hetero-reproductive imperative to carry on a family tree in a particularly mappable way (extending the tree at the front of the novel) and to maintain a political system that preserves hetero-patriarchy. A radical political shift, like that to statehood, might enable the shift to a democratic feminist ideal, as might statehood itself. But we end in a chiasmus that draws outlying, eccentric poles into a center and sends them back out the other side: desire between women enables the very things that it threatens and threatens the very things that it enables—repression, equality, freedom, chaos.

Conclusion

This book is framed by texts, and by analyses of those texts, focusing on failures and rejections of desire between women, and of Caribbean independence. This framing highlights the nagging concerns that I still have about the transformative power, the anticolonial potential, and the radical possibility of desire between women. Always already part of the mangled structure of desire and sexuality in the Caribbean, desire between women does not change radically. The similarities between Rosario Ferré's 1998 *Eccentric Neighborhoods/Vecindarios excéntricos* and José Martí's 1885 *Amistad funesta/Lucía Jerez* evidence not Ferré's regression but Martí's prescience, as well as the enduring power *and* insufficiency of the heterosexual model in the Caribbean. Nevertheless, focusing on desire between women initiates a more modest, yet effective, change in perspective, foregrounding the complex and intersecting structures of desire, sexuality, and family that both traverse and incorporate heterosexual structures—structures I identify with the mangrove. Indeed, if we can mark a clear change between the late nineteenth and the late twentieth century, it is not that desire between women increasingly reconfigures hetero-colonialism or hetero-nationalism but that neocolonialism and national "development" increasingly encroach upon the mangrove.

Binaries, thanks to both postmodern and postcolonial theory, have become notoriously problematic, even as they remain notoriously hard to escape. This difficulty remains endemic to this book: to argue, as I do, that the colonial binaries of man/woman, hetero/homo are insufficient in the Caribbean risks coming up with new binaries such as colonial/Caribbean or even binary/nonbinary. And noticing the curves and vulvar openings of the mangrove roots and branches, the soft wetness of the muck in the cover photograph, I am reminded of the difficulties of claiming various kinds of specificity for the mangle, and am brought back to my introductory questions about how to account for difference and specificity—of gender, sexuality, place—outside of the binary structures that have constituted them.[1]

This book begins to formulate an answer: the mangrove is not essentially womanly or queer in ways that depend on their excluded opposites. Looking in the mangrove swamp for and from the perspective of desire between women, we can see the many shapes of desires for "bodies similar to my own," as Tituba says, and for bodies "whose hollows fitted my curves and whose swellings nestled in the tender flatlands of my flesh" (122). In the mangle, we find the many alliances between girls and women that also contain and are traversed by and intersect with the many alliances based on other gender configurations or other vectors of desire and need and opportunity. But of course the mangrove is not inhabited by women who desire women, or by anyone. It is not hospitable to human, or even animal or insect, habitation; while the mangle houses many other plants and marine animals, it serves mostly migratory or "commuter" mammals, reptiles, birds, and insects.[2] As a model for things human, the mangrove insists on what passes between humans, on what blocks as well as what enables our connections, on how temporary, passing, and mobile are our desires, pleasures, and pains.

While this book foregrounds the specificity of the category "woman" and a set of longings and practices that are grouped into "desire between women," my avoidance of other specificities, such as "homosexual," runs another risk, one that Faith Smith identifies: namely, that "repudiating binaries" may "also foreclose and police, suggesting that particular desires, practices, and identifications are not quite or not at all Caribbean" (15). After I have argued that the hetero–homo model does not hold in the Caribbean, do I leave room for those who do identify, who want to identify as homosexual? Can Makeda Silvera, Achy Obejas, and their characters claim lesbian identity in the mangrove? The structure of the mangrove, insofar as it complicates the hetero–homo binary that forces all sexuality to be either the one or the other, should not exclude the possibility of homosexual practice or identity. In other words, just because not all or even most of women's desire, eroticism, and sexuality is either homo or hetero does not mean that none of it is. I agree with Antonia MacDonald-Smythe's point that a problem with the lesbian continuum is that, along it, everything is some degree of lesbian (*Macocotte*: 227). But even in more apt figures, like MacDonald-Smythe's "spectrum of passionate friendships . . . that, like a rainbow, has variations, latitude, and seeming boundarylessness" or like my mangle, it is not that nothing is any degree of lesbian, but that lesbian, like straight, ceases to be the primary measure or the determining structure (227).

I am repeatedly tempted to find the epistemology of the mangrove so perfectly fluid and so complexly accommodating that it offers an ideal freedom of intertwining and intermixing where everything is just "good," and where even the homosexual, the heterosexual, and the colonial have a place. I want to protect the glimmer of hope in Capécia's nostalgia for a Martinican idyll, to downplay the humorously fantastic in Condé's transnational transubstantial figuration of Tituba and Hester's relationship, to confirm the reality of Kincaid's dreamy normal, to ignore the necessity of immigration for Powell. Indeed, upon reading a very early version of this book, Brad Epps remarked on its idealism. My reaction to that, to both defend idealism and to return to the ways that it may produce blind spots in my analysis, is still with me. The mangrove is a strange kind of ideal, maybe even a sort of anti-ideal, muddy and mucky and mixed up as it is. Not only are barriers to perfect fluidity constitutive of the mangrove, but the mangrove itself is a barrier to the perfectly fluid encounter of sea and sand. I have had to take into account, in my readings, that Mayotte's ideal can only be constructed retrospectively, that Condé writes Hester as a parody of the very kind of reader I am tempted to be, and that *Me Dying Trial* ends in the United States.[3] To idealize the mangrove nonetheless might offer a kind of antidote to other idealizations of the Caribbean for its innocence and open beauty, its exploitability, and might even perform the kind of radical refusal of identification and "progress" that *Eccentric Neighborhoods/Vecindarios excéntricos* toys with. But I selected the photograph on the cover because the still water and thick mud in the foreground remind us that the mangrove can be an unpromising place, and a place that is constantly challenged to adapt to the "unpromising conditions" in which it grows.

However much the mangrove incorporates heterosexuality, the inverse is hardly the case: heterosexual structures that still play a prominent role in the Caribbean do not always incorporate the mangrove. As many of the essays in Smith's anthology demonstrate, there remains little tolerance for public discussions of lesbianism, homosexuality, and other less binary and more mangled expressions of desire between women in the Caribbean. This intolerance and public upholding of heteronormativity, I argue, have always been accompanied by the commonality of desire between women, and that strongly suggests that, far from being antithetical, the two may be perfectly compatible. Desire between women might then not be as powerful an anticolonial or anti-heteronormative force as Natasha Tinsley, in her own possibly idealizing move, finds; its very ability to survive might mark the ways that desire between women is complicit with, even supportive of heteronormativity. I have argued throughout this book that it is a strange kind of heteronormativity that is supported by and incorporates desire between women, but it is also, I would add, a strange kind of desire between women that can support and be incorporated into heteronormativity. Heteronormativity and desire between women coexist in ways that both make the former less normal or exclusive and the latter less radical and potentially transformative than we might otherwise think.

If public professions of heteronormativity can coincide with regular practices of desire between women, we may need to rethink public professions of heteronormativity. Even professions as official as Prime Minister Golding's may not run counter to tacit knowledge of desire between women but may instead operate alongside the mangled structure of desire and sexuality. The public profession of anything, in other words, serves a purpose other than to circulate knowledge about what is normal. It serves, rather, as part of a geopolitical positioning strategy, and perhaps even, in spite of itself, as a protection of tacit subjects. But of course these public professions of heteronormativity become codified into laws that do not protect, and set off international discourses that attempt to "save" the "oppressed" in ways that are deeply disruptive to the local structures that might limit or respond to oppression.

While I have argued that mangroves are emblematic of the Caribbean, they do not appear in many views of the Caribbean shore, as looking for the book's cover image of the mangrove vividly demonstrated. A search for "Caribbean" in an open source library of stock images turns up 64,814 images. The great majority of these repeat the public image of the Caribbean, in both national self-positionings and international imaginations, as some combination of sandy shores and clear waters (government-sponsored brochures and web pages, and international tour guides are similarly replete with images blazoned with bright white and blue, dotted with vibrant orange, pink, purple flora and fauna). A search for "mangrove and Caribbean" in the same stock image library turned up only 170 images. Of those, 30 do not actually show mangrove, 59 are views of the mangrove from the water (as if the viewer were on a yacht or out snorkeling), 27 show isolated clumps or outcroppings of one or two mangroves in clear sea or white sand, 26 are aerial or broad-angle views of the Caribbean coastline with mangrove, and 13 are top views of lush mangrove leaves. Only 14 are similar in perspective and content to the one that I selected. Visually marginalized, the mangrove figures as a minor object of (touristic) curiosity, to be consumed and enjoyed instrumentally, as if from afar.

The mangrove represents in many ways the back side of the Caribbean, and I am in many ways speaking of the back side and the underside of the mangroves—what you see when you look from the perspective of the cover image. I selected the image in large part for its perspective: looking out from the edge of a mangrove forest across a cove to another mangrove forest and also beyond to the sea. A few trunks rise up, visible in the left corner of the photograph, lush foliage appears across the bay on the far side of the photo, but front and center are the tangled, intertwining brown roots and branches and mud. On this side of the mangrove, the water appears stagnant, populated by a few fish; it is not easy to thrive, let alone to make a home in the West Indian mangle, and yet the mangle may be what makes making home in the West Indies possible (to borrow the title of MacDonald-Smythe's book). The possibilities for growth, for creativity and survival and interspecies epiphytical and parasitical mutuality are, at least, matched by the possibilities for getting stuck or else sold off to make room for white sand and tall, swaying palms.

The mangrove protects the coastline, in part responsible for the stretches of sandy beaches elsewhere, because it can survive the winds and tides where the sandy beaches and palms cannot. Privileging resort-style beaches over mangroves, prioritizing "development" over the preservation of the mangle, endangers not only the mangrove itself but also the "front view" of the Caribbean, for without the messiness of the mangroves, the white beaches will also be spoiled, and swept out to sea. Promoters of tourism, developers, and Western lookers of all kinds too often overlook not only the *other* possibilities that the mangrove offers, but also the ways that the mangrove is essential to those most pristine and prejudiced, apparently singular and binary, structures. The mangrove both supports binaries such as homo/hetero and undermines their claims to singularity and binarity, showing them to be always already dependent on and intersected by the mangle.

Although I describe the mangrove as the barrier that filters what goes in and out of the islands, this book pays little attention to the recent transnational flows of bodies and desires manifested in tourism or diaspora. Primarily, this book is interested in what remains in the Caribbean in spite of or even thanks to so much human and financial traffic. However, the desire for more traffic directly threatens the mangroves, with "development" and aquaculture looming as the main causes for the over 3 percent annual decline in Caribbean mangrove populations.[4] It may well be that the literal mangle is in greater danger than the structure of desire and sexuality for which it is the metaphorical model. Mangroves are literally being torn up to make way for beachside developments for a tourism industry that brings an increasing volume of Euro-American bodies and monies and desires for certain kinds of sexuality imagined to be in the Caribbean.

The depiction of the Caribbean as "a highly sought after vacation destination," as Patricia Saunders notes, involves its status as "a proverbial sexual playground" where Caribbean women and, increasingly, men serve the sexual and relationship fantasies of Europeans and Americans ("Buyer Beware," 23). The makeup of tourist populations is changing: Saunders writes about African-American and Black European tourism; Tinsley notes that "LGBs have become visibly and globally mobile, travelling on organized tours to gay-owned hotels with new confidence that the world has space for queers to move comfortably" (137). But the diversification of tourists seems to have little impact on their view of the Caribbean. Thus, Olivia Companies, "the largest promoter of lesbian travel services in the world," now offering regular trips to the Caribbean, becomes one of the latest participants in a tradition, extending from Columbus through the United Fruit Company, of seeing the Caribbean as simultaneously a savage population in need of Euro-American civilizing and a bountiful source of Euro-American profit and pleasure. Tourism emerges as but one of the latest incarnations of colonialism. The rise in tourism in the Caribbean, especially since the 1980s, may mark a return to influx of money and ideas for the "development" of the Caribbean unparalleled since the height of colonialism. But colonialism, as I have argued, is precisely what resulted in the mangled structure of desire and sexuality in the Caribbean. And so even as I fear that tourism might destroy the mangle, I think it is more likely that it will alter it, and thus allow—or even enable it—to persist. The mangrove has survived in the Caribbean since the Paleocene epoch because of its ability to adapt to an almost endless series of "unpromising conditions."

The conditions of tourism in the Caribbean are the subject of a growing number of texts, from Kincaid's scathing book *A Small Place*, to Condé's characteristically tongue-in-cheek text for the guidebook *Guadeloupe* and Powell's consideration of the touristic component of the diasporic Caribbean's return home in *The Fullness of Everything*. Critical work is just beginning to address the literal and poetic, the structural and metaphorical results of tourism in and for the Caribbean. I hope that this book will help to direct future critical attention to how stories of desire between women in the Caribbean interact with tourism and vice versa. The texts that I have explored in this book, however, show more attention to other parts of recent transnational flows: the Caribbean diaspora and the increasingly wide reach of Euro-American attention to transnational homosexuality and global queerness.

The increasing openness of the Caribbean to Euro-American-style homosexuality can be as destructive of the mangrove as heteronormativity, and perhaps even more so, for while imposition and repression force the mangle to fill in, openness can cause it to empty out, rendering what remains readable as retrograde, unenlightened (it is hard to resist narratives of a certain kind of progress, toward ever-increasing openness—which, however, also entail a clearing of mangroves). I hope that this book has shown that the preservation of the mangle is progressive if we understand progress to include the continuation of Caribbean adaptations and mutations for survival in the "unpromising conditions" that have always characterized it.[5] The mangle remains the place where colonial and neocolonial traffic and progress are the least attempted and most slowed. Exemplary might be Condé's *Traversée de la mangrove*, where Carlos leaves Haiti and his lover, Désinor, for the United States. While Carlos's letters begging Désinor to join him are Désinor's most treasured possessions, Désinor is caught in the mangle in Guadeloupe, tragically unable to imagine how to get to the United States and heroically accepting the ties that bind him to other men "without wife, without children, without friends, without father or mother, with nothing under the sun" over the promise of free jobs and free love in New York (168). Even many Caribbean writers who use Euro-American identitary terminology such as lesbian or queer and who take their stories and themselves to the United States or Canada in part in order to live away from the oppression of postcolonial national heteronormativity (this especially is true of writers from Jamaica and Trinidad and Tobago) locate the fullest expression of their desire and sexuality in the Caribbean and in Caribbean terms. Thus Dionne Brand's *In Another Place, Not Here* refers not to Canada where the story is set, but to the islands for which Elizette and Verlia long, indicating that although the relationship between them takes place in Canada, it belongs to and finds belonging in the Caribbean.

Homophobia in the Caribbean hinders some relationships and causes some women who desire other women to leave, but this rejection of (or by) Caribbean homophobia is not necessarily an embrace of Euro-American-style homosexuality. Kincaid's Lucy, for example, describes kissing an American girl not as the culmination of her childhood *macocotte* relationships that in America have the chance to develop into full-fledged lesbianism, but rather as an experiment with something entirely new. Inasmuch as kissing an American girl makes Lucy think back to her *macocotte* relationships, it makes her think about the distinct qualities of those relationships. Certainly, some Caribbean diaspora writing depicts and embraces international homosexual or queer identity, like Nalo Hopkinson's *The Salt Roads*, but much of it continues, both from within the Caribbean and from the diaspora, to depict mangled visions of desire and sexuality, as in the work of Shani Mootoo, Edwidge Danticat, and Erika Lopez.

This book has tended to focus on how the mangroves grow; as it concludes, I am repeatedly struck by their location, by where they grow, the mud and muck in the foreground of the cover photograph. Looking at them from the land side, we see the ways that these lovely rhizomatic structures are guided not only by desire, by some kind of nebulous reaching toward what can never be had, but also by necessity, by desperation even to survive, to find support and nourishment in a strange mix of waters and soils and winds. Tinsley critiques Glissant's view of the mangrove for its failure to "retain the swamp's dangerous, sticky femininity" (24). If the damp stickiness of the mud is gendered female, we might strategically extend that interpretation to the curving, vulvar roots, so that what we see when we look at images such as the one on the cover is a figure for the touching, penetrating, producing between women, where women or the feminine is not homo(geneous) and where what happens (or passes) between them is hard wrought, not always pretty, and threatened by the very things that enable it—including attention to the ways that, in the mangle, men and women, homosexual and heterosexual, colonial, postcolonial, neocolonial, anticolonial all traverse one another.

This book looks back over established, even "canonical" Caribbean literature. The novels and analyses considered here contextualize new work that increasingly strives for the time when a Caribbean child will, as Thomas Glave writes,

> be able to walk past the mountains that slouch over her/his town, along the glistening shores that stretch just beyond, secure in the knowledge that s/he has never had, could never have: that no one, not anyone at all, will come crooning at her/him with a few pennies, lately grown to dollars, for a prolonged taste of his/her various parts; that no one will run shouting at him/her, wielding a machete, because s/he possesses not only breasts, but blue ones; not only a penis but a green one.
>
> (*Words*, 45–46)

Glave is spokesperson and activist for a growing group of writers who create works like *Our Caribbean: A Gathering of Lesbian and Gay Writing from the Antilles*, which "exist for the passing along, the making known from consciousness to uttered word to the next watchful, waiting eye," and for groups like the Jamaica Forum for Lesbians, All-Sexuals, and Gays (J-FLAG). These authors join and push the limits of the writers of the mangrove such as Martí, Capécia, Condé, Kincaid, Powell, and Ferré (1).

Looking back at the authors and texts that are the focus of this book reveals the difficulty as much as the promise that desire between women poses for knowing desire and sexuality in the Caribbean. In a literary, theoretical, and political world dominated by gazes and structures that expect and want binary hetero/homo models, it is difficult to sustain, let alone to promote the epistemology of the mangrove, and yet the epistemology of the mangrove derives from the endless combination and recombination of native, African, South and East Asian, and colonial structures and models that pass in and out of the Caribbean. The epistemology of the mangrove is especially precarious in the face of the more blatant efforts to establish national models and structures, as seen not only in Martí's foundational failure and Ferré's teetering on the edge of the same in *Eccentric Neighborhoods/ Vecindarios excéntricos*, but also in the Jamaican national discourses of heteronormativity that so impact Powell's characters in *Me Dying Trial.* Sometimes, as in Capécia's *Je suis martiniquaise*, colonial structures are so powerful that the epistemology of the mangrove can survive only through nostalgia, or through the rendering impossible of the colonial ideal that they still cannot overturn. But even in these texts, desire between women and the epistemology of the mangrove survive in some form, often in stories that we can read, or that aunty/mothers like Cora can tell to daughter/nieces like Peppy. And sometimes rather than always and only reacting to the colonial as a threat against the epistemology of the mangrove, stories like Condé's *Moi Tituba sorcière . . .* demonstrate how the colonial is also created by and through the epistemology of the mangrove.

Notes

Introduction

1. Most critical material on Columbus's "Matinino" concerns itself with studying the possible sources for Columbus's claim about its inhabitants. Those who examine the Amerindian sources include Astrid Steverlynck, who studies, from an anthropological, archeological perspective, the "reality" of all-female societies in the Americas prior to Columbus's arrival, and William F. Keegan, who turns to Taino mythology to understand the symbolism of "Matinino." Julius Olson and Edward Bourne's annotations of Columbus's letters cite both Marco Polo and Arawak myths recorded by later explorers as sources for Columbus's "Matinino." A few critics such as Peter Mason consider Columbus's description of the women of "Matinino" in the context of his view of native bodies and gender roles in the New World.
2. Albrecht Rosenthal cites the myth of all-female Amazon societies from classical Greek literature in support of his argument that "many of the *merveilles* encountered by Marco Polo, Mandeville, Columbus, and other travelers reveal themselves . . . as being conscious or unconscious reminiscences of stories related in the romances and chronicles which shaped the medieval conception of distant lands" (257).
3. As might be expected, the most well-known Caribbean theories, such as those of Glissant, Fanon, James, Walcott, and Benítez-Rojo, either do not mention desire between women at all or else do so primarily to dismiss it. The work of Patricia Mohammed, Evelyn O'Callaghan, Gloria Wekker, and M. Jacqui Alexander, although at times limited by identitarian discourses to poles of unification and marginalization, initiated critical recognition of desire between women in the Caribbean. While more recent studies attend to gender and sexuality in more subtle ways, they still overwhelmingly treat desire between women as an embattled other opposed to a heterosexual norm. Caribbean sexuality receives a new kind of treatment in a series of publications in the second decade of the twenty-first century, including books by Thomas Glave, Lawrence La Fountain-Stokes, Faith Smith, Mimi Sheller, Donette Francis, and Omise'eke Natasha Tinsley. Tinsley's book and this one, as well as a special issue of *Contemporary Women's Writing* on

Caribbean queer, are the first to take as the primary focus desire between women in Caribbean literature.

4. Activism and scholarship overlap and intersect in this area, as O'Callaghan makes clear when she observes that "there has been an increase in the number of locally informed academics, teachers, LBGT activists, health and social workers, lawyers, artists, and students who recognize that engaging with queer theory and writing makes possible difficult but important discussions" ("Sex," 233). See also Denise deCaires Narain and Emily Taylor for incisive articulations of the intersections of Caribbean and queer studies.
5. In one of the most recent and exhaustive biological studies, *The Biology of Mangroves and Seagrasses*, Peter Hogarth explains,

   > At the level of the individual tree, mangroves show complex adaptive structural and physiological responses to the immediate environment, particularly to physical factors such as salinity . . . At a larger scale, local variations in these physical factors help to determine the overall structure of the mangrove forest. Such local variations, and the structure of the forest, are profoundly affected by the environmental setting in which it grows. Finally, the species present are a subset of those available in the geographical region, so over-riding biogeographical factors must be taken into account. (49)

6. I did not learn of Tinsley's work until 2009, when I was already well into this book project; the difference in the texts I selected for study develops not out of a wish to cover things she did not but out of a coincidental turn to other texts. In the one novel that we, coincidentally, both consider, Mayotte Capécia's *Je suis martiniquaise*, the difference in our readings of that text—Tinsley's focus is on the anticolonial qualities of the story and on the biographical and historical questions surrounding the author and text, while I focus on the imaginative and idealizing qualities of the first half of the story and on the intertextual and critical contexts of the book—shows that not only are there a wealth of texts to be read with attention to their representations of desire between women, but each of these can be understood through a wealth of readings.
7. Similarly, when Denis deCaires Narain explores the valences of queer and the possibilities of other terms, she suggests "that a creolizing interpretive practice might be more historically and culturally attuned to the *particular* proliferation and intersection of differences in the Caribbean than a queering one" and that terminology such as "creolizing" "might also avoid the anxiety attendant on *inclusion* that causes Donnell to hesitate over 'queer' as an 'imported' category and take us further toward the more 'affirmative term' she seeks" (196, emphases in original).
8. Evelyn O'Callaghan explores what I am calling the betweenness of desire between women in "Sex, Secrets, and Shani Mootoo's Queer Families," where she analyzes desire as transforming the individual subject into a relational subject, and desiring as always being in relation to others.
9. Donnell (2012: 224) exemplifies thinking outside of sexuality as identity in her analysis of Shani Mootoo's *Valmiki's Daughter* as she argues that

by focusing on lives that are so clearly messy, compromised, and incomplete, yet vibrant, pleasurable and rewarding, *Valmiki's Daughter* reaches beyond an imagined extension of sexual normalization (in which homosexual subjects enter into marriage, child rearing, and so on) to provoke an acknowledgment of pervasive queerness and to question the identity-making.

10. Other terms include *zamiez* in St Lucia, *malnomme* in Dominica, *jamette* in Trinidad, *man royal* in Jamaica, *wicca* in Barbados, *kambrada* in Curaçao, and *tuerca*, *parcha*, *bombero*, *capitán*, and *general* in Cuba.
11. Smith (2011: 9) also points out that it is important to maintain "a suspicion about the liberatory capacity of Creole speech" for "while it has been used to draw the line between fluent insiders and clueless outsiders, . . . Creole speech is a repository for sexual slurs and sexual violence."
12. O'Callaghan importantly notes that although "The 'ideal' nuclear, the extended, or the noncoresidential kinship network models appear to maintain a relatively unremarked coexistence" both in regular practice and in literary figurations, "Caribbean discourses on the preferred forms of sexual relationships and family life . . . tend to be strongly prescriptive and endorse traditional [heteronormative] notions of what is 'natural' " (2012: 236).
13. Derek Walcott offers the image of the Caribbean as broken or cut apart and glued or pasted back together in *Fragments of Epic Memory*. Glissant argues for opacity and a relation as integral to Caribbean poetics throughout his writings, and Antonio Benítez-Rojo develops a theory of *The Repeating Island*.
14. This work is becoming so widespread that I cannot list it all here, but it includes the novels of Gisèle Pineau, Shani Mootoo, Nalo Hopkinson, Magali García Ramis, Mayra Santos-Febres, and many of the contributors to Thomas Glave's anthology *Our Caribbean: A Gathering of Lesbian and Gay Writing from the Antilles*.
15. In a section of *Black Skin, White Masks* that compares the treatment of blacks to the treatment of Jews, Fanon cites Henri Baruk's descriptions of "anti-Semitic psychoses." In one of Baruk's cases, a man accuses Jews of homosexuality. The following is what Fanon annotates it with:

    > Let me observe at once that I had no opportunity to establish the overt presence of homosexuality in Martinique. This must be viewed as the result of the absence of the Oedipus Complex in the Antilles. The schema of homosexuality is well enough known. We should not overlook, however, the existence of what are called there "men dressed like women" or "godmothers." Generally they wear shirts and skirts. But I am convinced that they lead normal sex lives. They can punch like any "he-man" and they are not impervious to the allures of women—fish and vegetable merchants. In Europe, on the other hand, I have known several Martinicans who became homosexuals, always passive. But this was by no means a neurotic homosexuality: for them it was a livelihood, as pimping is for others. (180)

16. Sommer describes as one of her underlying concerns the ways in which naturalized heterosexual romance is a figure for nation formation in mid-nineteenth-century Latin America. As Sommer develops this analysis in her book *Foundational Fictions*, she also reveals the assumption of singularly heterosexual romance in the theorists with whom she engages, notably Benedict Anderson and Eric Hobsbawm. René Girard's analysis of *Deceit, Desire, and the Novel* similarly offers a key reading of romance plots but that insists on an assumption of heterosexuality.
17. For critiques of the hetero-patriarchy of the *créolistes*, see A. James Arnold's "The Gendering of Créolité" and Price and Price's "Shadowboxing in the Mangrove." Even Chamoiseau, in his reading of Condé's *Traversée de la mangrove*, acknowledges that the Caribbean literary figuration of desire and sexuality ought to not to be hetero-patriarchal, writing, "we have a literature to build on love, and... we have to build it in unprecedented terms, far from French/Western patterns" (391).
18. Mangroves are considered native throughout the tropical zone. The original distribution of mangroves dates back to the Paleocene through the Miocene epochs, at which point tectonic distribution was different than it is now; current mangrove distribution is the result of tectonic shifts and the increasing cooling of the earth throughout the Pleistocene epoch, which limited a once much larger distribution to the Tropics.
19. According to Peter Hogarth,

    > True mangroves comprise some 55 species in 20 genera, belonging to 16 families... From this we can infer that the mangrove habit—the complex of physiological adaptations enabling survival and success—did not evolve just once and allow rapid diversification by a common ancestor. The mangrove habit probably evolved independently at least 16 times, in 16 separate families: the common features have evolved through convergence, not common descent. (3)

20. For detailed investigations of slavery in the Caribbean with special attention to issues of gender, see Shepherd and McD. Beckles. For a collection of essays on Caribbean history especially attentive to colonialism, see Stephane Palmié and Francisco Scarano.
21. The work of Stefanie Dunning, Ernesto Javier Martinez, and Ian Bernard addresses the ways that queerness might operate on and through race as much as gender in the African-American context.
22. For detailed discussion of the violent regulation of slave sexuality, see Hartman.
23. Inge Dornan is among a small group of historians working to retrieve and to analyze the voices of slaves. Fanon lays out his theory of internalized colonization in *Black Skin, White Masks*. Albert Memmi as well as Aimé Césaire in his essay on colonization offer similar analyses. Du Bois's concept of double consciousness demonstrates how African-Americans always see themselves through both white and black perspectives.

24. Lacan's theories of jouissance have been developed and reworked in myriad ways by, among others, Julia Kristeva, Hélène Cixous, and Deleuze and Guattari.
25. Describing the mangrove's ability to grow in mud and saltwater along hurricane-swept shorelines, Peter Hogarth (2007: 10) writes, "Mangrove trees have adapted to survive in such unpromising surroundings."
26. Antonia MacDonald-Smythe also critiques the applicability of Rich's lesbian continuum to a Caribbean context in "*Macocotte.*"
27. See for example the history of the denial and imposition of marriage for slaves, as documented in Shepherd and McD. Beckles.
28. M. Jacqui Alexander develops a similar argument.
29. For a more detailed study of Caribbean religions, see Zora Neale Hurston, Margarite Fernández Olmos, Joseph Murphy, and Lizabeth Paravisini-Gebert, and Nathaniel Murrell. Smith includes Caribbean religions along with Caribbean musical traditions in "the arena of performance" where

> it may very well be . . . that sexual desires are given a wider range and reign than they are in other areas of life, and attending to this might show us that regional conversations about the affirmation of all sorts of desires predate our present moment and therefore exceed the imprisoning limitations of defending or impugning the region's honor against charges of homophobia. (2011: 14)

30. In 1830s Antigua, the Moravian Reverend J. Curtin, for example, although dedicated to ending slavery and Christianizing and educating blacks, and credited by Mary Prince with teaching her to read and write, could only officially offer religious instruction to slaves and had, "when any adult slaves came on week days to school, to require their owners' permission for their attendance" (Prince 1831: 36). Hilary McD. Beckles discusses scarcity and the power of slave literacy in "The Literate Few."
31. Other articulations of the Caribbean "us" appear in José Martí's "Nuestra América" at the turn of the twentieth century, and Césaire's *négritude*, Glissant's *antillanité*, and Bernabé, Chamoiseau, and Confiant's *créolité*.
32. Rosamond King's analysis of Carnival positions it as a regular space for the public performance and pronunciation of what are otherwise tacit subjects, potentially a key component for understanding tacit subjects and the circulation of community knowledge in the Caribbean. Vanessa Agard-Jones refers to something like the tacit subject as "discretion," which, she writes, might be understood as the kind of "radical passivity" that Halberstam enjoins.
33. The "tacit subject" of course also functions to keep certain knowledge from being articulated in other ways, thus perpetuating certain forms of silencing, as O'Callaghan points out in "Sex, Secrets, and Shani Mootoo's Queer Families." However, while silencing entails stopping the circulation of information, tacit knowledge operates in precisely the opposite way, to allow what may appear silent to be known, breaking silencing without "breaking the silence."

E. L. Johnson compellingly articulates the delicate balance to be understood between the calls for "examining the nature and legacy of oppression as a silencing force," "represent[ing] silences that cannot be broken," and "going beyond the longstanding goal of breaking silence to reconsider the silence/speech binary altogether" (270).

34. Tinsley similarly shows that the yard is a space of what I am calling tacit knowledge of desire between women (30–67).
35. Naipaul repeats this claim in different ways in different works, but perhaps most clearly in *Middle Passage*, where he writes, "History is built around achievement and creation; and nothing was created in the West Indies" (20). Many have responded to Naipaul, perhaps most famously Derek Walcott in *The Antilles: Fragments of Epic Memory*. Importantly, however, Naipaul uses his claim not to refuse history as a useful concept for the Caribbean but to call for the creation of Caribbean history. For analysis of Naipaul's ideas about Caribbean history, see Bridget Brereton.
36. This view of epistemology approaches what deCaires Narain elaborates as "a creolizing hermeneutics." DeCaires Narain draws on "the entanglement of epistemologies" but suggests "that it is in detailed, intimate engagement with a text that we might approach a more modest hermeneutical practice" (201).

Chapter 1

1. Critics vary in the title they use to designate the novel. My choice to use both reflects my belief that the titular concern of the novel is both "fatal friendship" and the character of Lucía, as well as my understanding that many aspects of the novel were troubling, undecided, and subject to revision for Martí at the time of his death.
2. For a detailed analysis of Juan and Lucía's characters and their symbolism, see my "Dark and Dangerous."
3. For example, Anderson Imbert focus on stylistics in *Amistad funesta*/*Lucía Jerez*, and Mercedes López Baralt on questions of genre; Paulette Beauregard analyzes the gender presentation of the protagonists; Jesús Barquet reads the novel biographically, and Fernández Rubio politically.
4. At the age of 9, Martí reported to have seen a group of mistreated slaves, an experience that he eventually immortalized in poem XXX of *Versos Sencillos* (OC 16:106–107). In January 1869, Martí published his first newspaper article criticizing Spanish rule (OC 1:31–36). The same month, Martí helped to create the newspaper *La Patria Libre*, in whose only edition his poem-play *Abdala* appeared. *Abdala* tells the story of a young boy who fights for the freedom of his enslaved country (OC 18:11–24). In February 1869 Martí published the sonnet "10 de Octubre," expressing his enormous support and admiration for the war of independence (OC 17:20). In October 1869, Martí was arrested for a letter he wrote denouncing the Cubans who joined the Spanish "volunteers" fighting against Céspedes. He was condemned in 1870 to six years in a hard labor camp, but

in 1871 his father succeeded in having the sentence commuted to deportation to Spain.

5. At various times, Martí also visited and wrote on Costa Rica, Argentina, Colombia, Honduras, Nicaragua, Uruguay, Paraguay, Santo Domingo, Haiti, Jamaica, and Puerto Rico. Martí's chronicles are collected in OC 5:83–335, and OC 6–13. For detailed consideration of Martí's chronicles, see Aníbal González, *La crónica modernista hispanoamericana.*
6. Luis Baralt, in his 1966 translation of a selection of Martí's chronicles, translates the title *Amistad funesta* as "Untoward Friendship" (xxv). Baralt does not translate any part of the novel beyond the title, and all translations here are my own. Although "untoward" gestures to the illicit nature of the friendship that I explore in this analysis, I prefer to translate "*funesta*" with "fatal" to highlight the foreshadowing of the novel's deadly denouement that is present in "*funesta*" and throughout the story, and also to allude to the *femme fatale* that the protagonist turns out to be.
7. Matei Calinescu provides one of the most extensive studies of *modernismo.* Carlos Javier Morales, Henríquez Ureña, and Roberto Fernández Retamar, among many others, examine Martí's work in the context of *modernismo.* An increasing number of studies address the importance of *Amistad funesta/Lucía Jerez* in the context of *modernismo.* See, for example, Rosario Peñaranda Medina, Klaus Meyer-Minnemann, and Dolores Phillipps-López.
8. Mauricio Núñez Rodríguez: 8–11.
9. *El Latino Americano*'s header announces a "newspaper for families" containing "literature, science, art, travel, music, theater, fashion, useful information, general interests." Along with the first installment of *Amistad funesta*, on the front page of the May 15, 1885, edition are "Idilio," a poem by Ginés Esoanamires de Binares in celebration of a wedding, and a moralistic tale by Francisco Reyes about a princess who is extremely exigent in her choice of a husband and ends up as "*La desposada de la muerte*" ("Death's Wife").
10. The publication of novels in serial form and under pseudonyms was quite common during the *fin de siglo*, and Martí had used pseudonyms previously. However, most of the gender-crossing pseudonyms come from women who signed their works as men. By 1885, Martí had publicly condemned the use of pseudonyms. Martí signed some of his 1875 articles in Mexico's *Revista Universal* with the name Orestes (OC 6:191–356; OC 14:19–23), and others with his initials (OC 14:15–16). On his brief return to Cuba in 1879, Martí published his contributions to the clandestine Club Revolucionario Cubano under the pseudonym "Anahuac" (Ottmar Ette, 143). Martí signed his articles for Venezuela's *La Opinión Nacional*, dated August to December 1881, "M. de Z." instead of his customary "José Martí" or the less frequent "J. M." (OC 14:37–289). For analysis of some of these pseudonyms, see Ette, "Apuntes para una orestiada americana." After the *Revista Universal* (where Martí had published under the pseudonym Orestes and under his initials) was shut down by the dictatorship of Porfirio Díaz, Martí published two articles in another Mexican newspaper, *El Federalista*,

under his true name. In the second, he "came out" as Orestes, and condemned the use of pseudonyms (OC 6:360–363). The clandestine nature of the Cuban paper where he subsequently signed articles as "Anahuac" suggests that Martí used that pseudonym in order to protect himself from persecution. He subsequently employed "M. de Z." in articles for Caracas's *La Opinión Nacional* at the request of the paper's owner and director, Fausto Teodoro de Aldrey, following Martí's expulsion from Venezuela by the country's dictator, Antonio Guzmán Blanco (Mañach: 187).

11. This is repeated in the planned prologue. Quesada y Aróstegui reports Martí repeating similar information to him upon his (re)discovery of the manuscript (v–vi). The information presented in the works of biographically inclined critics such as Barquet seems to draw from these sources, as well as on the memoir of Blanca Zacharie de Baralt, Adelaida's niece. Martí met Adelaida Baralt through her brother, Dr Luis A. Baralt, who was a close friend of Martí's both in Cuba and in New York. Living in exile in New York at the same time as Martí, the Baralt family hosted the Sociedad de la Cultura Harmónica, which drew together many of the Latin American intellectuals in the area, and, according to Núñez Rodríguez, may have been responsible for the direction of *El Latino Americano* (personal conversation June 23, 2003). Adelaida Baralt was herself a regular contributor of prose and poetry to *El Latino Americano*.
12. Leonard Koos's analysis of the pseudonym confirms its association with posing. Molloy develops her analysis of posing in relation to Oscar Wilde, but in response to criticism she received for her "Too Wilde for Comfort," which details Martí's fascination with Wilde. Molloy explains that posing refers

    > equivocally to the homosexual, for it refers to a theatricality, a dissipation, and a manner (the uncontrollable gesturing of excess) traditionally associated with the non-masculine or, at the very least, with an increasingly problematic masculinity. Posing makes evident the elusiveness of all constructions of identity, their fundamentally performative nature . . . it increasingly problematizes gender, its formulations and its divisions: it subverts categories, questions reproductive models, proposes new models of identification based on recognition of desire more than on cultural pacts, offers (and plays at) new sexual identities.
    >
    > ("The Politics of Posing": 187)

13. The exact date of the prologue and of the corrections made to the story by Martí is not known. Martí's literary executor, Gonzalo de Quesada y Aróstegui, reports finding "a few loose pages of *El Latino Americano*, here and there corrected by Martí," in Martí's office at 120 Front Street, at an unspecified date in the 1890s (v). Quesada y Aróstegui published it in 1911 under Martí's name and with some unspecified corrections made to the original serial by the author, but that edition does not include the new title, the prologue draft, or the poem Martí sent to Adelaida Baralt along with the novel. It is not until Gonzalo de Quesada y Miranda's 1940 edition of Martí's complete works that the prologue and poem

appear in print. That 1940 edition (volume 25 of Martí's *Complete Works* edited by Quesada y Miranda) still entitles the novel *Amistad funesta*, but provides an introduction that mentions the planned new title, *Amistad funesta/Lucía Jerez.* Manuel Pedro González' 1969 edition, published in Madrid by Gredos, is the first to use the title *Amistad funesta/Lucía Jerez.* The 1979 edition published in Havana by Editorial Gente Nueva is the last to use the title *Amistad funesta.* Carlos Javier Morales's 1994 edition, published in Madrid by Cátedra, also employs the title *Amistad funesta/Lucía Jerez,* as do Núñez-Rodríguez's 2000 editions, published simultaneously in Havana and Guatemala. The latter also compare the text originally published in *El Latino Americano* to that offered in subsequent editions in order to elucidate the exact changes planned by Martí. Summarizing the revisions, Núñez-Rodríguez writes: "Martí did plan substantial changes for the structure of the discourse, but rather concerned himself with bettering or perfecting the hurried writing in hopes of achieving greater clarity" (39), which amounted to grammatical corrections.

14. "El poeta Walt Whitman" was published in 1887 simultaneously in *La Nación* in Buenos Aires and in *El Partido Liberal* in Mexico City (OC 13:131–143).
15. For example, Martí writes, "the pollen scatters; the cooing and billing are hidden among the pleached branches; the leaves seek the sun; all exudes music; in this language of raw light Whitman spoke of Lincoln" (*The America of José Martí,* 243). Although the words are credited to Whitman, no quotation marks are used. The passage is also representative of the very loose references to and translations of Whitman which Martí tends to use; although Whitman's poems to Lincoln are full of the kind of imagery Martí cites, the closest in exact words are: "Lilac and star and bird twined with the chant of my soul,/There in the fragrant pines and the cedars dusk and dim" (Whitman, *Poetry and Prose*: 467).
16. Ben Heller makes a similar argument about the presentation of homosexuality in "Nuestra América."
17. Carlos Javier Morales's edition, which I use, offers voluminous introductory material, beginning the story itself on page 114.
18. In this depiction of the heterosexual romance, Martí seems to anticipate Evelyn O'Callaghan's observation that "the ideal model of the 'natural' family remains the heteronormative, patriarchal, nuclear family . . . In the field of recent [Caribbean] fiction, however, the 'natural' family is also portrayed as 'unnatural' " ("Sex," 236). Denise deCaires Narain also offers a similar reading of Kincaid as depicting "damaging" heterosexual relationships "as an index of the utter failure of all human relationships, but particularly as they are encoded in the ideal of the heterosexual romance narrative, and the family" (204).
19. From the beginning of the third chapter, the narrator and all of the characters take up Lucía's nomenclature and refer to the girl as Sol. In Morales's edition of the book, an editorial footnote informs readers that "from now on Leonor will always appear with the name Sol, given the symbolic function that such a name performs" (155). The note is superfluous, for the narrator makes clear that "Sol" ("sun") is an accolade as much as it is a name.

20. The imperfect form of the verb *lucir* "to shine," "Lucía" translates as "shone" or "was shining," but also has a meaning that corresponds to the English "glitter, sparkle." The name Lucía also evokes Saint Lucy (Santa Lucía), patron saint of light and vision as well as of the blind, famous for ripping out her eyes in order to avoid an arranged marriage to a pagan. For a full discussion of the symbolism of Lucía's name, see my "Dark and Dangerous."
21. See, for example, Anderson Imbert (101); Fernández-Rubio; Morales (81); Fina García Marruz (287); Gladys Zaldívar (63); Aníbal González, "El intelectual" (141).
22. The twists and turns that these arguments must make indicate that the subject requires further investigation. Aníbal González' case for Lucía's jealousy is sweeping and by his own admission under-substantiated: González asserts that Lucía interacts not only with Sol but with the entire world in a jealous mode despite the fact that Juan offers her no reason to be jealous of Sol ("El intelectual": 141). Zaldívar draws on symbolic traditions when she finds Lucía's jealous character represented in the camellia with which she is often associated, but then adds that Martí's is the only text to employ the camellia to symbolize jealousy (63). Morales refers to the structure of the love triangle to confirm that Lucía and Sol relate via jealousy, but his assertion is so fraught with unnecessary qualifiers that it asks for reconsideration. Morales writes: "Juan is, without a doubt, the object that the two appear to dispute" ("Introduction": 81). The unnecessary interjection of "without a doubt" suggests the very doubt that it denies, while the qualifier "appear" allows that there may be another relationship between the women that is hidden beneath appearances. Furthermore, the presence of the two qualifiers in the same sentence draws attention to the tentative quality of the assertion.
23. Sedgwick works from René Girard's analysis that "jealousy and envy imply a third presence: object, subject, and a third person toward whom envy is directed . . . true jealousy contains an element of fascination with the insolent rival" (12).
24. Uribe similarly analyzes Lucía's jealousy as one which "allows a glimpse of a desire which goes beyond that which is strictly limited to her gender" (35).
25. Elizabeth Meese and Monique Wittig elaborate this idea, already present in Freud's descriptions of female sexuality and of the perversions.
26. Torres-Pou notes that the references to the moon and to Paris add elements of female sexuality or eroticism to the scene, while José Gomáriz also points out that in this scene Lucía resembles Salomé, "the saturnine man-eating woman" (181).
27. An excellent discussion of "transgressions," including female–female eroticism and sexuality, in *fin de siècle* Paris can be found in Eugen Weber (36–39, 52–53). Felski also finds that "in modernist culture the metropolis will increasingly come to be depicted as a woman, a demonic femme fatale whose seductive cruelty exemplifies the delights and horrors of urban life" (75).
28. In addition to the now clichéd association of women with flowers, used in the opening description of the cousins where each girl is associated with a particular flower, Lucía is linked with roses in particular earlier in the novel when she gives

that flower to Sol and later in Ana's symbolic painting of her friends where Lucía appears as a rose.

29. Torres-Pou, unwilling to imagine that sexual violence could take place without the presence of a man, argues that "it could be concluded that the flower-eating monster [the animal hidden inside every woman], caressed by the moon's rays [by sexuality], causes the destruction [the insanity] in the girls" (52). Destructive insanity caused by one woman in other women, however, only brings us back to *fin de siglo* psycho-medical explanations of female homosexuality.
30. Uribe similarly observes, "the opposition between Ana and Lucía is not static or one-sided, since on a content level they function not as adversaries but as companions, friends, sisters" (28). Even a model of triangulation may suggest a relationship more distanced and static than the one that actually exists between Lucía and Ana.
31. Several critics, including Uribe, Martínez-San Miguel, and Campos, contend that Sol represents the ideal of romantic femininity that Lucía destroys. While my analysis of Sol, as desiring Lucía, troubles her neat identification with that ideal, the underlying concept of such analyses is similar to mine: Lucía shoots not at an individual but at a symbol.
32. Martínez-San Miguel (38); Masiello (276).
33. In "La mujer en la novela modernista hispanoamericana," Rosa Pellicer explains: "throughout the work there has been an insistence on Ana's pale, dry lips, which were 'a fountain of pardon', her prayerful eyes and priestly soul; at the moment of climax she approaches Lucía Jerez, who everyone contemplates in horror, and gives her the kiss of pardon" (295). Similarly, Uribe reads the kiss as "the blessing of Martí, the blessing of the artist" (37).
34. Morales recognizes the open nature of the novel's close: "the denouement comes in the form of a crucial act that, nonetheless, does not succeed in definitively truncating the romantic relationship, since in the mind of the reader, it remains open to various future possibilities" (71). Although it refers to the romantic relationship between Lucía and Juan, Morales's statement can equally apply to the romantic relationship between Lucía and Ana. The second possibility seems more likely, given the disposition of the characters at the end of the last page: Juan in Pedro's arms in one room, Lucía in Ana's in another.

Chapter 2

1. One early critic, the Martinican Jenny Alpha, gives *Je suis martiniquaise* an unfavorable review in 1948, objecting in advance of Fanon to what she sees as the protagonist's preference for white men and her missing revolutionary spirit. For further discussion of Alpha's review, see Stith Clark (4).
2. Capécia serves as the prime example for Fanon's analysis of "the woman of color and the white man" in *Peau noire, masques blancs* (*White Skin, Black Masks*).
3. Fanon's choice of terminology, "lactification," plays on the white color of milk. That all mothers who nurse their children, not only those impregnated by white

men, do so with milk either is strangely ignored by Fanon or else implicates all childbearing women, regardless of the race of their partner, in the attempt to produce more "milky-white" children.

4. See for example Duffus, Hurley, Sparrow, Nya, and Makward.
5. One library, worldwide, has a digitized version of Stith Clark's translation; digitized versions of the original and the translation are not available for sale.
6. Any translation must, by virtue of being a translation, use words different from those in the original and any other choice besides "I Am a Martinican Woman" would have added or subtracted other implications to the original, as evidenced by the titles of the Swedish and German translations, *Mayotte Fran Martinique* (1949) and *Ein Mädchen von Martinique* (1951), respectively. By virtue of pioneering work on Capécia, Stith Clark becomes a target of later developments, but the immensity of her contribution should not be underestimated. However, since Stith Clark's necessary decisions tend to elide the very aspects of *Je suis martiniquaise* that I wish to highlight, I use my own translations.
7. As mentioned in Chapter 3, Suzanne Césaire writes in *Tropiques* (4: 50): "Come, true poetry is elsewhere. Far from rhymes, complaints, breezes, paroquets. Bambous, we decree death to doudou literature. And shit to the hibiscus, the frangipani, the bouvanvillea. Martinican poetry will be cannibalistic or it will not be" (cited in Sourieau: 69). "*Doudou*" in Creole means both girlfriend and traditional women's dress and referred in the 1930s and 1940s specifically to Antillean women who served as the exotic mistresses of colonial French.
8. This is perhaps most obvious in the *Code Noire*, and more specifically in its insistence on the social prestige and moral superiority of marriage. María Lugones analyzes powerfully the connections between heterosexualism and the "coloniality of gender."
9. This is demonstrated in *Je suis martiniquaise* with Mayotte's twin sister Francette being raised by an aunt. For detailed discussions of Caribbean family structures, see Edith Clark, Michael Garfield Smith, Raymond Smith, and Cecile Accilien.
10. Haigh, in her analysis of Michèle Lacrosil's *Cajou*, has already suggested some of the shifts in Fanon's model that follow when the Caribbean woman's desire to be the white woman is accompanied by a desire to have her: "Not only does Lacrosil succeed in representing the lesbian desire unimaginable for Fanon but, in depicting Cajou's refusal of compulsory heterosexuality and of compulsory motherhood, she succeeds also in suggesting that black female desire for whiteness cannot be reduced, as Fanon seems to imply, to a simple desire for literal miscegenation" (35).
11. Women appear, for example, a few very brief times in Césaire's *Cahier d'un retour au pays natal* as the possessors of the wombs that will grow the men's seed (46) and as the owners of the *pagnes* that decorate the Caribbean landscape (35), while Césaire's new black leader will be a distinctly male character: "and of myself make neither a father/nor a brother nor a son/but the father, the brother, the son/do not make me a husband, but the lover of this unique people" (*Return* 77).

12. For a detailed reading of *Je suis martiniquaise* and *La Négresse blanche* in the context of Martinique's place in World War II, see Cheryl Duffus.
13. It was during this time that Fanon fled to Dominica, where he joined de Gaulle's army and made his first trip to Algeria.
14. In theory, a *département d'outre-mer* is like any of the 94 departments in hexagonal France. However, the special name, *d'outre-mer*, not only distinguishes those departments from the others by geography, but also specifies the extreme distance, geographical as well as cultural and conceptual, between France and its overseas departments. *Outre* derives from the Latin "ultra," which expresses excess or exaggeration, similar to extra-, hyper-, and super-. The *Robert* dictionary defines *outre* as "*au delà de*" ("beyond"), suggesting that *outre-mer* is not simply a location different from France, but one that is almost insurmountably far from a France that is at the same time constituted as the center from which things are or are not distant. The famous recitation of "Our ancestors the Gauls" that forms the basis of the history curriculum in all French-administered schools reveals the limits and contradictions of the universalism on which French colonialism and French republicanism are based.
15. Clarisse Zimra's mode of distinguishing between the two by referring to the author as Capécia and the character as Mayotte has become standard critical practice.
16. Christiane Makward cites Jean Duché, in a 1948 interview with Capécia, saying "It is the first time we have a woman novelist of color" (29).
17. For consideration of the possible meanings of the name Mayotte Capécia, see Tinsley (144–145).
18. Critics differ on how to use the biographical information revealed by Makward. Jack Corzani, in his preface to Makward's biography, offers a scathing critique of Fanon's conflation of Capécia the author and Mayotte the character (7–12). Tinsley, in her reading of Makward's revelations about the ways that *Je suis martiniquaise* draws from André's account and about the probably significant editorial work of Correa staff, argues that "In the end, the *I Am a Martinican Woman* that went to press in 1948 was a hybrid, multiauthored text" and cautions that "it is difficult to attribute too much agency to Capécia as tale teller" (143, 155). Stith Clark finds that "it is difficult . . . to imagine that Frantz Fanon . . . was unaware of her true identity" (x), but recommends that critics not "succumb to the lure of probing the factual existence of Lucette Combette née Ceranus" but rather "let Mayotte Capécia remain her fictional self" (xi). It is in agreement with this recommendation that, aside from the short introduction of her biography, I refer to the author as Capécia and that I analyze the text as a novel with no necessary correspondence between the story and the author's fictional or factual self.
19. Sibyl Jackson Carter argues that *Je suis martiniquaise* is a direct parody of the writings of Lafcadio Hearn and other explorers and ethnographers who perpetuated precisely those stereotypical ideals of the Caribbean and its women.
20. Tinsley reads the bananas as "a ripe cluster of phallic symbols" (153). The Banania images and slogan so actively marketed in France as early as 1914 assure a primary

association between bananas and colonial produce. Although the most famous Banania image is of a Senegalese man, the first Banania image, used from 1914 to 1915, was of an Antillean woman. The Banania slogan "y'a bon," launched at the 1931 Exposition Coloniale, was meant to repeat the "pidgin" French of the colonial subjects.

21. Vincent Byas's 1942 article arguing for US annexation of Martinique offers a particularly blatant example of the conflation of island and woman: "Martinique is the tiny island gem crowned with the mass of bluish-green emeralds that are her mountains, delicately set in an incredible sapphire sea. The constant trade winds, playing lustily about, serve in a mighty way to enchant her life in the equatorial sun" (277). For discussion of Capécia's interactions with stereotypes about Caribbean women, see Lizabeth Paravasini-Gebert.
22. "*Amoureux*" refers to someone who is in love with the subject. Stith Clark's translation, "sweetheart," conveys the way that it generally connotes a love which is accepted by the subject, but misses the clear specification of the source of love coming from outside the subject.
23. In this I follow Henry Drewal's analysis of Mami Wata devotees, who, he writes, " 'study' others-overseas visitors . . . Their study of our 'ways'—our lore, writings, possessions, or patterns of worship—is actually a resymbolization of them" (160).
24. For more detailed analyses of Maman Dlô, see Drewal, Revert, Haigh's "Between," Bastian, and van Stipriaan.
25. Maman Dlô stories are quite common in Caribbean folklore and oral literature. Written Maman Dlô stories include Patrick Chamoiseau's play *Maman Dlô contre la fée Carabosse*, Alain Mabiala and Bernard Joureau's graphic novel *Petit Jacques et la Manman Dlo*, Trinidadian historian Gérard Besson's "Ti Jeanne's Last Laundry," and Alex Godard's young adult novel, *Maman Dlo*, which figures Maman Dlô as the mother who has left a young Guadeloupean girl to go work in France.
26. This distinction, which is the enforcer of heterosexuality, is taken from Freudian psychoanalysis, especially as Sedgwick, Butler, and Fuss have interpreted it.
27. The possibility that blacks could be aligned with slave owners is made apparent in the servile manner in which Mayotte's father treats her; questions of all sorts of collaboration are particularly near the surface of *Je suis martiniquaise* through its setting during the Vichy rule in France. For a detailed analysis of the war in *Je suis martiniquaise*, see Duffus.
28. The gender rift in *Je suis martiniquaise* which Sparrow and others analyze puts Martinican men and women not only at odds in general but particularly in different positions in relation to the colonial powers.
29. Here Capécia anticipates *antillanité* and *créolité* with their recognition of the heterogeneous nature of "Caribbeanness." Marie-Agnès Sourieu argues that, over the course of her writings in *Tropiques*, Suzanne Césaire also "opposes to the rejection of the Other—the White—as advanced by the philosophy of négritude—at least in its beginnings—the recognition of the complementary relationship with the Other" (70).
30. Jeffrey Theis's details of specificity of the sylvan pastoral in early modern British literature can be extended to the colonial context.

31. The French grammatical necessity of gendering all nouns and pronouns might render the feminization and personification of the moon slightly less pronounced in the original. "*Sa lumière*" can be translated as "its light" rather than "her light," but the impassioned address of the moon and Mayotte's descripton of her feelings play up and play on the grammatical tradition in a way that would be obscured by a translation of "its light."
32. Ernest John Knapton's probably remains the best biography of Empress Joséphine. Paul Guth also offers an extremely popular version of Joséphine's life story.
33. Slavery was repeatedly abolished and reinstated in Martinique between 1794, when the French Convention abolished slavery, and 1848. During that time, Martinique shifted between French and British possession several times; France and Britain abolished slavery and the slave trade at different times, and France changed its position on slavery and the slave trade several more times during that period. Napoleon reinstated slavery, reversing abolition of the French Convention, in 1802. The British, who had outlawed the slave trade, but not slavery, in 1807, took possession of Martinique in 1809 and held it until 1814. In 1815, Napoleon abolished the slave trade but, perhaps at the urging of Joséphine, left intact slavery itself. Slavery was definitively abolished in Martinique in 1848. The statue of Empress Joséphine was beheaded in the early 1980s and has since often been doused with blood-colored paint and covered with graffiti protesting her role in the history of the island. For a discussion of the symbolism of the statue of Empress Joséphine and its beheading, see Natasha Barnes.
34. For detailed studies of Carnival aesthetics, see Esiaba Irobe, Patricia Alleyne-Dettmers, and Pamela Franco. For a discussion of the expression of "unrespectable" female gender and sexuality at Carnival, see Rosamond King.
35. Carnival can be a site for much more subversive, mangled, play with gender identities and roles, as King shows in the case of "Nineteenth-Century Jamettes" in Trinidad. The differences between the islands and the time periods may account for real differences in Carnival practice, but the Carnival in *Je suis martiniquaise* also must be understood as part of the narrative more than as documentation of the event.
36. The misrepresentation of Martinican Carnival, blending together the *diablotins* who parade during the week leading up to Mardi Gras and the *guiablesses* who walk the streets on the day after, either signals a disingenuousness to Mayotte's explanatory position or else marks the fictional quality of the work. Either Capécia strategically rewrote Carnival for literary effect or else Capécia wrote a Mayotte who did so. For detailed descriptions of Martinican Carnival, see Louis Achille and David Murray.

Chapter 3

1. Condé says in an interview with Ann Scarboro that she only read Petry's book "when I was already halfway through *Tituba* because her book was difficult to find . . ." (200).

2. Maroons, *marrons* in French, are slaves who escaped the plantations and lived in the hills or woods fomenting rebellion; the practice of flight, survival, and revolt is *marronnage* or marooning.
3. This plays with the generic conventions of autobiography and the eighteenth-century traditions of *accréditement* (where an author claims to have written a story imparted to them by someone else). Paula Barnes, Haigh, and Leah Hewitt (*Autobiographical Tightropes*: 189) discuss the conventions of the slave narrative and their repetition or parody in *Moi, Tituba sorcière*. . . . Spear and Hewitt examine the ways in which the epigraph toys with *accréditement* (727; *Autobiographical Tightropes*: 189).
4. Condé discusses these details in numerous interviews (with Pfaff, Elizabeth Nunez, Ann Armstrong Scarboro, and others) and presents them at length in *Coeur à rire et à pleurer: contes vrais de mon enfance.*
5. Condé speaks at length about her biography and her marriage with VèVè Clark in "Je me suis réconciliée avec mon île."
6. My reading of Célanire can be found in "Parodic Métissage." For additional discussions of women's sexuality in Condé's novels, see Arthur Flannigan; A. James Arnold, "The Novelist As Critic"; Susan Andrade. To a lesser extent, Condé also explores male sexuality and consistently includes male characters who desire other men: Pierre-Gilles in *Hérémakhonon* (1975), Dénisor and Carlos in *Traversée de la mangrove* (1989), Aymeric in *La migration des coeurs* (1995), and Dieudonné and Luc in *La Belle Créole* (2001).
7. See, for example, Lisa Bernstein, Carolyn Duffey, Mara Dukats, Lillian Manzor-Coats, and Michelle Smith.
8. Duffey remarks on the minimal critical attention afforded to Tituba and Hester's erotic desire for one another, but does not follow up on her own suggestion that it "might bear some scrutiny" (106–107). Jeanne Garane notes that "Tituba and Hester even seem to engage in a sexual relationship which remains more or less implicit" but does not elaborate (162). Thomas Spear mentions in passing "the loves of Condé's Tituba, which include a Jewish man and her prison mate, Hester" (728). Michèle Vialet parenthetically notes "alienation in or by sexuality is a trial that forces Condean characters to understand that the pleasure they search for in the 'procession of men' (or women) in their beds is only an escape from the self" (76). Haigh notes briefly that after Hester's suicide, "the relationship between the two women becomes overtly sexualized" (183). Robert McCormick ends his description of Hester's role in the novel with the sentence, "Hester also vaguely evokes 'bodily pleasure' between women" (278). Moss dismissively harks back to these when she remarks, "some feminist critics want to see the jailhouse encounter between Tituba and Hester Prynne as a parody of contemporary Anglo-feminist liberal discourse—complete with lesbian separatist overtones" (14).
9. "*Doudou*" in Creole means both girlfriend and traditional women's dress and referred in the 1930s and 1940s specifically to Antillean women who served as the exotic mistresses of colonial French.

10. Among the most famous cannibalistic Caribbean texts, Aimé Césaire's *Une tempête* and Roberto Fernández' *Todo Calibán* both re-present William Shakespeare's *The Tempest*, while Jean Rhys's *Wide Sargasso Sea* recounts Antoinette (Bertha) Harris's story up to the point where she becomes the madwoman in the attic of Charlotte Brontë's *Jane Eyre*. Condé cannibalizes Emily Brontë in her later novel, *La Migration des coeurs* (*Windward Heights*). *Moi, Tituba sorcière*... digests and redeposits Hawthorne and a whole tradition of historical and literary texts about the Salem witch trials.
11. When asked about her reasons for including Hester in *Moi, Tituba sorcière*..., Condé tells Scarboro:

> First of all, I like the novel *The Scarlet Letter* and I read it often. Second, it is set in roughly the same period as Tituba. Third, when I went to Salem to visit the village, the place where Tituba used to live, I saw the house of Nathaniel Hawthorne, the House of the Seven Gables... meaning there was a link between Tituba and Nathaniel Hawthorne. I didn't know whether I wanted to subvert existing versions of history because all those kinds of reflections are observations from a critical point of view. When you are involved in writing, you do not have that distance between yourself and your text and you cannot answer this way. (202)

12. Sedgwick describes a similar project in *Epistemology of the Closet*:

> The analytic move it makes is to demonstrate that categories presented in a culture as symmetrical binary oppositions heterosexual/homosexual in this case—actually subsist in a more unsettled and dynamic tacit relation according to which, first, term B is not symmetrical with but subordinated to term A; but, second, the ontologically valorized term A actually depends for its meaning on the simultaneous subsumption and exclusion of term B; hence, third, the question of priority between the supposed central and the supposed marginal category of each dyad is irresolvably unstable, an instability caused by the fact that the term B is constituted as at once internal and external to term A. (9–10)

Taking on the story of a Caribbean woman who desired other women and who was crucial in the Salem witch trials, Condé at once joins Sedgwick in suggesting that the "homosexual" is constitutive of the heterosexual and adds that likewise the "black" (African or Afro-Caribbean, slave, "Other") is constitutive of the Anglo (Puritan, "American," "Western"), and that, furthermore, neither black nor Anglo is equal to either homosexual or heterosexual (as in sets of binaries that are listed as sets of parallels), but each category is interpenetrated by the others.

13. Dukats and Jane Moss make similar arguments. Dukats writes: "the imaginative encounter between Tituba and Hawthorne's Hester Prynne enabled Condé to

think about the way that her heroine, Tituba, had enabled Hawthorne to produce the 'true beginning' of American prose fiction" (56). Moss finds that Condé's novel becomes a "rewriting of *The Scarlet Letter* 'avant la lettre' or before the fact, to play on the two French meanings of 'lettre' " (14).

14. Elaine Breslaw's *Tituba, Reluctant Witch of Salem* was published more than a decade after Condé's novel.
15. The first French edition (Mercure de France, 1986) does not feature the ellipses; however, the font size and color of the title create uncertainty as to the relationship between "Maryse Condé," "*Moi, Tituba sorcière*," ("I, witch Tituba") and "*Noire de Salem*" ("Black [woman] of Salem"). In French, adjectives follow nouns, and, as in English, black can either be an adjective or function as a noun (standing in for black woman or black man, necessarily gendered in French), so that "*Moi, Tituba sorcière*" alone could be read as "I, witch Tituba" while "*Moi, Tituba sorcière Noire de Salem*" could be "I, Tituba, black witch of Salem" or "I, witch Tituba, black woman of Salem." Condé's name appears in the same color and font size as "*Noire de Salem*." "*Moi, Tituba sorcière*" separates the two but in a different font and color, so that "*Noire de Salem*" appears to modify "Maryse Condé" as much if not more than it does "*Moi, Tituba sorcière*." For a more detailed analysis of the title of this first edition, see Manzor-Coats. In the second and third French editions of the novel (Mercure de France/Folio, 1990 and 1996), ellipses follow "*Moi, Tituba sorcière*..." on the front cover while "*Noire de Salem*" appears only on the first page. The capitalization of "*Noire*" indicates a further separation and makes it less clear what exactly "*noire*" modifies. The Québecois edition (Beauchemin, 1995) combines the two different French versions, with *Moi, Tituba sorcière*... on the cover in bold font and centered directly below it *Noire de Salem* in italics. When asked by the editors of the Québecois edition about the meaning of the ellipses, Condé responded: "It is a question of elegance in the layout of the title" (1995: 9). The English editions of the novel all omit entirely the ellipses, and almost any other separation between the first and second halves of the title. The first English edition (University Press of Virginia, 1992) displays the title on the front cover as "I, Tituba Black Witch of Salem." The second English edition (Ballantine Books, 1994) adds a comma after Tituba, and the third English edition (Faber and Faber Limited, 2000) removes it again. Condé tells Ann Armstrong Scarboro: "I wanted to call it simply *I, Tituba* but the publishers said that was a bit laconic as a title and added Black Witch of Salem" (205). The interview with Armstrong appears in the afterward to the novel's first English edition, so that it is unclear whether Condé refers here to the English title or to the original title. Perhaps Condé could clarify her referent, but the ambivalence over the exact content and format of the title, which changes with each edition of the book, extends to its every invocation and, furthermore, underlines the problems of interpretation featured throughout *Moi, Tituba sorcière*.... In all of its incarnations, the title draws intertextual connections with any number of other texts published around the same time, many of them fictional autobiographies, which employ a similar titular formula, including Aimé Césaire's collection

of poetry, *Moi, Laminaire* (1982); Paul Guth's extremely popular biography of the Martinican wife of Napoleon, *Moi, Joséphine Impératrice* (1979); Marie-Claude Leduc's collection of poems and stories, *Moi, la Réunionnaise* (1983); Michel Foucault's *Moi, Pierre Rivière, ayant égorgé ma mère, ma sœur et mon frère... un cas de parricide au XIXè siècle* (1973); Michel Domage's *Moi, Cadet, maréchal de l'empire* (1982); and Robert Graves's account of the Roman Empire from Augustus to Claudius as told by the dying *I, Claudius* (1934).

16. Probably the most important Christian document on witchcraft, Heinrich Kramer and James Sprenger's *Malleus Maleficarum* concludes: "all witchcraft comes from carnal lust, which is in women insatiable" (1:6 [47]). *Malleus Maleficarum* served as the basis for much of the inquisition, and was a significant influence in the writings of American proponents of the seventeenth-century witch hunts.
17. For further discussion of the witch or Obeah woman in Caribbean folklore and culture, see also Paul, Beverley Ormerod, and Condé, *La parole des femmes*.
18. No dates are specified in *The Scarlet Letter*, but scholars agree that the story is set between 1642 and 1649. Writing from his present in 1849, Hawthorne opens the main story of *The Scarlet Letter* on "The grass-plot before the jail, in Prison Lane, on a certain summer morning, not less than two centuries ago" (73) where

    > The door of the jail being flung open from within, there appeared... the grim and grisly presence of the town-beadle... Stretching forth the official staff in his left hand, he laid his right upon the shoulder of a young woman, whom he thus drew forward; until, on the threshold of the prison-door, she repelled him, by an action marked with natural dignity and force of character, and stepped into the open air, as if by her own free-will. (76–77)

19. The notion of skin and skin color as a cover that hides feelings is one of the main subjects of Fanon's text. Condé affirms in an interview with Pfaff that she intended ironic references to Fanon throughout *Moi, Tituba sorcière...* (*Entretiens*: 92).
20. For further discussion of Tituba's eroticization, see Mudimbé-Boyi.
21. In her relationships with men, Tituba demonstrates a preference for the non-white. White men figure, in sexual relationship to black women, as rapists from the first line of the novel: "Abena, my mother, was raped by an English sailor" (IT: 3). Tituba's first lover, John Indian, is of mixed Amerindian and African heritage. Her other male lover in Anglo-America, Benjamin Cohen d'Azevedo, is a Jew with a marked racial and cultural distinction from the Puritans. When she returns to Barbados, Tituba's two male lovers are both black maroons.
22. Considering how to distinguish desire between women in texts that are not explicitly lesbian, Barbara Johnson looks to "overinvested and underexplained" relationships between women that create "the effect of irresistible magnetism that is precisely *not* grounded in friendship" ("Lesbian Spectacles": 162, emphasis in original).

23. Elizabeth Meese explains: "as the logic goes, the lesbian woman must be 'narcissistic', loving her own image, because she is in love with 'the same', since her love object is not a man" (67).
24. In "Of Mimicry and Man," Homi Bhabha presents reiteration with difference as a tactic of postcolonial resistance.
25. Experiences of divine love are often described as unutterable because they exceed all language, as by Saint Theresa of Avila. The impossibility of speaking certain kinds of love also recalls Lord Alfred Douglas's "love that dare not speak its name."
26. "*Morne*" derives from the Spanish "*morro*" ("round hill") and has no etymological relationship to the French "*colline*" ("hill"), which designates the same geographical formation in France. The Creole "*morne*" is equally unrelated to the French adjective "*morne*" ("morose") or to the French noun "*morne*" ("impediment"). For a detailed discussion of the importance of "*morne*" in Caribbean literature, see J. Michael Dash.
27. Evelyn O'Callaghan explores the erotic complexities of maternal relationships as they relate to desire between women in "Compulsory Heterosexuality."
28. For Castle, ghosts are "made to seem invisible" (4) as a form of erasure, while for Condé "the invisibles" are forever present, simply not visible. Thus Castle seeks to "rematerialize" the lesbian ghost, while for Condé ghosts are already perfectly material, if differently than the living. Condé explains to Rebecca Wolff in an interview:

    > There is an idea in the Caribbean that people who are dead are still with you. Normally the room is full of dead people, close to me, who like to see the way I live now, how I go on with my life . . . Some people are trained to see them. Those people belong to what we call Santeria, or Kimbwa, or voodoo, and if I had their services, they could well come in here, and say, "yes, your mother is sitting there, looking at you." The idea is that we are always trying to be in communication with the souls of the people that we love and who have left us. (80)

    Similarly, when asked whether Tituba really believed in ghosts, Condé affirms that: "All Negro-African culture rests on the belief in spirits. In Africa, in the Antilles, in Brazil . . . it is a fact that has been studied at length by any number of specialists" (*Moi, Tituba sorcière . . .*, 1995: 8).
29. McCormick similarly notes: "Hester becomes one of the 'life-giving forces'—the only white non-African one and the only woman of Tituba's own generation" (278).
30. The water lily is native to the Caribbean, Europe, and North America. For an analysis of Mallarmé's poem, see Johnson, *The Critical Difference*. Possibly drawing himself on Mallarmé's "Nénuphar blanc," or on the French fame of water lilies provided by Monet's famous paintings of Giverny, Césaire refers to the water lily as a particularly European figure, writing: "In my memory are lagoons./They are covered with death's heads. They are not covered with water lilies" (*Return*: 64). According to Chevalier and Gheerbrant, in Africa and the

Caribbean, the water lily, associated with mother's milk and hence the woman's bosom, symbolizes abundance and fertility through or as women's sexuality (1090).

31. This distinction draws from Barbara Johnson's remarks on the unknown:

> Far from being a negative or nonexistent factor, what is not known is often the unseen motivating force behind the very deployment of meaning. The power of ignorance, blindness, uncertainty, or misreading is often all the more redoubtable for not being perceived as such. Literature, it seems to me, is the discourse most preoccupied with the unknown, but not in the sense in which such a statement is usually understood. The "unknown" is not what lies beyond the limits of knowledge, some unreachable, sacred, ineffable point toward which we vainly yearn. It lies, rather, in the oversights and slip-ups that structure our lives in the same way that an X makes its possible to articulate an algebraic equation.
>
> ("Critical Difference": xii)

32. Following Johnson's model, the desire between Tituba and Hester would create a crypto-lesbian plot less because of any way in which it is known than because of the ways in which it is so repeatedly not known. Or, in Sedgwick's formulation, to the extent to which the unknown in Tituba and Hester's relationship has a content, it is a content of desire between women. Glissant's notion of opacity, which he develops throughout *Le Discours Antillais*, offers a description and response to the problem of content in Caribbean identity.
33. For further discussion of Abena's disapproval of Tituba's relationships with men, see Carolyn Duffey.
34. Many Condé critics share this opinion. Hewitt writes, for example: "Condé is more often concerned with tracing [the] complications and intersections [of racial, sexual and political oppressions] than with the clarity of their definitions" ("Inventing": 80). Thomas Spear concurs: "For Condé's characters preoccupied with self-discovery, the 'search' itself is more important than any point of arrival where one's supposed 'authenticity' would be found—that is, where one's past, or individual identity, would become clearly defined" (724).

Chapter 4

1. The interplay of Western, Indigenous, African, and Asian traditions in Caribbean literature and in Caribbean literary history renders the specificities of Caribbean narrative structure difficult to systematize and to generalize, but studies of individual Caribbean novels repeatedly encounter formal deviations from Western narrative conventions. See, for example, Barbara Christian, Jan Bryce, and Monica Hanna.
2. See, for example, Diane Cousineau, Leigh Gilmore, Brenda Berrian, and Helen Pyne-Timothy. MacDonald-Smythe's analysis of the desire between girls in

Kincaid's later novel, *Lucy*, as a "*macocotte*" relationship is similar, although as I argue in the introduction, it is also more suggestive of other readings ("*Macocotte*").

3. For more detailed discussion of the complex relationship between "truth" and "fiction" in Kincaid's work, see Donnell, Braziel, and Gilmore (*The Limits of Autobiography*).
4. In *My Brother* and also in *Mr Potter*, Kincaid describes how she learned that another man, Mr Potter, was her biological father.
5. Sources differ as to the exact year and age at which Kincaid left Antigua. Paravisini-Gebert lists it as 17 (*Jamaica Kincaid*: 9); in an interview with Selwyn Cudjoe, Kincaid says that it was in June of 1965, shortly after her 16th birthday (215–216).
6. For more detailed biographical information, see Paravisini-Gebert (*Jamaica Kincaid*), or interviews with Kincaid that touch on her biography: "Jamaica Kincaid and the Modernist Project"; "I Come from a Place That Is Very Unreal"; "Interview" in *Conversations with American Artists.*
7. Barbadian historian, cultural critic, and poet Edward Kamau Brathwaite elaborates: "Shakespeare, George Eliot, Jane Austen—British literature and literary forms, the models that were intimate to Great Britain, that had very little to do, really, with the environment and reality of the Caribbean—were dominant in the Caribbean education system" (*Roots*: 262). For further consideration of the content of the colonial curriculum, see Helen Tiffin; Walcott, "An Interview with Derek Walcott"; Silvio Torres-Saillant; Paravisini-Gebert, *Jamaica Kincaid: A Critical Companion.*
8. In this, I disagree with Denise deCaires Narain's assessment that "sexual relationships in [Kincaid's] texts are invariably (hyper) heterosexual," although certainly the sexual relationships that deCaires Narain examines, as well as many others, are between women and men and contend with heteronormativity and all of the gender and sexual extremes that entails (203).
9. Thus, Judith Halberstam argues, "queer subcultures produce alternative temporalities by allowing their participants to believe that their cultures can be imaged according to logics that lie outside of those paradigmatic markers of life experiences—namely, birth, marriage, reproduction, and death" (2).
10. Braziel reads in this projection into a future of being married to a woman a transformation of the speaker into a man (22). That would indeed be the only way to maintain a heterosexual frame for the story, but nothing in the story suggests that the narrator changes gender. The use of the first person avoids the need for gendered pronouns, but the narrator has previous to this moment clearly identified herself as a girl and does not in any way change how she talks about herself or remark on any gender change. The narrator of "At Last," the next story in *At the Bottom of the River*, does shift between a daughter and a husband position in relation to a mother, remarking "sometimes I appeared as a man," but even this mutability is described not in the context of maintaining heterosexual coupling but rather in the context of shape-shifting Caribbean beings, for this

narrator continues, "Sometimes I appeared as a hoofed animal, stroking my own, shiny back" (17).

11. See also Covi, "Jamaica Kincaid's Prismatic Self"; Roni Natov; Niesen de Abruna.
12. Originally conceived in an eighteenth-century satire by John Arbuthnot, John Bull has come to personify England, and to represent "the typical Englishman," much like Uncle Sam in the United States. For a history of the figure of John Bull, see the article on "John Bull" in the *Encyclopaedia Britannica.*
13. The one difference between Kincaid's quotes and Kingsley's text is minimal: where the first quote in "Wingless" reads "Once upon a time there was a little chimney-sweep, whose name was Tom" (20), the first line of *The Water-babies* is "Once upon a time there was a little chimney-sweep, and his name was Tom" (5). Moira Ferguson finds a very different set of implications to the *Water-babies* reference, referring to the book as "Charles Kingsley's political allegory about nineteenth-century British industrial poverty and child abuse that fore-shadows everyday situations in twentieth-century England" (*Jamaica Kincaid*: 8). Ferguson's reading allows for an interesting analysis of Kincaid's story where "the narrator longs for the same drastic transformation experienced by the protago-nist, Tom, a psychologically and physically abused chimney sweep who becomes a water baby" (*Jamaica Kincaid*: 8). However, it involves ignoring the quite explicit racist and colonialist aspects of *The Water-babies*, and also the stories' position, within "Wingless" as part of the colonial curriculum.
14. Between being canon of Chester and being Canon of Westminster, Kingsley spent two years in the West Indies, which prompted the writing of *At Last: A Christmas in the West Indies* (1871).
15. For further discussion of the moral lessons of *The Water-babies*, see Charles Muller.
16. Arthur de Gobineau crystallizes many of these views in his four-volume *Essai sur l'inégalité des races humaines* (1853–1855), while Anténor Firmin's 1885 *De l'Égalité des races humaines* responds to the theories of de Gobineau and others like him. Lisa Wade gathers many of the most striking examples of eighteenth- and nineteenth-century racial theories. For more analyses of nineteenth-century racial discourses, see John Haller and Herbert Odom.
17. In an interview with Bill Moyers, Morrison explains, "The Master Narrative is whatever ideological script that is being imposed by the people in authority on everybody else."
18. Ferguson finds that the narrator's description of herself "swimming in a shaft of light, upside down" likens her to Tom swimming in the river after his transfor-mation into a water-baby. Ferguson takes this connection as one more piece of evidence for the similarity between Kincaid's narrator and Tom (*Jamaica Kincaid*: 8, 24). To support that analysis, we could also refer to Kincaid's narrator's descrip-tion of herself as "wingless," which is also one of the characteristics of Tom in his water-baby state (*The Water-babies*: 60–63). However, if this connection is a fac-tor, I would suggest that it demonstrates the important differences rather than the similarities between Kincaid's narrator and Tom, for Tom must spend the

entire fairy-tale learning to see himself clearly, and one of his many lessons is that he is not like the caddis that will transform into a winged dragonfly. While I agree with Ferguson that "Wingless" has extensive interrelations with *The Water-babies*, I would suggest that the connection between the two is, like that between so many Caribbean and European texts, cannibalistic.

19. Alison Donnell offers a similar remark about Kincaid's style, referring to her "devious simplicity and complex clarity" (123).
20. In this, I respectfully disagree with readings that unequivocally reduce "the woman I love" and the mother to one and the same person, as in Paravisini-Gebert, *Jamaica Kincaid*; Ferguson, *Jamaica Kincaid: Where Land Meets Body*; Diane Simmons, *Jamaica Kincaid*.
21. Allusions to boys and men include the figure of Tom and the "cruel and unloving master" to a dog that the narrator might become (24).
22. British poet and songwriter Thomas Haynes Bayly wrote "Gaily the Troubador Touched His Guitar" in the 1820s.
23. The narrator in *Mr Potter* explains:

> The open sky, stretching from the little village called English Harbour to way out beyond the horizon, was familiar to Nathaniel Potter, and this sky was a blue unimaginable to people who had never seen it before; the eminence that was the sun, traveling with such a vast distance, reaching the village of English Harbour as harshness of light and temperature, if you were overly familiar with it, or as a blessing of light and temperature, if you were not familiar with it at all. (37)

Chapter 5

1. My translation draws heavily on "Murder Inna Dancehalls." "Rude boy" originally referred to Jamaican gangsters, then to rebellious nationalist youth in the 1960s, often connected to nationalist ska music, and most recently taken up by dancehall singers to refer to themselves.
2. See, for example, Carolyn Cooper, Timothy Chin, Donna P. Hope, Peter Tatchell, Akim Ade Larcher, and Colin Robinson. It is certainly easy to find similar lyrics in other dancehall music, such as Beanie Man's "Damn," Bounty Killer's "Another Level," and Elephant Man's "A Nuh Fi Wi Fault" (addressed specifically to women with "When yuh hear a Sodomite get raped/But a fi wi fault/It's wrong/Two women gonna hock up inna bed/That's two Sodomites dat fi dead"). Carmen Gillespie makes a compelling argument for the influence of US music culture in and on similar songs, but still concedes that they reflect Caribbean perspective in the musical "call-and-response."
3. Articles 76 and 77 of Jamaica's Offences against the Person Act make "the abominable offense of buggery" illegal and punishable by up to ten years in prison, and article 79 states that

> Any male person who, in public or private, commits, or is a party to the commission of, or procures or attempts to procure the commission by any male person of, any act of gross indecency with another male person, shall be guilty of a misdemeanor, and being convicted thereof shall be liable at the discretion of the court to be imprisoned for a term not exceeding 2 years, with or without hard labour.

Although "gross indecency" is not defined in the law, it has been interpreted to include any kind of physical intimacy between consenting adults even in private. For more information, see J-FLAG, "Know Your Rights." Jamaica's legal position on homosexuality is not the most restrictive in the Caribbean. In Barbados and Guyana, sodomy is illegal and punishable by life in prison. In Trinidad and Tobago, the 1986 "Sexual Offenses Act," strengthened in 2000, makes both male and female homosexuality punishable by up to 25 years in prison, and the Immigration Act makes it illegal for homosexuals to enter the country. For analysis of the penal code debates in Trinidad and Tobago, see Yasmin Tambiah.

4. Human Rights Watch's 2004 "Hated to Death" provides extensive documentation; Amnesty International's " 'Battybwoys affi Dead': Action against Homophobia in Jamaica" concurs. These reports emphasize the violent crime against homosexuals, the frequency of extrajudicial police participation in those crimes, and the infrequency of investigation and prosecution in cases of reported anti-homosexual crime. Cecil Gutzmore offers important contextualization for this judgment:

> a certain clarity is required in characterizing and comparing Jamaica internationally in relation to homophobia. A difference between Jamaica and certainly the urban sector of metropolitan societies is undeniable and is largely explainable in terms of social change in the latter over recent decades. But neither in Jamaica nor in any other non-metropolitan society has a formal, systematic statistical study been conducted of the attacks and threats in all their variety such as might produce results constituting reliable evidence upon which to make well-founded comparison that might then provide a sound basis for declaring Jamaica the worst offender, or among the worst offenders, in this specific regard. (122)

5. "What Jamaica Wants," *Jamaica Gleaner News*, May 21, 2008.
6. Stressing the importance of Simpson's position on homosexuality, Warren Sibblies writes in a December 31, 2011, "Letter to the Editor" published in Jamaica's major newspaper *The Gleaner*, "The president of the People's National Party (PNP) recently said she would not exclude persons from her Cabinet on the basis of sexual orientation. Few seem to appreciate how profound the comment is. One newspaper sprang into attack mode with its bold headline, 'A idiot thing that'."

7. Dane Lewis, executive director of the Jamaican Forum for Lesbians, All-Sexuals, and Gays, reported in October 2012 that murders of gays were increasing, with at least nine already that year (Bowcott and Wolfe-Robinson).
8. Dancehall singers Elephant Man and Beenie Man, for example, associate "battymen" with "Miami men," "Arabians," and "Canadians" in hits such as "Ah Nuh Fi Wi Fault" (1998) and "Damm!" (1999). For scholarly examination of the persistent, if at times contradictory, links between homosexuality and "the West" throughout reggae and dancehall lyrics, see Hope, Cooper, Lewis and Carr, Thomas, and Patricia Saunders's "Is Not Everything Good to Eat Good to Talk." The role of the British group Outrage in the protest against "murder music" has served as a focal point for discussions about the place of Euro-American gay and lesbian organizations in regards to Jamaica and to Jamaicans labeled as homosexual. See, for example, Larcher and Robinson. The literature of J-FLAG touches on similar concerns in its explanation of its full name, Jamaican Forum for Lesbians, All-Sexuals, and Gays. Most explicitly, the "Definition of All-Sexuals" on the J-FLAG website from 1997 to 2008 read: " 'All-Sexual' is a term used in the Caribbean Forum for Lesbians, All-Sexuals & Gays (C-FLAG) network to indicate that it considers all-sexual behaviour to be part of a sexual continuum in which classifications such as 'gay', 'lesbian' and 'bisexual' often cannot be rigidly applied" (J-FLAG, "Definition of All-Sexuals"). The 2013 updated language is somewhat more subtle, but conveys similar attempt to define Caribbean terminology, identification, and activism that is distinct from Euro-American terminology, identification, and activism: "the term all-sexual was adopted in 1997 to reflect a continuum in sexual identity, which captures the consensual bisexual and transgender experiences of sexual minorities more so than any sexual activities or behaviours" (J-FLAG, "Meaning of Acronym J-FLAG").
9. See, for example, Donna P. Hope. The Jamaican Offences against the Person Act, derived from the British Offences against the Person Act of 1861, was established in 1864 when Jamaica was a British colony. The 1962 constitution of the newly independent Jamaica maintained the language of the act. Revisions to the act in 1969 maintained the language of the sections in question.
10. Cooper in her analysis of dancehall culture makes a similar claim: "Jamaicans are generally socialized to recognise the fact that antihomosexuality values are entirely compatible with knowing acceptance of homosexuals within the community. This is a fundamental paradox that illustrates the complexity of the ideological negotiations that are constantly made within this society" (162). Powell herself suggests that there may be another side to her depiction of Jamaican homophobia when in answers to a question about response to her second novel, *A Small Gathering of Bones*, she tells Faith Smith: "A few people thought I was portraying Jamaicans as incredibly homophobic" (328).
11. Often taught and maintained, as Althusser demonstrates in "Ideology and Ideological State Apparatuses," by family, school, church, and cultural institutions.
12. In this way, it might be helpful to pair *Me Dying Trial* with Magali García Ramis's *Felices días, tío Sergio*, where a young girl uses reflections on her uncle, who is

rumored to be gay, to understand her own desires and options. Lawrence La Fountain-Stokes's analysis of *Felices días* points to such an analysis.

13. Personal conversation.
14. In her review, Palmer Adisa writes, "In Jamaica, when people exclaim, 'See me dying trial', they are calling on a higher being to witness the trouble they have to bear" (322).
15. Even when she becomes afraid about the results of her affair, "Gwennie start up prayer meetings with God at night. And she would lie down there and ask Brother Jesus if him could please not let Walter find out, for only the Heavenly Father up above could help her if him ever know" (10).
16. Gutzmore finds in his research in Jamaica "the overt virulence of the homophobia at the expressive level within both secular and religious popular culture," although he also cites Bishop Blair in a 2003 televised sermon stating "Some of you think that homosexuality is a greater sin than malicekeeping. No way in the sight of God" (TVJ), March 3, 2003.
17. Patwa is the Jamaican vernacular. Although Powell writes in her own version of a Jamaican-inflected standard written English, the Jamaican inflections that she uses can best be understood through their Patwa meanings.
18. Various English translations of the Bible rely in widely divergent ways on the term "natural." While it never appears in Genesis 18–19, it often appears in other references to non-procreative sex (e.g., Jude 1:7; Romans 1:26; 1 Corinthians 6:9; Leviticus 18:23; 1 Timothy 1:10; 2 Kings 17:17). Sex acts between men are expressly prohibited in Jamaica in the Offences against the Person Act under a section entitled "Unnatural Offences and Acts of Gross Indecency."
19. Lewis and Carr survey historical material to come up with a similar argument about a policing of manliness being central to a policing of homosexuality in Jamaica.
20. After her brief affair with Luther, for example, Gwennie prays to Jesus that Walter not find it out (10). Of course, requesting personalized assistance from Jesus is a central tenet of many Church of God, Adventist, Pentecostal, and Baptist traditions, but it is my contention that Gwennie's particular request shows evidence that she understands personalized attention as potentially superseding or at least offering a particular understanding of scriptural commands such as not telling lies.
21. *The King James Bible*; Gwennie does not quote directly from any Bible.
22. Many other books of the Bible refer back to the destruction of Sodom and Gomorrah, suggesting that other places and people can and should be dealt with in like manner, making Sodom and Gomorrah even within the Bible as much a metaphoric as a literal reference.
23. Although since John 8:7 addresses judgments by humans and Genesis 18–19 addresses a judgment by God, the two are not contradictory, the potential for them to become conflated can be seen in the lyrics of Prodigal Son, another Jamaican dancehall singer, that use Luke 10:19 to confer on a human (in this case, Prodigal Son) the right and obligation to make and carry out judgments

and punishments against "b-men." For more sustained discussion of the ways in which dancehall lyrics and Jamaican Christian fundamentalism use and perhaps misuse human and divine judgments, see Gutzmore (126–128).

24. Comments made during a Writers Series reading and talk at Salem State College, December 2005.
25. To date, only Palmer Adisa's review focuses solely on *Me Dying Trial.* A similar perspective on Powell's work generally and on her other novels can be found in Timothy Chin ("The Novels of Patricia Powell"), Jason Frydman, and Tzarina Prater.
26. Thanks to the students in my Spring 2006 Contemporary American Literature course for pointing out the Family Tree and its failure to represent the important family configurations in *Me Dying Trial.* Further thanks to those students for asking Powell about her intentions with the family tree. Powell explained that she composed the family tree at the suggestion of a writing teacher, who thought it might help readers to sort out the characters and their relationships to one another. She had not thought of its other implications, she said, but remarked that at the time she was not even sure of the proper composition of a Family Tree.
27. Skip and Miss Elsie seem to have a similar family life, for MaDee is described as living "in Maroon Town calling distance from her oldest boy, Skip, his wife Miss Elsie, and them six out of thirteen children" (43), but those children are absent from the opening family tree. It might be argued that Old Tom and Ma Mait's family also lives out the idea, but MaDee rather than Ma Mait is described in the novel as "Clara and Cora's mother" (43). The most heteronormative explanation is that although her name on the Family Tree is Ma Mait, she actually goes by MaDee. However, another explanation equally supported by other uses of "Ma" in front of a name to depict nonbiological mothering (Peppy refers to Cora as MaCora) is that Clara, Cora, and Skip count MaDee as their mother because she is the one who raised them while the family tree lists a biological mother who did not play a role in their lives. It is also possible that the difference results from some kind of an error, where Powell changed the character's name in the text but not in the family tree, but even this explanation points once more to the strange place—at once authorizing and important but also irrelevant—of such normative structures as the family tree.
28. This tension is plotted through Gwennie's escape to school followed by her return to Walter and then her escape to the United States followed by her relationship with Clive. The body of scholarship that investigates how the very women who are caught by patriarchal norms are those who most directly perpetuate them is relevant here.
29. When anthropologist Edith Clark studied Jamaican families, she found a predominance of households like Cora's. In *My Mother Who Fathered Me,* Clarke explains that such households are based on affective and economic relationships between women who share household and child-rearing duties, and occupy both traditionally male and traditionally female positions in providing for and maintaining the family. These arrangements grow out of the frequent absence of men,

due to high mortality rates, economic conditions that force them to look for work in big cities often in the United States or Canada, and the common practice of outside children.

30. Glissant, albeit somewhat problematically, draws the connection when he suggests that "sexual indifference" in Caribbean women, resulting from the history of brutal rape of so many women during the Middle Passage in conjunction with a "short-circuit between an appetite for orgasm and the profit of pleasure," which slavery induced in Caribbean men, has made it so that Caribbean women "developed attitudes of responsibility that allow them what we still call deviancies or singularities (homosexuality, status as single women, communitary attitudes)" (511–512).
31. Most of the historical information about Nanny comes from oral sources. While specific accounts very significantly, most concur that Nanny was born in West Africa and brought to Jamaica as a slave in the early eighteenth century. She escaped from slavery along with a group of men often referred to as her brothers, and founded a maroon encampment. Living in remote areas difficult for colonists to access, the maroons survived on their knowledge of the land, the cooperation of urban slaves and free blacks with whom they traded, and supplies they gathered in plantation raids. They supposedly helped many other slaves to escape. In order to better survive, Nanny and the men set up separate maroon towns around the island, with Nanny and Qua controlling the Blue Mountains (a large mountain range just behind the capital port city of Kingston). Nanny was reported killed in 1733 by Captain Sambo (William Cuffee). She was named a national heroine in 1975 and her face is on the 500 Jamaican dollar bill. For more detailed accounts of the Nanny legends and accompanying historical material, see Madeleine Burnside and Rosemarie Robotham, Mavis Campbell, and Karla Gottlieb.
32. For more detailed discussions of Nanny and female independence in Cliff, see Fiona Barnes and Griffin.
33. In her introduction to the second edition of *Me Dying Trial*, Edwidge Danticat extends Cora into a Caribbean institution, asking: "what would many of us be without our Aunt Coras, who lovingly take us in when our mothers must surrender us for a while?" (x).
34. A by-product of cane sugar, rum is the local and national drink in Jamaica as well as much of the Caribbean.
35. The limitations, in Jamaica, on *any* public representations of sex and sexuality, also minimize the differences between the circulation as tacit knowledge of the details of what women or men in same-sex relationships do and the circulation of details of what women or men in opposite-sex relationships do. Lewis and Carr discuss in detail the limitations on public representations of sex and sexuality in Jamaica.
36. In "The Novels of Patricia Powell," Timothy Chin makes a compelling argument for understanding Powell's writings in the context of the Caribbean diaspora, but this diasporic context maintains Jamaica as the focal point even as the characters move from it.

37. Donna P. Hope makes a similar argument specifically about Jamaica, writing "My research shows that this rise in anti-homosexual dancehall lyrics is a direct result of the progressive unmasking of (male) homosexuality since the late 1990s" ("Clash").

Chapter 6

1. For discussions of Ferré's feminism and the ways she connects it to Puerto Rican independence, see Helene Carol Weldt-Basson.
2. The spatial metaphor of eccentric neighborhoods extends what Jessica Magnani calls the "colonial ambivalence" in the metaphor of marriage that Ferré employs to articulate Puerto Rico's national status in other novels. For analyses of marriage as a metaphor for statehood in *House on the Lagoon*, see Elena Machado Sáez, Irene Wirshing, and Jessica Magnani.
3. My formulation of these questions as well as my attempts to answer them are informed by the many theorists who have asked them, or versions of them, in other contexts. Adrienne Rich, Audre Lorde, Judith Butler, María Lugones, Susan Stryker, and M. Jacqui Alexander are among the most influential ones here.
4. The possibility, or impossibility, of writing a national romance without a nation leads to differing opinions about whether there exist Puerto Rican foundational fictions, the place of failure in the national romance, and the definition of nation. Sommer, finding that the most likely candidate, Eugenio María de Hostos's *The Peregrinations of Bayoán* (1863), does not qualify as a national romance in large part because "its contradictory affairs with politics and passion founder in the rather un-American competition between erotics and duty" (50), does not analyze a Puerto Rican national novel. To fit Puerto Rican foundational fictions, Zilkia Janer develops a special subcategory of "impossible romances." Dara Goldman makes a compelling argument for reading Hostos's novel, and also Salvador Brau's, as articulating a particularly Caribbean version of the national novel.
5. Sommer recognizes this when she writes, "a variety of novel national ideals are all ostensibly grounded in 'natural' heterosexual love and in the marriage that provide a figure for apparently nonviolent consolidation during internecine conflicts at midecentury" (6). Their re-inscription of colonial gender and sexuality is what makes M. Jacqui Alexander refer to many independent Caribbean nations as neocolonial (64).
6. The most recent plebiscite took place in 2012. The plebiscite contained two questions: the first asked if voters wanted to maintain Puerto Rico's current status as a Commonwealth; the second listed three options for change: statehood, independence, or "sovereign free association." Fifty-four percent voted "No" on the first question. Of those who answered on the second question, 61 percent chose statehood, 33 percent chose free association, and 5 percent chose independence, but 26 percent of the ballots either left the second question blank or wrote in statements of protest. For analysis of the results, see Charles Venator-Santiago.

Ferré was too ill in late 2012 to participate in public activities. In response to both the plebiscite and to complaints about the process, the Obama administration included $2.5 million dollars for a federally funded plebiscite, to be preceded by massive voter education, in its 2014 budget. In May 2013, the "Puerto Rican Status Resolution" bill was proposed to the US House of Representatives, inviting Puerto Rico to become a state; if passed, the bill will allow for a binding Puerto Rican vote on statehood.

7. Ferré's comparison of the bilingualism of a Puerto Rican state to the coexistence of two languages in Hawaii reveals some potential flaws in her argument. Hawaii has two official languages; however, according to the 2000 census, almost 75 percent of Hawaiians speak only English at home. Furthermore, it is only with great struggle that, in limited forms and with still inconclusive results, Hawaiian-language instruction is allowed in Hawaiian public schools, and no Hawaiian-language newspapers have been in print since 1948. For more detailed discussion of bilingualism in Hawaii, see William Wilson.
8. Perhaps most explicitly, linguistic tensions played out in the first half-decade of Puerto Rico's association with the United States in regulations about language of instruction. In 1901, a Department of Instruction of Puerto Rico was created under the control of the US Federal government, and English was imposed as the language of instruction in Puerto Rico. In 1915, the commissioner of education allowed that Spanish be the language of instruction through grade 4, and instruction be in both Spanish and English in grades 5–7 and in English only after that. In 1934, Spanish was reinstated as the language of instruction throughout all public elementary schools, with English as a second language starting in first grade. Two years later, however, following statements by President Roosevelt, the commissioner of education reverted to a graduated system with Spanish as the language of instruction in the first and second grades, and then English-language instruction gradually increasing, until high school where the only language of instruction was English. In 1949, Spanish was reinstated as the "vehicle of instruction" in all public primary and secondary education. In June 2012, the Puerto Rican secretary of education Edwin Moreno announced an initiative to make English the language of instruction in all Puerto Rican schools by 2022; the policy faces opposition from the Puerto Rican Teachers Association. For a detailed discussion of the political, social, and pedagogical debates surrounding the history of the language of instruction in Puerto Rico, see Pablo Navarro-Rivera. A recent iteration of the combined debate about Puerto Rico's political and linguistic status can be found in discussions of the 2010 Puerto Rico Democracy Act. See, for example, Katherine Skiba's coverage of US representative Gutiérrez' position on the bill.
9. The New Progressive Party (PNP) and the Popular Democratic Party (PPD) both call for bilingualism in Puerto Rico, but in ways that favor English and Spanish, respectively. The difference in positions can be seen not only in their different views on language of instruction but also in positions on the official language of Puerto Rico. In 1991, PNP governor Rafael Hernández Colón declared

English as the official language of Puerto Rico but did not change the language of instruction in schools. In 1992, Hernández Colón did not run for reelection and his party did not with the governorship. In 1993, PPD governor Pedro Rosselló's first official act was to make both Spanish and English official languages of Puerto Rico.

10. Gayatri Spivak's consideration, for example, of translation as a surrendering to the source text and to its use of language suggests a rather different distribution of power than Venuti's description of translation as domestication.
11. Foreign and domestic are constituted by the languages, not the interpreters, so that "the fact that the author is the interpreter doesn't make the interpretation unmediated by target-language values" (6).
12. Ferré published her first work of fiction, the short-story collection *Papeles de Pandora*, in Spanish in 1976. She began writing English versions of her work in 1989 with *Sweet Diamond Dust* (from her 1985 *Maldito Amor*). In 1995, Ferré published her first book written first in English, *The House on the Lagoon*, which she wrote in Spanish in 1996. *Eccentric Neighborhoods/Vecindarios excéntricos* was published in English in 1998 and in Spanish in 1999. The first Spanish edition of *Vecindarios excéntricos*, from Planeta in 1998, carries the notes "*traducido por la escritora*" ("translated by the author") and the 1999 Vintage Español edition's copyright page reads "*este libro ha sido publicado en ingles*" ("this book has been published in English"). In 1997, Ferré published the novel *Lazos de Sangre* and a children's book, *La sapita sabia y otros cuentos*, in Spanish; they have yet to be translated into English. In 2001, she published another novel, *Flight of the Swan*, in English and a collection of essays, *A la sombra de tu nombre*, in Spanish. Her Spanish version of *Flight of the Swan*, *Vuelo del Cisne*, was published in 2002. Also in 2002 Ferré published her only traditionally bilingual book, the poetry collection *Duelo de language/Language Duel*. For the next decade, she published essays and poetry in Spanish. In 2011, *Memoria* came out in Spanish; in 2012, it came out in English as *Memory*. For further discussions of Ferré's language choices, see Charles Hanley, Cristina Garrigós, and Irma López.
13. This scenario plays out in *Eccentric Neighborhoods* as well in the family of Elvira's maternal uncle Roque. When he dies, the story goes, Titiba Menéndez comes to Roque's wife Clotilde with a proposition: "Titiba asked her if they could share Roque Vernet in death as they had in life" (292). Rather than jealousy, Clotilde experiences solidarity: "She was touched by the fact that Roque, a man of simple tastes, had chosen Titiba, a woman of humble origins like herself, as his paramour" (292). Clotilde allies herself with Titiba against the patriarchal Catholicism of Roque's family. With Titiba at her side, Clotilde can insist on Roque's cremation and reassert the primacy of the matronym: "Tía Clotilde ordered two adjacent chapels at Portacoeli to be filled with flowers—one for the Vernet and Rosales families and one for the Menéndez family" (293). Clotilde and Titiba's families, as much as either woman and Roque, will be next to one another for the passage into what might be an afterlife of complementary love between women. No longer locked into heteronormativity by religious or legal

apparatuses, no longer oppressed by the decorum to which Roque and they had acceded, the two women stand at the threshold of unbounded possibility. Theirs no longer needs to be a family mappable onto the erect tree at the front of the novel. However, Roque remains the focal point of their connection, and the structure of complementarity that unites them is still binary. As fits the pattern, Clotilde is white, dour, and repressed, while Titiba is Taína, happy, and voraciously sexual. At the ceremony they will sit not together but "adjacent," under separate names. In the English, in one chapel we find "Vernet and Rosales" and in the other "Menéndez." In the Spanish, while both families are described as Roque's, the patronym is attached to neither chapel. In both cases, their particular resistance to the patronym underlines the women's different nomenclatures as much as it does their similar position outside of the patronym. And although Clotilde describes herself as from a humble family, her family name is a "rich" one, while Titiba's is so common that it is even interchangeable in the Spanish version, which alternately calls her Titiba Menéndez, Titiba Menénez, and Titiba Martínez (382–383). That the two women unite in spite of these differences suggests the strength of their connection and its potential to disrupt structures such as jealousy and competition. But the promise of equality is rendered suspect by the lines of division, and the possibility of a union where the parallel lines lay right on top of each other is held at bay or redirected.

14. Treacy argues that in many Latin American texts "a female narrator images a man's desire in order to permit her own desire for another woman" (204), supporting a reading of these relationships as themselves potentially destabilizing the hetero–homo binary.
15. In this I differ from Fernández-Olmos, who finds that the "possibility of recognition and communication and of going beyond a social system which prevents women from a true realization of their potential, and from each other" is realized structurally in Ferré's works. The possibility is most promising in the stories in *Papeles de Pandora,* which Fernández-Olmos analyzes, but even there I find it to be only a promise, while in subsequent works it becomes an almost formulaic aside that haunts but does not structure women's relationships with one another.
16. Biasetti makes a similar claim that in *La casa de la laguna* Ferré renders central the marginal. Benítez-Rojo's passing reference to the disappearance of the center in the Caribbean machine,

> the notion of polyrhythm (rhythms cut through by other rhythms, which are cut by still other rhythms)—if it takes us to the point at which the central rhythm is displaced by other rhythms in such a way as to make it fix a center no longer, then to transcend into a state of flux—may fairly define the type of performance that characterizes the Caribbean cultural machine, (18)

offers another view of the paradox of center and eccentric in and as the Caribbean. Fátima Rodríguez and Laura Eugenia Tudoras argue that eccentric in *Vecindarios excéntricos* refers to the United States and Europe while Puerto Rico is the center defined by these ec-centers. Eccentricity in the novel is certainly polyvalent, and the United States and Europe help to position Puerto Rico and the characters, but I maintain that Ferré focuses on eccentricity in, perhaps even as, Puerto Rico.

17. Peter Brooks's *Reading for the Plot* unveils a profoundly ideological, normal, and universal plot structure that moves inexorably from a beginning of (unsatisfied) desire though a middle period of searching to a reproductive end in (heterosexual) marriage, childbirth, and death. Any potential undoing of the narrative (of) progression in its detours and backtracking is always already recuperated in the final denouement that not only straightens out but also explains as necessary any kinks in the scheme.
18. Clarissa's husband never has an affair. Elvira learns of her paternal aunt Clotilde's arrangement with Titiba from her paternal aunt Celia and there is no mention of Clarissa having any knowledge of it.

Conclusion

1. As I want to claim a certain womanly specificity to the structure of the mangrove, I am reminded of playful warnings that Barbara Johnson often gave me, in the early stages of this project, about finding what I am looking for, that my finding of desire between women everywhere has as much to do with my desire as with anything in the texts. And I have often wondered about making some kind of exculpatory self-positioning statement that speaks to that as well as to other aspects of where I am looking from and how that affects what I look for and how I look for it. That it must be in part because I am always in a sense looking for desire between women that I see it in these texts is the answer as well as the problem: we need to read from and for many perspectives and biased views, views from various outsides, see things that other views miss or take so fully for granted that they do not bother mentioning them.
2. For detailed discussion of the population of the mangle, see Hogarth (especially 60–100).
3. Evelyn O'Callaghan analyzes the sexual freedom and the limitations that migration offers Powell's women characters in "Caribbean Migrations."
4. Valiela, Bowen, and York find a 3.6 percent annual rate of decline in Caribbean mangrove population in 2001. Ellison and Farnsworth's 1996 study finds the rate of decline in the 1980s to be about 1 percent. It is unclear whether the rise to an over 3 percent rate of loss is due to the time difference or to different research methods and findings. For more recent discussion of the decline in mangroves, see Polidoro et al.
5. Hogarth refers repeatedly to the "unpromising conditions" to which the mangrove has adapted (1, 10, 19).

Bibliography

Accilien, Cecile. *Rethinking Marriage in Francophone African and Caribbean Literatures*. Lanham, MD: Lexington Books, 2008.

Achille, Louis T. "Carnival in Martinique." *Phylon* 4.2 (1943): 121–129.

Agard-Jones, Vanessa. "Le Jeu de Qui? Sexual Politics in the French Caribbean." In *Sex and the Citizen: Interrogating the Caribbean*. Ed. Faith Smith. Charlottesville: University of Virginia Press, 2011. 181–198.

Alexander, M. Jacqui. "Not Just (Any) Body Can Be a Citizen: The Politics of Law, Sexuality and Postcoloniality in Trinidad and Tobago and the Bahamas." *Feminist Review* 48 (Autumn 1994): 5–23.

——. "Erotic Autonomy as a Politics of Decolonization." In *Feminist Genealogies, Colonial Legacies, Democratic Futures*. Ed. M. Jacqui Alexander and Chandra Talpade Mohanty. New York and London: Routledge, 1997. 63–100.

Alleyne-Dettmers, Patricia Tamara. "Black Kings: Aesthetic Represenation in Carnival in Trinidad and London." *Black Music Research Journal* 22.2 (2002): 241–258.

Althusser, Louis. "Ideology and Ideological State Apparatuses." In *Lenin and Philosophy and Other Essays*. Ed. Louis Althusser. New York: Monthly Review Press, 1972. 85–126.

Amnesty International. "'Battybwoys affi Dead:' Action against Homophobia in Jamaica." *Amnestyusa.org*. Web. January 19, 2006.

Anderson Imbert, Enrique. "La prosa poética de José Martí. A propósito de *Amistad funesta*." In *Crítica Interna*. Ed. Enrique Anderson Imbert. Madrid: Taurus, 1961. 93–139.

Andrade, Susan Z. "The Nigger of the Narcissist: History, Sexuality and Intertextuality in Maryse Condé's *Heremakhonon*." *Callaloo* 16.1 (1993): 213–226.

Anzaldúa, Gloria. *Borderlands/La Frontera*. San Francisco: Aunt Lute Books, 1987.

Arnold, A. James. "The Novelist As Critic." *World Literature Today* 67.4 (1993): 711–716.

——. "The Gendering of Créolité; the Erotics of Colonialism." In *Penser la créolité*. Ed. Maryse Condé and Madeleine Cottenet-Hage. Paris: Karthala, 1995. 221–240.

de Baralt, Blanca Zacharie. *El Martí que yo conocí*. Havana: Editorial Trópico, 1945.

Barnes, Fiona. "Resisting Cultural Cannibalism: Oppositional Narratives in Michelle Cliff's *No Telephone to Heaven*." *Journal of the Midwestern Modern Language Association* 25.1 (1992): 23–31.

Barnes, Natasha. *Cultural Conundrums: Gender, Race, Nation, and the Making of Caribbean Cultural Politics*. Ann Arbor: University of Michigan Press, 2006.

Barnes, Paula C. "Meditations on Her/Story. Maryse Condé's *I, Tituba, Black Witch of Salem* and the Slave Narrative Tradition." In *Arms Akimbo: Africana Women in Contemporary Literature*. Ed. Janice Lee Liddell and Yakini Belinda Kemp. Gainesville: University Press of Florida, 1999. 193–204.

Barquet, Jesús. "Revelación y enmascarameinto de la personalidad de José Martí en *Amistad funesta*." In *La Chispa '83: Selected Proceedings*. Ed. Gilbert Paolini. New Orleans: Tulane University, 1983, 35–43.

Barthes, Roland. *The Pleasure of the Text*. Trans. Richard Miller. New York: Hill and Wang, 1975.

Bastian, Misty L. "Nwaanyi Mara Mma: Mami Wata, the More Than Beautiful Woman." Web. January 31, 2013.

Beauregard, Paulette Silva. "Feminización del héroe moderno y la novela en Lucía Jerez y El hombre de hierro." *Revista de critica literaria latinoamericana* 26.52 (2000): 135–151.

Beckles, Hilary McD. "The Literate Few: An Historical Sketch of the Slavery Origins of Black Elites in the English West Indies." *Caribbean Journal of Education* 11.1 (1984): 19–35.

Benítez-Rojo, Antonio. *The Repeating Island: The Caribbean and the Postmodern Perspective, Second Edition*. Trans. James E. Maraniss. Durham, NC: Duke University Press, 1996.

——. "A View from the Mangrove." In *A View from the Mangrove*. Antonio Benítez-Rojo. Trans. James E. Maraniss. Boston: University of Massachusetts Press, 2000: 170–189.

Bernabé, Jean, Patrick Chamoiseau, and Raphaël Confiant. *Éloge de la créolité/In Praise of Creoleness*, bilingual edition. Trans. M. B. Taleb-Khyr. Paris: Gallimard, 1993.

Bernard, Ian. *Queer Race*. New York: Peter Lang, 2004.

Bernard, Louise. "Countermemory and Return: Reclamation of the (Postmodern) Self in Jamaica Kincaid's *The Autobiography of My Mother* and *My Brother*." *Modern Fiction Studies* 48.1 (2002): 113–138.

Bernstein, Lisa. "Écrivaine, sorcière, nomade: la conscience critique dans *Moi, Tituba, sorcière . . . Noire de Salem* de Maryse Condé." *Études Francophones* 13.1 (1998 Spring): 119–134.

Berrian, Brenda F. "Snapshots of Childhood Life in Jamaica Kincaid's Fiction." In *Arms Akimbo: Africana Women in Contemporary Literature*. Ed. Janice Lee Liddell and Yakini Belinda Kemp. Gainesville: University Press of Florida, 1999. 103–116.

Besson, Gérard. "Ti Jeanne's Last Laundry." *The Caribbean History Archives*. Paria Publishing, 2011. Web. January 31, 2013.

Bhabha, Homi. "Of Mimicry and Man." In *The Location of Culture*. Homi Bhabha. London: Routledge, 2004, 121–131.

Biasetti, Giada. "El poder subversivo de La casa de la laguna y La niña blanca y los pájaros sin pies: La centralización de la periferia." *Hispania* 94.1 (March 2011): 35–49.

Blau DuPlessis, Rachel. *Writing beyond the Ending*. Bloomington: Indiana University Press, 1985.

Bost, Suzanne. "Transgressing Borders: Puerto Rican and Latina *Mestizaje*." *MELUS* 25.2 (Summer 2000): 187–211.

Bowcott, Owen and Maya Wolfe-Robinson. "Gay Jamaicans Launch Legal Action over Island's Homophobic Laws." *Guardian*. October 26, 2012. Web. January 31, 2013.

Boyce Davies, Carole. *Black Women, Writing and Identity: Migrations of the Subject*. London and New York: Routledge, 1994.

Brathwaite, Edward Kamau. "History of the Voice." In *Roots*. Edward Kamau Braithwaite. Ann Arbor: University of Michigan Press, 1993. 259–304.

Braziel, Jana Evans. *Caribbean Genesis: Jamaica Kincaid and the Writing of New Worlds*. Albany, NY: SUNY Press, 2009.

Brereton, Bridget. "Naipaul's Sense of History." *Anthurium* 5.2 (Fall 2007). Web. January 31, 2013.

Brezlaw, Elaine G. *Tituba, Reluctant Witch of Salem Village: Devilish Indians and Puritan Fantasies*. New York: NYU Press, 1997.

Brooks, Peter F. *Reading for the Plot: Design and Intention in Narrative*. Cambridge, MA: Harvard University Press, 1984.

Bryce, Jane. "A World of Love: Reformulating the Legend of Love." *Caribbean Studies* 27.3/4 (1994): 346–366.

Burnside, Madeleine, and Rosemarie Robotham. *Spirits of the Passage: The Transatlantic Slave Trade in the Seventeenth Century*. New York: Simon and Schuster, 1997.

Byas, Vincent W. "Whither Martinique?" *Phylon* 3.3 (1942): 277–283.

Byrne, K. B. Conal. "Under English, Obeah English: Jamaica Kincaid's New Language." *CLA Journal* 43.3 (2000): 276–298.

Calinescu, Matei. *Five Faces of Modernity*. Durham, NC: Duke University Press, 1987.

Campbell, Mavis C. *The Maroons of Jamaica, 1665–1796*. Trenton, NJ: Africa World Press, 1990.

Campos, Jorge. "José Martí y su novela 'Lucía Jerez'." *Insula* 24.275–276 (1969): 11.

Capécia, Mayotte. *Je suis martiniquaise*. Paris: Corrêa, 1948.

——. *I Am a Martinican Woman & The White Negress*. Trans. Beatrice Stith Clark. Pueblo, CO: Passeggiata Press, 1997.

Castle, Terry. *The Apparitional Lesbian*. New York: Columbia University Press, 1993.

Césaire, Aimé. *Return to My Native Land*. Trans. John Berger and Anna Bostock. London: Penguin Books, 1969.

——. *Discourse on Colonialism*. Trans. Joan Pinkham. New York: Monthly Review Press, 2001.

Chamoiseau, Patrick. "Reflections on Maryse Condée's *Traversée de la Mangrove*." Trans. Kathleen M. Balutansky. *Callaloo* 14.2 (Spring 1991): 389–395.

Chevalier, Jean and Alain Gheerbrant. *The Penguin Dictionary of Symbols.* Trans. John Buchanan-Brown. London: Penguin, 1996.

Chin, Timothy S. " 'Bullers' and 'Battymen': Contesting Homophobia in Black Popular Culture and Contemporary Caribbean Literature." *Callaloo* 20.1 (1997): 127–141.

——. "The Novels of Patricia Powell: Negotiating Gender and Sexuality across the Disjunctures of the Caribbean Diaspora." *Callaloo* 30.2 (2007): 533–545.

Christian, Barbara. "Ritualistic Process and the Structure of Paule Marshall's *Praisesong for a Widow.*" *Callaloo* 18 (Spring–Summer 1983): 74–84.

Clarke, Edith. *My Mother Who Fathered Me.* London: George Allen & Unwin, 1957.

"Le Code Noire." *Les 60 Articles du Code Noire.* Liceo di Locarno: Biologia, Presentazione della Martinica. May 2007. Web. August 15, 2008.

Columbus, Christopher. *The Four Voyages of Christopher Columbus.* Trans. J. M. Cohen. New York: Penguin, 1969.

Coisneau, Diane. "Autobiography: Innocent Pose or Naturalistic Lie? Jamaica Kincaid's *Annie John.*" In *Letters and Labyrinths: Women Writing/Cultural Codes.* Diane Coisneau. Newark: University of Delaware Press; London: Associated University Presses, 1997. 118–127.

Condé, Maryse. *Parole des femmes.* Paris: Éditions L'Harmattan, 1979.

——. *Une saison à Rihata.* Paris: Robert Laffont, 1981.

——. "L'Afrique, un continent difficile. Entretien avec Maryse Condé." *Notre librairie* 74 (1984): 21–25. By Marie-Clotilde Jacquey and Monique Hugon.

——. *Moi, Tituba sorcière . . . Noire de Salem.* Paris: Mercure de France, 1986.

——. *La vie scélérate.* Paris: Éditions Seghers, 1987.

——. *En attendant le bonheur (Hérémakhonon).* Paris: Seghers, 1988.

——. " 'Je me suis réconciliée avec mon île,' Une interview de Maryse Condé." *Callaloo* 12.1 (1988): 86–133. By VèVè A. Clark.

——. *Traversée de la mangrove.* Paris: Mercure de France, 1989.

——. *Les derniers rois mages.* Paris: Mercure de France, 1992.

——. *I, Tituba, Black Witch of Salem.* Trans. Richard Philcox. Charlottesville: University of Virginia Press, 1992.

——. *Tree of Life.* Trans. Victoria Reiter. New York: Ballantine Books (Random House), 1992.

——. *La colonie du nouveau monde.* Paris: Robert Laffont, 1993.

——. *Entretiens avec Maryse Condé.* Paris: Editions Karthala, 1993. By Françoise Pfaff.

——. "Order, Disorder, Freedom and the West Indian Writer." *Yale French Studies* 83.2 (1993): 121–135.

——. *I, Tituba, Black Witch of Salem.* Trans. Richard Philcox. New York: Ballantine Books, 1994.

——. *Crossing the Mangrove.* Trans. Richard Philcox. New York: Anchor Books, 1995.

——. *La migration des cœurs.* Paris: Robert Laffont, 1995.

——. *Moi, Tituba sorcière . . . Noire de Salem.* Laval, QC: Éditions Beauchemin Itée, 1995.

——. *Moi, Tituba sorcière . . . Noire de Salem.* Paris: Mercure de France/Folio, 1996.
——. *Desirada.* Paris: Robert Laffont, 1997.
——. "Entretien avec Maryse Condé: de l'identité culturelle." *French Review* 77.6 (1999): 1091–1098. By Marie-Agnès Sourieau.
——. Interview with Rebecca Wolff. *Bomb* 68 (1999): 74–80.
——. *I, Tituba, Black Witch of Salem.* Trans. Richard Philcox. London: Faber and Faber Limited, 2000.
——. "Maryse Condé: Grande Dame of Caribbean Literature." *Unesco Courier* 11 (2000): 46–51. By Elizabeth Nunez.
——. *La belle Créole.* Paris: Mercure de France, 2001.
——. *Histoire de la femme cannibale.* Paris: Mercure de France, 2003.
Condé, Maryse and Jean Du Boisberranger. *Guadeloupe.* Paris: Richer/Hoa-Qui, 1998.
Cook, Mercer. "Review." *Journal of Negro History* 34.3 (1949): 369–371.
Cooper, Carolyn. " 'Lyrical Gun': Metaphor and Roleplay in Jamaican Dancehall Culture." *Massachusetts Review* 35.3/4 (1994): 429–477.
——. *Soundclash: Jamaican Dancehall Culture at Large.* New York: Palgrave Macmillan, 2004.
Covi, Giovanna. "Jamaica Kincaid's Political Place: A Review Essay." *Caribana* 1 (1990): 93–103.
——. "Jamaica Kincaid's Prismatic Self and the Decolonialisation of Language and Thought." In *Framing the Word: Gender and Genre in Caribbean Women's Writing.* Ed. Joan Anim-Addo. London: Whiting and Birch, 1996. 37–67.
——. "Jamaica Kincaid and the Resistance to Canons." In *Jamaica Kincaid.* Ed. Harold Bloom. Philadelphia: Chelsea House Publishers, 1998. 3–12.
Danahy, Michael. *The Feminization of the Novel.* Gainesville: University of Florida Press, 1991.
Danticat, Edwidge. "Introduction." In *Me Dying Trial.* Patricia Powell. Boston: Beacon Press, 2003. ix–x.
deCaires Narain, Denise. "Naming Same-sex Desire in Caribbean Women's Texts: Toward a Creolizing Hermeneutics." *Contemporary Women's Writing* 6.3 (November 2012): 194–212.
Decena, Carlos Ulises. "Tacit Subjects." *GLQ* 14.2–3 (2008): 339–359.
Deleuze, Gilles and Felix Guattari. *A Thousand Plateaus: Capitalism and Schizophrenia.* Trans. Brian Massumi. Minneapolis: University of Minnesota Press, 1987.
Donnell, Alison. "Living and Loving: Emancipating the Caribbean Queer Citizen in Shani Mootoo's *Cereus Blooms at Night.*" In *Sex and the Citizen: Interrogating the Caribbean.* Ed. Faith Smith. Charlottesville: University of Virginia Press, 2011. 168–180.
——. "New Meetings of Place and the Possible in Shani Mootoo's *Valmiki's Daughter.*" *Contemporary Women's Writing* 6.3 (November 2012): 213–232.
Dornan, Inge. "A War of Words: Slave Women's Opposition to the Atlantic Slave Trade." *Symposium: The Transatlantic Slave Trade and Plantation Slavery in the Americas, Exploring Scottish Connections.* University of Glasgow, March 2010.

Drewal, Henry John. "Performing the Other: Mami Wata Worship in Africa." *TDR* 32.2 (1998): 160–185.

DuBois, W. E. B. *The Souls of Black Folk*. New York: Viking Press, 1986.

Duffey, Carolyn. "Tituba and Hester in the Intertextual Jail Cell: New World Feminisms in Maryse Condé's *Moi, Tituba sorcière... Noire de Salem*." *Women in French Studies* 4 (1996): 100–110.

Duffus, Cheryl. "When One Drop Isn't Enough: War As a Crucible of Racial Identity in the Novels of Mayotte Capécia." *Callaloo* 28.4 (2005): 1091–1102.

Dukats, Mara L. "The Hybrid Terrain of Literary Imagination: Maryse Condé's Black Witch of Salem, Nathaniel Hawthorne's Hester Prynne, and Aimé Césaire's Heroic Poetic Voice." *College Literature* 22.1 (1995): 51–61.

Dunning, Stefanie. *Queer in Black and White: Interraciality, Same Sex Desire, and Contemporary African American Culture*. Bloomington: Indiana University Press, 2009.

Dutton, Wendy. "Merge and Separate: Jamaica Kincaid's Fiction." *World Literature Today* 63.3 (1989): 406–410.

Ellison, Aaron and Elizabeth Farnsworth. "Anthropogenic Disturbance of Caribbean Mangrove Ecosystems: Past Impact, Current Trends, and Future Predictions." *Biotropica* 28.4a (1996): 549–565.

Eng, David, Ed. *Q&A*. Philadelphia: Temple University Press, 1998.

Ette, Ottmar. "Apuntes para una orestiada americana. Situación en el exilio y búsqueda de identidad en José Martí 1875–1878." *Revista de Crítical Literaria Latinoamericana* 12.24 (1986): 137–146.

Fanon, Frantz. *Black Skin, White Masks*. Trans. Richard Philcox. New York: Grove Press, 2008.

Felski, Rita. *The Gender of Modernity*. Cambridge, MA: Harvard University Press, 1995.

Ferguson, Moira. *Colonialism and Gender Relations from Mary Wollstonecraft to Jamaica Kincaid: East Caribbean Connections*. New York: Columbia University Press, 1993.

——. *Jamaica Kincaid: Where the Land Meets the Body*. Charlottesville and London: University of Virginia Press, 1994.

Ferguson, Roderick. *Aberrations in Black: Toward a Queer of Color Critique*. Minneapolis: University of Minnesota Press, 2004.

Fernández Olmos, Margarite. "Luis Rafael Sánchez and Rosario Ferré: Sexual Politics and Contemporary Puerto Rican Narrative." *Hispania* 70.1 (March 1987): 40–46.

Fernández Olmos, Margarite, Joseph Murphy, and Lizabeth Paravisini-Gebert. *Creole Religions of the Caribbean*. New York: NYU Press, 2003.

Fernandez Retamar, Roberto. *Introducción a José Martí*. Havana: Centro de estudios Martianos, 1978.

Fernández-Rubio, Francisco. "Importancia de *Amistad funesta* como reflejo de las inquietudes sociales de Martí." *Anuario Martiano* 5 (1974): 113–130.

Ferré, Rosario. *Papeles de Pandora*. Mexico City: Joaquín Mortiz, 1976.

——. *Maldito amor*. Mexico City: Joaquín Mortiz, 1986.

——. *The Youngest Doll.* Lincoln: University of Nebraska Press, 1991.
——. *Sweet Diamond Dust.* New York: Plume, 1996.
——. *La casa de la laguna.* New York: Vintage Books, 1997.
——. *Eccentric Neighborhoods.* New York: Farrar, Straus and Giroux, 1998.
——. "Puerto Rico, U.S.A." *New York Times.* March 19, 1998. A21.
——. *Vecindarios excéntricos.* New York: Random House, 1998.
——. "A Side View." Interview by Bridget Kevane. In *Latina Self-portraits.* Ed. Bridget Kevane and Juanita Heredia. University of New Mexico Press, 2000.
——. *Flight of the Swan.* New York: Farrar, Straus and Giroux, 2001.
——. *Vuelo del cisne.* New York: Vintage, 2002.
——. *Lazos de sangre.* Doral, FL: Santillana USA, 2009.
Firmin, Antenor. *De l'égalité des races humaines.* Ed. Jean Mélius. Montreal: Mémoir d'encrier, 2005.
Flannigan, Arthur. "Reading below the Belt: Sex and Sexuality in Françoise Ega and Maryse Condé." *French Review* 62.2 (1988): 300–312.
Francis, Donette. *Fictions of Feminine Citizenship: Sexuality and the Nation in Contemporary Caribbean Literature.* New York: Palgrave Macmillan, 2010.
Franco, Pamela R. " 'Dressing Up and Looking Good': Afro-Creole Female Maskers in Trinidad Carnival." *African Arts* 31.2 (1998): 62–67.
Frydman, Jason. "Jamaican Nationalism, Queer Intimaces, and the Disjunctures of the Chinese Diaspora: Patricia Powell's *The Pagoda.*" *Small Axe* 15.1 (2011): 95–109.
Fuss, Diana. *Identification Papers.* New York and London: Routledge, 1995.
Garane, Jeanne. "History, Identity and the Constitution of the Female Subject: Maryse Condé's Tituba." In *Moving beyond Boundaries, Volume 2: Black Women's Diaspora.* Ed. Carole Boyce Davies. New York: NYU Press, 1995. 153–164.
García Marruz, Fina. "*Amistad funesta.*" In *Temas Martianos.* Cintio Vitier and Fina García Marruz. Havana: Biblioteca Nacional José Martí, 1969. 282–291.
García Ramis, Magali. *Felices día, tío Sergio.* Río Piedras, PR: Editorial Antillana, 1992.
Garrigós, Cristina. "Bilingües, biculturales y posmodernas: Rosario Ferré y Giannina Braschi." *Insula: Revista de Letras y Ciencias Humanas* 667–668 (July–August 2002): 16–18.
Gillespie, Carmen. " 'Nobody Ent Billing Me': A US/Caribbean Intertextual, Intercultural Call-and-response." In *Sex and the Citizen: Interrogating the Caribbean.* Ed. Faith Smith. Charlottesville: University of Virginia Press, 2011. 37–52.
Gilmore, Leigh. *The Limits of Autobiography: Trauma and Testimony.* Ithaca, NY, and London: Cornell University Press, 2001.
Ginsberg, Judith. "From Anger to Action: Avenging Female in Two Lucias." *Revista de estudios Hispánicos* XIV.1 (1980): 131–138.
Girard, René. *Deceit, Desire, and the Novel.* Trans. Yvonne Freccero. Baltimore, MD: Johns Hopkins University Press, 1979.

Glave, Thomas. *Words to Our Now: Imagination and Dissent.* Minneapolis: University of Minnesota Press, 2005.

——, Ed. *Our Caribbean: A Gathering of Lesbian and Gay Writing from the Antilles.* Durham, NC: Duke University Press, 2008.

Glissant, Édouard. *Caribbean Discourse Selected Essays.* Trans. J. Michael Dash. Charlottesville: University of Virginia Press, 1989.

——. *Le discours antillais.* Paris: Gallimard, 1997.

De Gobineau, Arthur. *Essai sur l'inégalité des races humaines.* Paris: Firmin-Didot, 1853–1855.

Godard, Alex. *Maman Dlo.* Paris: Albin Michel Jeunesse, 1998.

Goldman, Dara. *Out of Bounds: Islands and the Demarcation of Identity in the Hispanic Caribbean.* Lewisburg, PA: Bucknell University Press, 2008.

Gomáriz, Jose. "Las metamorfosis del poeta e intelectual ante la modernidad en *Lucía Jerez*". *José Martí: Historia y literatura ante el fin del siglo XIX.* Ed. and intro. Carmen Alemany, Ramiro Muñoz, and José Carlos Rovira. Alicante, Spain: Universidad de Alicante with Casa de las Américas, 1997. 179–199.

González, Aníbal. *La crónica modernista hispanoamericana.* Madrid: Ediciones Porrúa, 1983.

——. "El intelectual y las metáforas: *Lucía Jerez* de José Martí." *Texto Crítico* XII.34–35 (1986): 137–157.

Gopinath, Gayatri. *Impossible Desires: Queer Diasporas and South Asian Public Cultures.* Durham, NC: Duke University Press, 2005.

Gordon, Angus. "Turning Back: Adolescence, Narrative, and Queer Theory." *GLQ* 5.1 (1999): 1–24.

Gosser Esquilín, Mary Ann. "Rosario Ferré y Olga Nolla: ¿manuscritos reconceptualizando la nación?" *Confluencia* 19.2 (Spring 2004): 58–68.

Gottlieb, Karla. *The Mother of Us All: A History of Queen Nanny, Leader of the Windward Maroons.* Trenton, NJ: Africa World Press, 2000.

Griffin, Farah Jasmine. "Textual Healing: Claiming Black Women's Bodies, the Erotic, and Resistance in Contemporary Novels of Slavery." *Callaloo* 19.2 (1996): 519–536.

Guth, Paul. *Moi, Joséphine Impératrice.* Paris: A Michel, 1979.

Gutzmore, Cecil. "Casting the First Stone! Policing of Homo/Sexuality in Jamaican Popular Culture." *Interventions* 6.1 (2004): 118–134.

Guzman, Manolo. " 'Pa la Escuelita con Mucho Cuida'o y por la Orillita': A Journey through the Contested Terrains of the Nation and Sexual Orientation." In *Puerto Rican Jam: Essays on Culture and Politics.* Ed. Frances Negrón-Muntaner and Ramón Grosfoguel. Minneapolis: University of Minnesota Press, 1997. 209–228.

Haigh, Sam. *Mapping a Tradition: Francophone Women's Writing from Guadeloupe.* Leeds, UK: Maney, 2000.

——. "Between Speech and Writing: 'La Nouvelle Littérature Antillaise?' " In *Comparing Postcolonial Literatures: Dislocations.* Ed. Ashok Bery and Patricia Murray. Basingstoke, UK: Macmillan; New York: St Martin's, 2000. 193–204.

Halberstam, Judith. *In a Queer Time and Place: Transgender Bodies, Subcultural Lives.* New York: NYU Press, 2005.

Haller, John S. "Race and the Concept of Progress in Nineteenth Century American Ethnography." *American Anthropologist* 73.3 (June 1971): 710–724.
Hammonds, Evelynn M. "Toward a Genealogy of Black Female Sexuality: The Problematic of Silence." In *Feminist Genealogies, Colonial Legacies, Democratic Futures.* Ed. M. Jacqui Alexander and Chandra Talpade Mohanty. New York and London: Routledge, 1997. 170–182.
Hanley, Charles. "Books and Authors: Rosario Ferré." *Puerto Rico Herald.* May 21, 1998. Web.
Hanna, Monica. " 'Reassembling the Fragments': Battling Historiographies, Caribbean Discourse, and Nerd Genres in Junot Diaz's *The Brief Wondrous Life of Oscar Wao.*" *Callaloo* 33.2 (Spring 2010): 498–520.
Hartman, Saidiya. *Scenes of Subjection.* Oxford: Oxford University Press, 1997.
Hawthorne, Nathaniel. *The Scarlet Letter.* New York: Dell Publishing, 1960.
Heller, Ben A. "Suturando espacios: comunidad, sexualidad y pedagogía en José Martí." *La torre* 1.1–1.2 (1996): 33–54.
Henríquez Ureña, Max. "Martí, iniciador del modernismo." In *Antología crítica de José Martí.* Ed. Manuel Pedro González. Mexico City: Publicaciones de la Editorial Cultura, 1960, 167–188.
Heredia Rojas, Israel Ordenel. "*Amistad funesta,* obra centenaria de Martí." *Islas* 79 (1984): 3–14.
Hewitt, Leah. *Autobiographical Tightropes.* Lincoln: University of Nebraska Press, 1990.
Hogarth, Peter. *The Biology of Mangroves and Seagrasses.* Oxford: Oxford University Press, 2007.
Hope, Donna P. *Inna Di Dancehall: Popular Cultures and the Politics of Identity in Jamaica.* Mona, Jamaica: University of the West Indies Press, 2006.
——. "Clash—Gays vs Dancehall." *Jamaica Gleaner.* October 5, 2004. Web. January 31, 2013.
Hopkinson, Nalo. *The Salt Roads.* New York: Grand Central Publishing, 2004.
Hoving, Isabel. "Jamaica Kincaid Is Getting Angry." In *In Praise of New Travelers: Reading Caribban Migrant Women's Writing.* Isabel Hoving. Stanford, CA: Stanford University Press, 2001. 184–237.
Human Rights Watch. "Hated to Death." *Hrw.org.* November 15, 2004. Web. January 31, 2013.
Hurley, E. Anthony. "Intersections of Female Identity of Writing the Woman in Two Novels by Mayotte Capécia and Marie-Magdeleine Carbet." *French Review* 70.4 (1997): 575–586.
Hurston, Zora Neale. *Tell My Horse.* New York: Harper & Row, 2007.
Ippolito, Emma. *Caribbean Women Writers: Identity and Gender.* Rochester, NY, and Suffolk, UK: Camden House, 2000.
Irobe, Esiaba. "What They Came With: Carnival and the Persistence of African Performance Aesthetics in the Diaspora." *Black Studies* 37.6 (2007): 896–913.
Jackson Carter, Sibyl. "Mayotte or Not Mayotte?" *CLA Journal* 48.4 (2005): 440–451.

Janer, Zilkia. *Puerto Rican Nation-building Literature: Impossible Romance*. Gainesville: University Press of Florida, 2005.

J-FLAG. "Definition of All-Sexuals." May 8, 2008. glbtqjamaica.blogspot.com Web. August 13, 2013.

——. "Know Your Rights." *jflag.org*. Web. January 31, 2013.

——. "Meaning of Acronym J-FLAG." jflag.org. Web. August 13, 2013.

Johnson, Barbara. *The Critical Difference*. Baltimore, MD, and London: Johns Hopkins University Press, 1980.

——. "Lesbian Spectacles: Reading *Sula*, *Passing*, *Thelma and Louise*, and *The Accused*." In *Media Spectacles*. Ed. Marjorie Garber, Jann Matlock, and Rebecca L. Walkowitz. New York and London: Routledge, 1993. 160–166.

Johnson, E. L. "Inventorying Silence in Michelle's Cliff's *The Store of a Million Items*." *Contemporary Women's Writing* 6.3 (November 2012): 267–283.

Julien, Nadia. *The Mammoth Dictionary of Symbols*. Trans. Elfreda Powell. London: Robinson, 1996.

Karafilis, Maria. "Crossing the Borders of Genre: Revisions of the Bildungsroman in Sandra Cisneros's *The House on Mango Street* and Jamaica Kincaid's *Annie John*." *MMLA* 31.2 (1998): 63–78.

Kincaid, Jamaica. *Annie John*. New York: Farrar, Straus and Giroux, 1983.

——. *A Small Place*. New York: Farrar, Straus and Giroux, 1988.

——. "Jamaica Kincaid and the Modernist Project: An Interview." In *Caribbean Women Writers: Essays from the First International Conference*. Ed. Selwyn R. Cudjoe. Wellesley, MA: Calaloux Publications, 1990. 215–232. By Selwyn R. Cudjoe.

——. *Lucy*. New York: Plume (Penguin), 1991.

——. *At the Bottom of the River*. New York: Plume, 1992.

——. " 'I Use a Cut and Slash Policy of Writing': Jamaica Kincaid Talks to Gerhard Dilger." *Wasafiri* 16 (1992): 21–25.

——. "I Come from a Place That's Very Unreal." In *Face to Face: Interviews with Contemporary Novelists*. Ed. Allan Vorda. Houston: Rice University Press, 1993. 77–105.

——. "A Lot of Memory: An Interview with Jamaica Kincaid." *Kenyon Review* 16.1 (1994): 163–188. By Moira Ferguson.

——. "An Interview with Jamaica Kincaid." *Clockwatch Reivew* 9.1–9.2 (1994–1995): 39–48. By Pamela Buchanan Muirhead.

——. "Columbus Was a Cannibal: Myth and the First Encounters." In *The Lesser Antilles in the Age of European Expansion*. Ed. Robert Pacquette and Stanley Engerman. Gainesville: University Press of Florida, 1996. 17–32.

——. "Eleanor Wachtel with Jamaica Kincaid: Interview." *Malahat Review* 116 (1996): 55–71.

——. *The Autobiography of My Mother*. New York: Penguin, 1997.

——. "Interview." In *Conversations with American Novelists*. Ed. Kay Bonetti, Greg Michalson, Speer Morgan, Jo Sapp, and Sam Stowers. Columbia and London: University of Missouri Press, 1997. 26–38.

——. *My Brother*. New York: Farrar, Straus and Giroux, 1997.

——. *My Garden (Book)*. New York, Farrar, Straus and Giroux, 1999.

——. *Talk Stories*. New York: Farrar, Straus and Giroux, 2001.

——. *Mr Potter*. New York: Farrar, Straus and Giroux, 2002.

King, Rosamond S. "New Citizens, New Sexualities: Nineteenth-century Jamettes." In *Sex and the Citizen: Interrogating the Caribbean*. Ed. Faith Smith. Charlottesville: University of Virginia Press, 2011. 214–223.

Kingsley, Charles. *The Water-babies*. New York: Harper Collins, 1997 [1863].

Kirkpatrick, Susan. "Female Tradition in 19th-century Spanish Literature." In *Cultural and Historical Grounding for Hispanic and Ludo-Brazilian Feminist Literary Criticism*. Ed. Hernán Vidal. Minneapolis: Institute for the Study of Ideologies and Literature, 1989. 343–370.

Knapton, Ernest John. *Empress Josephine*. Cambridge, MA: Harvard University Press, 1982 [1963].

Koos, Leonard. "Improper Names: Pseudonyms and Transvestites in Decadent Prose." In *Perennial Decay: On the Aesthetics and Politics of Decadence*. Ed. Liz Constable, Dennis Denisof, and Matthew Potolsky. Philadelphia: University of Pennsylvania Press, 1999. 198–214.

Kramer, Heinrich and James Sprenger. *Malleus Maleficarum*. Trans. Rev. Montague Summers. London: Pushkin Press, 1948.

Lacan, Jacques. *Écrits*. Trans. Bruce Fink. New York: W. W. Norton, 2007.

La Fountain-Stokes, Lawrence. "Tomboy Tantrums and Queer Infatuations: Reading Lesbianism in Magali García Ramis's *Felices días, tío Sergio*." *Tortilleras: Hispanic and US Latina Lesbian Expression*. Philadelphia, PA: Temple University Press, 2003: 47–67.

——. *Queer Ricans*. Minneapolis: University of Minnesota Press, 2009.

Larcher, Akim Ade and Colin Robinson. " Fighting 'Murder Music': Activist Reflections." *Caribbean Review of Gender Studies* 3 (2009): 1–12. Web. January 31, 2013.

Lebrón, Aníbal Rosario. "The Interregnum of Hegemonies: Reflections on the Recent Puerto Rican Shift in the Hegemonic Discourse of Heteronormativity." *Social Science Research Network Working Paper Series*. 2011. Web. January 31, 2013.

Leung, Helen Hok-ze. *Undercurrents: Queer Culture and Postcolonial Hong Kong*. Vancouver: University of British Columbia Press, 2009.

Lewis, Anthony and Robert Carr. "Gender, Sexuality and Exclusion: Sketching the Outlines of the Jamaican Nationalist Project." *Caribbean Review of Gender Studies* 3 (2009). Web. January 31, 2013.

López, Irma. "The House on the Lagoon: Tensiones de un discurso de (re)composición de la identidad puertorriqueña a través de la historia y la lengua." *Indiana Journal of Hispanic Litertatures* 12 (Spring 1998): 135–144.

López Baralt, Mercedes. "José Martí ¿novelista?: modernismo y modernidad en *Lucía Jerez*." *Revista de Estudios Hispánicos* 12 (1985): 413–425.

Lorde, Audre. *Zami: A New Spelling of My Name*. Freedom, CA: Crossing Press, 1998 [1982].

Lugones, María. "Heterosexualism and the Colonial/Modern Gender System." *Hypatia* 22.1 (Winter 2007): 186–209.

Mabiala, Alain and Bernard Joureau. *Petit Jacques et la Manman Dlo*. Lamentin, Martinique, and Petit-Bourg, Guadeloupe: Caraibeditions, 2011.

MacDonald-Smythe, Antonia. "Authorizing the Slut in Jamaica Kincaid's *At the Bottom of the River*." *MaComère* 2 (1996): 96–113.

——. *Making Homes in the West/Indies: Constructions of Subjectivity in the Writings of Michelle Cliff and Jamaica Kincaid*. New York and London: Garland Publishing, 2001.

——. "*Macocotte*: An Exploration of Same-sex Friendship in Selected Caribbean Novels." In *Sex and the Citizen: Interrogating the Caribbean*. Ed. Faith Smith. Charlottesville: University of Virginia Press, 2011. 224–240.

Machado Sáez, Elena. " 'Latino, U.S.A.' Statehooding Puerto Rico in Rosario Ferré's *The House on the Lagoon*." *Phoebe* 16.1 (Spring 2004): 23–38.

Magnani, Jessica. "Divided Loyalties: Latina Family Sagas and National Romances." Dissertation. University of Florida, 2007.

Mañach, Jorge. *Martí el apóstol*. Madrid and Barcelona: Espasa-Calpe, 1933.

Manzor-Coats, Lillian. "Of Witches and Other Things: Maryse Condé's Challenges to Feminist Discourse." *World Literature Today* 67.4 (1993): 737–744.

Martí, José. *The America of José Martí*. Trans. Juan de Onís. New York: Funk and Wagnalls, 1968.

——. *Obras completas*. 26 vols. Havana: Editorial Nacional de Cuba, 1963–1966.

——. *Martí on the USA*. Trans. Luis Baralt. Carbondale: Southern Illinois University, 1966.

——. *Lucía Jerez*. Ed. Carlos Javier Morales. Madrid: Catedra, 1994.

Martinez, Ernesto Javier. *On Making Sense: Queer Race Narratives of Intelligibility*. Stanford, CA: Stanford University Press, 2012.

Martinez-San Miguel, Yolanda. "Sujetos femeninos en *Amistad funesta* y *Blanca Sol*: El lugar de la mujer en dos novelas latinoamericanas de fin de siglo XIX." *Revista Iberoamericana* 62.174 (1996): 27–45.

Masiello, Francine. "Melodrama, Sex, and Nation in Latin America's *Fin de Siglo*." *Modern Language Quarterly* 57.2 (1996): 269–278.

Mason, Peter. "Reading New World Bodies." In *Bodily Extremities*. Ed. Florike Egmond and Robert Zwijnenberg. Burlington, VT: Ashgate Publishing, 2003.

Mawkward, Christiane P. *Mayotte Capécia, ou l'aliénation selon Fanon*. Paris: Karthala, 1999.

McCormick, Robert H. "Return Passages: Maryse Condé Brings Tituba Back to Barbados." In *Black Imagination and the Middle Passage*. Ed. Maria Diedrich, Henry Louis Gates, Jr, and Carl Pedersen. New York and Oxford: Oxford University Press, 1999. 271–279.

Meehan, Kevin. "Romance and Revolution: Reading Women's Narratives of Caribbean Decolonization." *Tulsa Studies in Women's Literature* 25.2 (Fall 2006): 291–306.

Meese, Elizabeth. *(Sem)Erotics Theorizing Lesbian: Writing*. New York: NYU Press, 1992.

Memmi, Albert. *Portrait du colonisé, precedé de Portrait du colonisateur.* Paris: Gallimard, 1957.
——. *The Colonizer and the Colonized.* Trans. Susan Gibson Miller. Boston: Beacon Press, 1991.
Meyer-Minneman, Klaus. "La novela modernista hispanoamericana y la literatura europea del 'fin de siglo': punto de contacto y diferencias." In *Nuevos asedios al modernismo.* Ed. Iván Schulman. Madrid: Alteas, Taurus, Alfaguara, 1987. 246–261.
Mistron, Deborah. "Literary Analysis of *Annie John*: Coming of Age in Antigua." In *Understanding Jamaica Kincaid's* Annie John. Ed. Deborah Mistron. Westport, CT: Greenwood Press, 1999. 1–11.
Mohammed, Patricia. "Towards Indigenous Feminist Theorizing in the Caribbean." *Feminist Review* 59 (Summer 1998): 6–33.
Molloy, Sylvia. "The Politics of Posing: Translating Decadence in *Fin-de-siècle* Latin America." In *Perennial Decay: On the Aesthetics and Politics of Decadence.* Ed. Liz Constable, Dennis Denisof, and Matthew Potolsky. Philadelphia: University of Pennsylvania Press, 1999. 183–197.
——. "Too Wilde for Comfort: Desire and Ideology in Fin-de-Siècle Latin America." *Social Text* 31–32 (1992): 187–201.
Morales, Carlos Javier. "Introducción." In *Lucía Jerez.* José Martí. Ed. Carlos Javier Morales. Madrid: Catedra, 1994. 9–98.
——. "Modernismo, modernidad, y posmodernidad en la poesía de José Martí." *Anales de la literatura española contemporánea* 23.1–23.2 (1998): 249–276.
Morrison, Toni. "Interview with Bill Moyers." *A World of Ideas.* March 1990.
Moss, Jane. "Postmodernizing the Salem Witchcraze: Maryse Condé's *I, Tituba, Black Witch of Salem.*" *Colby Quarterly* 35.1 (1999): 5–17.
Mudimbé-Boyi, Elisabeth. "Giving Voice to Tituba: The Death of the Author?" *World Literature Today* 67.4 (1993): 751–756.
Muller, Charles H. "*The Water-babies*—Moral Lessons for Children." *UNISA English Studies* 24.1 (1986): 12–17.
Muñóz, José Esteban. *Disidentifications: Queers of Color and the Performance of Politics.* Minneapolis: University of Minnesota Press, 1999.
Murdoch, H. Adlai. "The Novels of Jamaica Kincaid: Figures of Exile, Narratives of Dreams." *Clockwatch Review* 9.1–9.2 (1994–1995): 141–154.
Murray, David. "Re-mapping Carnival: Gender, Sexuality, and Power in a Martinican Festival." *Social Analysis* 44.1 (2000): 103–112.
Murrell, Nathaniel. *Afro-Caribbean Religions: An Introduction to Their Historical, Cultural, and Sacred Traditions.* Philadelphia, PA: Temple University Press, 2009.
Naipaul, V. S. *The Middle Passage.* New York: Vintage, 2002.
Natov, Roni. "Mothers and Daughters: Jamaica Kincaid's Pre-oedipal Narrative." *Children's Literature: Annual of the Modern Language Association Seminar on Children's Literature and the Children's Literature Association* 18 (1990): 1–16.
Navarro-Rivera, Pablo. "The University of Puerto Rico: Colonialism and the Language of Teaching and Learning, 1903–1952." *Journal of Pedagogy, Pluralism, and Practice* 4.1 (Fall 1999). Web. January 31, 2013.

Niesen de Abruna, Laura. "Family Connections: Mother and Mother Country in the Fiction of Jean Rhys and Jamaica Kincaid." In *Motherlands: Black Women's Writing from Africa, the Caribbean, and South Asia.* Ed. Sushiela Nasta. London: Women's Press, 1991. 257–289.

——. "Jamaica Kincaid's Writing and the Maternal-colonial Matrix." In *Caribbean Women Writers: Fiction in English.* Ed. Mary Condé and Thorunn Lonsdale. London: Macmillan, 1999. 172–183.

Núñez Rodríguez, Mauricio. "Prólogo." In *Lucía Jerez.* José Martí. Ed. Mauricio Núñez Rodríguez. Havana: Centro de Estudios Martianos, 2000 v–xxxi.

Nya, Natalie. "Fanon and Mayotte Capécia." *Caribbean Journal of Philosophy* 2.1 (2010). Web. January 31, 2013.

O'Callaghan, Evelyn. *Woman Version: Theoretical Approaches to West Indian Fiction by Women.* New York: St Martin's Press, 1993.

——. " 'Compulsory Heterosexuality' and Textual/Sexual Alternatives in Selected Texts by West Indian Women Writers." In *Caribbean Portraits: Essays on Gender Ideologies and Identities.* Ed. Christine Barrow. Kingston, Jamaica: Ian Randle, 1998. 294–319.

——. "Caribbean Migrations." In *Sex and the Citizen.* Ed. Faith Smith. Charlottesville: University of Virginia Press, 2011. 125–135.

——. "Sex, Secrets, and Shani Mootoo's Queer Families." *Contemporary Women's Writing* 6.2 (November 2012): 233–250.

Odom, Herbert. "Generalizations on Race in Nineteenth Century Physical Anthropology." *Isis* 58.1 (Spring 1967): 4–18.

"Offences against the Person Act." Ministry of Justice: Jamaica. Web. January 31, 2013.

Olson, Julius E. and Edward Gaylord Bourne. *The Northmen, Columbus and Cabot, 985–1503.* New York: C. Scribner's Sons, 1906.

Ormerod, Beverley. "The Representation of Women in French Caribbean Fiction." In *An Introduction to Caribbean Francophone Writing: Guadeloupe and Martinique.* Ed. Sam Haigh. Oxford and New York: Berg, 1999. 101–117.

Palmer Adisa, Opal. "Review." *African American Review* 30.2 (1996): 322–324.

Palmié, Stephane and Francisco Scarano. *The Caribbean: A History of the Region and Its Peoples.* Chicago: University of Chicago Press, 2011.

Paravisini-Gebert, Lizabeth. "Feminism, Race, and Difference in the Works of Mayotte Capécia, Michel Lacrosil, and Jacqueline Manicom." *Callaloo* 15.1 (1992): 66–74.

——. *Jamaica Kincaid: A Critical Companion.* Westport, CT: Greenwood Press, 1999.

Paul, Maritza. "*Pluie et vent sur Télumée Miracle* and *Moi, Tituba sorcière . . . Noire de Salem*: Two Francophone Antillean Women's Praisesongs for the Obeah Woman." *MaComère* 2 (1999): 114–124.

Pellicer, Rosa. "La mujer en la novela modernista hispanoamericana." *Actas del IX simposio de la sociedad de literatura general y comparada*, 18–21 November, 1992. *Vol. 1, La mujer: elogio y vituperio.* Zaragoza, Spain: Universidad de Zaragoza, 1994. 291–300.

Peñaranda Medina, Rosario. *La novela modernista hispanoamericana: estrategias narrativas.* Valencia, Spain: Universitat de València, 1994.

Phillipps-Lopez, Dolores. *La novela hispanoamericana del modernismo.* Geneva: Éditions Slatkine, 1996.

Polidoro, B. A., K. E. Carpenter, L. Collins, N. C. Duke, A. M. Ellison, et al. "The Loss of Species: Mangrove Extinction Risk and Geographic Areas of Global Concern." *PLoS ONE* 5.4: e10095, 2010. Web. May 25, 2013.

Powell, Patricia. *The Pagoda.* New York: Mariner Books, 1999.

——. *Me Dying Trial.* Boston: Beacon Press, 2003 (1993).

——. *A Small Gathering of Bones.* Boston: Beacon Press, 2003 (1994).

——. *The Fullness of Everything.* Leeds, UK: Peepal Tree Press, 2009.

Prater, Tzarina P. "Transgender, Memory, and Colonial History in Patricia Powell's *The Pagoda.*" *Small Axe* 16.1 (2012): 20–35.

Price, Richard and Sally Price. "Shadowboxing in the Mangrove." *Cultural Anthropology* 12.1 (1997): 3–36.

Prince, Mary. *The History of Mary Prince, a West Indian Slave.* London: F. Westley and H. Davis, Stationers' Hall Court, 1831.

Puri, Shalini. *The Caribbean Postcolonial: Social Equality, Post-nationalism, and Cultural Hybridity.* New York: Palgrave Macmillan, 2004.

Pyne Timothy, Helen. "Adolescent Rebellion and Gender Relations in *At the Bottom of the River* and *Annie John.*" In *Jamaica Kincaid.* Ed. Harold Bloom. Philadelphia, PA: Chelsea House Publishers, 1998. 157–167.

Quesada y Aróstegui, Gonzalo de. "Introduction." In *Amistad funesta (novela),* Vol. 10. José Martí. Ed. Gonzalo de Quesada y Aróstegui. Berlin: n.p., 1911. v–vii.

Ratsch, Christian. *The Dictionary of Sacred and Magical Plants.* Trans. John Baker. Santa Barbara, CA: ABC-CLIO, 1992.

Revert, Eugène. *La magie antillaise.* Paris: Annuaire Internationale des Français d'Outre-mer, 1977.

Rich, Adrienne. "Compulsory Heterosexuality and Lesbian Existence." In *The Norton Anthology of Theory and Criticism, Second Edition.* Ed. Vincent B. Leitch. New York: W.W. Norton, 2010. 1591–1609.

Rodríguez, Fátima and Laura Eugenia Tudoras. "Viajes azarosos: La aventura de la insularidad en la narrativa puertorriqueña: *Vecindarios excéntricos* de Rosario Ferré." *Revista de Filología Románica* 22 (2005): 193–199.

Roscoe, Will. *Changing Ones: Third and Fourth Genders in Native North America.* New York: Palgrave Macmillan, 2000.

Rosenthal, Albrecht. "The Isle of the Amazons: A Marvel of Travelers." *Journal of the Royal Anthropological Institute* 1.3 (1938): 257–259.

Ross, Marlon. "Beyond the Closet as a Raceless Paradigm." In *Black Queer Studies: A Critical Anthology.* Ed. Patrick E. Johnson and Mae G. Henderson. Durham, NC: Duke University Press, 2005. 161–189.

Salih, Sara, Ed. "Focus on Queer Postcolonial." Special issue, *Wasafiri* 50 (Spring 2007).

Saunders, Patricia. "Is Not Everything Good to Eat Good to Talk: Sexual Economy and Dancehall Music in the Global Marketplace." *Small Axe* 7.1 (2003): 95–115.

——. "Buyers Beware: 'Hoodwinking' on the Rise: Epistemologies of Consumption in Terry McMillan's Caribbean." In *Sex and the Citizen: Interrogating the Caribbean.* Ed. Faith Smith. Charlottesville: University of Virginia Press, 2011, 21–36.

Sedgwick, Eve Kosofsky. *Epistemology of the Closet.* Berkeley: University of California Press, 1990.

——. *Between Men: English Literature and Male Homosocial Desire.* New York: Columbia UP, 1985.

Sheller, Mimi. *Citizenship from Below: Erotic Agency and Caribbean Freedom.* Durham, NC: Duke University Press, 2012.

Shepherd, Verene A. and Hilary McD. Beckles, Ed. *Slavery in the Atlantic World.* Kingston, Jamaica: Ian Randle, 2000.

Sibblies, Warren. "Letter to the Editor." *Gleaner.* December 31, 2011. Web. January 31, 2013.

Simmons, Diane. *Jamaica Kincaid.* New York: Twayne, 1994.

Skiba, Katherine. "Puerto Rican Statehood? No Thanks, Gutiérrez Says." *Chicago Tribune.* May 2, 2010. Web. January 31, 2013.

Smith, Faith, Ed. *Sex and the Citizen: Interrogating the Caribbean.* Charlottesville: University of Virginia Press, 2011.

Smith, Faith and Patricia Powell. "An interview with Patricia Powell." *Callaloo* 19.2 (1996): 324–329.

Smith, Michael Garfield. *West Indian Family Structure.* Seattle: University of Washington Press, 1962.

Smith, Michelle. "Reading in Circles. Sexuality and/as History in *I, Tituba, Black Witch of Salem.*" *Callaloo* 18.3 (1995): 602–607.

Smith, Raymond Thomas. *Kinship and Class in the West Indies.* Cambridge, UK: Cambridge University Press, 1988.

Somerville, Siobhan B. "Feminism, Queer Theory, and the Racial Closet." *Criticism: A Quarterly for Literature and the Arts* 52.2 (Spring 2010): 191–200.

Sommer, Doris. *Foundational Fictions.* Berkeley: University of California Press, 1991.

Sourieau, Marie-Agnès. "Suzanne Césaire et Tropiques: de la poésie cannibal à une poétique Créole." *French Review* 68.1 (1994): 69–78.

Sparrow, Jennifer. "Capécia, Condé, and the Antillean Woman's Identity Quest." *MaComère* 1 (1998): 179–187.

Spear, Thomas C. "Individual Quests and Collective History." *World Literature Today* 67.4 (1993): 723–730.

Spivak, Gayatri. "The Politics of Translation." In *The Translation Studies Reader.* Ed. Lawrence Venuti. New York: Routledge, 2000. 397–416.

Steverlynck, Astrid. "To What Extent Were Amazons Facts, Real or Imagined, to Native Americans?" *Ethnohistory* 52.4 (Fall 2005): 689–726.

van Stipriaan, Alex. "Watramama/Mami Wata: Three Centuries of Creolization of a Water Spirit in West Africa, Suriname and Europe." *Matatu* 27/28 (2003): 323–337.

Stith Clark, Beatrice. "Foreword: An Update on the Author." In *I Am a Martinican Woman*. Mayotte Capécia. Trans. Beatrice Stith Clark. Pueblo, CO: Passeggiata Press, 1997. vii–xiv.

——. "Introduction." In *I Am a Martinican Woman*. Mayotte Capécia. Trans. Beatrice Stith Clark. Pueblo, CO: Passeggiata Press, 1997. 1–25.

Tambiah, Yasmin. "Threatening Sexual (Mis)Behavior: Homosexuality in the Penal Code Debates in Trinidad and Tobago, 1986." In *Sex and the Citizen: Interrogating the Caribbean*. Ed. Faith Smith. Charlottesville: University of Virginia Press, 2011. 143–156.

Tatchell, Peter. "The Reggae Lyrics of Hate." *New Statesman*. September 29, 2003. Web. January 30, 2013.

Taylor, Emily. "Introduction: Reading Desire between Women in Caribbean Literature." *Contemporary Women's Writing* 6.3 (November 2012): 191–193.

Theis, Jeffrey. *Writing the Forest in Early Modern England: A Sylvan Pastoral*. Pittsburgh, PA: Duquesne University Press, 2010.

Thomas, D. *Modern Blackness: Nationalism, Globalization, and the Politics of Culture in Jamaica*. Kingston: University of the West Indies Press, 2004.

Tiffin, Helen. "The Institution of Literature." In *A History of Literature in the Caribbean*, Vol. 2. Ed. A. James Arnold. Amsterdam: John Benjamins, 1994. 41–66.

Tinsley, Natasha Omise'eke. *Thiefing Sugar*. Durham, NC: Duke University Press, 2010.

Torres-Pou, Joan. "Las amistades peligrosas de José Martí: Aspectos de la representación de lo feminino en Amistad funesta." *Hispanofila* 108 (1993): 45–57.

Torres-Saillant, Silvio. *Caribbean Poetics: Toward an Aesthetic of West Indian Literature*. Cambridge, UK: Cambridge University Press, 1997.

——. "The Cross-cultural Unity of Caribbean Literature: Toward a Centripetal Vision." In *A History of Literature in the Caribbean*, Vol. 3. Ed. A. James Arnold. Amsterdam: John Benjamins, 1997. 57–76.

Treacy, Mary Jane. "Cherchez les Femmes: Looking for Lesbians in Spanish Class." *Modern Language Studies* 28.3–4 (Autumn 1998): 201–206.

Uribe, Olga. "*Lucía Jerez* de José Martí o la mujer como la invención de lo posible." *Revista de critica literaria latinoamericana* XV.30 (1989): 25–38.

Valens, Keja. "Desire between Women in and as Parodic Métissage: Maryse Condé's *Célanire cou-coupé*." *Journal of Commonwealth Studies* 10.1 (Spring 2003): 67–93.

——. "Dark and Dangerous." In *Changing Currents: Transnational Caribbean Literary and Cultural Criticism*. Ed. Emily Allen Williams and Melvin Rahming. Trenton, NJ: Africa World Press, 2006, 47–67.

——. "The Love of Neighbors: Rosario Ferré's *Eccentric Neighborhoods/Vecindarios excéntricos*." *Contemporary Women's Writing* 6.3 (November 2012): 251–266.

Valiela, I., J. L. Bowen, and J. K. York. "Mangrove Forests: One of the World's Threatened Major Tropical Environments." *BioScience* 51 (2001): 807–815.

Venator-Santiago, Charles R. "The Results of the 2012 Plebiscite on Puerto Rico's Status." *Latino Decisions: Everything Latino Politics*. Web. December 28, 2012.

Venuti, Lawrence. *The Scandals of Translation*. New York: Routledge, 1998.
Vialet, Michèle E. " 'Connais-toi toi-même.' Identité et sexualité chez Maryse Condé (1)." *Notre Librairie* 118 (1994): 70–76.
Wade, Lisa. "Whites, Blacks, and Apes in the Great Chain of Being." *Society Pages.org: Sociological Images*. July 12, 2007. Web. January 31, 2013.
Walcott, Derek. *The Antilles: Fragments of Epic Memory*. New York: Farrar, Straus and Giroux, 1993.
——. "An Interview with Derek Walcott. With Charles H. Rowell." In *Conversations with Derek Walcott*. Ed. Peggy Whitman Prenshaw. Jackson: University Press of Mississippi, 1996. 122–134.
——. *What the Twilight Says*. New York: Farrar, Straus and Giroux, 1999.
Weber, Eugen. *France, Fin de Siècle*. Cambridge, MA, and London: Belknap Press of Harvard University Press, 1986.
Wekker, Gloria. "What's Identity Got to Do with It? Rethinking Identity in Light of the *Mati* Work." In *Female Desires: Same-sex Relations and Transgender Practices across Cultures*. Ed. Evelyn Blackwood and Saskia E. Wieringa. New York: Columbia University Press, 1999. 119–138.
Weldt-Basson, Helene Carol. *Subversive Silences: Nonverbal Expression and Implicit Narrative Strategies in the Works of Latin American Women Writers*. Madison, NJ: Fairleigh Dickinson University Press, 2010.
" 'What Jamaica Wants'—Church, Gays Divided on PM's BBC Interview." *Jamaica Gleaner*. May 21, 2008. Web. January 31, 2013.
Whitman, Walt. *Whitman: Poetry and Prose*. Ed. Justin Kaplan. New York: Literary Classics of the United States, 1996.
Wilson, William. "The Sociopolitical Context of Establishing Hawaiian-medium Education." *Language, Culture, and Curriculum* 11.3 (1998): 325–338.
Wittig, Monique. *Le corps lesbien*. Paris: Les Editions de Minuit, 1973.
Zaldívar, Gladys. "Polisemia simbólica y fuente de la camelia en Lucía Jerez." *Circulo: Revista de Cultura* 25 (1996): 59–65.
Zimra, Clarisse. "A Woman's Place: Cross-sexual Perceptions in Race Relations (Mayotte Capécia)." *Folio* 11 (1978): 174–192.
——. "*Négritude* in the Feminine Mode: The case of Martinique and Guadeloupe." *Journal of Ethnic Studies* 12.1 (1984): 53–77.

Index

CPSIA information can be obtained
at www.ICGtesting.com
Printed in the USA
LVHW060827030319
609297LV00014B/463/P

9 781137 340078